PRAISE FO
BREAKING FREE FROM ˙

"Tell me a Story" and that is exactly what Marcus has done. Men don't respond to important facts like they do a good story. And a good story always holds the veins of gold that remind us of what is true. We all need to be inspired and invited to continue in this battle for the heart and *The Wilderness Project* is a story that will do both.
Michael Thompson, Best Selling Author of "Heart of a Warrior" and "Search and Rescue", Founder of Zoweh Ministries

"A great sense for the use of imagery"
Sarine Thomas, Author, Emergency Room Nurse

"He will answer and guide you through healing the wounds you experienced in your personal story." That is EXACTLY what it does. BAM!!! You have accomplished that, my friend.
Tammy Whitehurst, Author, Blogger, Speaker

"…a most creative way of dealing with abstract ideas as each chapter has its own memory of the past which is followed by a discussion between the sheep and the Shepherd."
Fleur Marie Vaz, Professional Book Editor

"After reading the first few chapters, I was compelled to call my birth father, who I hadn't spoken with in 26 years"
Jim Busler, US Army retired

ALSO BY MARCUS JOHNSON

My Personal Desert Storm: Eating Crow and Humble Pie

BREAKING FREE FROM THE SHADOWS

THE WILDERNESS PROJECT BOOK 1

MARCUS JOHNSON

Visit Marcus's website: www.thewildernessprojectexperience.com
Breaking Free From the Shadows - The Wilderness Project Book 1 – Marcus Johnson

Scripture quotations taken from the New American Standard Bible, Copyright @ 1960, 1962, 1963, 1968, 1971, 1972, 1973, 1975, 1995 by The Lockman Foundation. Used by permission (www.lockman.org).

Scriptures taken from the New King James Version®. Copyright © 1982 by Thomas Nelson. Used by permission. All rights reserved.

Scriptures taken from The Message. Copyright Â© 1993, 1994, 1995, 1996, 2000, 2001, 2002. Used by permission of NavPress Publishing Group.

Library of Congress Cataloging-in-Publication Data
Names: Johnson, Marcus, author
Title: Breaking Free From the Shadows
Series: The Wilderness Project, Book 1

Identifiers: LCCN 2020912861 | ISBN: Hardback: 978-1-64746-374-8 (hardcover) | 978-1-64746-373-1 (paperback) | 978-1-64746-375-5 (ebook)

Editor: Fleur Marie Vaz

This is predominantly a work of fiction. There are events based on actual events but names, locations, or specifics have been modified to protect those involved.

This book is dedicated to ALL men who have messed up, made significant mistakes, or otherwise lived a life believing they weren't good enough, men who were told that they weren't worth it. More importantly, this book is dedicated to ALL men who think they aren't good enough for Jesus Christ. I pray that they learn the truth – that they are wrong! They are loved! No matter what!

A BOOK WRITTEN BY DESIGN

THIS BOOK WAS WRITTEN by design, a non-fiction novel that tells a story rather than a book that will flood you with principles and spiritual guidelines. This book is intentional and conversational, using real events and real people (albeit with some modifications and name changes). While I categorize this as a non-fiction book, it reads like an epic generational story rather than a book of bible bullets and Christian principals. I knew that this book was different and I figured it was a book that would be targeted at men specifically; what I did not know was how much it would impact my beta readers, many of whom were women. Some have stated that they were suddenly convicted to take action in their lives. Praise God!

This book delves deep into the darkness of man and the spiritual warfare that takes place in that darkness: torment, fear, hatred, rejection, lust, pride, and self-destruction amongst others. I believe that too many Christians have tried to hide themselves away from it, they prefer books that have nothing but happiness, joy, righteousness, love, and grace. Unfortunately, while this is accurate and true to what is God and who God is, it is not the reality of where we find men in the world, where many men find themselves.

Men of the world feel isolated and helpless with no way out because they have come to believe the lie that they are worthless, that nobody can help them, that nobody loves them, not even God Himself. What a crock! And yet, Christians are lost in how to help men like this because they don't understand men like this, partly because they run away… from books like this. If they are lucky, they run into men who used to be like this and found the light, who've accepted Christ, and have hopefully been blessed to hear that man's story.

Why is this important? Because a fallen world is where a significant percentage of lost men are and this is where Christians need to go - where the lost are. Did God not say that He would leave the 99 and go after one lost sheep? God operates through people; therefore, people need to go where the lost are.

Many Christians are advised, or hold themselves to a standard, to only allow positive and uplifting words through their eye gates. I respect and honor this; time MUST be devoted to reading books that are positive and uplifting, else life would get depressing really quick. But, I would encourage Christians to also, carefully, read Christian themed books that also dig into the realities of the world in which we live. Part of the search and rescue mission is to understand the location where God's lost children are located and this book right here attempts to delve into that.

Now the good news - this book has a very happy ending and I am going to tell you what it is: the sheep is saved. But I believe this is not the most important part of this book, the most important part is the story of the journey that it took to get there. The journey is where many men get stuck in their demise, a crazy labyrinth, and they need help finding the way out. Perhaps there is something in the pages of this book that will help you understand how to guide a man, or woman, that you know out of that maze – or maybe you will learn something about yourself.

I wrote this book with a belief that many of those reading it might be new to the faith, or struggling to understand key concepts essential to their spiritual maturity. This book is also specifically targeted at men who believe they aren't worth it, they feel rejected, unloved, disrespected. Men like this feel as if the world is out to get them, that it is somehow personal and they have been cursed. Men like this may have, or had, daddy issues and are still carrying around these wounds with a belief system that they cannot be healed. This is a LIE, 100% untruth - I am a walking, living, breathing example that this is a lie. I walked that way for over 40 years.

After my born-again experience, I had books being recommended to me from people with different backgrounds and characteristics, different mind-sets and different heart-sets, a different "coming to Christ" moment than mine. They were also recommending books that they were reading now, not when they were first born-again years earlier. Bless their hearts, they could not relate to what I needed but they were trying. Man I wish I had been introduced to ministers early on such as John Eldredge, Pat Morley, David Dusek, or Michael Thompson for example. These type of ministers, with material I needed, ministers who understood men like me, came to my attention years later – ugh!

If you are mature Christian "spiritually" then you may find some of the early chapters written at a level you have already surpassed. Or you may find some of the dialogue lasting a little longer than you might prefer. However, you will also find that as you get through each chapter, the lessons the main character of the book learns build on each other, becoming more complex as the story unfolds. This was by design.

I want this book to be a conversation meshed in with stories shared from the heart. I want the book to speak to you, not lecture you or just fill you with principals with no understanding of how to apply them. I want you to feel like you are immersed as an observer of a story unfolding in front of you. This book is full of scripture because the great commission is to spread the gospel to all the nations. What if I told you, that regardless of your background, you have been living out portions of the gospel in your life already? I can see you shaking your head and saying, "nu uh!". You have, but it doesn't mean that you have been living out the right parts or the good parts and that my brother, sucks! It took me a few years to figure this one out. I had been living the bad parts.

WHEN YOU EXPERIENCE your own Wilderness Project, you will want to know Him on a much deeper level and what His plans are for you. But this also requires that you learn to hear God's voice. Bottom line is that you will find it challenging to explore and understand your own Wilderness Journey without hearing Him. This challenged me for years after my born-again experience, actually frustrating me at times and even giving me cause to give up and quit. It was too hard.

This book opens in the prologue with a middle-aged man praying and seeking wisdom from God, which requires that he be able to hear His voice. The scene described in the Prologue is based on an experienced believer who is confident and knows how to hear His voice; if you are not yet experienced in hearing His voice, this will provide a brief glimpse into what is possible for you, if you desire it. After the Prologue, the man is thereafter referred to as a sheep, because the Lord is our Shepherd and we are His flock.

If you require help and are frustrated with hearing God's voice like I was, there is a section in the back of this book titled "Call to Action". In that section, I will provide instructions on where and how to develop your ability to hear God's voice. Otherwise, I have listed some materials in the bibliography of this book that can serve as fantastic independent resources for you as well.

In Psalm 91:1, the Bible makes reference to a place called the secret place, a place of protection, safety, and communion with God. This is the place where every believer can meet with God face to face. This is a place where you can be comfortable and at ease with Him. Within this book, I describe a place where the sheep regularly meets with a man called Shepherd, this is the secret place where the sheep and the Shepherd discuss each event they witness through the journey.

Finally, Steve's journey through the Wilderness Project is accomplished through a series of visions. Visions are a biblically sound process that the Lord uses to communicate with us. (Acts 2:17, 18:9; Joel 2:28; 1 John 4:1; Psalm 89:19 and many more scriptures like them discuss the concept of visions). In the "Call to Action" section, I will share details on the idea of receiving visions from God.

Finally, I must provide warning that this book IS NOT suitable for children as there will be a few adult concepts and mature situations shared and discussed. I would not say that this book is rated R, but it is very likely a heavy PG-13. You will have to be the judge.

While I pray that you enjoy this book and my chosen writing style, I hope, more than anything, that the style of the book allows you to connect your own life to a life of Christ, no matter your past and background. I want you to visualize your own stories and your own wilderness journey to the path that is the River of Living Water, leading you to the Promised Land. If you have not given yourself to Christ yet, then it would be awesome if you feel His call after reading this book.

TABLE OF CONTENTS

PART 3: THE SHEEP WANDERS

PART 4: THE ROOSTER CROWS

For I know the plans I have for you, declares the Lord,
plans for welfare and not for evil, to give you
a future and a hope.

Jeremiah 29:11

PROLOGUE
THE REQUEST

"Indeed, I will make a roadway in the wilderness,
rivers in the desert"
(Isaiah 43:19)

PRESENT DAY

IT IS VERY EARLY IN THE MORNING and a middle-aged man is sitting comfortably in his favorite chair, a fresh cup of coffee resting on a coaster protecting his mahogany desk, contemplating and praying. After ten years of walking in Christ, he knew he had authority but he still didn't feel complete: something was missing. He understood his position in the next life, but, he was still living his life today and did not understand why he still felt lost. While he had given up much of his old self, his life "Before Christ," there were traits that he just could not seem to get over. They would still creep to the surface when he was triggered or certain buttons were pushed: brash, sarcastic, uncouth – areas that impacted his ability to build positive relationships. Why was this still a struggle after so many years? He had prayed with God often enough about it, but he just couldn't shake it.

"Well," he smiled to himself, "I definitely know that my character and my attitude have dramatically improved in some areas. The fact that I even care about this is a positive change. There was a day that I wouldn't care at all." This was something that he had been reminding himself of almost every day for the last ten years as it kept him motivated…minus his three-year dark period.

After a good devotional and prayer time, the man picked up a book sitting on the corner of his desk. He had read through it a few times; it had touched him deeply, and for some reason he was still unable to place it in its pre-established location on the bookshelf that housed a large book collection. This book made him cry, and he was not a crier. He opened it and scanned the pages, reviewing his highlights as well as his notes written in the margins, drinking in the details that touched his heart the most.

"Many men, strong believers, are still walking around with deep heart wounds. These wounds are keeping these men from living lives that God wants for them," the book read.

"Sometimes, the best way to heal a wound is to understand how it got there. Just like a gunshot wound, the doctors can best treat the wound if they know where the bullet is and where it entered. If the bullet was a through and through, then the doctor can best help the patient if he understands where the bullet entered, the path it traveled through the body, and where it exited. Without this knowledge, the doctor has to make his best guess, and it's possible that he may miss something. Therefore, he spends more time exploring the inside of the body, ensuring that he catches and cleans as much infection and foreign material as possible. In similar fashion, this is also true for a man who has received deep emotional wounds," the book continued.

The man looked at his notes, written in small print over several pages. "By God's grace, I have healed significantly from my past and I have forgiven those that hurt me – myself, mostly. But, perhaps I am still hurting from wounds because I don't know what they are. I haven't found them and fully healed from them. Does this mean that I don't fully understand my wounds? Do I need to seek healing that is more specific?"

OVER THE PAST FEW YEARS, the man recalls listening to messages about looking into the past. "We are people that have led sinful lives. For many of us, we have regrets, guilt, and remorse for things that we have done and people we have hurt. But, as God fearing people, we are to look forward, and moving forward does not require that we live a life constantly looking in the rear-view mirror. The Lord has forgiven you and He has forgotten…so should you."

The man continued reviewing a few highlights in the book, "If he's been carrying around unhealed wounds, then the answer for the man may lie in investigating himself more deeply, how he received the wound, even if he has to go back as far as his childhood. We are not doing this to revisit items in which we have been forgiven. We are on a search and rescue mission, to save the heart of the man, to find the wounds that are still festering like an unseen cancer."

The man sat back and pondered these words, just as he had a dozen times before. "I thought I understood how I received my wounds; I know I got most of them from my father, while others I brought on myself. However, there is something more there, something hidden. I think I need to understand what happened to Dad, why he was the way he was. After which, I need to understand how this impacted my life, my adulthood, and how this developed into my own relationships, particularly with my wife and my own children."

The man knew that he needed revelation, to hear from God, not just His voice, but he felt that he needed something more, something deeper and more revealing. He had read about visions in Scripture, there were dozens of examples in both the Old and the New Testaments. Acts 2:17, 18:9; Joel 2:28; 1 John 4:1; Psalm 89:19 immediately came to mind…but he knew there were more.

For a year, the man had been seeking and praying for revelation and visions that would reveal what he needed, but no answers came, causing some personal frustration. But he had also learned that it was necessary to be a patient man when it comes to the things of God. "If it is in His Word, then visions are a reality for Him. If they are a reality for Him, then they are for me as well," he figured, not for the first time. So, as he had done dozens of times previously, he acted out on faith that visions were for him, just as they were for the apostles and the prophets of old.

Before praying, he meditated on a few scriptures for several minutes, allowing them to resonate within and soak in his heart. Psalm 46:10: "Be still, and know that I am God." 1 Corinthians 2:12: "Now we have received, not the spirit of the world, but the Spirit who is from God, that we might know the things that have been freely given to us by God." Proverbs 2:3-5: "For if you cry for discernment, Lift your voice for understanding; If you seek her as silver And search for her as for hidden treasures; Then you will discern the fear of the Lord And discover the knowledge of God." Acts 2:17: "'And in the last days it shall be,' God declares, 'that I will pour out my Spirit on all flesh, and your sons and your daughters shall prophesy, and your young men shall see visions, and your old men shall dream dreams.'" Acts 1:8: "But you will receive power when the Holy Spirit has come upon you, and you will be my witnesses in Jerusalem and in all Judea and Samaria, and to the end of the earth."

THE MAN SAT BACK in his office chair, his office doubled as his quiet place in the early mornings so as not to wake his wife, who was still asleep. Closing his eyes, he focused on the Lord as well as imagined himself in his secret place, a place specifically reserved where he and God could communicate face to face. Quieting himself down both externally and in his heart, he began to pray, a prayer that he had memorized, one that he had written down several months ago.

> *"Father, You are the immortal, invisible God, Who has promised to lead and guide all those that are called by Your name... and You have undertaken to give godly wisdom and vision generously to all who come to You asking in faith – knowing that You have promised never to turn away those that ask in faith, or to find fault when we come to You trustingly and in humility of heart. I come now to pray for spiritual vision and to ask You to lead and guide me into understanding. Understanding that will help to reveal answers to the questions plaguing me: who am I and what am I? I am trusting You to fulfill all the desired petitions of Your servant as may be best for me – to Your praise and glory.*

> *"Open my eyes, Father, to see who my father truly was, not the man I remember. Prevent me from following after my own natural inclinations or allowing my fluctuating emotions to dictate what I believe, for I seek the truth. Why was my father the way he was? What happened between my father and his father? May I be led by Your Spirit to see only those things that are necessary for my understanding. For I believe that, only as I seek to live godly in Christ Jesus, will purpose for my life be fulfilled to Your praise and for my eternal benefit.*

> *"Lord, I am lost. Even though I know my future in the next life, in this life I feel lost in the darkness that surrounds me. What is my*

part in the larger story? My oldest son is no longer with us and his death consumes my soul as I fail to understand why I was not a better father to him. I tried, yet I feel like a failure and I don't understand why. Give me the knowledge and wisdom so that I can progress, change, and move forward in a way that I can better please You. So many emotions are plaguing me, Father. I believe that these burdens can be cast from me if I were to simply under-stand. Lord, I humbly pray that You would honor my request for wisdom in this because I cannot do anything on my own.

"Lord, You have full knowledge of everything in Your grasp. There is nothing that surprises You. Father, I need clarity right now. I can't rely on human intuition here, Lord. Father, I ask You now for clear and concise answers. I know that we are living in days when there is so much deception – not only in the world but in the Church that it is often difficult to know the truth – yet You have told us that if we know the truth, the truth will set us free. Thank You that I am already free form the bondage of sin and death and have my feet firmly planted on the Lord Jesus Christ – but I also ask that You grant me discernment and an understand-ing heart to know what is good and true and to be able to identify and reject what is false and deceptive.

"Help me to test every spirit to see and discern the difference between truth and error. I pray and thank You that You are not a God of confusion but the God of peace. Give me an understand-ing heart so that I may be open to hear Your voice and hear You say: this is the path, walk in it. Amen!"

WHILE REMAINING STILL, the man is determined to look for vision while he continues to pray, listening for the spontaneous thoughts that would alight upon his mind. With a pen and paper ready, he is prepared to write down everything that he sees. He knew that he could test it all later against scripture. As he continues to pray, he recalls the words of the prophet Habakkuk from Habakkuk 2:1-2:

"I will stand on my guard post and station myself on the rampart; And I will keep watch to see what He will speak to me, And how I may reply when I am reproved. Then the Lord answered me and said, 'Record the vision And inscribe it on tablets, That the one who reads it may run.'"

5

CHAPTER 1
THE QUEST BEGINS

"He who dwells in the secret place of the Most High
Shall abide under the shadow of the Almighty"
(Psalm 91:1, NKJV)

THE MAN FOUND HIMSELF IN A PLACE that was beautiful and crispy. The temperature was perfect and the sun was in a position that indicated it was mid-day with just enough clouds floating in the air, at just the right altitude, to magnify themselves in full display of their marshmallowy glory. The grassy ground was perfectly mani-cured and the grass was a deep rich green with a periodic daffodil poking up from between the blades of grass. He visits with the Lord regularly in the secret place, but something about this experience feels different from before. He could hear a tiny whisper in his heart, *"Welcome My sheep."*

Walking along a freshly raked path mixed with brown mulch and earth, he is on a search – but for what specifically he isn't sure. This was his normal secret place, at least he thinks it is, but something is different. Off to his right is a deep blue lake with small waves rippling against the shore offering a subtle and gentle sound carried across a soft breeze that soothingly graces his skin. "This day is perfect," he thinks to himself, "almost too perfect. Am I dreaming or is this real? Did I fall asleep at my desk?"

As he continued walking across the serene landscape, a tall man covered in a white robe and holding a staff in His right hand appeared in front of him. His face was covered in short stubble, like He hadn't shaved in a week or two, and His head was surrounded in shoulder length dark brown hair. He raised His arm that was not holding the staff, offering Himself to the man and showing that He was there for him. *"I'm the One you're seeking,"* He said, *"take a seat here next to Me on this rock."*

"Where did the rock come from?" the man thought for a second. But he humbly obliged as he sat next to Him, the rock perfectly fitting and much softer than it should have been.

"So, My Brother," the man in the white robe started, *"let Me introduce Myself. I am your Helper, here to guide you along your journey. You can consider Me your Comforter, your Teacher – whatever you like. But, you may call Me Shepherd. However, I am not to be confused with the Messiah, Who is Himself the Good Shepherd, but Shepherd may be the most fitting for our current purposes."*

"Wow, the man's voice, I mean Shepherd, His voice is like a song but He isn't singing. His voice is so…beautiful," the sheep thought. "The sheep? Why am I suddenly thinking of myself as a sheep?" he asks himself. "Weird."

"Because you are part of My flock," the whisper comes again.

As he looks at Shepherd skeptically, he notices a familiarity in the man, an aura surrounding Him, making the sheep feel safe, that he could do or say anything and this man would never belittle him. He was used to coming to the secret place to commune with God but he had never talked with the Shepherd before.

"You have questions," Shepherd noticed. *"The Lord has heard you, but go ahead, tell Me what you're seeking. What's troubling you?"*

"It's my life, Shepherd, I feel lost and confused. I feel as if my soul, or maybe my spirit, is struggling to understand how I got here and why."

Shepherd nodded His head, acknowledging the sheep, and letting him know that he could continue.

"It's as if I'm constantly under attack, but I can't see anything. And then, when I do see, other thoughts come against me…it hurts because I feel like I messed up, but I don't know what I did. I want to cry but I don't want to let others know what I'm feeling."

The sheep paused for a second; just sharing this much was already causing him to break down, and it had only been what…two minutes?

Shepherd didn't speak; He just kept His piercing brown eyes on the sheep in a gaze filled with both understanding and compassion.

After taking a few deep breaths, "It all started with my father," the sheep continued. "I hated him when I was growing up, but I did come to understand and discern a few years ago that the things I hated him for were not his fault. I forgave him and all, but I fear I'm still holding something in, that whatever he and I were dealing with is not over." The sheep began to stutter as his lips quivered and small droplets began to form in his eyes.

"I need to understand, Sir. Even though I've forgiven him, I sense that I need more healing, but in order for me to be properly healed, I need to know how I was wounded. I need to know why. I think that with this knowledge, I'll be able to better treat my wounds."

WHEN IT APPEARED that the sheep had paused, not knowing where to go from here, Shepherd spoke. *"I understand. You feel... obstructed. That you somehow can't move forward without under-standing your heart. But, there is more."*

"Yes, Sir, I think so. But I am not sure how to explain it," the sheep responded. "Why am I this way? Why was my father the way he was? What happened to him and how and why do I still feel the way I do? I am concerned about my own children, that I've somehow damaged them and I have no idea what to do or how to fix it. I sense, in my spirit, that my father and his before him passed something down, and that I now carry it myself, like a curse or something."

The sheep paused, but then he continued. "I need help and I..." he began to sob again. "I can't do it. My soul is getting pounded, pounded, pounded. And every time I experience a season of peace, it starts up again, out of nowhere and for reasons I don't see." He started to cry uncontrollably. "Is... there... something... wrong... with... me? Why... cant... I... get... it... right?"

The sheep paused long enough to catch his breath; he could actually feel Shepherd drawing confidences from him. "I've accepted Jesus and I believe I know who I am. I also know that we are a product of our experiences and I know that every step I've taken and every decision I've made has led me to this moment, right now. I feel like I'm supposed to do something with all of it but I am not sure I understand it."

He continued to ramble on while Shepherd allowed him to let it all out. This went on for a few minutes before the sheep could look up at Shepherd again, his eyes bloodshot, and his nose dripping with mucus. He was exhausted, he looked…finished.

Shepherd's eyes remained on the sheep, filled with sorrow but also with compassionate understanding. He smiled at the sheep, *"My Brother, it's OK. You can be at peace now. The Lord knows. You are on a quest to learn more about who you are, where you come from, and how you got here. Just like all men, you traveled the wilderness, but be comforted in the knowledge that you made it. You found the river and followed its life-giving water out of the wasteland and to the promised land. Be proud of that, but also give glory to Him."*

"Praise God!" they declared together.

"All men have walked through the wilderness, a vast desert landscape where they suffer the pangs of life, constantly looking for who they are, where they belong; in search of the answer to the question – why? On occasion, they come across an oasis in the middle of nowhere, a place of comfort and security, where they live for a season and feel they can be themselves. But over time, the oasis dries up and the man is wandering again, across the wilderness. He's on a quest to learn more about his identity, his purpose, a reason for 'all of this.' And, just when he thinks he has it, that it's within his grasp, he loses it."

The sheep was enthralled with what Shepherd was telling him, "But why does God allow that to happen? For example, why did it take me forty years for my journey, while for other men it could be shorter – or longer?"

SHEPHERD SHOOK HIS HEAD, *"God does not want men to spend one single second longer in the wilderness than they need, but most men spend much longer because of their choices, their decisions, and their hard headedness. And then there are men that walk around with heavy hearts, wounded to such a degree that they victimize themselves. They learn to live as a victim; they acclimate to it, feeling awkward when things are going right, or pessimistic that their world, at some point, is going to explode around them if they allow themselves to get too comfortable. So they always live on the edge.*

"Every quest for men is the same, though the journey for each man will be different. Paths traveled may be different, events will manifest differently, and the choices of taking a right or a left at each fork is left up to each individual. This is why the wilderness journey is different for each man and why time diverges independently for each person. Unfortunately, some men never leave the wilderness; they dry up inside until they eventually die."

"OK, but why does it seem that some men find it easier to get through the wilderness than others?" the sheep asked.

Shepherd nodded and thought for a second, *"Much of it depends on the individual, their upbringing, their belief systems, and more. But what makes you think that it was easy?"*

"I guess it appears easy because of the way they act, their testimonies...their strength."

"Haven't you heard that when you get through something, that it makes you stronger? That may answer part of your perception but, that is what it is, your perception. I doubt you know everything about those you are measuring. There's a danger in comparing yourself, and your experiences, to others just as it is dangerous for those that have gotten through the wilderness to compare themselves to those that are struggling, or even failing. This leads to pride for the latter, and regret for the former. Some of God's children may experience multiple wilderness journeys; it may not be just a one-time experience. Each man has his own personal experience with Our Creator, what one man walks through is different than the man standing next to him.

"Let me remind you, Brother," Shepherd continued, *"you yourself visited the wilderness again after your son left the earth."*

That one hit the sheep in the gut but he knew Shepherd was right. That was his "dark period," at least, that is how he referred to it.

"What matters is that men help other men. While God is involved, some of it depends on a team. Take yourself, for example; you had your wife and those around your wife. She had your back, even when you didn't have your own, or hers. Teammates do not quit on each other, no matter what. This is something that God loves, what He desires, and what He expects. Too many give up, both the man and those that had been cheering him on. They quit when they don't see results."

OK, I see some of that, but some of it goes over my head."

"Just know that the Lord is watching out for you; He loves you; He wants a relationship with you, and He wants to commune with you. He will never, ever, give up on you. But a lot of it does depend on you."

SHEPHERD SENSED that it was time to move on, so He brought the conversation to a close. *"You are curious about your wilderness journey; you are on a quest to learn more about yourself and how you got here. While understanding how you were wounded will help you to heal, you must also learn how to let the past go. You want to know how your story fits into the larger story, but you need to recognize that, as you get through each chapter of your life, you need to move on to the next one; don't dwell in it any longer.*

"You were hurt by your father but you are wise in recognizing that your father was hurt by his as well. As much as you try to be different, you tend to follow that same pattern. So, let's go back to your grandfather and see what we can glean from his past. From there, we will see how he affected your father and how your father's own experiences and belief system impacted you, and so on. Consider this a project of sorts, looking for certain milestones that reside in your heart and the hearts of your fathers. See where the Lord is speaking or operating in your life and the lives of your father and grandfather."

The sheep nodded in agreement. "OK, so we are going to go on a Wilderness Project. A quest to learn more about my identity, my purpose, and understanding."

"Yes. But I want you to consider that you will also experience the identity of God, as it applies to you and this journey, in order to understand where and how He operates. And how men like you can miss Him!"

"Fair enough! I'm ready!" the sheep said excitedly.

PART 1

They've Come to Kill the Rooster

CHAPTER 2
THE ROOSTER

*"Who has put wisdom in the [**bird**], or who has given
understanding to the rooster?"
(Job 38:36 LEB, clarity added)*

SHEPHERD SPOKE. *"Allow Me to share with you a lesson about
the rooster. You know what a rooster is, but what you may not know,
is that the rooster is like a calling card, a mechanism of communication that has been used to connect men with the Creator."*

"Huh? A rooster?" the sheep managed to cough out.

"Ha, that got your attention," Shepherd chuckled. *"Yes, a rooster.
Earlier you had mentioned that you were feeling something pounding on your spirit, so you already understand that you have a spirit
inside of you, placed there by Our Father the exact moment you
were conceived."*

The sheep gave Him a look acknowledging that he understood.

*"Your spirit communicates with the Creator's Spirit. Because
you are a believer in Him, this link is established, allowing Him to
speak to your heart. Are you with me so far?"*

"Yes, Sir, I believe so. But why my heart? Why doesn't He just
speak directly to me? Seems like it would've been easier – to me
anyway." The Shepherd tilted his head in observation, happy to see
that the sheep was getting comfortable, almost forgetting what he
went through just a few short minutes ago.

"Ah, but He does speak to your ears; in this case we are refer-ring to the ears of your heart. The heart is the gateway, Brother, the gate to your soul, which guides your emotions, your will, and your desires. Many think it's their head, but they are wrong.

"Your head is bombarded by your surroundings, the things you see, the things you hear, the things you perceive, and on and on. This allows your head to be clouded, confused, and misguided. Unfortunately, some of these things make it to your heart, contam-inating it with lies and untruths, causing you to react sporadically, emotionally, and impulsively.

"Nevertheless, the Creator speaks directly to your heart, filling you with His visions and experiences that bypass your head and all of the cloudiness buried there. The treasure of life is in your heart, Brother, not your head. Your spirit is in your heart; so is His Spirit. They reside together. But, if you allow the judgments of your head to get into your heart, they tend to blot Him out and bury Him in layers within so that you struggle to hear Him."

"OK," the sheep nodded. "But how do I get what He places in my heart to a point where I understand and can take the right actions, do the right things, say the right things? It seems so hard."

"Ah, wonderful questions! That makes me happy. Let's leave that for another time, though. First, let's explain the role of the rooster. This may help you understand how you got here and why. Is that OK?"

"Yes, Sir," the sheep replied. Something inside of him told him that he needed to listen; that he could trust the Shepherd.

"Wonderful. First, let me say that Our Father, Our Lord, can take anything bad that has happened to you and see that good comes from it, for you. Can I get you to agree on that?"

"I understand. I believe you took that from the Book of Romans. You cheated," the sheep laughed. "I'm kidding. But, I have to say that some things read better in the Bible than they are put into practice."

Shepherd was amused and the corner of his mouth curled up ever so slightly. *"Knowing Scripture, Brother, is experiencing God Himself. If you know His Word, and strive to understand His Word, then you will know Him. The more you know Him, the more you will trust Him. And the more you trust Him, the more you begin to act like Him. The more you begin to act like Him..."*

"The more I will experience Him and see Him operating in my life," the sheep concluded for the Shepherd.

"Bravo! Yes. All of which, begins and operates from your heart, and, your spirit. Not your head."

"OK, but back to this idea of the rooster. I am intrigued as to where it plays into this," the sheep wanted to know.

"SCRIPTURE TELLS US that the rooster is one of three creatures considered complimentary to a king, along with a lion and a goat. Are you familiar with that verse?" Shepherd was testing him.

"I believe that is a Proverb, but I can't recall the specific verse," the sheep answered.

"Yes, Proverbs 30:29-31 is where this particular bit of wisdom resides. Even the lowly rooster compliments a king. Each of these three creatures are marked by their confidence, the way they express it in their demeanor and their swagger as they walk into a room, as well as the dominions they oversee, the rooster over a hen house, for example. But the rooster, the Word tells us, is both proud and cocky. Does this sound like anyone you know?"

"I can think of a few, yes, Sir, myself included," the sheep admitted.

"Well, honesty is a good virtue. The good news is that the Word tells us that the Lord can use this. It is the rooster who crows every morning, signaling the rise of the sun; it also happens to get your attention and can wake you up if you are asleep as any farmer will tell you."

The sheep laughed, "Yes, I see that so far."

Shepherd continued, *"When the Apostle Peter was told by Jesus that he would deny Him three times, Peter responded with chagrin, telling the Savior that he would never deny Him. Yet, he did. Are you familiar with this event?"* Shepherd asked.

"Yes, Sir. As I recall, Peter did deny Jesus three times. And later, as he saw Jesus being scourged from nearby, he heard the rooster crow, reminding him of what Jesus had told him. It caused him to leave and weep bitterly."

"Absolutely! Peter's arrogance and self-sufficiency were exposed at the exact moment that the rooster crowed. He was asleep at the wheel and the rooster woke him up. He did not get this revelation

from a human, his spirit spoke to his soul when he heard that crow from the rooster. He remembered his denials, and he was immediately broken, allowing him to repent of his sins. And do you know what else is attractive to the Lord?"

"A broken spirit?"

"Yes. The Lord comes near the brokenhearted and will save those whose spirits have been crushed. There is something about brokenness that pleases the Lord. Now, many unfortunately think of this as odd because they are thinking naturally, not spiritually. It gives rise to conflict within them because they don't like the idea of being broken. They want everything working and all together, which is why they are drawn to the proud, the self-assured and confident, those that seem to have their act together. Do you understand so far?"

The sheep nodded. "Yes, Sir. But why is God that way? Why does He oppose the proud and give grace to the humble?"

"Our Creator wants to be close to the broken hearted so that He can save those who are crushed in spirit," Shepherd answered. *"Even our Savior, Jesus Himself, told us that He blesses the poor, those who weep, and those who are persecuted. The Apostle Paul said that his power is made great in weakness, not in his own strength. He even declared that he will boast happily in his weaknesses so that God's power will rest on him."*

Shepherd stopped to look at the sheep who was pondering everything that had been shared with him so far.

"OK, but what on earth is going on here?" the sheep asked.

"THE SIMPLE ANSWER IS that the Lord is drawn to the broken because He loves everyone, no matter who they are, where they are, or what they've done. And, make no mistake, My Brother, all are broken, though it may not be recognized or admitted to, not yet anyway. Too many people are like Peter, pretty sure that they've got their act together and, since God grades on a scale, all they have to do is stay one step ahead of the others."

The sheep stopped Him, "Wait a minute, God doesn't grade on a scale...does He?" he asked embarrassingly. "Maybe I missed something," he thought to himself.

Shepherd laughed. *"No, he doesn't. Have you heard the story about two men who were hiking in the woods when they came across a bear? One guy takes off his hiking boots and puts on his running shoes. The other guy calls him a fool and tells him that he can't outrun the bear. The guy responds that he doesn't have to outrun the bear; he just has to outrun him.*

"Some people think that in order to get to heaven, they have to get ahead of others. But that is not how God operates or how you will get to heaven. So, no, He does not grade on a scale. But, unfortunately, some think, men in particular, that others are somehow on a level with God that they are not. This is not true and is a result of bad teaching and theology. There are some who will place pastors on some higher level, or prophets, or minister teachers, or even the elders of their congregation. Though some may want to believe this, they are fooling themselves. Nowhere is this stated in God's Word.

"So, there you are, sitting pretty, confident that you have got all your act together and that everything is going to be OK. Most of the time, people are not actually cocky or walking around with a spiritual swagger, but their arrogance shows up as a symptom of selfishness. They love God but they aren't thinking about Him. They are just doing their thing and going along their way, without a care in the world; life is simply about them. That is, until like Peter, they hear the Lord's alarm system for themselves, waking them from their stupor...the crow of the rooster.

"It is also important that you understand this point: Peter heard the rooster with his ears, but the crow of the rooster spoke to, and within, his spirit."

The sheep jumped in, "The Holy Spirit is trying to get their attention, to wake them up from their sin or un-Christ-like behavior. Did I get that right?"

Shepherd smiled as he continued, *"Yes. Peter was focused on himself, his abilities, his understanding, his self-discipline, and his religion; this even after Jesus had personally spent three years with him, teaching him about humility and trying to make him understand that his relationship should be centered on Him. Peter didn't get it... until that rooster crowed. And then, all of a sudden, he recognized what Jesus had been trying to tell him all along. He learned it that fast, just like that! Peter had had a real-life experience with the real man Jesus Himself; yet he still missed it. This is an important lesson: that no one is immune to the entry of pride and arrogance, and this gets a lot of professing and lifelong Christians in trouble, even pastors and teachers."*

The sheep offered, "So, the Lord has His alarm system, the rooster, to wake us up to His reality. I get it, OK. And, to be clear, you are using the rooster as a metaphor of my spirit and my heart, the organ used to communicate with God through His Spirit. Am I right?"

"You are getting it, but there is a reason that I am using the rooster, both as a biblical example and to help you understand where this is going to lead us - the idea of Spiritual Warfare. You want to know what happened to your father and how and why you were impacted. This, My Brother, is because our enemy has worked hard to kill the rooster, particularly in men. By killing the rooster, the enemy can successfully cause men to ignore the Creator, to not hear His voice, and even to run away from Him. There are both spiritual and earthly impacts from this, but we are getting ahead of where we need to be."

"When Peter wept, he repented to the Lord; and when he returned to the other disciples, he was able to encourage them. Because Peter was now broken, God was able to use him and this is when the Spirit of God began to move in Peter. It would be a few weeks before Peter's ministry began, but when it did, Peter began his leadership as an exemplary servant of the church. Peter was now a humble man, no longer arrogant."

THE SHEEP LOOKED at Shepherd, "OK, but this seems kind of harsh in a way. God wanted Peter to become broken?"

"The key is that before Peter could experience this breakthrough in his life, something had to break in him first. God uses broken people, people like you, for example, to heal people that are broken, just like you," Shepherd answered.

Chills ran up through the entire body of the sheep. "So, this is why the evil one is adamant about killing the rooster. Kill the rooster, hamper the man's spirit. Hamper his spirit, the man is unable to hear from God."

Shepherd nodded and continued, *"To be clear, the rooster is not the direct path; it's more like a warning system. You can hear from God, learn from Him, and be comforted by Him, without the aid of the rooster. The rooster is a symbol of how God communicates when man is in deep trouble, in dire straits, or ready to fall off a cliff, if you will. Just like Peter, it is an opportunity to catch yourself immediately, just like that.*

"However, if the rooster is suppressed, that is the moment when man falls into his pit of despair, making it harder, but not impossible, for him to climb out of it. The rooster is crowing, but men are not hearing it."

"So, does this explain the pounding that I keep feeling on my soul?" the sheep asked.

"Sure, partially, but there was, and is, more going on in your life than just that, causing you to fear and isolate yourself. The devil is not always the one attacking you. Most of the time, to be honest, you are allowing the world to consume you and you are refusing to pay attention to the spiritual world. That pounding may simply be the Lord knocking on the door of your heart, asking for permission from you to allow Him to work through you, just as He did with Peter."

"God has a wonderful plan for all of His children but something inside each one has to break first. God has a breakthrough waiting for you, in your spiritual life, in your relationship with Him, and more. But, like Peter, something may have to break inside of you first."

"Everyone, regardless of what they believe, has something inside of them that God wants to let out, to pour out on others, an anointing with God's unlimited potential for you; but you must break first or what's inside of you cannot come out." Shepherd paused for just a few seconds to allow that to sink into the sheep's heart.

"So, unless I'm broken, there's no release for that breakthrough He has planned for me; my flesh, my pride, must first be broken," the sheep said, starting to experience a bit of revelation. "This is what Peter finally figured out after he heard the rooster crow. He realized that he had failed; however, he didn't use his brokenness for an opportunity to quit; it seems that he used it to actually persevere."

"Quite right," Shepherd replied. *"All because of the crow of a rooster – and Jesus warning to him previously."*

"Wow, OK, I have often considered all of the bad stuff happening to me as the end, that it was all over. I would put a few lessons learned into my rucksack and simply close that chapter of my life and walk away. But Peter was different: he went back and he was able to strengthen his brothers. And all because he saw his mistakes, repented, and forgave himself, after which, God was able to use that brokenness to make a difference. He was a different man, a different leader, and a different friend, husband, father. And all because He allowed God to use that brokenness in his life, allowing God to minister through Him. Wow, I never saw that before. I never want to ignore, or miss, the crow of the rooster!"

SHEPHERD SMILED and gave the sheep a hug, *"Yes, My Brother, you are getting it. You've been visiting God's house for several years now, but did you know that sometimes arrogance is shown in indifference, or self-absorption? Some go to church simply because they want something from God, or they pray when it is convenient for them. But they aren't doing anything to build a relationship with Him. There's a voice inside of you, trying to prevent you from destroying your life. Many don't always listen to that voice and they keep heading for disaster – until they finally reach that place of brokenness and then, if they choose to listen, they will hear the crow of the rooster."*

The sheep nodded. But then he realized that he was learning more about himself, which brought him back to his original question. "I get it and I believe I know what I need to do in order to move forward. But, what about my father and my grandfather? What happened to them? While I am lucky enough to be sitting here on this rock with you, they never did. Surely, the rooster was around, somewhere in their lives. I came to know Jesus later in life and my father came to Him just before he died; but I am not sure about my grandfather."

Shepherd weighed his next steps carefully. *"You spent four decades on this earth before answering the door, My Brother. Do you think the rooster wasn't crowing for you before that time? Of course he was, and you eventually answered. Unfortunately, your grandfather did not heed the call. His soul and his spirit experienced devastation that soured him."*

"The enemy wants to squash the rooster, the last line of defense. And sometimes men just give up. Unable to stop the attacks, they see no other way out but to simply give in and accept the fate the world is tossing at them. When this happens, this does not mean that the Lord gives up on them. He is still working, but man refuses to listen and eventually, the man dies."

"So, is this what happened to my dad and his dad? And is it because of this, that created the conditions between my father and me? Is this why I struggle with things in my life today?" said the sheep looking up.

"Partially so, but not all. Some of the conditions in your life, and your father's and his father's, were completely of your own making; don't give too much credit to the evil one: he is not that strong."

"The evil one has his minions constantly on the prowl, looking to kill that rooster, but they are also telling you lies that you choose to believe. These lies make their way into your heart and begin to formulate your belief system. As this false belief system becomes stronger, the crow of the rooster becomes fainter and fainter.

*"**SOME MEN TODAY**, men like you used to be, are walking as lost sheep through the wilderness, just like the Israelites did after their exodus out of Egypt. These men are on a quest, seeking their purpose, their identity, the reason for all of this. They are looking for their true names, how their tiny story is a part of the larger story."*

"As you walk through this wilderness, you are seeking the river of living water, the river that will take you out of the wilderness and into the Promised Land where you will find your identity and your purpose. Some men find it much sooner than others. For you, it took almost forty years. You didn't always hear his call, let's be clear on that, but you heard him on occasion and followed that sound to the river. Unfortunately, some men, like your grandfather, refuse to listen and they dry up in the desert, never finding the river that will sustain them."

"OK, I had been asked once why it took me forty years to come to Christ. It was that question that started me on a new path. But I sure struggled along the way, that's for sure."

"Yes you did, as well as numerous others. You are not alone. Sometimes, men think they are having some kind of experience that nobody will understand, that somehow they are unique. This is another lie and is a product of self-absorption. As you traveled through the wilderness, you built strongholds, but there are no unique strongholds. There are differences in how the strongholds manifest and how they are taken down, but they are virtually the same for all men."

"OK, I get it, but I feel like I am taking you off track," the sheep confessed.

"The point, My Brother, is that all men should be encouraging other men before they hear the rooster, before their world crashes around them. Men should WANT to hear the voice of the Lord today and open their hearts to Him. But they are confused by their world. Some people are broken by life, some are broken by circumstances, and some are broken financially. There are others that were broken by people that should have protected them or been with them in times of trouble."

"But, no matter what, the Lord is close to the broken hearted and He saves those that are crushed in spirit. God is drawn to the broken, to every situation. He is drawn to those that need to be saved and rescued. Jesus Himself tells men to come to Him and He will give rest to their souls."

"Some are hearing the rooster crow, Brother, the cry of the Spirit, to alter course or to change. But they are either deaf, or they are ignoring Him because they feel unworthy. And there are those that are openly defying Him, saying to themselves, 'I get this but don't tell me what to do.' The Lord does not want men to go through what Peter went through. Peter had plenty of opportunities to learn well before the rooster crowed, but he was too headstrong. Jesus wants men to understand that they don't have to wait until the world crashes around them or until they lose everything. Men do not need to wait for that rooster to crow, but we still want to protect it. Sometimes, the rooster is heard through other men."

Shepherd was on a roll. *"And this is what happened to your father. Your father is an example of a man that waited until his world was crashing around him: he was dying. Then, through you, he heard the rooster crow and heeded the call. If the accuser can snuff the rooster, do you now see the danger in this?"*

"But you asked to understand what happened. Let me take you on a journey and show you what happened to your grandfather and your father. As an observer of specific events, you may see how these experiences impacted you, placing you in the desert wilderness, impacting your own heart."

"How will that work? How can you take me back to these events in the past?" the sheep asked.

"The Lord is omniscient and omnipresent; He was there and is there. As His Spirit, I, too, was there and am there. The Lord tells

us in His Word that men will dream dreams and have visions. This is how you will be able to observe."

"Awesome!" the sheep replied.

"Be wary, little Brother. You may not like all of what you see and what you hear. But know that the Lord was there, working on those that are willing to listen, but, more importantly, those that obey. You will see where the rooster crowed as well as where the evil one worked against it."

CHAPTER 3
THE COYOTE STRIKES

"He who digs a pit will fall into it,
And he who rolls a stone,
it will come back on him"
(Proverbs 26:27)

THE COYOTE IS A SCHEMING TRICKSTER*, regularly designing and laying out a trap for the rooster. On this particular day, a day he has been planning and grooming for several years, the coyote is ready. His teeth are sharpened, his long-forked tongue sticking out of a mouth drooling with saliva. He wants the rooster in his paws, in his teeth, with the mind of everything that is filthy. He is ready to strike, for it has arrived, the day of the coyote, a day for his master.*

This coyote is chief of a band, each of whom goes by names such as Pride, Unrighteous Judgment, and Jealousy, amongst others. Their weapons are their jaws, their claws, and their scent, which, when used, create fear, intimidation, treachery, rejection, and unforgiveness.

At this moment, the coyote has hold of a large round stone that he will use in his attack, announcing out loud to his band, "We've got him!" The stone is a weapon named Hate; it is the strongest one in his arsenal. He crawls forward, and with every sweat-filled inch he turns the stone relishing the thought, "I can almost taste him. He's mine!" And then, he strikes and drops the stone.

▥

FORT DODGE, IOWA, MAY 1918

HE RAN, corn stalk brambles cutting and slapping him across his face and body, as if they were trying to intentionally hurt him, reaching out for him out of nowhere. The field was flat in most spots, but his feet would occasionally find the water paths, cutting through the field to water the crops, causing him to trip and fall, cutting his britches in the knees and making them bloody when impacting and scraping the hard earth.

But even a casual observer would notice that something was off, noticeable by his flailing arms and the terrified look in his eyes as he looked behind him, searching for whoever, or whatever, was chasing him. A stalk that was bent and falling towards the ground caught his shin and he fell once again, quickly recovering and staggering to his feet. He had been running in such panic that he was unsure where he was.

At nine years old, David was used to his pa's beatings, but today was different. It was his eyes. When he had approached David in the yard, his mouth was curled up in a snarl, as if possessed by a wolf, and his eyes, they were…black. He knew then that he had to run and the last thing he saw before he turned and ran into the field, was the red flush of his father's face, full of rage and anger. "What did I do?" he screamed as he entered the outer rim of the nearby corn field. He was confused, not sure what had happened.

"Run David, run!" an encouraging whisper.

David had seen his dad angry before, but something was off, different. "What is happening?" he screamed into his mind. His lungs were fighting for breath; all he could do was babble.

He could hear the man chasing after him, yelling, "Where're ya boy? Git back here, right now," he shouted. A second or two pause. "Come take your lickin' like a man, or are you just a lil ole baby?" He could hear the slur in his pa's speech. He was always drunk when he wasn't tending to the fields or the cattle.

28

As David ran, continuing to dodge the towering corn stalks as best he could, he could feel the pain of what will eventually become large bruises from the continued whipping of the increasing strands and the expanding ears of corn growing out of them.

Ed, his father, was chasing after him. A voice growls from a precipice in Ed's soul. *"You got em' Ed. He can't hide from you. He's yours!"*

David knew this field because he and his brothers would often play games in here, one large field set in the middle of the corn field bonanza located throughout the Fort Dodge and Webster County area. But today, the field felt like a maze: he was lost.

"I'm gonna git ya boy, I've got a wippin for you that you ain't never gonna forget!" That shout brought David back to his current predicament. "No, help me…help me…help me!" he cried. "Mommy…Mommy…Mommy!"

His cousin would normally protect him and his brothers from their pa, but he was off fighting in the war – the Great War they were calling it. All David knew was that his cousin was gone and he needed to fend for himself.

It was hot and dry in the fields. David was sweating in every nook and cranny, drenching his clothes. Ma was going to have a day cleaning them – she always did laundry on Thursdays.

"Keep moving David, don't stop," a voice buried behind fear and panic.

As David ran for cover, he wasn't sure where he was going. He was simply focused on dodging and turning, left and then right; right and then left again. At some point, he figured Pa would tire and stop chasing him, but he had longer legs than David's lanky legs. Plus, Pa could run through some of the stalks that David had to dodge around. So David needed to keep moving.

In the background was a sudden monstrous roar, "What was that? What was that?" David cried. It was close and getting closer.

At some point, David broke through an opening, and, not knowing where he was, he was surprised to find that he had come to the family barn, 50 feet in front of him. Somehow he had circled around as the barn was only 100 yards from the yard where this chase had started. So, he did what most kids do; he ran to hide in the barn.

"No, David, do not go in there!" a warning builds up inside of him.

HE KNEW EVERY SQUARE FOOT of this barn, having played in it with his brothers since he was two. As soon as he entered the barn, his knee's buckled, causing him to fall to his knees, impacting his already bloodied and painful kneecaps. He quickly recovered and thought about latching the barn doors but that would only make it obvious that he was in here. So, he made a split-second decision and dove for a large, but loose, pile of hay that was 12 feet tall and stacked up against one of the walls. As he dove for cover, he went as far back as he could into the stack until he hit a wall and dug down as deep as he could, covering every inch of his body so Pa wouldn't see him.

Back in the fields, Ed was on a steady pace. *"When you catch him, Ed, make sure you bloody him up good. Show him what a pathetic little bug he is,"* a sinister voice said in his head.

The hay was always itchy and sometimes bugs would be in it and crawl all over you, but David could not feel anything right now. He could hear his heart beating in his ears and he was still breathing hard and needed to calm down, or Pa would hear him. But, his hiding space quickly surrounded him, making it difficult for him to catch his breath.

"Peace David, be at peace, little Brother. Breathe," a calming voice tried to say to him.

After a few minutes, he could hear his pa stomping around outside the barn. David felt terror well up inside him and he started to cry. "Please don't find me, please, please, please. Where's Vernon and Tom – they were in the house? How come they aren't here to protect me. Damn them to hell (he had always heard Pa and Grandpa say this)."

David remembered the last beating; it took three days for the pain to dissipate afterwards. But Pa never had that look that he had seen today. "And what was that roar?" he thought to himself, finally starting to catch his breath.

Voices in Ed's head continued to press him, *"Lift your nose, Ed; you can smell him; you can smell the fear."*

"I know you're in there, Boy. You might as well come out; it will only get worse," his pa yelled angrily. David could hear in his voice that his irritation was increasing.

Off in a nearby house 300 feet away, a woman was staring through a window. She watched as her husband opened the doors and enter the barn that she had just watched her son enter a few minutes earlier. She closed the curtains to block the view and began to sob into her hands before collapsing to the floor, her back against the nearby counter, shaking and crying uncontrollably. "I'm sorry David, please forgive me," she whimpered.

Back in the barn, David's heart continued to race. "Please don't see me. Please don't find me. Help me, Mommy. Vernon, where are you?" But there was no one to hear his silent plea. No one that he could see anyway.

David listened as the barn door opened and his father entered. David laid down further, digging an imaginary hole in the hard earth beneath him. He could barely breathe again as sweat poured down his face and out of the pores of his body, drenching him more.

He could hear his pa walking closer; his heart started beating faster. It was at this point that he started to cry, so he placed his hands over his mouth. "Oh God, did the hay move?" The more he tried to control the crying, the harder it was to control the whimpers. His body began to quiver and he could not stop.

"You are going into shock, David. Peace, little Brother...peace," the whisperer was still trying to reach him, to comfort him.

Time seemed to move very slow and very fast at the same time. He could hear his pa and then...he couldn't. Time froze.

His whimpering was becoming more uncontrollable as the silence consumed him. "Where is he? Where's Pa?"

And then...

He felt hands viciously grab his ankles as he was violently jerked out of his hiding spot and dragged to the middle of the barn floor and tossed like a rag doll. He landed on his belly but got up to his knees and elbows, covering his head with his arms.

"I told ya boy, this was going to be worse if I had to hunt ya," he snarled as he pulled off his thick leather belt.

"Pa, stop...please!" David yelped.

"You don't know this but your cousin ain't going to save ya no more. He's passed on. Your ma and I got the message from your auntie this morning."

"You shouldn't a made me chase ya; now I'm tired and cranky," he growled more to himself than to David. He wrapped one end of the belt around his fingers and made a fist, the buckle of the belt across his knuckles leaving enough dangling leather to beat David.

David could smell the liquor on his pa's breath, even from five feet away. He could also smell, "matches?"

"No, Pa, please!" David cried.

"I'VE GRIEF TO RELEASE SON," he replied. And with that, he struck the first of several blows across David's back. After the fourth blow, his pa lost his balance and he fell to the ground for a split second; as he maneuvered to get back up, he punched David against his right side with his buckled knuckles. "Aah!" David screamed out as he fell from his knees and elbows to his belly on the ground.

"You got 'em, Ed, beat him, but don't kill him. Beat him until he passes out!"

Neither of them could see the two spiritual beings standing to the side, representatives of two different kingdoms, both competing for their souls. Shepherd watched on in sorrow and grief. *"Ed, stop. Do not be a willing party to his death."* But Shepherd knew that the coyote did not want the boy to physically die. He wanted his spirit, and this is what Shepherd was most dreading.

The coyote whispered into Ed's ear and licked the side of his face. He then giggled and looked directly at Shepherd as Ed spoke.

"You are better off not to have any boys of yer own," Ed said stoically, as he connected another blow across David's buttocks and upper legs, oblivious to his screams and cries.

"If you do, they, too, will suffer the wrath of the devil, boy," crack. "This world is evil," crack, "and we ought not to plague it with more men like us," snap, crack.

"That is not true David. The Lord heals the brokenhearted and bandages their wounds," Shepherd said. But, unfortunately, that healing would be left for another generation.

"Ed, children are a gift from the LORD; they are a reward from him." But there was no reaching Ed, the coyote had a complete hold on him. Ed had removed any semblance of God from his life years earlier, deaf to the groanings of His Spirit. Shepherd was dismayed because he could not intervene, while he watched the coyote continue to move Ed like a puppet, his dangly paws now meshed into Ed's mind.

After a few minutes, David's dad finished due to exhaustion. Panting as he worked to catch his breath, he put his belt back on, and then turned to stare at his son who had passed out on the floor, bloodied and bruised across his back down to the back of his legs.

The coyote pulled his paws from the mind of Ed.

"DANG," ED THOUGHT, " I really opened him up this time!" Tears temporarily filled his eyes, obviously thinking about what had just transpired, thinking what we will never know. His dark eyes began to slowly dilate back to normal.

As David began to stir, Ed spoke to him, "Your ma will have supper in an hour. Make sure you clean up before sittin at the table." And with that said, he walked out of the barn, leaving David on the floor, his shirt torn, shredded, and bloodied. The scars on his back would remain with him the rest of his life. That, and the emotional scars that came with it.

Shepherd spoke to David, *"Little Brother, don't let the hate consume you. You are young and your body will heal. So can your soul if you choose to accept Jesus Christ."* But David could not hear a thing; he was burying his spirit.

David had just experienced a lesson in hate, and he knew it. He lay there, his tears getting stronger as his terror ebbed into anger, his anger transitioning into hatred, his hatred bleeding into his heart, turning into rage.

"Hah, you see there, you god sniveling fool!" the coyote barked at Shepherd. *"His heart has hardened and darkened and it is sure that he will develop into a wrathful man. I don't understand why the Creator doesn't see the truth, that His children don't love Him, nor do they follow Him. They are so easily manipulated."*

Shepherd watched Ed as he walked out the barn door. *"It is written that whoever causes one of these little ones to sin, it would be better for him if a great millstone were hung around his neck and he were thrown into the sea,"* he cautioned. He knew that Ed's life would most likely end in only a few years.

The vision froze, now a spot in time as Shepherd and the sheep closed out this episode in the life of David. This would not be the last beating that David would receive from his pa; they would continue for another few years. But each beating would serve as nourishment, feeding the hatred in his heart, making him angry and tearing apart his soul that would be felt for further generations – just as his father had told him it would.

While the coyote sneered, *"This one is mine now,"* Shepherd looked at David with eyes full of love, but saturated in sorrow.

"The father made a choice, the son will also make a choice, but either way, the Father will turn this into a triumph," Shepherd declared.

"The Father will eventually recognize that these humans are losing their way. He is losing them more and more as each generation passes from this earth," the coyote said gleefully.

"No, all will fall into the plan that He has ordained, and the world will see that He is King and Savior. Whether in this generation or another, He will reign on high," Shepherd's voice rang.

"We shall see, you cowardly monkey brain. But for now, this battle is mine – you can at least concede that," the coyote snipped.

"Battles are fought every minute of every day," Shepherd said calmly back. *"Some are lost and some are won, but it is the war that matters, and victory in this war has already been ordained: it is a foregone conclusion. You know the truth but you allow the lies your master tells you to mask the truth."*

The look from the coyote made it clear that this was a discussion that they had obviously had a thousand times over several millennia.

As the coyote vanished, Shepherd remained for a few more seconds to whisper a prayer for David:

> *"Lord, I pray for mercy on the soul of David and those that follow him. Lord, there is no one besides You to help in the battle between the demons that torment him and his spirit, for he is young and has no strength; help him to ease his suffering, O Lord, we trust in Your name to come against this multitude. Father, You are our God; and nothing can prevail against You. Amen."*

His compassion for David was strong but, while He did not know everything, He knew that David would live the remainder of his life with a torn spirit. But this did not stop His prayer asking the Lord for mercy to ease David's suffering. He also knew that David would pass his broken spirit onto his sons, fortifying strongholds in their own spirits. As He dropped His chin in sorrow for David, He slowly faded, off to view the plans of a million other souls. While He could assist with words of love, warning, and compassion, He was not a part of David's spirit and could not remain.

Some would answer the call but many would not…too many!

David slowly got off the floor, vowing to himself that he would get back at the world. If he could share his pain with at least one other, to let them know what it was like, what his life was like, that would bring satisfaction to him. Even at nine years of age, David knew that he would never be happy, but, by golly, he would have his satisfaction! He was an angry child who was learning how to stir up conflict, and as an angry person, David would become a hateful adult, passing his hate onto others.

At that, David received and accepted the fate that his father had sown into him: he was nothing but a rodent!

THE ROOSTER MADE ONE final crow but David could not hear it, for it had just been squashed, buried in the pit of despair that he had fallen into. But the sheep heard it, bringing tears to his eyes.

"Oh my God, I had no idea!" the sheep cried. He could not take his eyes off the young child, bloodied and torn, frozen in place as he was stumbling to the barn door.

"This, My little Brother, is one episode of many that David will continue to suffer as a child," Shepherd said. *"But the truth is that David is not the only one. This is happening all over the world with some children getting it much worse than your grandfather will ever receive."*

"But the rooster is dead! His spirit buried. It doesn't seem fair; he's only a child!" the sheep sobbed.

Shepherd looked at the sheep with eyes filled with compassion and mercy. *"The story may seem bleak for the rooster, that it is all over. But the truth is that the rooster, your grandfather's spirit, has not died. He has just buried it beneath the rubble of his life. The rooster can never truly die, but it can go dormant, losing the spiritual connection needed to keep David spiritually alive and comforted in His grace, helping him, and lifting him up."*

"Will he ever have more chances to get himself together? To connect with God?" the sheep asked. "I don't believe that God gave up on him." The sheep already knew the outcome of his grandfather but he needed assurance that the Lord had not given up on him.

"The Lord never gives up on His children, but they must always choose. They can choose Life, or they can choose death, but the Lord never gives up. Just as you were a lost sheep, so was your

grandfather. Just as the Creator knocked on the door of your heart multiple times, He was always doing the same with David for the remainder of his life. But, just as his father did before him, he shut the Lord out of his life. He refused to listen. That was the choice he made."

AS THE VISION BEGAN TO CLOSE AND FADE, the sheep could see remnants of the Coyote's pack that had remained behind with David. They had been nipping at him and placing their scent on him, which seemed to cause further aggravation with David as he painfully struggled to the barn door.

A little earlier, they had watched the Coyote let out a long howl in victory after releasing its claws from Ed's mind, his pack joining in an eerie chorus. The coyote had dropped the rock of hate on Ed earlier which had initiated the chase. Instead of blocking the rock or stepping out of the way, Ed had accepted what the rock gave him – deep felt hatred.

As they returned to the original location where the sheep and Shepherd had first met, Shepherd contemplated His next words, listening for the Father to tell Him what to share with the sheep.

"Little Brother, you can be comforted in the knowledge that it is possible for the end result to be much different for the coyote and for his prey. It is possible to distract the coyote, draw him away, by allowing the Father to work through you and dupe the demon. If you will listen and follow His instructions, it doesn't take long before the coyote finds himself looking up at the rooster from the bottom of the pit, the rooster that he thought was his."

The sheep recognized that this was a complicated twist of spiritual warfare that he, as a novice, was starting to see. Nevertheless he was learning the truth of who he was, and what his Creator desired for him.

Shepherd continued His knowledge sharing, *"As you consider this particular disaster that you believe has taken out the rooster, the coyote will operate in the lives of others just like David, where we will find him doing the same thing all over again. Do you know why?"*

As the sheep pondered the question, a picture formed in his head. "I can see the coyote lighting a fuse that routinely explodes in his own face; but yet he has hope beyond hope, that one day the fuse will help him capture and defeat the ultimate prey, Jesus Christ Himself. I think the coyote thrives in an environment of lies and deceit that he will run straight into, trying to get the rooster that miraculously continues to elude him."

Shepherd nodded, *"Close enough for now. For each rooster that he does successfully bury, this spurs him on to believe that he can bury them all, even when the odds show that he fails the vast majority of the time. The devil's minions know the truth but the darkness in them convinces them that the truth is actually a lie, the truth that whoever digs a pit will himself fall into it, and whoever turns a stone, he will find it turning back on himself."*

Shepherd advised the sheep before moving on, *"As we move on to the next vision, pay attention to what is the same but also different. The coyote will stand aside and allow a new creature to enter the fold, a darker enemy for the rooster. This creature is just as filthy, with the mind of the devil, but with behaviors and characteristics that differ only slightly from the coyote. He is the wolf and the wolf prowls – he is the one that wants to kill, to destroy that rooster! Physically, and spiritually."*

CHAPTER 4
THE WOLF PROWLS

"Be on your guard against false prophets who come to you in sheep's clothing but inwardly are ravaging wolves"
(Matthew 7:15 CSB)

"The wolf that one hears is worse than the orc one fears."
—JRR Tolkien

THE WOLF PROWLS IN THE DARKNESS, *stalking the victim it intends to consume; but its weakness is the light and he will avoid it. Its preference is to take advantage of the young, the weak, or the injured, as those who are disadvantaged are the easiest to catch. Ironically, the wolf is both the most cowardly as well as the most fearless of the dominion of evil; it is sly and opportunistic, but it can be chased away with the right attitude and character of those that stand their ground. Nonetheless, it likes the challenge and prefers the chase. As the rooster watches his flock and rules his ground, it is a matter of determining if the rooster will hold his ground. Will he run, or will he concede and give up when the wolf finally pounces?*

This wolf rules his pack, each member going by names such as Hate, Vengeance, Envy, Violence, Arrogance, and Depression. As with the coyote, their weapons are their jaws, their claws, and their scent, which create a condition of lust, addiction, isolation, violence, entitlement, idolatry, and neglect.

As he prepares to take the leap, we are reminded of the nature of the wolf as a beast of waste and destruction. Regrettably, there are those that will concede and fall, while there are others who will actually decide to run with the pack – if they are invited, if they feel wanted, or when they feel helpless. Sometimes, a wolf will manage to infiltrate the flock unnoticed, ravenous for a taste. The wolf whispers into the ears of those willing to listen, guiding its victim with words masked as affirmation and exhortation, while all the while feeding lies and wanting nothing more than the target's destruction. He wants its soul. A wolf knows how to be polite when others around its quarry have no clue about politeness. However, while the wolf can change its coat or its skin, it cannot change its disposition. The wolf wants nothing more than to kill, steal, and destroy.

⑄

FT. DODGE, IOWA, AND FORT SAM HOUSTON, TX 1918-1942

AS SHEPHERD ALREADY KNEW, David had developed into a very vindictive and immature man and, unfortunately, his choices were bleeding over onto others in his life.

The effects of David's experiences were very apparent to Shepherd and the sheep. The strongholds of rejection, pride, and fear remained with David after his beating in 1918, vying for his uninterrupted attention. The wolf pack observed David with sharp toothed smiles and celebratory pauses after regularly whispering into David's ear that his family hated him, they had rejected him, but yet he was still somehow better than all of those around him. "*We have him, master,*" they would regularly report to their overseer.

His father had finally passed away on a cold blistering morning back in 1922 when David was 13. "Good riddance," David told everyone. By that point, David had adapted and learned to expect the beatings and all sorts of physical and emotional abuse from his father, along with things much worse that he had buried in the back of his mind. His childhood, no longer living under the protection of his cousin who was killed in WWI, had turned David into something dark, violent, isolated, and unnerving. Even though the death of his

40

father meant the abuse stopped, it did not quell the darkness that had developed and festered in David.

"You are better than everyone David. You deserve anything you want; all you have to do is go out and take it," the voices in his head would regularly tell him.

The coyote and the wolf would vie for David's attention, each one pressing David farther and farther into his pit of despair, each one trying to outdo the other, hoping to gain their master's attention as to who was the better at executing his plan on God's creations. As soon as the demon of fear finished with David, the demon of pride would jump in for a taste of his own, filling David with a loathing for others that would consume him and tear apart his heart. This would allow the demon of rejection a wide-open door, driving David further away from his family and his mother who truly loved him.

As observers of the vision, Shepherd and the sheep could hear gentle voices reach out to David, voices of mercy, empathy, compassion, and grace. But they could not penetrate his hardened heart.

For the sheep, the vision would fast forward at quadruple speed, like one of the digital videos he would watch, giving a picture of David living. As a pre-teen and then a teenager, David would capture animals and rodents around the farm and, rather than dispose of them the proper way, what he could not tear apart with his bare hands, he would slash and cut up with his pocketknife and place the remains in areas around the house to frighten and intimidate the family. His mother, full of guilt and remorse, would try to love him, but she would also observe him helpless as he gleefully cut the smaller animals open and rip out their insides.

She asked his brothers to talk with him, but they had grown weary of him, having dealt with their own issues with their father, though not to the degree that David suffered. David held a special place with their father. His mother, while fearful of her husband, was also relieved when he passed away; yet she had become even more frightened of her son, demoralized that he did not change after the abuse stopped.

"David, go to your mother. She loves you and she wants to care for you," the voices of compassion would continue, never to be heard.

As a matter of fact, his brothers had actually tried to talk sense into David early on but he would tell them to "shuck off" and threaten them with the same knife he used to gut the rats. As his brothers took on more responsibilities around the farm after their pa had died, they pushed David to the side more and more, always keeping him at arm's length. David was alone.

"You are stronger than they are David; they are weak. Vermin to be chewed on and spat out. They don't deserve you." These were the voices that David listened to.

AFTER THEIR PA DIED, the family was fortunate and extremely grateful that they were able to keep on a family of boarders who helped to manage and operate the farm as a condition of small pay, including room and board. David seemed to believe that the boarders got more respect than he. He could not understand why he did not have more authority around the farm when he knew he was supposed to be in charge; that's what the voices told him. It was at some point in his teen years that it became obvious to him that he would never be part of the farm; he was being pushed to the side. This only served to fuel David's hatred further, which he would take out on others.

The wolf pack continued to nip at David, pass their scent to him, and lick him, causing him to grow more despondent. He would neglect whatever miniscule responsibilities he was given, feeling that he was entitled to the services and chores that others on the farm were doing. This only promoted further isolation and distance from the family. The wolf pack howled in glee.

The sheep would watch as angels of God would work to soothe David's heart, working to feed it with the mind of God. But David's Will was consumed with bitterness and hatred of people in general. Shepherd would speak to David but his heart had become so cold, that he could not hear, ignoring the voice speaking up inside of him. The only saving grace for David, if that can even be stated, was his distaste for the ultimate of all evil actions, to take another human life. But this didn't stop the other demons that would work through David, causing him to vent his Will in other ways.

David grew into a short 5 foot 8, lanky body, making him look taller than he was. While not physically attractive based on most views, he learned how to be very charming and manipulative, and would be with several woman before he turned 30, only to leave them in the dust. The wolf pack would yelp and sing their songs to David, giving him a superhuman ability for manipulation, which would serve him for the greater part of his life. Feeling a degree of guilt for his actions, guilt that the wolf fed into, he found comfort in alcohol.

When Japan bombed Pearl Harbor in 1941, David was a 32-year-old drunk, having finally spurned the animosity of his semi-affluent family. To get away from them and his perceived drama, he enlisted in the Army in April 1942 before being drafted. At this, the sheep felt hopeful that this would give his grandfather discipline and straighten him out; but it actually made him worse. The wolf pack followed David, bringing his unfettered attitude and character with him into the military, which quickly gained him the reputation as someone to stay away from.

Shepherd was also walking with David, and spoke the following to him, *"It is the Lord's desire for you David that you be encouraged in heart and love. For that, My little Brother, will be the provision necessary for you to experience the full riches He has for you as well as to understand your purpose and His desires for you."* A crack appeared as David looked up and around him, thinking that he had heard someone say something. But he did not see anyone and continued about his business.

During his time in the military, his drinking became chronic and so was his addiction to tobacco. His emotional problems expanded into verbal abuse to those around him, continued isolation, and a deep-rooted bitterness, feeding insecurities that everyone was out to get him. He didn't trust anyone, nor did anyone trust him.

The wolf celebrated with his pack. *"Yes, he will not change, my pets. He's ours!"* he sang.

FORT SAM HOUSTON, TX, AND FT. DODGE, IOWA 1942-1958

AS DAVID CONTINUED on his very dry and bitter desert wilderness journey, the wolf pack, with eyes aglitter with the joy of consumption, continued to devour David's soul, surrounding David with animosity. But, if David were to look with the true eyes of his heart, he would see what the sheep could see, a small sliver of light that was trying to break through the barrier he had placed in front of himself; yet, he still allowed the demonic strongholds to overtake him.

In fast motion, the sheep watched David serve three years in the military, serving as a cook at a Dining Facility at Fort Sam Houston, TX, a training base prepping medical support soldiers for combat. But David would never see combat nor deploy to an overseas location. At some point, he would work with a team pushing prepared meals to the European Theater, and, at some further point, he would make enough people angry that he would be restricted to full time kitchen duties in the largest dining hall on the installation for the remainder of his military stint.

"That's fine. It's good to stay in the USA, " David told himself, "here I have regular access to all of the whiskey I want. And the girls…good for me!" While he failed to get along with the men in his unit, David had a charm that attracted women. At some point, he would hook up with a girl, but the vision the sheep was experiencing would not allow him to see her or hear her name.

David was discharged from the military in October 1945 and had plans to head back to Iowa where he had a job waiting as a Bater, tanning hides and skins from butchered cattle. He told his girl that he would eventually reach out to her and move her to Webster County, but he wanted to prepare his mother first as he had never told her about their relationship. What David did not know was that she was pregnant.

Upon his return to Ft. Dodge, David would not contact the girl for another two years. She would try to reach out to him via telegrams, informing him that he had a son, but he ignored them. When he got back home, he found that his family still refused to acknowledge him, but out of a sense of obligation, they segmented 25 acres of his own from the land, including a small house and barn. His brothers, uncles, and cousins had made it clear that they did not want him working on the family farm. They weren't aware that David assumed things were in a mess over there, and had already worked out the job of Bater upon his return.

A breeze gently touched David's skin, *"Come to Me."*

Instead of moving into the property set aside for him, David moved in with a married woman, but this only survived for a few months. In early 1946, he had met another married woman named Marie and they immediately started an affair. A few months later, Marie would learn that she was pregnant and leave her husband for

David. They would move in together in the small house that his family had set up for him.

Other than telegramming the girl from Texas that it was over, he would never talk to her again; nor did he ever acknowledge his son. Marie would informally change her common name to her middle name Beth, in a blind effort to manage the gossip that would unfold in town, thinking that a new name might somehow disguise what she and David had done. She too, had left two children with her ex-husband, never to talk with them again, nor acknowledge them until later in life when she was suffering from dementia. While shocked about the knowledge that his grandfather had an illegitimate son, the sheep was already aware of his grandmother's past.

David had a son whom he abandoned and they were now expecting another. But he never wanted children as he believed that they were a plague on the world. In the vision, the sheep could see into David's mind. David felt that he actually lived by some kind of moral code by not desiring to bring children into a world he hated. Eventually, he completely wiped all memory of his first son from his mind. In fact, he never told Beth about him, which the sheep observed in surprise. He and Beth had become blinded to the truth of their abandonment. But, as the sheep observed, Beth was easily manipulated by David.

BETH GAVE BIRTH to their first son in 1947 – and David was not a fan. *"He's a bug, David, someone to be trod on,"* the wolf whispered to him.

To add to his personal and emotional misery, they would conceive two more sons before they were finished, one in 1948, and another in 1950. After the birth of their third son something happened: that familiar small sliver of light reached through the hardness of David's heart once again, a breakthrough the shadow, *"Children are a blessing from the Lord, a heritage to marvel."* But just as fast as it appeared, the light was quickly extinguished.

David and Beth raised their sons on their small farm in Iowa until 1958, but until that time David was a terror to his two older boys, and moderately absent with his youngest. He abused his two older boys physically and emotionally, constantly reminding them that he hated them. But things got much worse for the two older ones as they grew up.

"The boys are yours to do with as you wish David," the wolf and his pack would say to him while nipping at his chest and backside. *"Remember what your father told you. Do not spare the rod David; this is the only way to discipline them."*

Beth remained indifferent to the abuse and would never stand up for either of her boys. David was very adept at control and it didn't help that she agreed with him about life in general. He would remind Beth regularly that, if they had not had the same outlook on life, he would have left her after Danny was born. The wolf pack would regularly place their scent on David, continuing to drive his lustful temptations. Instead of leaving Beth, he opted for numerous affairs instead as it made him feel euphoric and in control.

Though born a year apart, Danny and Roger went through puberty at approximately the same time. Unfortunately, once their father discovered these changes, he would abuse and humiliate them during this most intimate time in their still developing lives. David's drinking reached a point where he was rarely sober, wasting the family money on cheap whiskey and moonshine from home brewers in the area. Not only would he force the two oldest boys to drink with him, he would humiliate them as their bodies changed. While Beth chose to believe that the boys were fulfilling chores by taking care of their pigs, their father had other unmentionable ideas in mind, and these activities would haunt the boys for the remainder of their lives.

Then one day, there was a rumble in the center of Beth's gut. Her heart drops for just a minute, *"Stop what is happening, for it is an abomination, and you know it."* But the fear of her husband, and her love for him, was much stronger and she quickly brushed it aside.

The sheep continued to watch the vision, overwhelmed with grief and outrage at what he saw, unable to fathom what was happening. He remembered that Shepherd had warned him that he would not like all that he saw and heard, and this warning came back to the front of his mind. Based on what he knew, how was it possible that Danny, his father, would never discuss or share any of this with anyone, not even his wife? The sheep now understood that these events would allow demons to operate in Danny's life right up until he himself was lying on his own deathbed. Somehow, the wolf and coyote had been passed on to Danny, lying to him, betraying him, manipulating him, tormenting him, and cheating him of a life of joy. Danny would, unfortunately, learn to take these out on his own son later.

Towards the close of the 1950s, the sheep noted that David's health was taking a serious turn for the worse due to his drinking, his chronic smoking, and the lime he would breathe in while tanning hides. His mother and father were long gone and his brothers and sister had pretty much disowned him, rarely acknowledging him as brother. The gossip about David and Beth, along with David's reputation, had deteriorated to a point where they were completely isolated. So they decided to migrate from Iowa to California with plans to start an Ice Cream Truck business.

"Love your wife, David, love your children. Do not listen to the lies. You have the capacity to love. Repent and come to Me! I am at your heart, David, hear Me knock!" the soft whispers would gently continue. "Leave me alone!" David would shout out into the air. "I'm not worthy of that, my Pa told me so... I am nothing... I have nothing to give."

The wolf pack celebrated his destruction; they knew it was not them alone. David himself was submitting to his own temptations, his own internal desires, and his own merciless hatred of himself. They had reached a point that they only needed to push a little, and it was getting easier and easier. Simultaneously, Shepherd was offering David a fighting chance to defeat them, but David had instead decided to concede, placing his bitterness onto his own children.

THE VISION FROZE AND FADED, transporting the sheep back to his spot on the rock beneath a beautiful sky and still surrounded by a lush green landscape. However, he noticed that there was now a small grove of trees off nearby, perfectly manicured with not a dry leaf among them. And sitting directly to his left was the Shepherd.

The sheep was completely distraught and embarrassed for his father and his entire family. While the events he had just witnessed were earlier in his father's life, he already knew some of the events that were yet to come and how they would impact his dad. No wonder he was angry and bitter. The sheep broke down and started to cry.

While the sheep tried to compose himself, Shepherd spoke. *"David was not paying attention, Brother; he was not listening to His voice. The vision did not show it but there were men working around him during his military service and at the tanning facility,*

47

trying to get his attention and make him more self-aware. They could see his struggle and recognized that his spirit was speaking up inside of him as the Spirit of God was trying to reach him, more than once; but he had reached a point where his spirit was warped, allowing his soul to condemn him. Rather than receive their encouragement as well as their admonishment, he made fun of the guys that were trying to reach him. His belief system had convinced him that he was not recoverable."

"I didn't know," the sheep trembled, "what my father had gone through. It must have torn him up inside."

"Yes, your father would develop a warped sense of living, just as your grandfather did from his father."

Shepherd continued, *"You had mentioned before that you felt as if a curse had been passed down to you from your father and his father. But you need to know that the Lord removed all curses from you when He became a curse on the cross for you. You are no longer under a curse, nor were your father or grandfather; but, all of you did fall victim to generational sins. The sins of your grandfather were passed to your father and he, in turn, passed them on to you, and you to your children."*

"But I tried to be different and I believe that my father didn't want to be the kind of father to me that his was to him. Actually, now that I've seen it, I know that my father was nowhere as bad as his. But it still doesn't make sense," the sheep reasoned.

"All men are born into sin because of the fall, which you are aware of from the opening chapters in Genesis. You were born a slave to sin, but you were also saved from that slavery when you were born again, by accepting Jesus Christ into your heart. If you want proof of that, ask yourself this: do you treat your children today the same way you did before you were born again?"

"No, I am actually much more aware of my actions and my attitude."

"You see. You broke that tie to generational sins; you are no longer a victim of them. I know that you are still tempted and there are times that you may lash out, but, you are different, more con-trolled, and as you stated, more aware. And that is because He is operating in your life now."

Shepherd continued, *"Even though your father wanted to be different with you and your sister than his father was with him, his spirit was not connected to Our Creator. He was still connected to the generational sins passed on to him. While he was able to manage minor degrees of self-control by his own effort, your father was never truly in control; he was always under the control of his sin. The result was that he exhausted himself because he could not continually defeat the demons operating in his life on his own strength."*

"Wow, OK, I think I get it." The sheep appeared more relaxed and somehow comforted.

Shepherd remained silent for a few seconds before standing up. *"It's time we move on to the next vision the Lord has for you. But we'll talk more about struggles, sins, and temptations as we move along. I pray that the visions you have seen so far, and our discussions, are giving you a sense of understanding of who you are and where you came from along earthly lines. Perhaps, you are even beginning to see how some of your own behaviors and traits relate to your earthly heritage."*

"Yes, I think so, but I suspect more will come to light. While this has been painful, I feel that I am growing," the sheep admitted.

"Wonderful! Then as we allow the past to rest, onward and forward we go!"

▥

BE CAREFUL, FOR THE WOLF *knows that all it needs to survive is for someone to not want to shoot it. But if you stand your ground Sword in hand, you have a fighting chance and can defeat the wolf.*

The wolf wants nothing more than to shed blood and destroy lives in order to get its dishonest gain. Sadly, even the most worthwhile rooster will fall if it is found lacking in heart and spirit. Even worse, there are some roosters who do not want to shepherd their family. If they see the wolf coming, they will flee and leave the flock, allowing the wolf to snatch its prey. They prey on the young.

As our story continues, it appears that the wolf has captured one rooster and has buried its remains, so it now moves on to its next quarry. In the meantime, the wolf transforms its skin into that of a creature that displays an exterior of beauty, grace, comfort, and peace – but it is all false. It may have a new exterior, but its heart and its motives remain the same. For its skin may change, but the disposition towards evil does not. It maneuvers itself as it teases and plays with the young, making them think that they have the upper hand, waiting for the opportunity to leap. The wolf has become the fox.

CHAPTER 5
THE FOX MANEUVERS

"...foolish prophets who follow their own spirits and have seen
nothing are like foxes among ruins..."
(Ezekiel 13:3-4, paraphrased)

"Some Pharisees approached Jesus, telling him 'Go away, Herod
wants to kill You.' And He replied to them, 'Go and tell that fox
that I am casting out demons and performing cures today and
tomorrow, but I will reach my goal on the third day'"
(Luke 13:31-32, paraphrased)

THE FOX CREEPS CLOSE *to the ground as it sneaks up on the*
chicken coop. Just like its predecessor the wolf, it prefers the darkness
of night. Now that the wolf has successfully distracted the rooster,
the fox focuses its attention on the chicks. As soon as it gets close,
it pounces and pins a youngling down in its paws as it prepares to
deliver the killing bite. Be advised, my dear friend, that this sounds
as if the fox is taking out the flesh of the young one. But no, the
fox wants to get in the mind and the soul of the young one with its
parasitic infection, while it is still developing, still maturing, and
still learning. If successful, the infected soul will grow, develop,
and mature into one that will tear apart its own flesh through the
power of temptation, a hunger that drives the body to do things that

can, eventually, lead to regret, defeat, and emotional turmoil, or worse – eternal death.

Like the coyote and the wolf, the fox rules his clan, each going by names such as Unforgiveness, Self-Centeredness, Anger, and Strife. As with the coyote and wolf, their weapons are their jaws, their claws, and their scent, which, when used, create a condition of thoughtlessness, regret, shame, worthlessness, suspicion, and despair.

The fox is solitary, but since it goes after the young and weak, it can successfully operate alone. The fox knows that, if it can get them when they are young, it has an opportunity for some to grow into something akin to an anti-rooster, a new self-centered creature focused more on itself, knowing that eternal death is inevitable so "why not?" This creature is driven to succeed, but to succeed on his own legacy and his own behalf. The fox is smart; it knows that this will destroy the flock, the family unit.

As this festers, the parasite spreads like a virus to its neighbors, colleagues, and the community. Once grown, this new and infected rooster will pass its infection to its own young, aiming for the final victory – to destroy that which was created for good. When this happens, the fox will thump its chest with pride and declare to its master that "this one is mine," marking its territory with its scent to let others know that this one is taken.

▨

NORWALK, CA SEPTEMBER 1964

DANNY, A REBELLIOUS TEENAGER, locked himself away into his home away from home. At 16, his parents had allowed him to move into a small trailer in the backyard of their property. This also allowed his two younger brothers to share a bedroom in the house rather than the three of them in the same room.

His new home was a 22-foot 1950 Silver Streak Clipper that his father had purchased when they moved to California several years earlier – and Danny loved it.

"Yes, isolate yourself and allow the infection to spread," the fox hoots in laughter while Danny moans. If it weren't for his best friend William, he would be completely alone.

He hated his dad with such ferocity that even the thought of his father would bring tears of anger to him. So he avoided him as much as he could. His dad had continued to beat him until just before he turned 16, at which time Danny had threatened to kill him if he ever touched him again. This is when Danny moved into the trailer. David, his father, behaved as if he did not care what Danny thought of him and avoided him just the same.

"Hate feeds the soul, young one, yes. Feed it now, your soul hungers for a release from the mind," the voice says in his head.

About a year earlier, he had been introduced to marijuana – it made him feel that all of his problems were lifted away. Until the next day, anyway. He had also picked up cigarettes a year earlier when he was 15, which helped him to mask the herbal smell of marijuana from his parents; but they didn't really care what he did, when he did it, or who he was doing it with. They just didn't want to be embarrassed.

Shepherd stands nearby, working to reach into a small crack of light he could see in Danny's heart. *"Danny, fill yourself with love, not chemicals of destruction. Love is what you need."*

William had told Danny that he wanted nothing to do with drugs, but he did enjoy beer. "Butch, I have said it before Bro, we don't need that stuff. Isn't beer good enough?" William would often ask him. Danny, aka Butch, as always, would roll his eyes as he took another drag.

He spent a lot of time with William and William's girlfriend Virginia. Danny didn't have a steady girlfriend, but he was charming enough to manage pretty well. He really wanted to hook up with the girl across the street, but she was a little young and only giggled at him anyway.

The two youth spent a lot of time at William's house messing around with cars. Danny had grown quite adept at engine work and metal work but he really wanted to play baseball – that was his true love – not that his dad would care.

To support his habits, Danny had teamed up with a couple of roughnecks at High School that had taken to small time robbery; but he wouldn't participate in most of it. William would support him. However, they would usually limit their activities to the nearby city of Bellflower rather than their own city. "But hey," Dwyane would justify to himself, "we won't touch kids or women. They're out of bounds." This is where he and William differed from the other guys.

The fox raised his eyes at Shepherd standing next to him. *"OK, you got to a small part of him, but don't get cocky. See there, you butt kisser, I still managed to convince him that he is not sinning by masking his actions with false morality."*

Shepherd defended his charge. *"That's a sign that there is light shining into his heart. He is not yours; he is still open to the Lord's bidding and recognizes that he has options. His heart, though hardening, is still malleable and open to the loving hands of the clay maker."*

THE SHEEP OBSERVED as these scenes were playing out in front of him: it was surreal that he could see into both the spiritual and worldly dimensions. In particular, watching as Shepherd operated in both the present and the vision felt odd to him. He would interact with Shepherd outside of the visions, but Shepherd in the visions didn't seem to notice him at all.

Back in his trailer, as Danny drifted in his induced euphoria, he reflected on an altercation he had a few days ago with his dad that still burned him. Danny had gotten home a little later than he preferred. It was dark and, as he opened the gate into the backyard, it squeaked rather loudly. He had oiled the hinges several times but for some reason he could not stop the squeak.

His dad had been up and was smoking a cigarette on the same side of the house that Danny had entered. As Danny closed the gate and turned around, his dad was standing there about three feet away from him, startling him and causing him to fall backward against the now closed gate behind him, hitting his head on the gate lock. Danny reached back to the bump on the back of his head.

"What the hell, Dad?" Danny said. It was obvious that he was both drunk and high.

"Where ya been, Boy?" David asked.

"Out with William – what do you care?"

"Get him David, strike him," the fox egged him on.

"You been out drinkin and I can smell that funny stuff on ya, too." A slight pause. "Boy, you better never do anything to embarrass me or get into trouble. I'll have you out there on the streets faster than you can think or say go."

"Screw off, old man, I'll be out of your hair as soon as I graduate," Danny shrugged him off.

The fox smiled at Danny as he fought his flesh, fighting the urge to punch his dad in the face. The fox didn't even need to do anything; Danny was operating on his own.

"What did you say, you piece of crap?" David asked angrily. "You still think you can take me on. You didn't last year and you won't now. You're worthless and I'll beat your butt with the leather of my belt so hard, your future son, if you have any, will feel it."

The fox had his paws on the head of David, manipulating him like a puppet just like the coyote had done to David's pa forty years earlier. It was just as easy to manipulate David now because by this point he had completely surrendered. However, the Shepherd interposed himself between David and Danny, creating a spiritual barrier of protection.

Danny looked at his dad with deep hatred, his eyes turning red with anger as his blood started pumping. He still remembered the abuse he and his brother suffered at the hands of their father: how could they ever forget? "You pull that belt out and that will be the last thing you do." As Danny looked at his dad's eyes, waiting for a response, his dad's eyes turned solid black, something that he had noticed a few times over the years – and it scared him.

"You're worthless, Boy. I know it and you know it. The day after you graduate, your outta here. I don't care where you go or what you do, but you're no son of mine."

"That is a lie, Danny; the Father has plans for you." Danny felt an odd sensation, as if his mind was telling him to stop talking and just walk away.

It was obvious that there wouldn't be anything physical happening tonight. But it was a game they often played, searching for the harshest words that might strike at the heart of the other, trading verbal jabs and always seeking for that one phrase that would serve to be the final stab into the already gaping chest wound.

A few seconds after he spewed his last words, David turned around and walked into the house, leaving Danny standing there pondering his next move before finally heading towards the backyard. As he walked to his trailer, he started to cry in frustration and anger. His emotions were all over the map, a roller coaster: angry, sad, depressed, excited, flustered, and most of all, confused.

"Ah yes, there it is," the fox giggled to himself loud enough for Shepherd to hear. Both he and Shepherd watched as more dark figures started slithering around Danny, looking for the openings that Danny would create to allow them to enter.

"Why?" he asked himself repeatedly. "Why does he treat us this way? What did I do? Why doesn't he treat my youngest brother the same way? Why do I have to be his beating bag? Man, I hate that bastard."

Danny's spirit was breaking, providing an opportunity for the Shepherd to once again speak to him. As He approached, the power of His light amplified and hit the fox, causing him to screech loudly and run into the shadows.

Shepherd lighted upon Danny at that moment, speaking to his heart. *"Invite Me in Danny. I can comfort you. Let Me ease your suffering, Allow Me to fight your battles."*

Then, as he frequently did after events like that with his father, Danny relaxed, and then he strategized. He would graduate high school and he would try out for the Dodgers or the Angels. Maybe even an out of state team so that he could get as far away from California as possible. He did OK in school, perhaps college would be an option, but not in California. No way.

As with any man, Danny would plan. But forces beyond him would dramatically influence his plans for himself.

AS WITH THE PREVIOUS VISIONS, the last scene slowly faded while Danny was putting his plans together, allowing him to contemplate what he had just recalled from his memory. In an ironic twist, the fox had been out maneuvered by the independent will of its prey.

"Why did the Creator have to give them free will?" the fox ranted as it realized that it had done its job too well. Danny had come to rely on himself rather than God, but he was also ignoring the demons around him. While Danny, a maturing rooster, still held on to a version of the fox's original parasite, he had become self-determined. This meant that his soul was still open and receptive to both the good and the bad.

Danny had identified what he believed to be the single source of his pain, which he was now focused on eradicating, wiping away much of the scent that the fox had laid. However, his rebellious will still opened new doors for more predators and new infections, while also being susceptible to the desires of the Creator. This act of open defiance did not make the solitary and competitive fox happy – he was angry because this rooster was supposed to be his and his alone.

The sheep continued to observe as the fox broke off from its target, but they both watched as new predatory creatures approached Danny with their own variety of toxins, blending in with that which the fox had already laid. *"This guy is not prepared for what he is about to face,"* the fox applauds itself. *"He's done for now; his life will be changed forever."*

The fox is intelligent and knows that, even if he hands Danny off to these new creatures, all he has to do is go dormant for a season. He will not leave completely because a piece of him still exists in Danny, hiding just below the surface. There, his parasite will remain, allowing the fox to also remain, unless, that is, the dreaded Comforter comes to kill the parasite. *"Hah,"* the fox stutters, *"that is highly unlikely. He has been through a lot in his short life and these new demons are sure to push him over the edge."*

With the other creatures of darkness coming in, the fox knows that they are stronger, giving him the assurance that Danny is surely to be tormented and continue to fall from grace. *"But it was I that laid the foundation,"* it thinks pridefully. *"If the stronghold of torment crumbles and it all comes crashing down, it won't be my fault."* It is now up to the coyote and the wolf, the ones who have returned, to finish what they had originally started with David."

AS THE VISION CONCLUDED, the sheep was transported once more back to the beautiful terrain where his quest had started. As expected, the scenery maintained its beauty and the trees he noticed the last time were blending in harmoniously with the landscape. The sheep also noted flowers of varying colors and varieties bursting forth from the greenery around him. This is when he picked up an intoxicating fragrance floating in the air, carried in the soothing breeze. "Wow," he thought, "this is wonderful; I never want to leave!"

"But you will have to leave at some point," Shepherd said, startling the sheep back to reality.

"Holy cow, you startled me for a split second!"

"Sorry, little Brother, but our time is getting short and we need to move on," Shepherd said gently. *"So, did you pick up on anything from this last vision?"*

"You know, I think I saw an opportunity for my father to connect with his father, but, they both chose to grow more distant, more bitter," the sheep remarked. "They were stubborn. I could be wrong but I almost sensed an opportunity; if only my father had humbled himself, things may have been different. But I'm not sure. I think that my grandfather's past experiences had hardened his heart to a point that he probably wouldn't have received him anyway."

"Sure. You are partly correct. But where you are wrong is that, no matter the condition of a man's heart, love can conquer all barriers, even the stone in your grandfather's heart. The challenge for both of them would have been consistency. They weren't spiritually aware enough for commitment of any kind with each other, although their souls would have been receptive to it.

"Can you explain that further?" the sheep asked.

"Are you familiar with the Songs of Solomon?" Shepherd asked, looking at His companion.

"Only that it is a love story between a man and a woman. It is rather provocative from what I have been told. Each time I go to read it, I get distracted and focus on the erotic parts."

Shepherd laughed, *"Yeah, the Lord hears that a lot. Songs of Solomon is a love story about King Solomon wooing his lover in a vineyard. However, the Book can also symbolize the love between a father and son – without the provocative parts obviously."*

"No matter how exquisite a marriage may be, it still has its shares of ups and downs. Both partners in that relationship are human with a heart that is prone to sin. On occasion, both partners, or father and son, may do something that hurts their mate; therefore both partners will experience hurt in some ways. Are you with me so far?" Shepherd asked.

"Yes, Sir."

"A father and son relationship can be just as tenuous as a marriage, or worse, as we are dealing the competitive egos of two men. Most of the time, it will be the little issues that can spoil a relationship like this from blossoming. Here is where that sinister fox enters the story."

"Solomon himself noted that it was the fox, eating away at the grapes of his mate's vineyard, that took her attention away from him just when they were ready to enjoy each other's company. In the case of your father and grandfather, the fox was preventing your father from forgiveness, and the son from offering the love a son ought to give to a father. Now, in this case, your grandfather's spirit was already severely damaged as he had committed his life to misery and bitterness."

"What could Dad have done? Seems that Grandpa was already done for and finished."

"Never underestimate the power of love, Brother. It can break through any barrier if you are persistent and patient enough. While there is a special bond between a husband and wife, the bond between father and son is even more special. But it is precisely because of this special bond that they are both easily susceptible to hurt, pain, and anger. The father wants to be respected by his son, whereas the son wants to be loved and taught what it means to be a man. If your father had found a way to respect his father, to forgive him, and then operate consistently in that paradigm, he would have reached your grandfather."

"BUT WHAT ABOUT THEIR PAST? Grandfather did horrible and unspeakable things to Dad," the sheep argued.

"It is exactly because of that past that your father could have reached your grandfather. Believe me when I say that your grandfather was full of guilt and remorse and it was actually tearing him apart. Your father would have just needed to forgive him and love him, but he would have had to be consistent. And this is where neither of them was aware enough, within their soul, for that level of commitment. The fox in your father's life was hindering him and distracting him, apart from rejecting the voice of Our Father."

"In the vision, the fox wasn't all that dangerous, but he had infected your father with hatred, anger, and frustration. These feelings festered because neither of them would allow a good source to cleanse it from their lives. Just when they had an opportunity to connect, the fox would contaminate their vineyard, frustrating them and causing both of them to separate and dwell on their own problems."

"OK, I think I am getting it," the sheep interjected. "The negative feelings that my father had began to chew away at his life, hindering the possibility for them to resolve their relationship. I think you keep pointing out my father versus my grandfather. My father was more susceptible to the Lord's influence because Grandpa was so far gone. Am I right?"

"As the eldest son, your father was the one in the best position to reach out to your grandfather. His love, love that he did not really know how to give, would have been the medicine needed. So, yes. Your father had already sworn to himself that he was not going to be like his father, allowing some light to shine through. Except he just didn't know how. So instead, he allowed his pain to blot out the potential goodness. Instead, he focused on what he did know...how to hate his father."

"Could my father have broken through that if he had the right person in his life?" the sheep asked.

"The bible tells is that the human will is perverted, determined to serve itself and please itself. Your father's will was already doing damage to his life; he was being emboldened by a self-centered spirit. Which I think you and I might agree was passed on to you, yes?" Shepherd asked quizzically.

"Yes, Sir, ashamedly so," the sheep replied.

"Several years ago, a wise man published a statement on how to be perfectly miserable. It contained a list of 20 statements. We can't go through the list here, but one item of note is that the spirit of self-centeredness will chew away at your spiritual vitals, making you a difficult person to get along with. Make sense?" Shepherd asked.

"Yes, Sir, I actually recognized that in my own life and have been working on it. The solution is to repent of self-centeredness and deny myself as Matthew 16:24-26 advises. I learned that I needed to get out of my own way, though I do still struggle with that to this day."

"Yes, just as you learned in your own life, your father was developing habits, making it difficult for him to contain his negative emotions, even though he didn't want them. Anyhow, let's move on to the next sin the fox was helping your father develop."

"The fox had also infected your father with the root of bitterness. Hebrews 12:15 reminds us that men need to be careful that no root of bitterness grow and make trouble for them, for they can become defiled."

"Oh, I know this one intimately, " the sheep jumped in. "I found deep rooted bitterness in myself and it fed into deep resentment within, making me angry, negative, and hostile to others."

"Yes, I remember," Shepherd reflected. *"That attitude was eating deep into your father, as well as you, like acid in the heart. Out of this, grew jealousy, bickering and controversy. Bitterness is a sin of tremendous proportion. It was one of the primary sins operating in your father's life, impacting his ability to love and forgive his father. Which leads us to the next sin the fox was operating in your father's life. Unforgiveness."*

"I'VE GOT THIS ONE," the sheep said. "Forgiveness is the act of granting a pardon to another person, or persons, for anything they have done that hurt you or offended you. This refers to both God's pardon for our sins and our willingness to release others who have wronged us."

"Absolutely! We are to forgive others just as God has forgiven us. Jesus Himself said that if you forgive, then you will also be forgiven."

"Unfortunately, men like your father and grandfather never realized that God had forgiven them because they felt they didn't deserve it. This attitude carried over into their own heart behavior, where they would carry unforgiveness for others that they felt had wronged them. They confused forgiveness with the idea of forgetting the sin committed against them. They failed to see that to forgive does not always mean that you forget; it simply means that you choose not to dwell on the offense."

The sheep meditated on that for a few seconds, reconciling what he was hearing with what he had already been taught about forgiveness. "It seems that, if they had thought about it and listened to the people in their lives, they would have recognized that. I seem to recall that failing to forgive someone also holds them in some form of emotional bondage. That doesn't seem fair to the other person; it seems selfish and thoughtless."

"Yes," Shepherd added, *"thoughtlessness is a sin that lacks sensitivity to the feelings of others. Thoughtlessness eventually leads to terrible regret. Men must learn to recognize and fight the little foxes more vigorously, and pay attention to the rooster's crow that sounds the warning alarm,"* he concluded.

"We have seen and pondered on the effects of various sins on a man's life, but we can't forget about love. Love is the medicine for everything. If your father had simply loved his father, it would have eventually reached through the hardness of his heart and touched him. Simultaneously, if your grandfather had loved his children, your father would have been a different father to you in return. It would have mitigated the passage of generational sin passed from father to son. But, the most important concept, above all, is the recognition that God is Love. And if it is true that love conquers all, then what do you think God, who is Love, can do?"

"Praise God!" the sheep declared. "You know, with these visions, I am really learning to understand my heritage and how generational sins impacted my parentage as well as me, and how I have dealt with my own children."

"Hallelujah, little Brother! But the Lord has one more vision for you before we get to you specifically. I suspect you will glean more from this one, an event that happened just prior to your own birth."

"I'm ready," said the sheep sitting up.

CHAPTER 6
THE ROOSTER ATTACKED

"Therefore be alert, since you don't know when the master of the house is coming—whether in the evening or at midnight or at the crowing of the rooster or early in the morning"
(Mark 13:35)

AS THE FOX DRAWS BACK *into the shadows, the coyote and the wolf approach with new attacks and new problems for the rooster – at least that's what they want him to think. They have actually been with him the entire time, haunting his subconscious and dreams with things passed on to him from his father. They gleefully celebrate their success with the father, knowing that his son, a rooster now in his own right, is damaged. They laugh as they mock the fox, "He thought he was the strong one. Ha!" they scoff, "we have been there all along, pushing, jabbing, kicking, punching, and speaking to him to remind him about the low life that he is." They also reflect on what they did to his father with a sense of ego and pride in having successfully buried that one's soul. They chose to not let him die but let him live in his internal torment. But now, they have someone whose soul is tender and injured, having marinated since birth in its spiteful juices – and they could almost taste him.*

For a few short years, the coyote and the wolf have worked as a team, successfully placing the rooster in a position that will surely prepare him for an eternal life in pain and turmoil. They figure that if they gang up on him, they will get him to "that point," that singular moment in time, where the rooster is finally ready, tired of life, ready to succumb to the pressure and give in, give up, end it all. If he didn't give in himself, then they would ensure he was taken out, to send him to the home of their master. The wolf and coyote may wear different skins but they operate under the authority of the dark one, the one who filled them with their mission and their ways of operating. He has power over them because he is the one that initially rebelled against the Creator.

The foundation is laid and the plan is solid. The rooster has been placed in an environment that will finish him – an environment conditioned by the demon's master. There will be carnage, there will be destruction, there will be souls taken, and there will be some that shout that glorious scream "Finish it already!" And, in all of this, scornful eyes will remain on the rooster, soaking in the sights of what will assuredly be his marvelous death. With that thought, the coyote and the wolf stand back and watch in their standard state, saliva dripping from their forked tongues sticking through their sharpened teeth.

SOUTH VIETNAM, NOVEMBER 1967

THE AIR WAS MUSTY and the vegetation was thick as the platoon of 75 men walked a trail close to the border of Laos. It wasn't raining on this day but it was rainy season so the bugs were somewhat minimal; but it didn't stop the sweat from building in every orifice and cranny of the bodies of the men as they got closer to their ambush location.

The sheep observed two dark forms standing on a far-off hill. He could also see the Shepherd in the vision standing off in the distance, and wondered what he was thinking. The coyote and the wolf looked at each other and wondered out loud, *"Will He take any action?"* Their looks conveyed the silent answer, *"Nah, the godlickers rarely get involved because of that silly rule of choice and free will,"* but they also remembered that He did step in from time to time. Pre-destination was something that man had made up, thanks to demons like themselves, but sometimes the Lord has very specific plans for His children.

64

The sheep watched his father, as a young twenty-year-old machine gunner, serving his second tour in Vietnam. He had tried to complete his military obligation back in the States after his first tour, but both the stigma of soldiers at home coupled with the formal military standard of living were realities he could not accept. So, he figured he would complete another year in the bush, while continuing to contemplate whether to make the military a career, or perhaps a baseball career like he had originally dreamt about.

The sheep could hear his father's thoughts as he reflected on how his plans had changed when he was drafted eighteen months ago. He did think it very odd that he received his notice on his eighteenth birthday, but he didn't get overly upset about it. It got him away from that jerk-wad father of his.

OF THE FORCE OF 75 MEN, most were South Vietnamese soldiers, but there was a contingent of twenty Americans working with them. Earlier in the day they had received a report that a small force of Vietcong were walking a trail from Laos into the Southern region of Vietnam. Their mission was to meet them and kill them enforce once they crossed the border.

While the sheep could see the soldiers arrayed across what he knew would be a battlefield, he looked up and noticed a cloud appearing. Upon closer inspection, he saw this cloud transforming into a swarm of deformed vultures, circling over the men below. Their feathers were unusual and there were teeth along the rims of their beaks. This is when he realized that these were not normal vultures but demonic manifestations. He then looked over to the wolf and the coyote, who were also looking up with their arms raised in what appeared to be celebration.

After a few more clicks of walking, the soldiers got to their location and the men set up their fighting positions for the ambush. Danny found a good spot behind a fallen tree overlooking the trail, good overhead cover, too; he was on the forward edge of the team spanning an ambush site 50 meters long. It would be his job to start taking out the bad guys once the team on the other end of the ambush site started shooting the leading elements of the enemy force. He would be one of the first to see the enemy and would have to patiently wait, holding back his shooting finger, until the shooting started 50 meters away.

Shepherd, standing off a short distance away, was also prepared for the battle that was soon to follow. He had his orders and He was prepared to follow them. Glory be to Him! As He looked on, ethereal forces of majestic friends started appearing around some of the men in the ambush site. These glorious forms, covered in armor, held shields at the ready, while maintaining swords locked in sheaths at their sides. The sheep could see everything, watching all of this happening in front of him, noting that not all of the men had a protective guard; it was limited to a dozen or so. The sheep waited in eager anticipation of what was about to come. He knew what was about to happen because his father had told him portions of the story, but he had never shared everything.

Danny had been through this before but this was his first time this close to the Laotian border. As he lay there, waiting for the Vietcong to enter the site, he contemplated his future. "A military career or baseball? Which is the right one for me?" No answers came, but either one excited him. After a few agonizing hours, the first signs of the enemy appeared through the thick leaves of the jungle. They were walking silently and in pairs but it appeared that they were not aware that they were about to meet a force ready to take them out.

The vultures circled in closer to the ambush site, their feathers raised slightly away from their skin. The sheep could not bear to look directly at them now; their eyes had started to turn a fiery red, their beaks opening showing their teeth. Simultaneously, the angels lifted their shields in protective covering over their charges, while Shepherd remained still a short distance away with his arms folded in front of Him, head bowed. The sheep could see that Shepherd was praying but he couldn't hear the words.

THOUSANDS OF MILES AWAY, Thomas Mason from the city of Nicholasville, KY was suddenly awakened from a well-deserved nap. At 72 years of age, he had come to enjoy these respites from the honey-do-list his wife often provided for him. This was also the day that she spent several hours at their church, giving Thomas the luxury of napping guilt free. However, today, he was suddenly jerked awake from his nap, with deep spiritual pangs to pray right now. This had only happened a dozen times for Thomas but he had learned in his long life to never ignore the Lord. He had no idea what was happening, for who, or where, but he was comforted in the knowledge that the Spirit knew, and that was good enough for him.

"Father, I don't know the details but I can sense in Your Spirit that someone needs prayer right now, someone that either cannot pray for themselves or there is the need for two or more to pray together. So, in obedience, Lord, I declare now, in Jesus' Name, that the situation unfolding right now has a spiritual layer of protection over it. The person or persons involved are safe, in Jesus' Name. The situation has been washed clean via the blood of Jesus Christ. O God, there is a sinner's grief ready to spill out and I believe in Your Word that You love the sinner and do not desire his death. Therefore Father, I thank You for the protection of Your heavenly angels over that situation right now, where someone or some ones are exposed to the wiles of the evil one, in Jesus' Name. Allow the people involved to be strengthened by the assistance of Your grace through Jesus Christ our Lord, Amen."

Around the world, several dozen people experienced the same call as Thomas, but only a dozen answered it.

DANNY THINKS TO HIMSELF, "Thank God it is not raining, or this would be more miserable than it already is. Daylight, too, makes this even easier." His adrenaline was pumping and he could hear himself breathing as he prepared to fire but had to restrain himself from firing early. He would aim his M60 machine gun at each bad guy he saw but he would not start shooting until the first round went down range. Ten minutes after the first of the enemy passed about 10 yards in front of him, the rounds started flying.

The raised feathers from the vultures were shaken and then released from their bodies targeted at the men below, hitting some of the men on both sides of battle. The shields from the angels protected the men they were guarding, saving them from the feathers that would have otherwise hit them. The sheep noticed that the angels were not only protecting men in his dad's units, but there were angels protecting a small number of Vietcong as well.

Danny had 2000 rounds of ammo between him and his battle buddy, spanning several 100 round belts packed in canisters that his buddy would assist with loading as necessary. The tactic of the machine gunner at the time was take out as much of the bush and vegetation as possible to clear the line of fire – just keep shooting in the direction of the enemy; do not conserve ammo. On occasion, a round would hit a bad guy, but for the first few minutes, he was simply shooting in the general area. He could see some of the bad guys fall after he got them in the shoulder, the neck, or the abdomen; he always aimed for the middle of the man. Coupled with a few carefully placed claymore mines, the battle was heavy. Bullets flying, screams, death yells as men on both sides were pumping themselves up.

As the feathers from the vultures hit some of the men, they did not seem to notice, but they were suddenly overcome with paralyzing fear. They dropped their weapons and curled up into a ball on the ground, but this did not stop deadly bullets from opposing sides killing them where they lay.

Lying in a prone position, Danny would not move but the Vietcong were trying to approach him from all directions in front of him. As they were firing, he felt two hot searing stripes cross his back, like someone had taken a hot piece of rod iron and laid it straight across his back. He knew that he had just been hit – twice from what he could tell – but he ignored the pain and kept shooting. After 15 minutes, the firing was reduced to a minimum … and then a minute or so after that, it stopped. The ringing in his ears was immense. He had shot up a little more than half of his ammo. He could hear the agonized whimpers of men all around him; they had been shot and were making it known that they were out of the fight.

SHEPHERD REMAINED in his position, never raising his head as he stood calmly in prayer. However, the coyote and the wolf screamed as they jumped into the action themselves, running directly towards the angels.

And then, all hell broke loose.

Danny started taking fire from his rear. He could also hear the sounds of battle 60 meters in front of him as his friends on the other side of the ambush zone started taking fire as well. Danny shifted his position to shoot behind him and to his "new" left. This is when he realized that his battle buddy was missing the top of his forehead; he had taken a solid round above his right eye. Danny loaded another belt by himself and started shooting at anything he thought he saw.

THE ANGELS, who knew the dark ones were running towards them, quickly drew their swords with one arm while continuing to hold their shields over their human charges. The wolf and coyote were joined by dozens of members of their packs, intent on destroying the angels or distracting them long enough to remove their shields of protection from the humans. Simultaneously, the vultures continued to circle overhead, releasing a never-ending barrage of hardened feathers.

Thunk! A round took out Danny's right foot; this added to the searing pain across his back. He had no time to think about this as he was now fighting for his life. He continued to shoot when he felt his right elbow give way – "What the heck!" He had taken another round and his right arm was useless, but he kept firing while leaning on his left side. His weight, now pressing and pulling against his left arm, was pulling his machine gun off target. He could feel the heat of more rounds crossing his back but, when he took a bullet in his left wrist, he could do no more; the pain was too much. He gave up, rolled over onto his back and waited for it all to end. He could hear the yelling and closing sounds of battle as the Vietcong got closer to him and the positions of his other team members. After a few more minutes, all he could hear was one shot here and another shot there. His team was gone. They had been annihilated. The entire battle had lasted less than 30 minutes.

The spiritual fight was just as intense from the sheep's vantage point. Shepherd, still in prayer, lifted his head to the heavens and raised his arms in surrender to the Father. The wolves and coyote had reached their targets and were jumping on and over the angels, striving to lock their jaws on necks or swipe their sharpened claws into the meaty portions of backs, arms, and legs. The angels were obvious masters of sword and shield as they struck back with the sharpened edges of their swords, slicing open bellies or lopping off legs and the occasional head. It was majestic to watch. Although the odds were almost four to one in favor of the demons, the angels were significantly faster, taking down three at a time in a vicious barrage of slicing and stabbing. It was glorious.

Just as the human battle had ended, the spiritual battle was also over. The angels had taken out a vast majority of creatures but it did look like two angels had been…killed? The sheep wasn't sure as the spiritual forces on both sides would vanish into atomic particles when struck down. But he also noticed that, while some of the angels had done their best against extraordinary odds in the battle, some of the humans had taken some of the vultures' arrows and were killed or wounded as a result of the fear that had overtaken them.

As the sheep looked over towards his father, an angel that had been guarding him removed his shield. With everything the sheep was witnessing, he had lost sight of his father as the ferocity of the fight had suddenly exploded; but he could see him now, backed up against a tree. Having survived the spiritual side of the battle, the wolf and coyote remained as Shepherd walked towards the center of the battlefield. They kept their eyes on him, while yelping in victory but they were not sure what Shepherd would do now. He was not responding to their jaunts and attempts at ridicule for what had just transpired. With the exception of one angel, the remaining angels and surviving demonic packs vanished. Shepherd and two creatures also remained, watching as the Vietcong soldiers followed their barbaric desires.

Shepherd, distraught that Danny had suffered so many injuries, was nevertheless satisfied that he would live. He already had a good idea of what Danny's future would be like, and this grieved him; but he had confidence in what the Lord willed for His children. Meanwhile, He trained his sight on one Vietcong soldier in particular that was pilfering the battlefield. This one was not like the others.

AS DANNY LAY THERE, starting to dream about the two career options that he would never see, he watched as Vietcong soldiers walked around bayoneting every man they found. Some men would scream "No" as the large knife penetrated their chest to take out their heart. He watched all of this unfold around him as he waited for his own death. He was in pain and no longer cared. He was not afraid; he just wanted it to end and he swore to himself that he would not beg or scream.

At some point, a young Vietnamese kid walked up to Danny, the same one Shepherd had noticed earlier. While Shepherd bowed his head, Danny and the Vietcong stared at each other, eye to eye, as Danny waited for the bayonet pointed at him to enter his stomach or chest. It felt like minutes, but likely just a few seconds. The young soldier kept his eye on Danny as he reached down and grabbed the rucksack that was lying next to him. And then…he turned and walked away. "What? Why? Huh?" just before he passed out. "What just happened?"

Shepherd raised his eyes to the heavens, *"Thank You Father!"* He then released the one remaining angel to run off to ensure that nearby forces had the information they needed to find the ambush location quickly.

An hour or so later, a team of friendlies walked into the ambush site looking for survivors. They would find Danny semi-conscious due to loss of blood; but he was alive. Danny would later learn that the small enemy force they had intelligence on was a lead scout recon team for a significantly larger Vietcong battalion two clicks behind them – the American intelligence team had messed up bad. The Americans and South Vietnamese had been outnumbered by five to one and didn't even know it.

The coyote and the wolf now stood aghast at all that had just transpired; they watched as their ultimate victory was taken away. The plan was that ALL of the Americans would die, but some still lived. They watched Shepherd stand over Danny, and they watched as the enemy soldier left him to live. They had grown angry when the angels had originally appeared, standing guard with their shields over some of the men around the ambush site. *"He did it, He got involved,"* they growled when they charged into the battle. They wondered what their master's reaction would be.

The sheep had just watched the battle that his father had only shared with him in spurts, never telling him the full story. Ten men survived that day, including Danny, but the sheep was already aware that this battle would live with him for the rest of his life. Already emotionally wounded, his father would be further damaged, living the remainder of his life as if he had died that day in 1967, just a few months short of his twenty-first birthday. As far as Danny was concerned, there may be a heaven, but he was in hell. This became his life's philosophy and it came at a price in his relationship with his future son.

BLOODIED AND INJURED, the rooster climbs out from under the rubble of the carnage. He looks around and soaks in the gruesome scene around him. In the shadows, the wolf and the coyote watch in dread when the drama does not end the way it was planned. They are focused on the now, and right now the rooster is not dead. Instead

the rooster lives. This angers both of them as they do not get to consume the soul of their charge, but they also shake in fear. "Who's going to report this to the master?" the wolf asks. The smarter one, the coyote, hisses a reply, "I suspect he already knows." With that, they remain with the rooster, bent on continuing their attacks and their lies.

Realizing that the plan did not turn out as expected, they openly invite the fox to come back out of the shadows to participate in activities that will torment the rooster. Where once there was one, there were two; where once there were two, now there are three.

However, the wolf and the coyote are aware of the damage that was planted in the heart and mind of the rooster. It may not have gone as planned, but their agenda worked, just not the way they thought. Unlike his father, who did not die, this rooster believes that he truly did die, that he did not deserve to live, and this would plague him. The three demonic creatures would feed on and expand on this, ensuring that the seeds of pain and suffering were properly watered. However, just as the fox learned, the coyote and the wolf would also learn that sometimes the free will of the rooster does not always cooperate.

The rooster would become determined, taking on anything that would blot out his pain. Unbeknownst to him, his struggles would remain just below the surface of his skin, coming out under times of duress. Nonetheless, the rooster would eventually move on to his own flock and father his own chicks. The seed that was planted in him would begin to bear fruit, but this fruit was bitter and sour. The rooster had no love for a world that he now considered hell – love does not exist, at least this is what he told himself, because in his heart he did care. He just didn't know how to show it.

The three predatory creatures would follow along in the rooster's life, regularly feeding him with thoughts that would continue to sour his soul. And then, one day, the rooster fathered his first chick, and they smiled in delight. They dispatched the weaker fox to take care of the chick, while they remained with the rooster. The rooster had climbed out from the rubble and carnage, having been denied the glorious death that he wanted. His anger and frustration would fester and the rooster would take it out on his flock, with help from the coyote and wolf, of course. The coyote and the wolf ensured that a piece of them was passed on from father to son, while the fox would use that to ensure the future rooster would be self-righteous and work against the Creator.

ᛗ

THE FINAL SCENE of the vision was watching his father being picked up and placed on a litter to be carried away. In and out of consciousness, his father would say to the men carrying him, "Just let me die." And then without warning, the sheep suddenly found himself standing along the perfectly manicured path a few feet away from the rock where he and Shepherd had first connected. The scenery was continuing to evolve, more features, more flowers in full bloom. He could see bees, hovering over the flowers essential to their life calling. He could see fish leaping from the nearby lake, snapping at little flies that dared to fly too close to the water.

He noticed a bench that had not been there before, so he strolled over to it and sat there. As small tears formed in his eyes, he placed his elbows on his knees and bowed his head. What he had just witnessed, the earthly battle and the spiritual battle had changed everything he felt he knew about his father.

"O Heavenly Father, I have been wrong. My visions and experiences of my youth drowned out the truth of who my father truly was. I was misguided, thoughtless, self-centered, unfair. While all I wanted was the respect of my father, I was also the one that was pushing him away. Yes, we had our moments, but after watching his life flow before me, I see that he, too, had his moments and his father before him. We have all allowed sins to pass from father to son and we allowed those sins to fester. However, I see now that, if I had learned to respect my father, he would have returned that respect; honor would have ruled between father and son. I see that now.

"Father, I love my father and it thrills my heart to know that I was able to spend a few days with him before he slowly passed away. It excites my spirit to know that he came to Jesus Christ before he died and that he and I will one day be able to wrap our arms around each other in a fatherly embrace. But is also grieves my heart with the knowledge that we wasted many years drifting apart, never truly knowing each other, guessing at what the other

73

was feeling. Lord, I repent of my ill thoughts towards my father and grandfather, feelings of vengeance and hatred towards them. I lived with a blind eye.

"Thank You, Father, for Your protection in that time of conflict in Vietnam. Not only was I able to witness the battle that tried to ruin him, I also observed Your majestic Spirit operating in a moment where many would say You were not there. Thank You, Father, for sending out the call to prayer, to strangers, to pray in intercession for those that could not protect themselves. Thank You for allowing me to see that You do love sinners and want nothing more than to protect them from death. Thank You, Father, for giving my dad another chance at redemption and salvation.

"I know now that the struggle is not against flesh and blood, but against rulers, against authorities, against the powers of this dark world and against the spiritual forces of evil in the heavenly realms. I know now that there were deep rooted adversaries working against the plans You had for my father and my grandfather. Thank You for honoring your commitment to be a rock in their lives. Even if they rejected it, You never gave up. I know that You loved my grandfather and my father and were continually working to shape them to be the person that You had originally called them to be. Father, I pray that, as I continue my walk on this earth and as I grow older, that I will be content with where I am, seeking Your discipline so that I can be a better person.

"Lord, I am a firsthand witness that, just as You commanded the Israelites not to be afraid when they left Egypt, You also went before my grandfather and my father, that You fought for them just as You did for the Israelites in Egypt. You were walking before them in their Wilderness. You offered to carry them, even when You knew they would reject You. Your hand was extended before them telling them, "Come with Me;" yet they did not take it. Father, please do not hold it against me that I continue to carry concerns that my grandfather could have received better guidance that would have pulled him from the pit of darkness that he placed himself in. Yet, Father, I also move forward in confident faith that there were forces and principalities working on his behalf that I did not witness. For I know that You never quit, even when my grandfather did.

"Father, my heart fails at the terror that my father and grand-father experienced at the hands of their fathers, understanding that these experiences became a part of who they were as men. I feel for them and I cry for them, knowing that they were lacking the strength to uplift their spirits. Thank You for the revelation in understanding this, as well as who and how to get the strength that we ourselves don't possess.

"My father's injuries from his youth and the war would be a burden for him. Whatever sports career he thought he had was over. His back would retain the scars, just as the scars across my grandfather's back. His foot injury would never allow him to run and his right elbow and left wrist would never fully heal. I can recall several conversations with him where, as far as he was concerned, he died that day in Vietnam. I also recall him saying that he considered the world we live in to be hell. Every day since he received his injuries on that battlefield was a day of pain for my father – physical and emotional – and I don't believe he ever fully recovered until, just days before his death, he came to know You.

"Lord, I pray, right now, against the adversaries that were oper-ating in the lives of my paternal heritage, causing them to waver. I break those chains of bondage, those generational sins passed from father to son, now in Jesus' Name. These things have no place in my life or the lives of my wife, children, and loved ones. I watched the angels fight against demonic forces with odds tightly stacked against them. Thank You for their shields of protection and their swords of truth.

"Father, finally, the one area that is the toughest one of all. Thank You for the time that I did spend with my father, recogniz-ing that he did teach me positive traits that equipped me for my own life. I repent for not recognizing them before and declare that I both honor him and I honor those moments. My relation-ship with him, based on what I have witnessed over these series of visions, has helped me to understand the paradigm of my rela-tionship with You. Therefore, thank You for the life of my father and I pray that he is now dancing in the light of Your throne of grace. Amen."

WITH HIS PRAYER COMPLETED, the sheep began to weep. He didn't feel Shepherd come and sit beside him, placing his left arm across his back. But he did hear the words, *"That was powerful, My Brother, and a true lesson in humility. It is amazing what changes inside when you come to know and understand the truth of things that you had been previously blinded to."*

"I knew some of these things before the visions, but there were many details of both of their lives that I was oblivious to. The details change the entire perspective of what I had thought previously," the sheep said, comforted by his mentor's presence.

"They can, yes. The analogy is that, as you begin to understand the details of God, Our Creator, your views and perspectives also change. First comes understanding, then comes change. Without first understanding, you cannot change, be it your character, your conduct, or your belief system."

"Your father and grandfather never understood the life the Lord wanted for them; therefore, they struggled to change. Your grandfather actually rejected it. However, it was because of your grandfather that your father recognized that something was wrong, something was off, which is why he became a different kind of man than his father. Your father was a lost sheep for seventy years, wandering around the wilderness, but his wasn't due to ignorance; it was due to a lack of understanding. You brought that understanding to him in his latter days, even though you were still changing and learning to understand yourself, too."

"Praise God! One question: I get the idea of angels and such, but my father was not a believer? Why did the angels protect him, and, if they could protect him, why didn't they protect my grandfather?" the sheep asked.

Shepherd nodded. *"The Lord loves everyone, but sinners most of all. Did you know that?"*

"Yes, Sir, there are several verses in scripture about that, but I think the idea that Jesus died on the cross for us, as sinners, is the most telling of all."

"Very good. Because the Lord loves sinners, He does not want them to die. Now, to be clear, this is in reference to eternal death, not physical death. However, if a sinner dies a physical death before repenting or accepting Him, they will also die the eternal death. Therefore, the Lord will operate through intermediaries to protect

the sinner from physical death, giving them more time to turn from eternal death, to eternal Life."

"Now, about your question about why some people seem to be protected and not others, I will try to answer that bit by bit. It's a complex subject and cannot be explained in one sentence."

"Do you remember in the vision about Thomas receiving the call from Christ to pray an intercessory prayer? That was for your father, who was not able to pray for himself. Your father did not recognize Christ but he knew there was something greater. He had not accepted Christ, but your dad never rejected Him either, even after suffering his physical wounds I might add. Your grandfather, on the other hand, outright rejected Him and turned Him away, so the angels of God were powerless to help him."

Shepherd continued, *"There were many called that day to pray in intercession but, as the vision also showed you, some did not answer the call like Thomas did. Therefore there were men that died that day before getting to know Him, on both sides, and it could have been prevented. And this grieves the Father."*

"Wow, I wake up a lot in the middle of the night and struggle going back to sleep. It bothers me to think that this was a call from Him to pray in the Spirit, a lost opportunity to pray for someone," the sheep admitted.

"Repent and move forward, Brother, with God; that is what He wants. And then, strive to be obedient moving forward."

Shepherd paused for a minute while the sheep prayed and repented there and then. *"That vision concludes the last one that is specific to your heritage. It gives you understanding of your past which is intended to help you as we continue this quest of discovery about yourself. From here on out, the visions will be specific to you. And it is these visions that may pain you the most, little Brother. Nonetheless, what follows should serve to uplift you. Like any lesson you learn throughout your life on earth, these lessons are about your spirit, your walk towards expanding your relationship with Jesus, the Father and the Holy Spirit."*

"OK, I am anxious, but I think I'm ready. I suspect I am going to see many aspects of my father and grandfather in myself."

"Most assuredly, you will. Many people don't like to recognize or admit it, but they often judge others for the same things they them- selves also do. Some even deny it. But, let's conclude on something

that is extremely important before we move forward because we are about to make a transition that will be confusing otherwise. It's the idea of the rooster and the idea of the lamb."

CHAPTER 7
THE ROOSTER RE-LOADED

"But Peter said to Him, 'Even though all may fall away because of You, I will never fall away.' Jesus said to him, 'Truly I say to you that this very night, before a rooster crows, you will deny Me three times.' Peter said to Him, 'Even if I have to die with You, I will not deny You.' All the disciples said the same thing too"
(Matthew 26:33-35)

SHEPHERD WAITED ON THE LORD about how to conclude this part of the quest. *"We have been making reference to the rooster, a metaphor for the soul of men as well as the emergency communication system for God to get the attention of a man before he falls. But what we have not addressed is the idea of the sheep, which begins as a lamb. So, let's conclude our story of the rooster before we get to that.*

"We already know that Jesus told Peter that he would deny Him three times, before the rooster crowed, but Peter felt differently, telling Jesus "No way, not me Lord!" However, as you are aware, Peter did in fact deny any connection with Jesus three times, and when he recognized this, he wept bitterly. The result was that Peter became a broken man who quickly repented and experienced grace. This message is powerful and it is important that this be understood: God's pardon extends to sinners who repent. Repentance is often expressed from the position of a broken spirit. Your grandfather, for example, could have repented at any time in his life, right up to his death, and the Lord would have pardoned him. Sadly, he did not."

"It is significant that the story of Peter's denial of Christ and the rooster crowing three times is recorded in all four gospels. But, this story would not be complete if we did not share the specifics of how Peter came to realize that, even though he had denied Christ, he was still valuable to the church. You must understand this very critical point: everyone is valuable to the church, no matter their past, who they are, or where they are in their walk."

"We mentioned that Peter had repented, but what did Jesus do with that repentance? In John 21:15-19 there is another interchange between Jesus and Peter. Peter denied Jesus three times; thus, Jesus asks Peter the same question three times, 'Do you love me?' Peter responds, 'Yes, I love You.' Three denials, three times to repent. Everyone is valuable; everyone still has a purpose. But they have to let go of self and ask Him to forgive. It's that easy."

"But we also see that Peter is finally grieved the third time Jesus asks – as would anyone if they recognize where they made mistakes. Being asked three times reminded Peter of his failure, but, after his repentance Jesus doesn't condemn him, nor does He disqualify him. Instead, He calls Peter to feed the sheep of God, to be a part of God's great plan of redemption. Jesus gives Peter a picture of his future and then leaves him with these words, 'Follow Me.' Peter grasps the cross of Jesus Christ and carries it every step of the way. Now there is a picture of the redeemed, the people of God, the Bride of Christ, the Church, sinners clinging to the cross of our Savior. And due, in large part, to the rooster."

THE SHEEP JUMPED IN, "You know, I think roosters are almost always associated with Peter in Christian art, obviously based on the gospel accounts of Peter's denial of Christ and his subsequent restoration. I think there are paintings of the rooster in ancient Christian burial tombs in both Rome and Israel. I'm not sure where I learned that but now I see it everywhere."

"Yes, Christianity has many symbols associated with it: the fish, the dove, the lamb, and, of course, the cross. However, the one symbol that can be found on top of many church steeples in Europe, is the rooster. In your city of Manhattan, the logo for the Presbyterian Church also happens to be the rooster, this one clinging onto a cross. The rooster is considered by many to be a picture of God's grace to sinners, the sinner's acceptance of a divine pardon through Jesus

Christ. It is an image of Peter's failure and Jesus Christ's triumph, a symbol that many use to help them go back to Him, where He will receive us with open arms. But look, this tends to get a tad religious, into areas of legalism, a trap that you do not want to get caught up in. It can also lead to a form of idolatry if you are not careful.

"The rooster is again mentioned in Mark 13:35. The Lord says that men need to watch and be careful, because they don't know when the master of the house will be home – in the evening, at midnight, or at the crowing of the rooster... Men must be on guard and watchful for their Lord, Jesus Christ. Throughout scripture, when the rooster is mentioned, though not often, it's a warning, a sign, or piece of wisdom. Therefore, perhaps, just maybe, men ought to pay attention to the rooster, to their soul, for their salvation. You can't really kill a rooster – let's be clear about that – but you can disguise it, you can ignore it, or you can allow it to be buried. Whichever way, the dark one wants to snuff it out and men should not let it – or else!"

The sheep could not help himself and jumped in again to show that he understood. "The rooster can only die when the man physically dies, but, a man can bury his spirit deep, blotting out the light that can lead to his salvation. The death of the rooster means the death of salvation for the man, and that only happens if the man dies before recognizing Jesus Christ as his Lord and Savior. By killing the rooster, by snuffing the rooster, those that are of the anti-Christ, both people and demonic forces, convince the man that his worth is in himself: to have faith in himself, and eventually to be bitter and rejected, to hate instead of love. The rooster gives an emergency call to 'Follow Him!'"

"You are getting it, little Brother. The spirit of your grandfather was buried to a place of total obscurity. He had no idea who he was and became a very vile and cruel man, empty of anything that could be called love. The coyote, the wolf and the fox are demonic representations of the demonic forces that were operating in his life, forces that he bowed down to and allowed to control him. As he never recovered; he never recognized these attacks for what they were, so they literally became a part of him. Unfortunately, as time took its course, he passed these creatures, these generational sins, on to his son – your father."

"I see it," said the sheep. "I know that my father grew up despising his father, a feeling that he retained up to the day he died. My father never spoke about my grandfather with me – the visions I witnessed explain why. My father was shamed by his dad and was never shown what love was, or how to love. But, glory to God, there was a crack in my father's heart and I believe that love was seeping into his heart, slowly, over years and decades. Unlike my grandfather, that crack was allowing a bit of light to shine in. My father would not recognize this light for what it was, but he did know that something was wrong, that his life was meant to be different than his father's. That there was just…that little something. He wanted an answer to the question 'Why?' But he never sought the answer for himself."

"YOU KNOW, I THINK I always instinctively knew that my father was a very hurt man and his wounds were very heavy, but I never respected that, or him, for that matter. I wonder how many other men, like me, are out there missing the same things that I did. Or worse, how many fathers are out there, like my dad, leading their sons down a path of rejection, humiliation, or pain. I think there are a lot of guys out there that need to figure out how to forgive their fathers and love them, without being misguided, or that it doesn't mean that they need to forget," the sheep wondered.

Shepherd smiled. *"We touched on some of that earlier. Love, My Brother, love is the cure for everything. It is hard to love if you have not forgiven – we spoke on unforgiveness and the seed it plants earlier. But, there is one more thing before we move on: repentance. Repent, forgive, and then love. There you go. These three things would have helped your grandfather, your father, and even you, little Brother, much sooner than it did."*

"The rooster was buried in your grandfather, while it was covered up in distractions and events in your father. As a result, they could not hear it crow, which would have allowed them to repent, forgive, and then love…the Shepherd then turned to the sheep. "So, what is the one significant thing that is different about you, from your father and grandfather?"

The sheep looked off in the distance for a bit, seeking that answer. "I think it is the fact that I have accepted Jesus Christ as my Lord and Savior, as well as received the gift of the Holy Spirit. Is that it? I can't think of anything else because I think I still carry around some of the negative emotions and feelings still."

"Yes, because you have accepted Jesus Christ, you were made a lamb under God, one of His sons. I am His Shepherd, guiding you along your path with Him. Great observation, that is revelation knowledge right there!" said Shepherd patting his friend on the back.

"When you were born again, you were born a lamb under God. Over the years you have matured, never perfect but always maturing, into a sheep. We'll dig deep into that topic later, but, for now, I want you to capture the idea, as we commence with the next phase of your visions, that you are a lamb of God. Keep the idea of the rooster in the back of your mind, though, as we won't discuss it again until much later."

"OK, I got it – I think anyway. If I get confused, I'll ask."

"The Lord is not about confusion, but I will provide clarity where needed," Shepherd assured him.

"You bet, Sir."

"Good. As we move forward, hold on to the understanding of what you have learned thus far from the past, but don't dwell on any of the negative or bad stuff any longer. Understood? It's good to understand who you are, but too often, men cannot move past their mistakes or those of their fathers. They become consumed by them and it kills their souls. So, don't do it."

"Yes, Sir. Understood."

After the sheep provided his confirmation, Shepherd bowed his head and prayed, *"Lord, He is ready. By Your grace and righteousness, Father, allow him to see his wilderness journey to the River. Let him be changed by it, filled with love and all of the fruit that the Spirit has to offer."*

PART 2

A Little Lamb Is Born

CHAPTER 8
THE LAMB

"Before I formed you in the womb I knew you,
And before you were born I consecrated you…"
(Jeremiah 1:5)

"If a man has a hundred sheep and one of them gets lost,
what will he do?" He'll go out and search for the
one that is lost until he finds it"
(Luke 15:4)

*"**THE SHEEP IS AN ADULT** while its children are most often called 'lambs.' If the sheep strays, what does this mean for the lamb? Where the sheep goes, the lamb is sure to follow."*

"A sheep knows that, without the instruction and care of the shepherd, it will be lost. Nevertheless, because of temptation or curiosity, it strays anyway, wandering away from the shepherd. The lost sheep is representative of the foolish and thoughtless wanderer from God, to whom He says, 'Do not listen to anything that will lead you away from Me and My truth.' The caution in Proverbs 19:27 – 'Cease listening to instruction, my son, and you will stray from the words of knowledge'– is for those who still choose to follow their own desires and look for teachers who will tell them what they want to hear, selecting verses that pander to their imaginations. Too often, God's sheep are allowing themselves to be enticed away by their own

intellectual vanity. When this happens, God will correct this type of person's straying by allowing the result of his sins to fall upon him.

> *"But each one is tempted when he is carried away and enticed by his own lust" (James 1:14).*

> *"They will bear the punishment of their iniquity; as the iniquity of the inquirer is, so the iniquity of the prophet will be, in order that the house of Israel may no longer stray from Me and no longer defile themselves with all their transgressions..." (Ezekiel 14:10-11 NIV).*

> *"Cease listening, my son, to discipline, And you will stray from the words of knowledge" (Proverbs 19:27).*

> *"For the time will come when they will not endure sound doctrine; but wanting to have their ears tickled, they will accumulate for themselves teachers in accordance to their own desires, and will turn away their ears from the truth and will turn aside to myths" (2 Timothy 4:3-4).*

STILL SITTING ON THE BENCH, the sheep and Shepherd continued their conversation. Shepherd was speaking, *"So far you have experienced the lives of two generations and have witnessed how the sins of one generation can be passed on to the second. From this point forward, we will look at the beginning of the third generation, that is, your birth and upbringing."*

"Yes, Sir, I am thankful for the Lord having shown me the events and attitudes that have already transpired, and passed from father to son. It does explain a lot as well as increase my understanding of own heart. I guess I am more anxious now than I was before as I think I'm going to witness my own shortcomings and when I missed God reaching out to me."

"Probably, but that's OK. While the truth can be painful, it can also be liberating. I suspect that you will be a changed person by the end of this – I can see changes in you already. Look around you, here, in this place. What do you see?" Shepherd asked looking around with a sweep of his hands.

"Well, when we first started, the landscape was already beautiful. The colors, the smells, the soft breeze, the sky, and the soothing sounds of the water. But I also noticed that the environment changed after each vision. New things were added, such as the flowers, the bees, and the fish in the water."

"Yes. If you were not aware, but I believe you are by now, this place was created by you, from your own heart. This...secret place... is a picture of what is in your heart. As you gain understanding, you're changing, and as you change, your heart changes, as your heart changes..."

"My secret place changes," the sheep jumped in. He could not help himself.

Shepherd smiled, *"Yes, Brother, for the purposes of this project, it will change. You are seeing changes that add to the beauty of this place because you are seeing your heart as beautiful, just as God sees it. You are seeing yourself in a new way, learning to love who you are. But, this place can also lose beauty if you allow it to be con- taminated by the judgments and grievances of your head. Therefore, it is paramount that you guard our heart because everything you do, act, and behave, flows from it. Men can guard their heart by loving God 'with all their heart' AND 'all their mind.' Do you know why I am bringing this up?"*

"Well, you opened this conversation by talking about the sheep and the lamb. You refer to me as a sheep, even though I am not covered in wool, because I am a follower of something greater than me. In my case, it's God. I am a sheep because I am grown and responsible for my own thoughts, my actions, and the condition of my heart. As a sheep, You are the Holy Ghost, responsible for passing me guidance and instruction from the Good Shepherd and the Father. However, when I was young, I was under the care of others, so I was a lamb, the child of a sheep who was responsible for my care and instruction," the sheep explained.

"Excellent, continue," said Shepherd, happy that his student was catching on so fast.

"If the sheep does not guard his heart against sin, he falls into temptation and becomes lost. If he has lambs under his care, he is not caring for them or instructing them in God's Way, so they, too, become lost. I think this is worse because the lamb is not learning; he may not even have an opportunity to learn. This means the lamb is born into an environment where he is automatically lost, with no foundation," the sheep answered.

"Yes, good. In that example, the sheep has not taught the lamb how to guard his heart the way the Lord tells us, neither by example nor instruction, let alone what it is that he is supposed to be guarding it from in the first place...Let's bring this to the topic of you."

"THOUGH YOUR CIRCUMSTANCES and surroundings were different, like your father before you, you were born into the wilderness. Now, this is predominantly due to the fall of man that you read about in the opening chapters of the Book of Genesis: we need to be clear about that. But, in your case, you were born to a father who was not guarding his heart, because he was not taught by his own father how to guard it. So you were raised up in a spirit of bondage while also inheriting the sins of both."

Nodding his head, the sheep agreed. "I see that, so I started with an unfair disadvantage, at least it seems that way. I know we keep referring to the Wilderness, a journey through life, as a wandering. How is this similar to the Israelites' exodus from Egypt? I sense there is something there."

"The Israelites suffered during their exodus because of their disobedience and unbelief even after the Lord had rescued them from slavery in Egypt. The Lord told them to take possession of the land that He had promised them, which He promised was 'flowing with milk and honey.' On their part, they saw giants and scary looking people in the land, and were convinced the Lord was wrong: no way could they take that land. This lack of belief in Him made God angry, so He cursed them to wander the wilderness until that entire generation had died off, a wandering which took forty years," Shepherd recounted.

"In the case of your father and grandfather, they roamed the wilderness their entire lives because they did not believe and were convinced that the Lord was wrong, or did not exist at all. Now..." the Shepherd smiled and declared, *"the good news is that you are free from curses because of the New Covenant. When Jesus died on the cross and bled for you, He washed away curses under the law, establishing a new beginning, a new Way. That Way is through Him."*

"But, man is still operating in a corrupt world; therefore, man is still under the influence of sin. You were not born into a world

where you have received curses from your father – that is nonsense that some people are teaching. But, you were born into a world of sin and did inherit sins from your father. That is different than generational curses that many people talk about. The bondage of sin is broken by coming to Christ, which is what you did when you accepted Him," Shepherd explained.

"I think I recall a verse from Ezekiel that tells us *"the son will not share the guilt of the father, nor will the father share the guilt of the son,"* the sheep piped in.

"Yes,", Shepherd continued. *"The curse of sin is not the same thing as a generational curse, but sin is passed on from father to son. Because of Adam, all men have sinned and fall short of the glory of God. But, because of Jesus Christ, who is also known as the second Adam, all men are offered atonement. Paul wrote in Romans 5:18 that, while through Adam all men may have been condemned, it was the righteous act of Jesus Christ, the second Adam, that brought the justification needed to bring life back to all men. It's not your fault that you were born condemned, but, at the same time, it is not your own actions that will save you."*

The sheep was already aware of most of this, but he thought on it for a few seconds before speaking up again. "You know, I lived a huge number of years believing that I was cursed, that my father had passed things on to me that I had no control over, no choices, no options, no vote, no way out. I always figured it wasn't fair and it would make me angry, complacent and despondent. Thank God I have been delivered from that foolish belief system!"

Shepherd smiled, which the sheep noticed He did a lot. *"Yes, Brother, yes! Praise God! I want to offer another observation for you before we move on with your Wilderness Project. You were once a lamb instructed in the ways of a lost sheep until the day you became a sheep yourself. However, even a lost sheep can find its way back, even one not taught His Way. You see, the Lord will leave ninety-nine sheep to find the one that is lost and He will not stop until He finds you or... you die."*

"One question before we move on," the sheep came in. "Why does Scripture refer to Jesus as the Lamb and us people as lambs, too? It's kind of confusing."

"When Jesus is called the Lamb of God in John 1:29 and John 1:36, John is referring to Him as the perfect and ultimate sacrifice

for sin. However, in order to fully understand who Christ was and what He did, we begin with the Old Testament, which contains prophecies concerning the coming of Christ as a guilt offering, for example, Isaiah 53:10."

"For the Jewish people, the sacrifice of lambs played a critical role in their religious lives when they were offered as a temporary atonement for sin. It is through Jesus' death on the cross as God's perfect sacrifice for sin, and His resurrection, that men can now have an eternal life. This is why He is referred to as the Lamb of God, God's perfect sacrifice."

"Also at the end of the Book of John, we find where Jesus Himself commanded Peter to 'feed My sheep.' After preparing a meal for the disciples, Jesus commissioned Peter with the task of feeding His sheep and tending to His lambs. Additionally, we also find in Psalm 95:7, where God's people are referred to as sheep, the flock under His care."

"Peter would later follow the example of Jesus in his first letter to the elders of the churches in Asia Minor, telling them to be shepherds of God's flocks He places under their care. Therefore, the elders are commanded to tend to, care for, and provide spiritual food for God's people, from the youngest lambs to full-grown sheep."

"Wow, OK. Ask and you shall receive, praise God!" the sheep exclaimed. "So, is it fair to call us sheep, or lambs, if we are not followers or believers of God?"

"You are all God's children; that will always be the case, no matter what one believes. When you state that a sheep is a non-believer, or someone that is not following Him, that is a lost sheep, but a sheep nonetheless," Shepherd answered matter of factly.

"OK, got it, thank You." After an awkward pause, the sheep wasn't sure where to go from here. He looked up at the Shepherd for guidance.

"God knew you as you were being formed in your mother's womb, little Brother. Your father was operating blind, being influenced by his false belief system and not welcoming the One that was nourishing and positive. He was a wanderer, adrift in a sea of winds and currents, and the dark forces in his life used this against him. Regardless of what you thought of him in your youth, he did recognize you and your sister as gifts. He was cold because he felt that everyone was living in a lawless world. Because he was a wandering spirit, you

were born into that wilderness, walking alongside him in the arid desert that he initiated, but it would be one that you yourself would develop and expand on."

As Shepherd made that final statement, the world around the sheep began to dissolve, eventually blanketing the sheep in a thick misty cloud, where he could not see his hand in front of his face. After what felt like a few minutes, He noticed a light off in the distance and started to walk towards it.

CHAPTER 9
THE JOURNEY BEGINS

"Jesus said, "Let the children alone, and do not hinder them
from coming to Me; for the kingdom of heaven
belongs to such as these"
(Matthew 19:14, NASB)

THE SNAKE SLITHERED ALONG THE GROUND, *unnoticed to*
those around it, its forked tongue sensing and feeling, looking for
the best route to accomplish its objective. "Heeessss mmminnne,"
it hissed to the fox sitting nearby. Even though he had sensed some-
thing coming, the fox was startled, not realizing that its master had
sent another one of its kind. He knew that his master had thousands
of forces at his disposal, but he rarely knew when, or if, any would
show up until they were there just like he was surprised when the
wolf and coyote reappeared years earlier.

But, the fox remained in his observation post, hiding in the back-
ground, eyeing the new lamb that had been born. He would wait and
bide his time, allowing the wolf and coyote to continue to devour
the sheep. But he was morbidly curious: what would the serpent do?

The snake continued along its course, planning, strategizing,
envisioning the best way to latch on to its target. Then he saw the
lamb running through the yard and this is when he decided to play,
to taunt him – the sheep, that is. Who knows, maybe this would be
the start of a new kind of torment for a sheep who had ignored his

Shepherd. When the snake got close enough, it bit into the arm of the sheep.

NORWALK, CA, OCT 1974

AS FIVE YEAR OLD STEVE ran around the corner of his house to the front yard, he saw his father on the far side of the yard watering the lawn. Steve was playing with their dog as he froze about ten feet from his dad, "What is Daddy going to do?" he wondered.

"Squirt him. Make sure he feels your desire to drown him," the snake relaxes his bite and wraps itself around the head of the father.

Shepherd immediately cried out at the father, *"No, don't listen to him. The serpent is the craftiest of all the beasts. It's a deception. You need to show Stephen, teach him the right way to live, so that he won't depart from it."*

It only took a second but his daddy looked up and saw Steve standing there. An angry grin appeared on his face and his eyes looked scary. This is when he raised the sprinkler in his hand and squeezed the trigger at Steve, while snarling, "Get away from me, you little a-hole!"

"Yes. That's it! Make him pay for your faithlessness."

Shepherd lowered his head, *"Lord, forgive him. He is not aware that he is leading his child in a direction that will provoke and discourage him. Show him, Father, that children are a blessing to the parents."*

When the water hit him, Steve turned and ran back to the side of the house to the backyard, scared to death at what had just happened.

He asked himself a question, one that he would ask for many years, "Why does Daddy hate me?" He had fading memories of when his dad would hug him, but these were quickly being replaced with memories of anger as his dad was mean to him most of the time. "What am I doing wrong?"

"You have done nothing. You are a child of God," Shepherd stated. The snake could sense Shepherd, but he could also sense the seed that was planted in Steve.

Steve was becoming afraid of his father and avoided him as much as he could. He was learning how worthless he was because his father would frequently remind him, "You are worthless! You will never amount to anything!"

Even at a young age, Steve was intelligent enough to ask himself the question, "But why am I worthless? What does it take to be worth something?"

"You are a blessing and are worth the great sacrifice," Shepherd whispered into his heart.

"When Daddy hits me, I deserve it when it happens," Steve figured to himself. He was worthless: this is what his daddy told him, and worthless things don't deserve to be happy.

Steve exhibited above average intelligence, having taught himself how to read before attending kindergarten earlier in the year. His parents had bought him a dictionary with little pictures next to the words and he was able to learn how to read by associating the pictures with the words, such as dog, horse and house.

"You were created for a purpose, Stephen. You have a discerning heart; soon you will turn it into understanding."

The snake and the fox could not hear it but they felt the voice speaking up in the child's heart.

Steve had just started attending a Christian school, but he was confused and was struggling to understand. His teacher was telling him one thing but his mom and dad were doing something else. He was learning about love and God and Jesus at school and how this was supposed to work in his house. But his daddy kept telling him that they were living in hell, that God didn't care. He respected his parents and knew they wouldn't lie to him, so he figured they were right and his teacher was wrong.

"Your parents are neglecting the way, Stephen, but this is their choice, not His desire. Learn from this, for it will be a valuable lesson for you later. They have been swayed by the world and the false laws that guide it," Shepherd cautioned.

"Blah, you're a rodent!" the fox snarled at him.

His daddy didn't seem to want anything to do with him, which didn't line up with what he was being taught in school. Steve supposed he could walk up to his dad but he was definitely afraid of him. Plus, his daddy would always tell him to get away from him, that he was a piece of poop, so he was confused while soaking it all in.

He would spend time with his best friend Jerry across the street. They either hung out or played on the street or they were at Jerry's house. Jerry would spend time with Steve in his house but only when his dad wasn't there. The other kids on the street thought Steve's dad was weird and sometimes they would tease Steve about it. But, luckily, this was rare and he was learning how to just let it go.

Steve was learning to hate his father by the example he was setting; but he also loved him. His father made him feel stupid but Steve knew that he was smarter than other kids his age. His dad was wrong about him – he could feel it. "Daddy's stupid! I'm not," Steve figured. And this thought would remain with Steve for a long time to come.

The snake removed itself from the father and started slithering away. It could sense what Steve was feeling. *"Yes, there it is! Hate him, little lamb, let your hate feed your heart"*.

Shepherd eyed the snake with a disgusted look before glancing back over at Steve. *"Stephen, hatred is death. Love is life. Love is truth. Love is the way. Let love guide your heart. Cling to that which is good."*

THE VISITING SHEEP COULD DO NOTHING as he was simply an observer of the vision, but it did not stop him from breaking down as he recalled this memory.

"Hahahahaha, that was fun!" the snake whispered to the others of his realm. "Whatever!" the coyote snarled back. "We have already infected the father. You couldn't have done anything if it weren't for us."

"Some truth, some exaggeration!" the snake retorted. "You and I know that some of that was the father's own flesh guiding his hand. Infected, yes, but the father did some of that on his own accord. He is angry. My bite did little but antagonize him."

The snake continued his hissing speech. "The father has become a prisoner of his own sin. He is at war within himself; it is your job to use that and not allow any inner peace to enter his heart due to his tribulation.".

"But be careful of that lamb," the snake breathes as he crawled back towards the hole he came from. "He has a sense of understanding about him. Though watering is limited, seeds about his identity are being planted into that one." The snake then allows the hole he entered to swallow him up.

The fox listens attentively to this exchange, for the lamb was his charge, his keep having been passed from father to son. He knew a seed had been planted and he knew where it was happening. It was very upsetting when his parents had planted Steve in...that.... school. It was still unclear to the fox how that light had entered the home, most likely from the mother, he figured.

Anyhow, now that Steve was being fed some Word, the fox would still remain in the background, allowing his "peers" to work on the father, who would in turn work on his son himself. It was a strategic plan to destroy the family unit, and so far, it looks like the plan was working.

The fox even admired the child a little bit, for he was, as the snake hinted, an intelligent one. He figured things out on his own, but the fox knew that Shepherd was working on Steve as well. If he could figure out how that bootlicking Shepherd was infiltrating him, he could then exploit it and block it. But, for now, the fox could not sense any of the good news permanently entering Steve's heart – that was something.

As the visiting sheep looked on, he could see what the fox could not. The fox could not see the seeds of Truth being planted in a corner of Stephen' heart because they were reserved by the Creator. They had not yet bloomed or borne fruit; this would be the only thing that the fox could sense.

Shepherd was, in fact, watching, always monitoring, always trying to inject influence, operating through both direct and indirect ways.

The visiting sheep knew, what the fox did not, that it was the neighbors that had been guided by Shepherd to advise the mother about sending Stephen and his sister to that school. The dark ones could not see it because the discussions were shielded by the love exhibited by the neighbors, and demons are driven away by love.

Once Stephen had gotten into the school, it was easy for the seeds to be planted undetected. Some of the seeds would sprout but only to be quickly killed by the lack of watering and feeding at home. However, there were also seeds planted into Stephen' heart that would lie dormant, hidden in that reserved corner of his soul, ready to sprout when needed, some not for several more decades.

Shepherd smiled as thoughts of the future flowed. He walked up to Stephen, allowing the fox to see him this time, and cupped his face between his hands. "Soon, My little Brother, you will have trials and you will experience tribulations. But you will also experience choices, triumphs, and victories."

The Shepherd then turned and disappeared through a mist, a veil that the fox could not see through.

⊞

AS SHEPHERD VANISHED, the vision faded and the sheep was transported back to the secret place.

Shepherd observed the sheep as he managed his emotions regarding the vision. *"How are you doing, Brother?"* He asked.

"That vision is one of the earliest clear memories I have of my father, so there weren't very many surprises," the sheep answered. "But, I was struck by how little the demonic influences affected my father. There was the snake that bit him but it still seemed that it was more him than it. You heard the snake, he even said as much," the sheep blurted. "I'm not sure what to think of that."

Shepherd stood next to the sheep and held him. *"Why do you believe your father would act that way of his own accord? Do you believe that your father did not love you?"*

The sheep grew despondent, "That vision, that memory. It shaped me," he answered. "This is one of the events that I have forgiven him for, but it is hard to see love there. I had always felt that he did not want me. I was an accident, an event that happened in his life requiring him to turn away from something else he would have preferred to do."

"Did you ever hear him say that?" Shepherd asked.

"Not in those words, but he would say to me that I wasn't worth it. That I was a waste," said the sheep looking dejected.

Shepherd comforted him. *"Brother, know that your father did love you. Men, boys included, see an outward appearance of other men and make judgments based on what they see. However, the Lord sees the heart and the heart is the truth of the man. He knows the heart of man because it was He that fashioned it. So know this, your father loved you, more than you know."*

The sheep pondered these words; he wanted to believe that but was having a difficult time with it. "That vision, that moment in time, was only three to four minutes of my lifetime; yet it is burned into my memory like the other events, some that are a little cloudier. If my father loved me, then why did he treat me that way?"

"The Lord would never deny that something was desperately wrong with that moment, or the other moments you are referencing. Understand this, your father was not your grandfather; your father was better, but he was also damaged. He was hurt and was carrying things around inside of him that were always churning, always welling, always reminding him of his wrongs, his shortcomings, and his weaknesses. Your father never felt like a full man; he felt inadequate even though he looked gruff and gritty on the outside. He always felt limited, though he would either hide his limits, or ignore them. Your father never let his physical wounds stop him from his career, but his physical wounds coupled with his emotional scars were always a source of intimidation when it came to you."

"I intimidated him?" the sheep asked astonished.

"Yes. You've recognized your intelligence, your drive for knowledge. Even as a five-year-old you were always experimenting, testing new things, reading beyond your age, being creative. These are things that your father was not, nor could he relate to you. When it came to physical things like baseball, football, or even frisbee, things of a physical nature; your father never learned how to overcome his physical wounds to do those things with you. When he looked at you, you reminded him of all of that. While he was proud of you, it would also torment him. You intimidated him because you were the one he wanted to be the closest with, but, you were becoming something that he believed he was not, but so wanted to be."

"Unbelievable! I never thought of that. However, why did he never bring me close to him? Instead, he pushed me away?"

"Ah, but there are events that you do not remember, that you have forgotten or have chosen to forget. In Jesus' Name, with Him in your heart, you need to tear down that wall that surrounds the stronghold blocking positive memories. That is a ploy of the dark one, to mislead you into believing only one aspect of your life, while forgetting what made you happy. You have forgiven your father, but you haven't finished your part in removing the strongholds that continue to wound you," Shepherd explained.

"Let's do that right now:

Lord, look into the heart of Stephen and see that he is true. We know that the weapons of our warfare are not of the flesh, but that they are divinely powerful for the destruction of strongholds. We are destroying them, right now in Jesus' Name, every thought and every lofty thing that has been raised up against the knowledge of God, we are taking you captive to the obedience of Christ. All thoughts, all memories, whether good or bad, belong to Stephen, in Jesus' Name.

"Father, we remove those walls surrounding and locking away the happy memories for Stephen right NOW, in Jesus' Name. We take authority over all of them, right NOW in Jesus' Name. The evil one must release them right NOW in Jesus' Name. Heavenly Father, these lies of the enemy no longer have a hold on Stephen. We declare and decree that he is a child of the living God! Jesus died for his sins! He has been redeemed and forgiven.

"Renew his mind in this area, Father. Let him recognize the need to know Your Word, more and more. He wants Your Word to be written, engrained, tattooed on his heart. Oh Father, we pray that You change his heart as well. Shield his mind and keep him safe and focused on You and Your Word. Show him the love of Your embrace, in Jesus' most precious, mighty, and powerful name, Amen."

The presence of God was strong. Shepherd could see Jesus' arms surrounding the sheep tightly, the sheep's head snuggled into the chest of Jesus. Shepherd allowed the sheep to meditate and marinate in God's love.

The sheep could not move as old, but also new, memories flooded his mind. His body was shaking as he saw things that he had forgotten for over forty years. His father playing with him as a baby. Him falling asleep on his father's chest as they napped together in the family couch. His mother wrapping him tight to her chest as she cleaned the house, or placing him lovingly into a baby rocker while she performed more strenuous chores.

He saw his father looking at him by his bedroom door with tears rolling down his face, angry at himself for not knowing what to do. The photographic memories continued to flash in his mind and through his heart. "I didn't know," he mumbled in between sobs. He saw his father in a new, fresh light. And he sympathized with the pain, experiencing new mercies and compassion for his father that he never had before. Then he wept uncontrollably.

"Stephen, what your father did was not right but, more importantly, know that he loved you, he hungered to know you. He struggled

because he was trying to do it all in his own strength, never allowing the Lord to operate in him or through him," Shepherd said gently.

"Your father fought a horrific war in Vietnam, but it was the war inside himself that was the hardest, the most difficult, the most painful," Shepherd consoled him.

The sheep was finally able to speak, "I came to the realization years ago that my father's mistakes were not his fault, but I always speculated as to why. Thank You, Lord, for allowing me to see him in a new light. Thank You, Father, for allowing me to witness his inner turmoil, for this has shown me the battle he fought – for both of us. While he may have lost most battles, the thought that he was fighting for us is all the encouragement I needed."

"You have forgiven him, but true repentance is not just lip service. True repentance is a change of the heart that comes with a new mindset, Brother. This is a huge step for you; the Lord can see it. Allow Him to continue to mold you, shape you, and change you so that you can live your life continuing to be more like Christ, to act like Him, and think like Him. The Lord says that true peace is found by taking up His yoke and learning from Him, because He is gentle and lowly in heart and you will find rest for your soul."

Shepherd kept His eyes on the sheep, waiting patiently as memories continued to feed into his mind and in his heart. After a few minutes, He placed His hand on the sheep's head, *"When you are ready, it will be time for us to continue, Brother, for He has more to show you. He is continuing to renew your mind and your heart, which will allow you to witness what He still has to share with you – with a renewed spirit. This will be critical as some of these visions will be difficult. It is important that you understand this before we move forward. And, as always, as we complete each milestone of this quest, you must never view them again with a critical spirit. It is done."*

The sheep looked up at Shepherd after He removed His hand. "Yes, Sir, I feel refreshed and at peace. I can already visualize other bad memories but they don't tear me down like they used to. Thank You, Lord."

Shepherd held His hand out pointing down the path that bordered the quiet pristine lake. *"Praise God, Brother. Now, walk with Me further down this path. Look and see the birds of the air of different colors and varieties, vibrant in the environment they are best suited for. When you can see them, that's when the next vision will begin."*

As the sheep walked alongside Shepherd, he looked around at the things he had already viewed. The grass, the flowers, the trees that seemed to be growing more majestic. And as Shepherd mentioned, this is when he noticed the birds flying around the trees, cardinals, blue jays, and sparrows, amongst others. It wasn't until he saw them that he was able to hear them singing their songs. It was hypnotic as if the birds seemed to sing the following words in harmony, "Glory to God in the highest!"

The air around him began to tingle…warm, comfortable, majestic. He was swallowed up in it, forgetting where he was…

CHAPTER 10
CONFUSION REIGNS

"God is not a God of confusion but of peace"
(1 Corinthians 14:33)

THE WOLF AND THE COYOTE *stood back and admired their handiwork. They had deceived the grandfather, worked to blot out the truth by tormenting him with lies about his inadequacies and allowing the bitterness towards his family to fester, replacing any thoughts of forgiveness with resentment and hate. They had fulfilled what their master desired, the same that he has for all of His creation – their destruction. He died not knowing who he was supposed to be – he died an orphan. The coyote and the wolf were now free to spend all of their time on the next in line.*

Meanwhile, the crafty fox was engaged in a meddling campaign of his own against the lost lamb. The fox figured that he could take advantage of this physical death and sow seeds of confusion.

NORWALK, CA, DEC 1976

STEVE WAS OVERWHELMED. At the age of seven, he did not recall ever being in the same place at the same time with all of his uncles and his dad's friend William. It was December, and just as they were preparing for Christmas, his grandpa had died.

"He will never return, Steve. You are born to die, gone forever. That is the cycle. Forget about him, just like the rest of the world will forget him and know him no more," the fox sneaked in.

But Shepherd knew better. *"Stephen, death is at work in you, but you can allow life to work...do not lose heart." "Memories of you may fade from the world, but you can set your name in remembrance in Him, to live in His memory forever."*

"Dad, how did Grandpa die?" he asked his father.

"Cancer" was the only reply.

Nothing else was said and at seven Steve did not understand. "What's cancer? How did it kill him? Why are you and my uncles laughing?" His questions went unanswered. In his young life, he had never seen death before, but he knew that his daddy's dad was dead and he was confused, Steve was always confused when it came to his family. Grandpa was gone and he would never see him again; this was what Steve was dealing with and nobody would explain it to him.

Steve didn't really know his grandpa, other than he drove an ice cream truck and he got free ice cream when Grandma and Grandpa drove through their street. His mommy and daddy rarely took him and his little sister to see Grandma and Grandpa and they, in turn, never came over to their house. This was different than his mother's mommy and daddy, whom they spent a lot of time with, and they lived directly across the street from his father's mom and dad. It was overwhelming and it all added to the extreme level of confusion that Steve was not yet mature enough to deal with. It made him sad.

"Look at your daddy, Steve. He is thrilled that your grandfather is dead, happier than he has ever been before," said the fox, planting that thought in his head.

What was strange, at that moment, was that his dad was happy that Grandpa was gone. And so were his uncles. They were smiling a lot and laughing. "Why is Daddy not sad that he won't get to see his dad anymore," Steve wondered. So he asked his mother.

"Mommy, why is Daddy happy that grandpa is dead? I think I would be sad if Daddy were gone forever."

"Your grandpa was a horrible man, Steve. They did not get along when your daddy was growing up," his mother replied. She did not elaborate further.

The fox took the advantage. *"Remember this, Steve. Your grandpa was a bad man. Isn't your own dad also a bad man? You will be happy when he dies, too. You will desire the same thing that your father desires."*

In his brief span of years, even though Steve had not spent much time with his grandpa, he had a natural affinity with him and he knew that Grandpa was still family.

"Yes, Stephen. Do not be deceived. You should care for your family, love your family, no matter the circumstances or how they behave," Shepherd spoke into his heart.

Steve's father would never talk about his grandpa with him – ever. This shallowness would be one of his items, one of the episodes of life that would stay with him for many decades to come. This single event, his grandfather's death and his father's reaction to it, would stick with Steve, perplexing him but also creating a level of inquisitiveness in him that would become a part of his character.

"Do not be confused, Stephen; that is not from God. Physical death of your body is inevitable, but your spirit can live forever in peace. It is an unrighteous deception being planted by those around you, the same ones that will also perish if they don't come to know the love of the Truth, that you can be saved."

Steve continued to observe, soaking everything in. "I guess I'm supposed to be happy when daddy and mommy die," he told himself. Nonetheless, Steve knew that something was off; but he had no one to talk with about it.

THE VISION FOR THE SHEEP WAS STRANGE. *He could see Shepherd in the vision as he was at that time, but he could also see Shepherd standing back watching him as he watched the vision. Being omnipresent meant that Shepherd could be in multiple places and multiple times at the same time. Even though the sheep had gotten used to seeing Him like this, it was hard to get used to. Shepherd never conversed with him during the visions, nor did He ever react to anything happening in the vision. "Of course, He was already there and had already seen it. Good God, this was hard to wrap his mind around! The things of God are foolish to a man."*

Shepherd in the vision watched the scene play out, whispering truth into Steve as false statements were made to him. Steve was young and would not realize it for many years, but Shepherd knew that Steve would come to understand that, while there is a way that seems to be right to the adults around him, the way they were behaving can only lead to death.

He smiled in the knowledge that Steve would eventually come to know that he should not lose heart, that even though his body is wasting away, his inner body could be renewed. But he would experience challenges along the way.

Nonetheless, Shepherd also stood in grief as David finally passed away not knowing the truth before he died. He knows the truth now and this brought tears to His eyes, but it was his decision, his choice, and it was too late. He chose to ignore wisdom.

"Ha, I can see you contemplating a hopeful future," the coyote sniveled at Him. "It's a lost cause. When are you going to realize that these humans are a waste of effort? The Creator is wasting His time; His creation does not love Him. They don't even recognize Him."

"You do what you do," Shepherd responded, "but the Truth can set them free. There are those that will learn that if they fix their eyes in hope on our Savior, the Living God, they will receive the righteous grace that He has promised.".

"Yes, but they must believe. This gabble here does not. Some of them actually hate Him."

"Some don't believe, but they will come to understand and recognize that they have a choice, that it is not a one-way street. Most of them will choose the life that He wants for them over the death you desire for them."

The coyote shook his head. "Now that the old one is gone, I can now focus all of my attention on his son. This will be fun!" He then vanished in a spray of stinking mist that hung around for a few seconds. The Shepherd watched over the family for one last moment as he whispered a prayer over them. "Prepare your minds for action, keep sober in spirit, fix your hope completely on the grace to be brought to you at the revelation of Jesus Christ."

He then directed his eyes on Steve as he slowly faded, "Steve, there is no need to be confused; the Lord will give you the understanding you need".

As expected, the vision faded and the sheep and Shepherd were once again standing on the path alongside the lake.

"YOU KNOW," THE SHEEP IMMEDIATELY STARTED, "the concept of death would be something that would confuse me for years. My grandfather died and everyone was happy; yet in a few more years my grandmother on my mother's side will die and everyone will be sad and torn apart. I could not wrap my mind around it. So, in some sense, death became an anomaly to me, a thing that happened – I never knew how to react. At least, until I joined the military. It was war that changed my perspective."

"Do you know why the experience of your grandmother's death was different than your grandfather's?" Shepherd asked.

"Love," the sheep concluded. "My grandmother exuded love over all of us. I remember being happy around her, while feeling differently around others."

"Yes, love. As we have discovered a few times already and we will see several more times, love is the medicine that is the cure for all ills. Did you pick up on anything else based on your grandfather's passing?" Shepherd asked.

The sheep pondered within himself, looking to his spirit for an answer. The revelation suddenly hit him like a brick. "Grief, " the sheep started softly and deliberately: "grief is an experience common to everyone, but the depth of our grief comes from the depth of our love for the person who passed."

Shepherd smiled, warmed by what the sheep was concluding. *"Yes, to lose a parent is to lose the past, and as you learned later in your own life, to lose a child is to lose the future. So your grief is based on your responses in how you deal with your past, present, and future lives."*

"You cannot change yesterday, but you can live today. You will want to learn to replace 'if only' with a more grateful phrase such as 'nevertheless.' For your grandfather, you could say 'Sure, we could have done more together; nevertheless, I am happy for the time we did have together.'"

"Were you aware though, Brother, that Scripture does not speak in the language of 'if only' but it does speak in a language of 'nevertheless.' Your father could not change his painful past with his father, no more than you can bring back your son. Nevertheless, you can live with gratitude for the love you had and shared – even if it was only a little."

"However, it is also OK to grieve in the spirit for a spirit that is lost. The Lord grieves over a lost soul, for they are all precious to Him," Shepherd continued.

"I don't understand how people can believe that when we die, we die into nothing. That is sad to me," the sheep said. "We all have a purpose, an identity, something driving us on the inside for something greater than simply living."

"Remember, Brother, you, too, held that belief once. Be careful about judgment. Those people are still souls with a spirit from God inside of them, reminding them that they ought to be living for something greater than themselves. They simply cannot hear God's voice, which is why Jesus commanded the great commission to spread the Gospel message. Your mission is to allow God to work through you and save them before they die the physical death, sending them into eternal death," the Shepherd warned.

"I understand, thank You for your correction."

"IT TAKES COURAGE to grieve the loss of a person who was not well liked or respected on earth, but, if you look to God and see it through His eyes, you will grieve," Shepherd said.

"Your father may have always appeared to be happy about his grandfather's death, but the Lord sees all and knows all. Your father grieved, Brother. He grieved over what should have been, over a relationship that never bloomed, and over the loss of a father that he wished he had. And his grief carried over into his relationship with you."

"Huh?" the sheep retorted.

"Your father wanted a glorious death, but his glory required that he build a relationship with you, one of honor and respect. His father's death reminded him of his own legacy, and his legacy was you. But, instead of building him up, this desire fed into his inner struggles, convincing him that he could not do it, adding into his belief system that he could never be what he wanted to be – a father."

The sheep was flustered, overwhelmed. "I never saw it that way before. And all of this from the death of my grandfather?"

"The Lord has a plan, Brother, and while stones are tossed to thwart the plan, they are temporary. The issue breaks down to obedience. If you are obedient to Him, then His plan for you will became a

reality for you in your life. I suspect we will learn about this as our quest continues," Shepherd responded, followed by a long pause.

Then Shepherd looked directly at the sheep. *"How do you feel?"*

"That I still have a lot to learn. I know that these visions are progressing through my life, but I can already see where my thinking and my heart were flawed. I held incorrect views based on false perceptions. I'm starting to feel remorse for things that I suspect we will see during this Wilderness Project. Kind of odd – to be honest."

"Good, good. You are growing," Shepherd replied heartily. He then leaned forward, *"As we continue, I am going to ask you to look for something, something that is more important than anything else you gain along this quest. I want you to answer this question: do you see God?"*

"God?" the sheep asked in return. "You mean in these visions?"

"I want to know if you can you see Him operating in the lives experienced in these visions? Can you see His identity, His fingerprint? These visions are about recognizing the identity of Jesus Christ along the path, equally, if not more so than your heart wounds. He is the One you need to heal your heart. If you don't see Him, then how can you heal the wounds you continue to carry?"

As they had been talking, they had also been walking further along the path, the sheep being so enthralled in their discussion that he missed it. They stopped walking, while the sheep reflected on what he was asked as well as the visions he had witnessed thus far.

"Yes, Sir, I agree and I understand. I have a relationship with Him today because of what He has done in the past. While I see Him today, it is just as important that I learn to see where in my life He was operating before I accepted Him."

"Good. While we progress through these visual milestones, open your heart to Him and experience Him. Invite Him and receive Him into the stories of your past, and you'll receive the healing you are looking for."

They started walking down the path again and after a few minutes they came across a black iron gate attached to gate posts positioned on both sides of the path. They could easily walk around the gate as there was no fence, but Shepherd guided the sheep up to the gate just the same.

"Lift the lever and open the gate. As we walk through it, we will enter the next rung along your quest," he told his charge.

The sheep did as Shepherd instructed and opened the gate. He felt a degree of apprehension for a few seconds…but slowly took a step across the threshold of the gate…

CHAPTER 11
FLAMING ARROWS

"Never pay back evil for evil to anyone.
Respect what is right in the sight of all men..."
(Romans 12:17)

THE SINISTER ONE HAS NUMEROUS FORCES *at his disposal, all serving his bidding. Yet, he only shares with them what he wants them to know; they don't know the entire plan he has for the earth, only his desires. He is aware of prophecy because he has spent more than 2000 years reading the Bible in the various forms in which it has existed. Most of his chief lieutenants are familiar with prophecy, but only what their master allows them to know. Most have limited knowledge of God's Word, again, only what he allows them to know. He never denies that the Bible is true, but he knows how to manipulate it.*

He has learned over the millennia that, if one of the Creator's children is contemplating something unethical or dangerous, then all he has to do is mockingly whisper to those willing to listen, "Go ahead, do it. God Himself says that no matter what you do, He will order his angels to save you and hold you up." He knows that this isn't what God intended, but those that listen to him don't know that. This is one of the things that the deceiver is good at; he even tried this with Jesus Himself.

Unlike the Creator, Satan is not omniscient, so he has to operate through the demonic and spiritual forces at his disposal. For 6000 years, he has watched humans and he has become a master at how to manipulate them. He does not know everything, but he has learned by his own reason and observation the most probable outcome of a situation. He knows what to do to get men to corrupt themselves; he knows what to do to push men over the edge. He is not a master of men. He is a master of deception.

But those that know the Word can see his deception for what it is, and they can combat it. This is why the nasty one pulls every string to blot out scripture, to hide the truth, to cleverly disguise the Lord's intent with his intent. He recognizes the war for what it is and he hungers to defeat the Creator above anything else. But this also means not allowing his minions to know the full picture. If they did, they would know that Lucifer has already been defeated, and that he has already lost everything.

The wolf and the coyote are now focused on the father, while the fox is focused on the son. On this day, the fox is alone with the lamb and he has found an opportunity to muster others to disrupt the peace of his charge. Since his lamb was being fed some of God's Word at school, perhaps a little melee would shake things up, string him out, make him doubt. So, he frames a gathering of lamb versus lamb, man versus man, with no sheep or shepherds around, and sits back and watches.

BELLFLOWER, CA, AUG 1982

STEVE'S FAMILY HAD MOVED to the city of Bellflower, about 12 miles from their last home a little more than a year earlier. He had listened in on some of the conversations his parents had about why they were moving; it had something to do with a new group of people that were moving onto their street that his dad did not like. Steve and his sister had still been attending the same Christian school at the time. He had just started the 6th grade and his sister the 4th, but getting to school now required that they use the school bus, which was very visible to the other boys on the street.

Steve was thinking about this as he was walking with his cousin Tyrone to the street corner. Their street was a cul-de-sac with one way in and one way out. Some of the other boys that lived on the street lived at the corner entrance and were throwing a football back and forth. He and Ty were walking to a liquor store a few miles away to play some video games as a new exciting game had just come out, Dragon's Lair.

The boys that were already living on this street when Steve's family had moved in had not taken to Steve. They had pushed him away rather than seek him out as a new friend. He recalled one time where four of the boys had confronted him and his sister when the bus had just dropped them off.

The sheep, who had been observing his young self and his cousin walking down the street, could see the flashback in Stephen' mind as he reflected on the event a year earlier – in fact, the sheep could see both timelines.

AS THE BUS ENTERED THE STREET, there were several pairs of glowing eyes that observed it stop and drop off Steve and his sister. In one voice of many, the pack of foxes whispered to their lambs, *"Get him, show him who runs the street!"*

All of the boys were roughly the same age as Steve, perhaps a year younger or so, but two of them were taller. The sheep watched as the boys walked up to his younger self and threatened him and his sister. A fight was brewing as eleven-year-old Steve pushed his nine-year-old sister behind him and prepared to defend them as best he could.

"Why do these guys hate me? What did I do to them?" he wondered.

A small breeze gently brushed Steve's hair. *"Change the conditions, Steve; you are safe. The Lord will fight for you; let Him in. This quarrel is not about you; it is coming from the desires of the boys to show off their strength to someone they don't recognize."*

Words were exchanged, challenging Steve to a duel of sorts until he finally relented. "OK, we'll fight, then, but I get the option of choosing who I fight first." He pointed at the kid he figured to be the weakest, "I will fight him first and then you can choose who fights next."

"Excellent, Steve, show strength and you can disarm them," urged Shepherd.

The fox could see Shepherd speaking and was trying to counteract His influence, but he could not reach Steve.

"How did we get into this? I won't let them hurt my sister but I am not sure this is going to end well. Why do they want to fight me?" Steve thought to himself again.

While the other foxes worked to manipulate their lambs, the lambs were still independent boys that felt fear; they were still allowed to choose. The foxes spoke as one, *"Jump him as one; he cannot overcome all of you."*

Shepherd stood beside Steve. He wasn't there to protect him: this was Steve's opportunity to display courage and strength against the boys. However, Shepherd was there as a show of strength against the fox.

Steve felt a sudden surge of confidence. The kid that Steve pointed at, a kid named Roger, who he had intuitively figured was a wimp, looked at his friends, suddenly showing fear. Steve presumed that the other kids might say no but they were actually agreeing to his suggestion. "They're testing me," he figured. This is when Roger said, "No way, man," before turning around and starting to walk to his own home across the street.

The foxes laughed at the fox that had lost his charge, *"Coward,"* they scoffed.

Steve stood there, waiting for the three remaining boys to say or start something. He then turned his head and glared at the next smallest kid in the group, while not saying anything: his look was enough. This one, named Donald, looked at him and then at the other two, one of whom was his brother Kenneth.

The fox charged with working Steve started to snarl, gritting his teeth as he tried to fight off Shepherd standing beside him. *"He's mine,"* he snapped and then immediately recoiled. *"This is just an innocent fight; why not let them figure out who is the stronger? Don't you want to know? You know you do."*

"The strength is in the Lord. There is no need to pursue what is already known. Peace requires more courage than throwing a fist. Fighting is easy; getting out of one is harder."

"Yeah, but shouldn't he protect his sister? Isn't that what a man is supposed to do? This could be a good lesson for the little lamb."

Shepherd looked at Stephen, *"You don't need to fear them, young one, for the Lord is with you. Sense Him in your heart; you will see."*

Donald looked around again and didn't see any action on the part of Nick or Kenneth. "Forget it," he said and then walked away.

A FEW SECONDS LATER, the remaining two looked at Steve, shook their heads and followed after Donald. Steve then told his sister to walk in the house with him following right behind her.

At this, the foxes all snarled at each other: *"You coward; it's your fault…you let them go…you failed…"*

Shepherd looked on with a smile. But the Lord had already revealed to him that there would be more of these events in the future. *"Great job, Stephen! You kept your words to a minimum and remained silent when necessary. The Lord is your strength; you have nothing to fear with Him by your side."*

This would not be the last encounter. There would be another altercation a few months later, with Steve and Tyrone versus the brothers Kenneth and Donald that would consist of boards up against heads. Now, one year later, Steve laughed at that memory as he watched the same boys tossing a football. "Oh boy, how is this going to go?" he wondered.

Both Shepherd and the fox watched, allowing this event to run its own course. The fox knew Shepherd would stop him if he tried to influence Steve.

Shepherd, with the foreknowledge provided Him, knew where this would go. Steve was about to enter into a relationship that would challenge him and take him down a path of temptation. Steve was reaching an age where his choices would be his responsibility, and he would make some poor ones.

As he and Ty continued walking to the end of the street, the nerf ball landed near Steve, so he stopped and picked it up. Kenneth looked at him, "Hey dude, toss it over here," to which Steve responded with a good toss.

"Steve, in your heart, you are going to learn and recognize that bad company will corrupt good morals."

Before he knew it, he and Ty were fully engaged with tossing the football around with three of the boys from the same violent altercation a year earlier. This was a turning point; a friendship was immediately sparked that late afternoon. Steve was now part of the crew of boys that owned the street. Steve, Nick, Kenneth, and Donald would become friends, terrorizing their street as well as the neighboring ones for the next five years. This was also the turning point where Steve would fully turn away from family, his sister included.

THE FOXES WANDERED in a circle, planning their next move. They had finally gathered this gaggle of human fools together, but there was an underlying blanket of protection on some of them. They glanced at the location where Shepherd had been standing but was now gone. "What is He planning?" they wondered to themselves. It was uncharacteristic of foxes to gather together as each preferred their own den, but they occasionally gathered to hunt together.

They had tried to victimize Steve with violence, a way to turn him from the Creator's ways that he was learning in that Christian school; but that plan had failed. They had then heightened the mistrust within this group of boys thinking that Steve would be tackled but, surprisingly, Steve was the one who had become determined. He was able to mobilize his own cousin to work with him to attack Kenneth and Donald, chasing them into a neighbor's garage, where they smacked heads with boards conveniently located on a workbench.

Oh, that had been a glorious day, watching Steve turn to violence. It was not what they had planned, but it was wonderful. They knew that the Creator guided His children to seek and pursue peace, but Steve had come to the conclusion that day that peace was not an option.

And now, this ironic twist of fate that even the foxes did not see coming. A friendship had been fostered among those that had once been enemies. "That was odd about the football landing near the feet of Steve," they observed. "But we can use that," they agreed. And with that, the foxes decided that they would continue the hunt together, in the belief that this was all consistent with the master's plan.

THE SHEEP AND THE SHEPHERD completed their step across the gates threshold as the gate closed behind them. The sheep turned around as he heard the metallic clink of the gate snapping shut, and then he watched as the gate slowly vanished, as if it had never been there. As he turned back around to look down the path they were walking, he noticed that the landscape had changed. The lake was still to his right, flowers were still blooming, birds were still chirping their song and the trees still danced with the movement of the wind. However, he also noticed animals of various kinds grazing peacefully in new meadows laid out before him.

The pathway was transitioning from neatly raked mulch and earth into a beautiful path of cobblestones, neatly placed side by side with no imperfections to be seen. He noted rolling hills, with a brook gently running down the hills into the nearby lake.

"This place continues to change based on your observed earthly maturity," Shepherd suddenly remarked, shaking the sheep from his euphoria. *"You have a little way to go but as you observe yourself change from a lamb into a sheep, your secret place will change as well. As a lamb, you are guarded and under the perfect care of Him that walks with you. That's why this place feels so perfect... majestic...glorious. But at some point you will become responsible for your own choices and you will see how this place changes based on your decisions...your choices...your actions."*

"What was the deal with the gate?" the sheep asked.

"The gate represented you transitioning from a past life into a new life. As we crossed the threshold, you were entering into a new phase of your life. As the gate vanished behind you, it represented that which is done, finished. You are still a product of your past and your experiences; but your past is just that; it's past – no longer to be dwelt on. There will be additional gateways and doorways, but that is for tomorrow and tomorrow will have its own worries...and rewards."

The sheep looked at Shepherd as they were both stalled on the pathway. *"As we take our next step, you will transition from a path that was beautiful even in its basic natural form of mulch and earth. The new path is more matured, formed, and put together. You will be walking on more solid ground but, if you should stumble as you walk, it will be more painful if you should trip, stub a toe, or scrape a knee."*

The sheep chuckled in acknowledgment as the metaphors and analogies were tossed out by Shepherd. "OK, I get it; I love how the Lord speaks in parables and metaphors. I found it confusing in my early walk, but I find it amusing now."

"Jesus Himself stated that He tells things in parables so that people will hear with their ears and see with their eyes, while understanding in their heart. You are blessed because you hear and because you see," said Shepherd patting his back.

"So, onward and forward, My Brother. What did you learn from that last vision and, more importantly, did you see the identity of

God?" And with a forward motion of his arm, Shepherd guided the sheep on the path again.

As the sheep took his first step on the cobblestone path, he started to address Shepherd's question. "Well, I noticed an aura of protection from Him when the boys on the street confronted my sister and me. That's one thing. I also felt my courage increase; I felt no fear, even at the thought of potentially fighting all four of them."

Shepherd nodded, *"The Lord says to fear not, for He is with you. He declares that He is your God and that He will strengthen you and help you with His righteous right hand. It was His personal declaration that you experienced."*

"Yes, Sir," the sheep wholeheartedly agreed, "I receive that. He also says that He is my Helper, so what can man do to me?"

"Yes," Shepherd agreed. *"You noticed that you had no fear. But did you also feel a sense of power, love, and self-control?"*

"Yes, now that you mention it. I felt that I had complete control of the situation. It was because of the love of my sister, and because He was with me. I do remember feeling powerful, which matches what I saw as I watched it in the vision. The Lord was with me – but I also noticed that He was actually guarding me from the spirits, not from the boys themselves."

"Yes, you needed exposure to dealing with your peers with Him by your side. He gave you confidence through His guidance, but it was your will to obey that led to victory. Do you recall how the experience with the four boys was different than the altercation a year later, where there was more violence with boards and fists?"

"Yes, Sir, embarrassingly so. There was no self-control and there was no love. I had had enough; I was angry and I wanted to hurt them," the sheep admitted

"Yes, the fingerprint of God was present in the first altercation in the vision but He was completely missing in the second. You wanted to physically hurt them and you followed through with it."

"But they kept pressing me and pressing me; they were constantly taunting me. Wasn't it my right to defend myself?"

"Did they threaten you with physical harm? They were just throwing out words, were they not?" Shepherd asked.

"No, they didn't threaten me physically, I guess. But what else was I supposed to do?"

"It was your flesh that wanted to hurt them; you wanted what you thought would be satisfaction because you were offended by their show of a lack of respect. The Lord is not into that. What you should have done is forgive them," Shepherd advised.

"But I did forgive them – multiple times, which is why I didn't do anything before. If I had not done anything, they would have kept it up. Their taunts did stop after that," the sheep argued.

"You should keep forgiving them, Brother. In Matthew 18:21-22, Peter asked Jesus Himself how many times he should forgive a brother. Jesus answered him 'up to seventy times seven times,' which means as often as it takes," Shepherd explained.

"Nonetheless, this is not necessarily a rebuke as much as it is a lesson. So, what happened at the end of the vision?"

THE SHEEP HAD THE URGE TO CONTINUE ARGUING with Shepherd about the fight. But he was also smart enough to know that God's answer was final. The main thing was to reinforce the need for love, repentance, and forgiveness. The Lord's desire was for him to be more Christ-like, not like ordinary men. The sheep suddenly felt convicted and wept.

"Forgive me for my brashness, Shepherd. I was brazen and uncouth. I could sense that old anger rising up again inside of me. I could feel a desire to defend myself rather than support and defend the Lord's truth," said the sheep lowering his gaze.

"You are forgiven, Brother. The anger rising up in you was not just because of that fight and your remembrance of it; it is something that you continue to carry inside of you. A desire to be recognized, respected by other men, and loved. If you don't get that, then you are hurt and offended, causing you to lash out spontaneously and erratically. But we will deal with that again before this is over. He forgives you and loves you. Accept His forgiveness and know that His compassion and mercy for you are complete."

"Now, tell Me, what stands out to you at the end of the vision?" Shepherd asked, as if the sheep had never blundered.

"The football!" exclaimed the sheep. "It landed at my feet, creating a situation for me to interact with the boys again. But this time, there was peace and…teamwork? Even the foxes in the vision seemed surprised that it landed near me."

"That simple act of the football landing at your feet created a situation that allowed peace to spring up between warring factions. A little melodramatic, perhaps, but you don't know what may have transpired a year later, or two, or three, if you and the other boys had not found peace together at that moment along the path," Shepherd commented.

"You could have kept the football yourself, or tossed it in the opposite direction – all out of spite, I may add. But, you chose to toss it back, sparking a shift, a change. Do you see that?"

"Yes, I do. As always, praise God! You continue to show me a different perspective that I had not thought of before. However, if I may, it was also that friendship that took me down a darker path, a path that was definitely not of God," the sheep added.

"Wasn't it?" Shepherd remarked.

"Huh? How could that be of God? I got into some bad things and got involved with some really bad people."

"Brother, just as no one knows your true thoughts and motives except your own spirit, no one knows the ways and thoughts of God except the Spirit of God. You may have been introduced to people and events that many people would frown upon, but, you were also a personal witness to how far man has fallen, how far removed men are from God, and how the temptations of man lead him astray when he neglects the spirit inside him. Would that be a fair assessment?"

"Why do you do that to me?" the sheep asked jokingly. "You always seem to make bad things into something good. Was God in control? Did He direct me to take that path?"

"The Lord can make something good from anything bad. But in answer to your control question, this is one that men have pondered for millennia. It all comes down to your definition of control," Shepherd explained.

"WAS THE LORD GUIDING YOUR FEET? *No. He may have lit the path for you but you chose to follow it. Did the Lord take control of your hand when you threw the football back to the boys? No, but He may have suggested it to your heart. You chose what to do with it. Did the Lord push and pull people to gather at that spot, at that time, ensuring that you would all meet up? He speaks to people's hearts, but they all make choices of their own accord."*

"The Lord does not possess you, or anyone for that matter. But He is always speaking, suggesting, and guiding. He has a plan for everyone and He has a direction that He desires everyone to move in," argued the Shepherd. *"However, He is a gentleman and has given everyone the gift of free will. There is a vast difference between what the Lord knows as compared to the erroneous theory of men that He is somehow manipulating you and taking control of your mind and body."*

"The Lord has a plan for you and all men, but that does not mean that men always accomplish that plan. Men go astray – as you already know intimately," Shepherd concluded.

"OK, I get that. I can even recall having heard several messages on that topic."

At this point Shepherd stopped in his path and beckoned the sheep, *"What do you see around you now, in this place?"*

Shepherd's discussions were always deep, thoughtful, and revealing, consuming the sheep's attention. So when he looked up, he wasn't surprised to see that the landscape was changing again. He could now see vegetable gardens and fields of wheat on the opposite side of the path from the lake.

"I see more growth, more development, more depth to our surroundings," the sheep reported.

"Yes," continued Shepherd. *"These gardens and these fields require tending, work, and effort to keep them thriving. A thriving garden can produce nourishment for the body and the wheat fields will produce an ingredient necessary to bake bread. Just like you, these gardens and fields need regular feeding and watering to stay alive. But, just as importantly, there are weeds growing in the middle of them. If you don't pull them out, they will grow and choke out the roots of the plants, killing them slowly, and painfully."*

"I see."

Shepherd pointed to the garden, *"Can you see the weeds growing in that garden over there?"* He asked.

"Yes, Sir, I can. I've worked in gardens before, so I know how to find the weeds and pull them out without hurting the plants."

"When you see another man that has been wounded, hurt or holds a questionable past, can you spot or discern him?" Shepherd asked.

"Yes, Sir, because I have been hurt, I can usually spot another man that has been wounded," replied the sheep. "My wife has remarked in amazement how easily I can spot them."

"Just like weeds in a garden, you can spot other men filled with wounds, turmoil, strife, and rebellion choking their spirit because you've experienced them yourself; even when other people cannot. At the same time, you can help other men recognize these weeds in their life, help them pull them out, without damaging the inherent goodness still in them. You have been there and done that. Can you see that?" Shepherd asked.

"Yes, Sir, I have made similar analogies in the past," replied the sheep.

"Do you think you could have helped these men if you had not experienced it yourself? Also, let's not forget the nourishment that men require after their weeds have been pulled. They require the Bread of Life, which is His Word, and they require the River of Living Water, which is Jesus Christ. Are you not prepared to help with that as well?" Shepherd asked.

"Yes, Sir, I believe so."

"Do you think any of this would be possible if you had not walked the path you walked, experienced the things you experienced, made the choices you made, or lived the life you lived?"

"No Sir; at least, it would have been significantly more difficult for me to relate to them and for them to relate to me. I think it is this relatability that allows us to connect," the sheep reflected.

"Quite right...so do you still have questions about how the Lord was an influence in your life, your walk, or why things happened the way they did? Such as you making friends with those boys, the football episode, or the events that followed?"

"Ugh!" the sheep scoffed, "No, Sir."

Shepherd laughed and pulled the sheep to Him tightly. *"The Lord loves you, Brother. I can see His revelation percolating in your head; but don't allow your mind to manage what you know to be true in your heart. He is a good God, Brother, and He never takes the lives of His children for granted. He may not have preferred for you to do the things you did, but He will turn that into good and use it – for you and your eternal spirit. All He wants is for you to follow Him!"*

Shepherd paused, waiting on wisdom from the Lord before continuing their walk along the path. *"It's time for us to move on once again, Brother. He has much more to reveal to you."*

A thin curtain appeared in front of the sheep, levitating in the air but blocking their path. *"When you are ready, pull the curtain aside and walk through,"* Shepherd instructed.

The sheep took a few minutes in order to digest all that had been revealed to him thus far. He wanted to make sure that he didn't have any more questions for Shepherd before moving on.

After a short period of time, the sheep took a deep breath and pulled the curtain aside to his left. He then walked through the opening before him....

CHAPTER 12
EVERY BREATH YOU TAKE

*"You have authority to walk on serpents and scorpions
and none of them will harm you"*
(Luke 10:19)

THE FOX COULD NOT SEE HIM but he could sense that the serpent was back. Following its scent, he found it slithering towards the sheep. "Yesssss, I'm back," it hissed. "You stay with the son while I have another tassste of the father."

The fox headed back to the lamb, but he stopped to hide around the corner to see what the snake would do. He was not left disappointed as he observed the snake enter the mouth of the sheep. The sheep, which had been napping, woke with a start, eyes wide open, wondering what it was that awakened him. It was then that he heard the sounds off in the distance – thump, thump, thump!

His heart rate accelerated and his skin tightened. With a heavy breath, the sheep got up and walked towards the sound that he believed had awoken him from his slumber.

BELLFLOWER, CA, JUNE 1983

STEVE AND CHARLENE WERE IN HIS BEDROOM, lying on the floor simply enjoying each other's company. Though Charlene was not the first girl he had hung out with, she was his first girlfriend. They had recently shared their first kiss in the middle of a bowling alley a few days earlier, and this memory exhilarated Steve.

He had given Charlene a necklace that day, but she did not know that he had stolen it from his mother's jewelry box a few days earlier. He figured his mother would never know as he had never seen her wear it, much less any jewelry for that matter.

The fox could see the thoughts running through the mind of Steve as he regaled the memory of the temptation to steal. The fox snickered as he recalled placing the thought into his mind that his mother would never discover the theft as she never wore the necklace.

Charlene was wearing it now and this only helped to fuel his memory about that kiss. He wondered what the next step would be.

As they lay on the floor of his room, touching their foreheads, the radio was playing *Every Breath You Take* by The Police. Kind of a romantic song, Steve supposed, but he and Charlene weren't doing anything that their parents would frown at. The fox was disappointed as he had been feeding perverse and sexual thoughts into Steve for a few years already.

The bedroom door was open and his father was home in the living room on the other side of the house.

"Oh, can't you see you belong to me
How my poor heart aches with every step you take
Every move you make, and every vow you break
Every smile you fake, every claim you stake, I'll be watching you"

Shepherd appeared, startling the fox. It seemed to the fox that Shepherd liked doing this to him, that it gave him some degree of personal satisfaction or something. Shepherd spoke in Marcs' direction, *"The wicked might think that the Lord is not paying attention, Steve, but the truth is that He is watching and examining everyone."*

"Do you want to get together next week sometime? Maybe we can hang out at the Lakewood Mall or somewhere closer to your house," Steve asked her.

"Sure, I would like that. I like hanging out with you," she replied.

"Man, how can someone like her like me?" he wondered. "She's so pretty and I'm ugly."

Steve marveled that they were actually laying there on the floor, just enjoying being around each other. His friends were most likely out smoking a joint, that's what they always did and Steve was always out there – normally. But he would rather be here than there.

They continued to hold each other's hands, head to head, listening to the music and relaxing in each other's company. Steve was still pondering on that kiss at the bowling alley, wondering what their next kiss would be like.

The fox could see that Steve was becoming aroused. *"Yes, go for it. You know she wants to."*

Shepherd continued to focus his attention on Steve, *"No, Steve, do nothing. Any action would hurt both your heart, and hers."*

The song on the radio changed to a song by Duran Duran. Steve thought it was titled *New Religion* but they did not play it very often, so he wasn't sure. "What a crappy song!" he whispered to Charlene, "I don't like this one."

"I've been now sauntering out and down a path sometime
Come on, it takes me nowhere which I knew"

SHEPHERD AND THE FOX COULD SENSE A CHANGE in the spiritual realm. Knowing this was coming is why Shepherd had arrived. The fox, already aware that the serpent was about, waited in eager anticipation.

As they lay there, Steve heard footsteps stomping towards his room. They had a hollow crawl space below their house and some-times, as people walked across the floor, the pounding of footsteps would sound like a beating drum, echoing from the bottom.

"Faces everywhere pulling grins and signs and things
Telling me not there man, it's no go (don't go there boy)"

Boom, boom, boom, the steps got closer.

"Oh great, he is coming. What did I do now?" he wondered.

The fox grinned and looked at Shepherd. *"He's in for it now,"* he laughed.

"Guard your heart, Steve; do not allow what is about to happen to provoke you into further sin."

Steve's anxiety increased; his heart started beating so fast he thought it was going to burst from his chest. Steve would do everything he could to stay away from him, but he could not always hide from him.

As his father entered the hallway that connected the living room to all three bedrooms of the house, he made a dramatic turn into Steve's bedroom. That look, on his face.

"Oh crap!" his thoughts screamed loudly in his head. "What did I do?"

His father's eyes were red and his face was curled up into outrage. It was only two steps to Steve from the door, and then his father picked him up by his shoulder and shirt, lifting him to his feet.

"Punch him, knock his teeth out!" the fox yelled. But he knew that there was another restraining Danny.

A heavy burst of wind entered through the open window. *"Danny do not do this! This is not discipline, this is violence! Spare the rod!"*

It happened so fast that Steve didn't have time to react before he felt the slap on the side of his head and fell to the floor.

"Do it again! Do it again!" the fox was hysterical.

After picking him up again, his dad slapped him upside the head harder than the first time, knocking Steve about four feet across the room, where he stumbled over his bed and into the wall. Danny didn't even see or notice Charlene cowering in fear against the opposite wall.

"I told you to turn that radio down!" he bellowed as Steve tumbled. "Turn it down!" he yelled once more before turning and walking out of the room.

"Yes," the dark one yelped. *"That was awesome!"*

IT TOOK STEVE A FEW SECONDS to get his bearings, but it felt like hours. "What just happened?"

"Dad has hit me before, but never in front of someone," Steve cried to himself. "He usually only does that when no one is around!" And then, he looked at Charlene. She was shaking, embarrassed and humiliated by what had just happened, still trying to bury herself in the wall.

"Only get one look before you die
Don't know why this evil follows me"

The next 30 minutes were a blur. Words were shared between Steve and Charlene, but he forgot them as soon as they were said. He was there but absent. He was distraught. He could barely hear the song that was now playing on the radio, still at its current volume.

"Ain't no sound but the sound of his feet,
Machine guns ready to go"

As he gave Charlene a hug, she walked out the front door to a waiting car and her mother. That would be the last time that Steve would ever see Charlene: she would disappear from his life.

"Steve, your mind is currently whirring with thoughts of death, but guard your heart with all diligence. Allow your mind, right now in His great name, to be governed by the Spirit of life and peace."

Steve did not know it, nor would he have understood it anyway, but a new seed, a bad one, had been passed to him from his father. With a look of fierce determination – outrage – Steve looked in the direction of his father lying on the couch. "He will never, ever, do that to me again!" he willed. "I'll kill myself first!" The seed that entered him served as the foundation of a new stronghold that had just taken form in his heart. And it came in the name of Rejection.

"How long can you stand the heat?
Out of the doorway the bullets rip
To the sound of the beat
Another one bites the dust"

AFTER TAKING CARE OF WHAT HAD WOKEN HIM, *the sheep trundled back to his hooch and lay down – in exactly the same position he was in before. To the sheep, it was as if he had just woken from a dream. He closed his eyes and was quickly back into a deep sleep.*

The snake crawled out of the sheep's mouth, down the belly, and to the ground. He was in no hurry, the sheep would not waken, nor would he remember what he did. "Thank you for being such a willing and welcome vessel!" he said to the sheep.

The fox turned the corner to greet the snake before he left. "That was awesome!" he cheered the snake.

"Watch the lamb; he has received a seed of the knowledge of rejection. He has awoken to a new foundation. Others will soon join as the seed takes root."

"He is a logical one, that lamb. What about Shepherd, he likes to intervene and get in the way?" the fox asked.

"Temptation is of mankind and the Creator has given them free will. He will not get in the way of man to make his own choices," the serpent hissed back. "Shepherd may provide a guiding hand but the seed that has been planted will infiltrate the lamb's thoughts and he will become a slave to his flesh."

"Understood," the fox agreed.

And with that, the serpent disappeared into his hole.

As the fox turned around, he noticed Shepherd standing a few feet away. He had overheard the entire conversation. "You know you will not win," He told the fox. "This one already has the indwelling Spirit; he has just forgotten he has."

"Something forgotten is something missed," the fox replied slyly.

"Perhaps. But something forgotten is not something lost. It simply needs to be found again. It will." With that, Shepherd walked towards the lamb who had just returned.

"Steve, one day you will recognize the peace of Christ in your heart; this is what you have been called to. You see the pain and tribulations of today as something that will be a part of your eternal future, but you will see that all of this will be turned around for good, thanks to the grace and righteousness of our Lord Jesus Christ."

SHEPHERD AND THE SHEEP stepped through the curtain and found themselves in a room that appeared to be a temple, or a worship room of some sort. It was immaculate.

The sheep looked around in awe. "This is fantastic!" The room was designed with beautiful wooden furniture in a variety of woods he could not identify, polished to a glorious shine. There were bowls, cups and trinkets clearly made of gold sitting on the tables and in the cabinets lining the room. The floor was of marble with spots of solid granite while the floor was raised up to a tub that looked to be made of bronze, filled with the clearest and purest water he had ever seen.

EVERY BREATH YOU TAKE

Placed strategically around the room were large pillows and cushions for relaxation and comfort. Bowls of fruit were arrayed around the room, different varieties of bread and meats, and ancient looking bottles of what looked like wine sitting near flasks of water. He had not experienced such peace and tranquility.

"What is this?" the sheep asked. "It looks like a fancy temple, what an extravagant temple might look like, though I've never been to one."

"Very perceptive of you to notice, Brother. Yes, this is a temple. But, this is a temple unlike any other that you will find anywhere because this is what is inside of you," Shepherd revealed.

"Oh, OK, I think it is found in 1 Corinthians 3:16 where we are told that our bodies are the temple of God and the dwelling place of the Spirit of God."

"Yes. That passage also continues in verse 17 that, if anyone should defile the temple of God, God will destroy him. To be clear, it doesn't mean that He will physically kill him, but it does mean that if anyone should allow the temple, a holy place, to remain defiled, then that person is allowing themselves assured destruction for eternity. Do you know the relevance of this to the vision you just experienced?" Shepherd asked.

The sheep thought about it for a few seconds. "The vision showed the serpent, a demonic entity, enter my father's body. Does it relate to that?" the sheep asked.

"Yes. Your father was already defiled before the serpent appeared. But it was because of that that the serpent was allowed to enter and speak to his heart. Then it could easily manipulate him into doing something that – let's be clear – your father would not normally want to do."

"You know, that was the last time that he ever did anything like that to me, at least that I can remember. Now that I think of it, I don't think we ever spoke about it; he acted like it never happened," the sheep added.

"Oh, your father remembered, Brother, and he was humiliated. He cried about it several times over the years, knowing that it was an event that solidified your lack of respect for him. He didn't bring it up because he knew it dishonored you and this tormented him. He wanted to forget about it and hoped that you would, too. He never forgave himself for it."

This triggered the sheep to start weeping. "If he had come to me to apologize and ask forgiveness, I am not sure how I would have responded. I hate to think that I would have turned him away."

"It's past, but you can be blessed in the knowledge that you have forgiven him now. If that is good enough for the Lord, then it should be good enough for you as well. But...there is one more lesson to take away from this."

"Your father could have taken this opportunity to repent to God and ask for His forgiveness. And God would have granted it. This would have compelled your father to talk to you about it. You would have seen the love in him and how much it hurt him, and you, too, would have fallen into God's grace and mercy. I believe you would have forgiven him. It's very similar to the vision you witnessed earlier where your father and his father confronted each other," Shepherd explained.

"Once your father recognized that he had defiled himself by his actions towards you, this could have served as an opportunity for him to start cleansing himself of all that was unfit, and to serve as a vessel of honor to you, and God. The Lord could have used this to start preparing your father for more good works. But, alas, your father chose to take the left in the fork along his path and not the right."

"If he had cleansed that which was unfit, then your father would have recognized that he had the authority to trample on that serpent, which would have prevented it from further defiling him. Of course, this would only operate if your father would have accepted Jesus Christ as His Lord and Savior."

SHEPHERD PAUSED FOR A BIT, allowing the sheep to soak in the lesson. *"Look around you. You have seen all that is beautiful and elegant. Do you see anything else? Remember, this is your body serving as the temple."*

The sheep looked around and could not see anything beyond what they revealed on the surface. "I am not sure; I see the furniture, the food, the water and all that. What am I missing?"

"Look into the corners of the ceiling, look closer at the tables and the utensils," Shepherd hinted.

The sheep meandered around the room and it was then that he noticed spider webs in the corners, scratches and dents in the wooden furniture, and tarnish starting to appear on the metallic objects. "Oh man, I see it. There's contamination, dirt, dust and wear marks," he remarked.

"Yes, these shortcomings represent the things that continue to hamper your walk with God. Sometimes, even mature Christians fail to notice the blemishes in their own lives, while they can point them out in others. They believe they are well, that things are perfect – but they aren't."

Shepherd could see that the sheep was troubled by this and he patted the sheep on his back and gripped the sheep's shoulder. *"It's OK, Brother. Your temple will always have blemishes because you are human and not yet perfected. The key is that you maintain your self-awareness and rely on His assistance to spot the blemishes so that you can cleanse them before they spread."*

"Nonetheless, if you fail to see these imperfections and do not deal with them, they will spread, which would allow foreign matter, such as negative influences, to infiltrate your temple and defile the holiness the Lord desires."

"Wow, another heart metaphor!" the sheep exclaimed. "I am seeing a trend that the heart is the key to everything. I can't count how often this has been represented in this journey thus far."

"The heart is the key to everything, Brother. Too many rely on their minds, but they are misled. Love resonates from the heart, but so does hate. If your father had kept his heart clean, the serpent would not have been able to manipulate him and strike out. When the snake did that, he hurt not only you, but also your father. That is how the dark one operates. Your father did not hate you – please know that in your heart – but he did hate himself, and he hated the world for it. Your father was not an evil man: he was just deceived."

ON THAT NOTE, the sheep wept again, barely able to maintain a semblance of composure. "I can't tell you how much I hated my father for that event. I carried that with me for decades." The sheep fell to his knees and buried his face in his hands. He began to pray.

"Lord, thank You for all You are doing in my life. Thank You for all You provide for me and the direction You have given me so far in this quest. Thank You for protecting me over the years and being my strength every day. Lord, today I lift up my heart to You because I had filled it with hatred that I couldn't seem to control,

and I still see signs of it in me today. There were times when I knew I should have let go of it, but it just kept grabbing onto me. Every time I think about this event and others like it, I just get angry all over again. I can feel the rage inside me build, and I just know the hatred is doing something to me.

"I ask, Lord, for Your forgiveness of my past hate, and, Lord, I also ask that You intervene in my life to help me overcome this hatred when it reappears. I know You warn against letting it fester. I know You ask us to love rather than hate. You forgive us all for our sins rather than allow us to be angry. Your Son died on the cross for our sins rather than allowing You to hate us. Jesus couldn't even hate His captors. No, You are the ultimate in forgiveness and overcoming even the potential for hate. The only thing You hate is sin. But sin is a thing, and You still offer Your grace when we fail.

"Yet, Lord, I'm struggling with this situation, and I need Your help. I am not sure I have the strength right now to let all of this hatred go. I am hurt and I have hurt. It is distasteful. I get distracted by it sometimes. I know it is taking hold, and I know You are the only one strong enough to get me beyond this. Help me go from hatred to forgiveness. Help me walk away from my hatred, and temper it down so I can see the situation clearly. I no longer want to be clouded. I no longer want my decisions to be biased. Lord, I want to move on from this heaviness in my heart.

"Lord, I know hate is much stronger than just a dislike for things. I see the difference now. I recognize that hate is strangling me. It is keeping me from a freedom that I've seen others experience when they've overcome hatred. It draws me into dark thoughts, and it keeps me from moving forward. It's a dark thing, this hatred. Lord, help me let the light back in. Help me come to an understanding and acceptance that this hatred isn't worth the weight it has placed on my shoulders.

"I am struggling right now, Lord, and You are my Savior and my support. Lord, please let Your Spirit fill my heart so that I can move forward. Fill me with Your light and let me see clear enough to come out of this fog of hatred and anger. Lord, be my everything at this moment so I can be the person You desire for me.

"Thank you, Lord. In Your name, Amen."

As the sheep concluded his prayer, he continued to weep, but now he was weeping with joy rather than regret and remorse. He felt Shepherd kneel down next to him and place His arms around him, embracing him with love and empathy.

"Yes, Lord, help My Brother cleanse his temple of blemishes. Help him to see where they are and give him the strength, courage, and reliance on You to remove them when they appear, before they spread and further contaminate this holy place. Yes, Lord, he sees Your love for him. Continue to show Yourself to him. Allow him to see the love his father had for him, even when he rarely showed it. Allow this man to replenish his respect and honor for his parents; free him from this bondage. Hold his hand, Father. Give him security when he feels that he will fall. Yes, Lord, love conquers all. Love is the enemy of hate. Love is light and light removes darkness. Thank You, Father, for Your love, grace and mercy. In His Holy Name. Amen."

When Shepherd had finished His prayer over the sheep, they heard the sound of a door opening. The sheep looked up from his kneeling position and noticed an open door along one of the walls, allowing the light to shine in, and inviting him to enter.

"It's time, Brother. The Lord has more to show you."

The sheep and Shepherd stood and crossed over to the open door. The sheep looked around the temple one more time, taking it all in. He then turned and looked through the open doorway, but, blinded by the light coming in, he could not see what was on the other side.

Shepherd took his hand giving him needed confidence and together they walked through the door.

CHAPTER 13
THE CHAMBER OF SECRETS

*"Do not get drunk on wine, which leads to debauchery.
Instead, be filled with the Spirit."
(Ephesians 5:18)*

THE LAMB WAS BECOMING A MAN, *yet not quite a sheep. He was now growing to be personally responsible for his own choices, his own decisions, and his own soul. This development now allowed the wolf to move in and join with the fox in leading the lamb astray – and they were a formidable pair.*

The lamb broke rules, participated in debauchery, gave into lust, associated with criminals, and was a thief. But the wolf, who was the stronger of the two spiritual forces at work, was also contending with the Shepherd, an invincible foe who was working to lead the lamb away from the evil one's plan, holding his hand, and giving him directions. This created a challenge for the wolf, since the lamb was able to discern that something was off, that he did not belong where he was. This is not what his master wanted.

Shepherd, on His part, was lighting a path and working on the eyes of the lamb to see the path in front of his feet. He was also working on the ears of his heart so that the lamb could hear His voice, and the mind of his heart so that the lamb could attain wisdom and revelation. But the lamb was still thorny ground.

The seed of truth had been planted in his youth, so even though the lamb did not recognize Him for who He was, the lamb could still partake of Him, sense Him, allow his spirit to connect with the Spirit. But each time the seed sprouted, the thorns of his heart would choke off the life-giving nourishment to the seeds planted in the corners of his spirit. The lamb would toss things off as odd, bizarre, or simply coincidence, and then go back to his worldly ways.

But things were changing: the Lord had been getting through to the lamb. The lamb was getting tired of being used, abused, and still not feeling like he belonged. He was frightened by some of the unsavory characters in his life. He had no one to lead him, to guide him, to tell him his true name, to help him understand his nature. He was lost in the wilderness and was feeling a call to search for his true purpose, his true identity, the reason for "all of this." The seeds may not yet have fully bloomed, but they were still firmly planted in the secret chambers of the lamb's heart, away from the prying eyes of the wolf and the fox.

NORWALK, CA, AUG 1986

THE DAY WAS HOT AND DREARY, but this was typical for mid-August in this Southern Los Angeles community, and Steve's senior year of high school was just a few weeks away from starting. He and his friends were hanging out at Nick's oldest brother's house, right next to the Los Angeles River, a concrete riverbed transporting waste from the city to the ocean 12 miles away. They were smoking weed as was their usual pastime.

They were spread out amongst a couch and cushioned armchairs in the tiny living room, lost in the euphoric haze of bluish green smoke, dazed and most definitely confused. The song *Paranoid* by Black Sabbath was on the record player, playing at almost full volume in the background blasting their ear drums with the Speed Metal band Slayer stacked on the record rack, ready to play after *Paranoid* finished.

Steve had started smoking weed when he was in the 8th grade, and while he had succumbed to the peer pressure of using Crystal Meth two years earlier, he drew the line at anything that required needles or acid. The guys had added Acid to their "drug buffet" about six months ago and Steve had been refusing to touch it; he had even refused to contribute money into buying it, which pissed off his friends.

Shepherd had been working in Steve to halt his drug habit since before he had even started, *"Drugs are a mockery, Steve; they block Him from you while allowing you to be led astray from the wisdom He has and desires for you."*

The wolf had been working with the fox for the last year and had thus far successfully convinced Steve that it was OK. *"But it allows you to break away from the world, Steve. Why would God create something that is natural and not want you to use it? Doesn't make sense. And besides, your grades in school are good, so why do you need to quit?"*

The four friends each had their hands somewhere in the drug trade. Steve was the connection for pot and could usually get a dime or quarter bag anytime he wanted, and for free sometimes, as the dealers were friends of his.

Nick, who Steve considered to be his best friend, had the Crystal Meth connection and could get it whenever they wanted, but his connection wouldn't give any away for free. This was Steve's drug of choice and, since he couldn't get it for free, he had decided to join in when the guys decided to start breaking into houses in search of cash.

"Leave, Stephen! Leave now! This life is not for you; it's time to follow the One who truly loves you, the One who can save you, the One who can redeem you and rescue you from this life. The boys around you do not love you."

Steve had been growing more and more upset, angry, and bitter about how his friends had been treating him and talking to him. There was a distance growing between them that he could not explain; it was just happening. So, he took advantage of them whenever he could in a way to get even with them. Since he was the one who could get weed whenever they wanted, they had been getting high most days for the last two years. As he had been growing fed up with the guys, he started lying to them about needing money when he knew he could get it for free. He would sometimes give a few dollars to his dealers, even if they didn't ask for any, and then he would pocket the rest. This is how he funded his crystal meth habit.

The wolf loved this betrayal and lack of integrity. He hadn't even thought of it; Steve had done this on his own. *"What they don't know won't hurt them, Steve. They would have to buy it anyway without you and you are actually getting it cheaper. It's all good."*

Shepherd, on the other hand, was not surprised, but this didn't negate His disappointment. *"Steve, you have taken a turn along the path that will lead you to misery, regret, and death. Turn away from this life now before it is too late."*

WHILE STEVE AND NICK HAD THEIR CONTACTS, it was Donald that had somehow started using acid along with a reliable supplier. His brother Kenneth just ran along on everyone else's coat tails.

The sheep, watching the vision run its course around him, shook his head. "So there we are," he said to himself, "a ragtag group of drug users, each with their own connections into the drug market, placing themselves in more danger than they realize." The sheep knew that a friend of theirs would be found dead in the trunk of an abandoned car a few years later. "That could have been me," he figured.

"Steve, come on dude, take a stamp," Donald pressured.

"Don't do it, Stephen! Remember, your body is a temple, it is not your own. It was bought at a price."

"No, man. Don't want it," he replied.

The wolf looked at Shepherd and growled. Shepherd avoided his gaze and spoke again into Steve's heart. *"Remember, Steve. Review your life choices and what they truly mean – the ugliness, the rage. Your values are better than this."*

After taking a hit from the bong and holding it in, Steve passed it to Kenneth. During the slow exhale, he started to dwell on the things they did to support their habits, or, to add excitement. When they had started breaking into houses, Steve never took anything himself, but he did enjoy the rush of the act. None of them took things like jewelry or other belongings, but they would steal alcohol or cash if they found it.

At some point, Donald had started breaking things like mirrors and dishes, dumping garbage all over the carpets and throwing stuff against the walls that would stain or stick. Steve laughed but he did not really think it was cool; he thought it was stupid and served no purpose other than ruin the lives of whoever owned the homes and make them feel more violated than they already did. Steve also recalled his taking money from his mother's purse, or his father's coin collection. This bothered him more than breaking into other people's homes, but every time he tried to stop, he would do it again.

The wolf spoke at Steve, *"Yeah, but, Steve, you get your weed for free so you aren't really stealing for drugs. And alcohol? You hate alcohol and never drink any of it, so you are clean, dude. The other guys, on the other hand, they are the ones that are really stealing, drinking the booze and using any money found to buy acid. Your mom will forgive you if she ever finds out – you're good, Bro."*

Shepherd, with the gracious touch of a feather, placed his hand against Steve's chest, *"Steve, the truth is being creatively disguised between half-truths and half lies. Do you not use Meth? Aren't you in the homes at the same time as the others? You are equally culpable and a contributor to the crimes. You are allowing your habits to deceive you."*

Shepherd pressed in, *"Steve, have you not felt the tug of my hand on yours? Have you not sensed the force pulling you away before the acts are committed? Come with me now. Take my hand and follow me."* Shepherd extended his hand, reaching for the hand of Steve's spirit.

The wolf could no longer contain himself, *"Get away from him you stupid light bug! He's mine by right because he has denied Him."*

"You cannot deceive Me, wretched one. He has not denied the Creator; he is simply indifferent. No matter, he is still a child of God and he is still free to choose."

Donald's continued mocking of Steve brought him back to the present. The acid debate had popped up about three times over the last few months but Steve remained vigilant against succumbing while his friends were relentless in teasing and mocking him for not taking it. It always ended with them calling him names as the acid took effect, just as it was now.

The sheep noticed other wolves in the room, each one licking, nipping, and spraying their scent on the other boys. *"Don't give up, you rat turds; he'll cave sooner or later. Keep offering it to him."*

"Man, look at all the spiders climbing up the walls," Kenneth stated hysterically.

"No way, dude; the walls are melting," Nick responded laughing.

Donald just looked like he was in a state of shock, staring into space at nothing in particular after having just demanded that Steve take a stamp.

"Take it, Steve. Feel the rush!" the lead wolf invited.

"No, Stephen. Keep your hands where they are," Shepherd said firmly. *"Come away with me. The time is now."*

THE SHEEP NOTICED THAT THE WOLF AND SHEPHERD were becoming more aggressive, more vigilant, and more urgent in managing and directing Steve's temptations. While Shepherd consistently remained calm and composed, the wolf was becoming more erratic and impetuous. He could see that the wolf knew he was losing him.

Kenneth started laughing at Steve and the other two immediately followed. "You're such a twat Bro; you don't know what you're missing out on."

The boys starting repeating, word for word, what their wolves were telling them.

"Yeah right, acid looks like fun dip wads," Steve gave it back to them sarcastically. "Looks like you are all having a lot of fun watching the walls melt and stuff."

"Dude, you're a wimp – come on man," they pretty much called to him in unison. Donald was typically the one that always started it; he tended to be the most unpredictable, mean, and arrogant. Steve regularly fought the urge to do something about it, remembering the thrill of banging that board against his head almost 5 years earlier.

"It was inevitable, always happens with these guys," Steve thought to himself. "They think I am an idiot for wanting to be an astronaut." Steve had been holding onto his dream of being an astronaut since he discovered books about the Space Race as a toddler. He had been told, somewhere, that acid never truly went away – that it was always locked away in some part of your brain, to come back when you least expected it.

Shepherd was thrilled when the Lord guided him to that understanding, while the wolf continued to bare his teeth and growl.

Steve had enough sense to realize that the last thing he needed was an acid attack when being launched into space aboard the space shuttle. It might be a silly dream, but it was real to Steve and he

THE CHAMBER OF SECRETS

was serious about it enough to manage his drug habit; this is why he refused to take acid.

The sheep shook his head as he recalled his naïveté and gullibility at thinking his drug habit would be OK. "Man was I stupid!"

Shepherd spoke to Steve again, *"Steve, the Father wants you to inherit the Kingdom of God. Come with me now, Steve."*

His friends were still laughing uncontrollably when Kenneth walked over to one of the walls and started to pee on it. He was apparently trying to get one of the spiders he saw crawling on it. The wolf worked to convince Steve that this is just what boys his age are supposed to do. *"Look how free they are, Steve! They are having fun while you watch like a little old lady."*

"They will end up being wanderers, Steve. You should leave now before they lead you further away from Him," Shepherd warned.

THE SHEEP CONTINUED WATCHING as the battle for Steve's will commenced between wolf and Shepherd. The wolf couldn't know it but Shepherd knew: if Stephen didn't turn away today, he would give in to temptation and fall a level deeper into his drug-induced pit.

Nick's laughter faded quickly to fear as he screamed that the walls were caving in from the lava flow. The other guys started laughing at him as Kenneth stumbled back to the couch, forgetting to zip up his fly.

"Thank God these guys don't shoot up!" Steve thought to himself. His urge to get up and walk away from them forever was getting stronger; but something was holding him back.

With dazed eyes, full of inspired confusion, the other boys looked around as if they could sense something they could not see, and then they all started to gang up on Steve again, continuing to call him names and tell him what an idiot he was. "Astronaut. What a moron!" The sheep watched as the wolf pack were at it again, biting and nipping at the other boys, working themselves up as if they, too, were on the same drug as the boys.

"What kind of friends are these guys?" Steve thought to himself for the hundredth time. "Why couldn't they be supportive? I already get this from my dad. I don't need this from them, too."

"They are not your friends, Steve. Yes, the veil is being removed from your deception. Open the eyes and ears of your heart and you will be able to judge truthfully."

"No, Steve, these are the only guys that get you; they understand you; they know you. Where else are you going to go? You've been hanging out with these guys since the 7th grade."

Today was different though. Something in sparked in Steve's mind, his heart nearly jumped from his chest. It was as if he had suddenly woken up from a coma. He was high from the weed, but his mind experienced a sudden clarity that was new to him. He'd had enough; he was done with them!

Steve pushed himself up from the chair with his arms and stood up. He berated the other guys as he walked towards the door leading him outside. "Screw you guys! I'm gone!" Steve did not turn around and look back as he walked the few steps to his Schwinn bike, picked it up from the ground, and rode off for home a few miles away. He wasn't sure if the guys heard him or cared, but he definitely didn't care.

There was no trepidation, no pause; he was moving on instinct as if some force was pulling him away. The sheep watched as an invisible hand slowly reached out from Steve and grabbed the hand of Shepherd, his spirit lovingly smiling up as Shepherd smiled back with pride and approval. "This part of the path is done," Shepherd said with finality

With Shepherd floating slightly above, leading Steve away from the chaos, the wolf was giving chase behind them, snapping at his heels but unable to catch up.

A few weeks earlier, a school friend named Dan had contacted Steve about getting some cocaine. Steve was able to get it for him but Dan had also shared with Steve about a group he was in called DeMolay.

"Yeah, man, bunch of guys! We get together, do some community projects and such," he shared. "We also go to a lot of parties, but beer is about as hard as it gets, but not always. Never any hard stuff. And there are always girls around. We also go out a lot for pizzas, games and more," he added. "It's a lot of fun; you ought to consider joining."

AS HE RODE HIS BIKE HOME, Steve decided that he was going to join DeMolay, start something new. He didn't need those jerks anymore – "bunch of buttheads!"

"They are sheep that have gone astray, Steve, and have gone their own way," Shepherd told him. *"The Lord loves them just as much as He loves you. They require saving just like you do; but that is not your call."*

Steve was determined that he was going to do something with his life and a life of drugs, crime, and constant partying was no longer in it. He knew it would end at some point – might as well be now.

The wolf was still chasing after him as the distance between them increased. *"You know you can't give it up Steve; the temptation is too strong. Even now you can feel your body crying out for meth."*

Thirty minutes later, Steve was back at his house, the effects of the THC long gone and forgotten. He walked to the phone and called Dan, "Hey, man, it's Steve. You told me about DeMolay a few weeks ago. Where and when do I need to be, Dude? I'm in."

SHEPHERD STOOD BACK, observing the lamb as he followed the path he had decided upon. The wolf had materialized a few minutes after they got to the house, the Shepherd watching as it continued to prod and poke at the lamb to remind Steve of what his flesh wanted.

"Father, the lamb is still in the wilderness, but he has made one of the turns that You desire for him. He has begun his search for the highway, the River of Life, that will lead him away from the wasteland." The Shepherd watched as the lamb ignored the flailing of the wolf – for now anyway. The Lord had shown Shepherd where the lamb would go.

The visiting sheep suddenly realized that the one thing forgotten in this part of the story was the fox. The sheep could see him now, hiding in the shadows and remaining silent, allowing the wolf to do his thing.

The fox sat back, fully relaxed. This had been the wolf's chance and he had failed; the master would not be pleased, if he found out or even cared. The fox had been watching and observing the lamb since he was born and he knew the lamb intimately, whereas the wolf did not.

The fox knew Steve's character and his habits. He knew his inner-most desires and cravings. But, more importantly, because he had been observing the lamb for so long, he knew his strengths – and his weaknesses. The fox knew that Steve's struggle with his temptations was just getting started.

Shepherd knew the fox was there and he knew what the fox would do; the Creator had already told him. Stephen was not out of the Wilderness yet; he, too, would experience the bite and sting of the serpent before it was all over just as his father had.

The fox, too, was patient, and would strike at the opportune time.

SHEPHERD AND THE SHEEP stepped back out into the sunlight from the temple. The sheep immediately noticed that they were back on the cobblestone pathway just as he heard the door shut behind him.

"You know, I had forgotten about some of that. I remember feeling free and super energized as I rode away from that house. But I also remember the anger, resentment, and rejection. I kept asking myself why they made fun of me but, as I look back on it now, I was at a loss as to why they kept rejecting me, disrespecting me. It was if they were intentionally chasing me away," he pondered.

"Do you know why?" asked Shepherd.

"No Sir, it is still a burning question."

"Because they knew that you didn't belong. They could see, they could sense, that something was different about you, something that did not necessarily align with what they valued," Shepherd advised. *"You knew it, too, on the inside. You were searching for something that they could not give you – a clear heart, a sense of belonging, your identity."*

The sheep nodded. "Sure, OK. I do remember things feeling foreign to me. Is that related to me being lost in the Wilderness?"

"That sense of belonging is not as straightforward for those that are not Christians. A sense of belonging is something that all men crave, especially in a world where the feeling of disconnection from others is common; displaced men, in particular, are a huge problem. You may have initially felt that your relationship with the other boys was good, but, you had actually started feeling disconnected years earlier, around the time that you allowed them to pressure you into experimenting with drugs," Shepherd disclosed.

"For the other boys, drug use was something they connected with and something they bonded over. You, on the other hand, weren't connecting with the drug use; you were trying to connect with the social club. They could sense that, so, they subtly started pushing

you aside, making you feel isolated. Can you determine why this was the case?"

"Because I was asking for something from them that they could not give me?"

"Yes...and no. You had the seed of God planted in you at a young age, a seed that you accepted, I may add, and this seed was seeking nourishment, and honest godlike love. Your flesh was seeking physical companionship but the seed inside of you was seeking spiritual companionship, and this is where the disconnect was. You figured those boys were the companions you wanted, but in actuality they were not. You had surrounded yourself with a company of fools and were, as a result, incomplete and suffering spiritually. You weren't whole."

The sheep stopped in his tracks. "So, I was operating based on what I thought was right, because I thought I needed this friendship. That was my flesh talking. In fact, what I needed was to nourish my spirit. OK. You know, I now believe that my spirit was crying out but I kept shutting it down. But, I also can't think of where I could have gone to feed my spirit. Who and where could I have gone?" the sheep wondered.

"Brother, there were opportunities, but you were blinded to them. I wouldn't dwell on it but trust me when I say that I had placed people into your life that would have had a better influence on you and your spirit. These were the ones that could sense the seed in you and were drawn to it. But, you turned them away or allowed the negative influences in your life to take you down a different path. I could share with you several instances, before the time of this last vision, where if you had selected a different path, you would have developed differently, matured differently, and experienced a more joyful life. However, would it make any difference in your life today if I did? Or, should we recognize and be joyful and thankful, praise God, that you are where you are right now? Filled with the love of Jesus Christ, saved for eternity, because of His righteous sacrifice for you?"

The sheep didn't hesitate to say, "Yes, Sir, you're right. My past choices don't matter because they won't change anything today as much as create guilt. I am thankful that He found me and redeemed me, no matter where I was or how old I was. Praise You, Father! Thank You for Your unfailing love! Your strength is in Your showing how much You care." The sheep prayed, feeling warm while his skin actually tingled as if electricity were passing through his body.

"*Amen!*" Shepherd added. "*The Lord knows you, Brother. You are His and you are a part of His people, a sheep of His pasture. You listened to His voice that day in 1986 and you followed Him. Did you notice that when His Spirit grabbed your hand, the wolf could not catch up?*"

"Yes, I actually thought it was funny as I watched it. The wolf was in a panic, afraid."

"*Yes, when you follow Our Creator and follow Him, you will not perish and no one will snatch you out of His hand. On the day you accepted Christ as your Savior, your body was no longer your own because your body was bought at a price. That price was His crucifixion on the cross, His death – for you.*"

"*The Lord knew that if He could not get you away from those boys on that day, that you would have surely died, physically and spiritually. That is why the Lord worked hard to save you that day, and, if I may remind you of a past lesson, the rooster was crowing, Brother – loudly!*

"*Sadly, too many men are failing to hear His voice. They mark it off as hallucinations or they are operating from what their flesh wants to do and not their hearts. They can hear the voice of Reason, the voice of Wisdom, but they choose to ignore it, not knowing who that Reason was. You could not see it in the vision because it did not apply to you, but the Lord was also knocking on the hearts of your friends on that day as well,*" Shepherd revealed.

"*What you should have noticed was how the wolf pack was behaving around them. They were in a battle with the Spirit just as the wolf was around you. You just chose differently and followed the voice in your heart. Your walking away that day was also a call to them to question their choices, but they chose to blow you off and continue down their chosen path,*" Shepherd lectured.

"You know, maybe they did, but I can't recall them ever talking with me and asking me about that day. We would see each other on the street and we would wave, but we never spoke. I remember feeling good and proud of myself as I started hanging out with my friends at DeMolay. And I had more fun and more laughs than I ever did when using drugs," the sheep admitted.

"Yes, Brother. That is because He was in you and He is greater than the one who is of the world. But, since you brought it up, what are your thoughts about DeMolay?" Shepherd asked.

The sheep was prepared as he had often thought about this. "I have a lot of positive memories of my time with that organization and made some great friends. In fact, I have often testified that DeMolay saved my life. However, I now recognize them as they are, a cult, an organization on par with the Pharisees, a group that pretends to be religious but has surrounded itself with rituals in progression. I would never recommend them to anyone, but at the same time, I have to recognize the part they played in saving me from myself," the sheep confessed.

"Yes, very wise of you on all counts. The Lord knew that you needed them, that they were a group of your peers that could help you, save you, and redirect you. They opened your eyes to other opportunities beyond the world that you had been living in, offering you new experiences that are still a part of you today."

"Nonetheless, the evil one has penetrated that organization, turning boys away from the true God, a true relationship, and a true spiritual awakening. They mask it under the guise of mentorship, making men from boys. They are adulterous, making the world their friend and God there enemy."

"Yes, I see that in DeMolay as well as in their parent organization, the one for adults – the Masons. I have a few close acquaintances in the church who are members, who are under its spell, unfortunately. I see the Masons for who they are," the sheep admitted.

"Awesome, Brother! Now, before we move on to the next phase of your journey, we need to make sure you recognize, in your heart, how your hunger for companionship and acceptance blinded you to the truth," said Shepherd.

"Yes, Sir. I had been following the desires of my flesh and ignoring the desires of my spirit. I was looking for relationships with people but ignoring my need for relationships with people that could help me nourish and nurture my spirit. I also believe that this hunger in me was because of the void I felt regarding the relationship with my father and other members of my family," the sheep answered.

"Yes, very good, Brother. As we move into the next phase, you are going to witness your transition from lamb to sheep as you move out on your own. However, there will be a hunger inside of

you that will also create great pains that distract you, mislead you, and misguide you. Your hunger will be from your heart, but your heart has developed a pattern of self-reliance, selfishness, and self-centeredness. You will forget the lessons from your past, and repeat them over and over again along your Wilderness journey. I share this because what you will witness moving forward may be the most difficult for you to see. But they will also enlighten you further as to what requires additional healing and restoration. The Lord knows," said Shepherd intently.

"I think I have an idea, "the sheep offered. "I can already feel my heart weeping."

"Good. You will weep but I want you to weep for joy that you are no longer the person you will see in these visions. Open the ears of your heart to hear, the eyes of your heart to see, and the mind of your heart to ponder."

The sheep nodded in agreement, already sensing his heart relaxing, experiencing the love of Jesus through the voice of the Spirit in front of him. He felt peace, comfortable in who he was today and no longer concerned. He looked up at the Shepherd who was looking at him with compassion – no judgment, no ridicule, no guilt. The Shepherd took the sheep's left hand in his right hand and started guiding him along the path.

The sheep was anticipating another gate or a door, but this time there was nothing. They were just walking, soaking in all of the goodness of God. The sheep was so consumed by the love he was feeling that his surroundings no longer mattered. All he wanted was to experience more of Him. He did not want to leave His presence, but he knew he had to.

Then Shepherd spoke to the sheep in a soft and soothing voice. *"Brother, before you go on, the Lord wants you to meditate and ponder on what you have learned. What does your heart say to you, right now, at this moment, about your experience? What have you been awakened to? Use your own words but also listen for His revelation as you speak. It's OK; there is no judgment here. The Lord wants you to share from your heart ... Go ahead."*

The sheep looked down in prayerful contemplation of the vision experiences thus far. "Yes, Father. I understand." He looked up at Shepherd with tears in his eyes.

"The Lord wants me to understand how my experiences up to this point, those passed on to me from father to son and those of my teenage rebellion, were a part of me as I moved on into adulthood. He wants me to understand that I was operating under a belief system that I had been taught, both verbally and by example. He reminded me that my life up to this point was as a child, and that I should allow myself a break for mistakes made, poor judgment, and brash decisions. He wants me to keep in mind that, just as He was with me in my youth, He was also with me when I started my Wilderness Journey."

"He wants me to describe, to share……"

CHAPTER 14
THE LAMB REJECTED

"He found him in a desert land, And in the howling waste
of a wilderness; He encircled him, He cared for him,
He guarded him as the pupil of His eye."
(Deuteronomy 32:10)

"THE LORD WANTS ME to describe and share what I believe I have under the New Covenant and how this is reflective of our relationship. Yes, the Lord wants to be intimate; He wants a relationship. He wants me to focus on Him and not allow myself to reflect on Him as simply words written down in the book," the sheep started.

"Under the New Covenant, we are identified as His children. Our position as children of God is confirmed by the special care the Lord gives us, particularly when we are lost in the Wilderness. God's love is so great for us, that even sinners can be called God's children," he continued.

"I believe it is in 1 John 3:1, where John advised us to see how great a love the Father has bestowed on us, that we are to be called children of God; and as such, we are. John continues to explain that it is for this very reason that the world does not know us; because the world does now know Him. There are many people who don't recognize that they can have a relationship with God because they don't know Him.

"The Lord's desire for us is that we would experience joy and happiness and that He will pull out all of the stops to help us achieve it. He feels so strongly about it that He will spend time on each one of us."

The sheep paused, taking his time to listen for what the Lord was revealing to him and Shepherd took this opportunity to ask, *"Do you believe that your friends and family did not sense the same thing?"*

"You know, I think they did sense it, that He was talking to them just like He was talking to me. The difference is what we choose to do with what we hear on the inside of us. Some, unfortunately, ignore it, while some like me finally choose to follow it, at least in some part. I think that unbelievers may refer to it as instinct, or a "sixth sense." Whatever you want to call it, the Lord is showing me in these visions that too many people are following their flesh instead of their deeper instincts – while the reality is that His Spirit is talking to your spirit, knocking on the door of your heart. And it is our responsibility, our choice, whether to follow it or not.

"I also noticed that You, and the Father, were referring to me as a lamb and my father as a sheep, which I see as a spiritual context. I recall from John 21:15 that Jesus commands Peter to take care of His lambs. In this context the lamb is a new as well as immature believer, which is how I defined myself. As a child, I attended a Christian school for seven years, a time that I believe His seeds were planted in my heart. In Luke 15:4, Jesus shares a parable about a shepherd that leaves his well-cared flock of ninety-nine to find "one" lost sheep. While it might be considered reckless to leave an entire flock in search of one, this emphasizes God's love for every lost sinner."

THE SHEEP PAUSED, looking to see if Shepherd was in agreement with him so far.

"Yes, *keep going, Brother; don't stop,"* Shepherd encouraged him. *"You are speaking to Him, not to Me. He hears you. He is your Judge."*

The sheep nodded in acknowledgment. "I know that sheep are animals that have no inherent defense system; therefore, they are lost without a shepherd. My father, an adult, was a lost sheep who was not following the instructions or guidance of a shepherd. As the father in the family, it was his responsibility to teach me how to live in a way that would not deter me from right living. That meant teaching me values, a solid belief system, and giving me an identity.

Even though I was receiving some grounding in my Christian School, since my father was lost, I, too, was lost. The difference is that I had the seeds of Jesus Christ planted in me, even if I did not recognize them for what they were. However, as my father, the one responsible for my spiritual care, was not watering and feeding those seeds, they would never blossom. Therefore, it was up to the Holy Spirit to get my attention.

"When the visions first started, I witnessed scenes showing how my grandfather had been groomed to be the man he became. I did not believe it before, but I now know that he did cross paths with people who were designated to show him the error of his ways, either vocally or by example; but he ignored and shrugged off everything. He learned how to hate, amongst other sins, and passed those generational sins to my father. My father would exhibit similar sins; however, his sins would manifest in different ways. I believe that my father wanted to be different and wanted to be better than his father, something that I believe, today, that he did achieve. However, he was never given the seeds of love, mercy, or compassion by his own dad. My father was a very prideful man who showed very little humility – until he got much older, and lonely…filled with regret. As a result, he was not equipped to be the man, the father that he wanted to be – and this frustrated him.

"My father had dark spiritual forces at work within him. He developed strongholds in his soul and his spirit that hardened his heart to true spiritual revelation. This further allowed the demonic spirits to stomp on his heart. Some of this was due to his childhood, but I can see that Vietnam was the catalyst that finally pushed him over the edge, causing him to live a long life of deep emotional pain. I could see my dad's physical wounds, but his inner wounds were buried.

"He was a master of disguise with many of those around him, but he could not hide his weaknesses from those that lived with him, or were close to him. He was abusive, a control freak, an alcoholic, a damaged soul. But he was also a man that wanted to connect with me, his son. But he couldn't connect with me because we were two completely different males and had nothing in common beyond blood. And, I believe, this frustrated him even more because he could not show me what he wanted to show me. So, he reacted and took it out on me instead.

"I now see my father as a sheep that had wandered away from God's flock. His only chance of survival, or to get through what he was experiencing, was via the care of a competent Shepherd. However, he decided to ignore and disavow the Shepherd. As a result, he was overconfident, while also lacking confidence; he was rebellious while also desiring someone to teach him; he was distracted while wanting something good to focus on. All this caused him to be erratic and wander farther away. He failed to notice, or at least follow, the flock that would lead him to joy, to righteousness, to love.

"Because he missed it, he fell victim to the devil who prowls around like a lion, looking for something to devour; and the devil took a large chunk from my father's soul. The devil had found the ideal prey: that lone solitary sheep who had wandered away from the Shepherd. This is why I now know that nothing about my father was his fault. He was simply not equipped to be the man he needed to be, or the father I needed him to be. But, good news! He accepted Jesus Christ as his Lord and Savior in January 2017. Glory to Him!

"I see that my father's behavior and conduct with me created a line of tension and friction causing a gap that widened the older I got. The gap had gotten so large that I rarely saw my father and had reached a point where I would never receive guidance or instruction from him, no matter how hard he would have tried – which he rarely did. My solution was to avoid him and his solution was to give me all of the space I wanted. I became orphaned, never knowing who I was or who I was meant to be. I started making up stories and telling lies (or at least highly exaggerating things). However, I always sensed that something was not right. I felt physically being pulled in one direction while emotionally pulled in another. So, I followed others, regardless of how dangerous and foolish that was." He paused for breath and reflection.

"Go on, My dear Brother," said Shepherd patting his back. *"You are certainly learning very fast!"*

"Whether or not it was a false sense, I felt rejected by my father and this was a burden on me, even though I thought I felt differently at the time – I simply ignored it. As I started to hang out with my 'friends,' I never truly felt like I belonged with them either. I was out of place, even though we did a lot of things together and I did have fun. I was a very lustful young teenager and spent time with girls that were just like me. In order for me to properly fit in, I followed the herd and started smoking pot and using Crystal Meth at a very young age. As I continued moving with the flow, I started connecting with the criminal underground. It was thrilling to me, but also very scary," the sheep admitted.

"BUT I KNEW, I ALWAYS KNEW that I had a voice inside of me, telling me to do things differently, and on some occasions I followed that voice. I tried connecting and hanging out with people who were not part of the drug or criminal crowd. I even held honest relationships with a small number of girls that were not into my lifestyle. I wanted out and I got close, but I would soon find myself sucked right back in. The Lord was with me, but I was failing Him.

"Ironically, when I was with certain groups in my wanderings, I would often be the one who was picked on or frequently chosen for slap fights. I remember on one occasion, me and another guy actually had a knife fight after getting high, and I ended up taking a blade through my foot. I remember the goofy tactics I took trying to hide that one from my mother and father even though I needed stitches. And, there were numerous occasions where I was that one guy not invited to some events or parties. I can see now that it was the times of not being included that hurt me the most, much more than the physical wounds I took on. I can now see that the strongholds of rejection and insecurity were the strongest forces working in me. These forces would remain in me for many years – to some degree even now."

The sheep paused again, but Shepherd knew that the Lord had just opened his heart to another revelation, so He remained silent.

"Wow, OK Father! I see it. These strongholds of rejection and insecurity caused me the most problems well into my adulthood. They made me erratic, impulsive, willing to follow whatever would give me attention, even if bad. I had a void inside of me that needed desperately to belong, to be accepted by my peers. But I was missing it, I misunderstood it. I was seeking the wrong influences in my life. That void was the space set aside and occupied by You, Jesus Christ. It was You that was asking to belong, to accept You. My fears of rejection blinded me and I allowed myself to follow other herds that were also lost, leading me further way from the path set before me.

"Wow, that explains a lot now!" the sheep said with a sigh of relief.

THE SHEEP BEGAN TO WEEP.

"Praise You, Father! Thank You for Your compassion for me and thank You, Lord, for planting those seeds in me at a young age that allowed Your Spirit to communicate with mine. I now see that You knew that I was struggling spiritually and was in deep distress. I was in need of a shepherd and You did Your best with me in the condition I was in, insecurities and all," and the sheep began crying tears of joy.

"It was You that had filled me with the courage to walk away that summer of 1986. It was You that brought to my memory that discussion I had with Dan regarding DeMolay. It was You that had fostered that connection to begin with. However, I also know that You did not make the choices for me; You did not make that phone call for me, You did not predestine that I would take the paths that I did. It was my choice, my will, my decision. I recognize that You have a plan for me, a desire for me, and a destiny for me; but You will not violate Your promise of free will.

"Lord, as I prepare my heart for the visions you are about to show me, I know that I will see myself operating in a condition where I felt the world was not cooperating with me. When I was attending that Christian school in my youth, it seemed that everything was coming together for me, that I was king of my world and everyone was doing what I needed – for me. I was the man; I was the popular one and everyone wanted to be around me. This was very comforting for me as I was missing much of that at home. I missed it before but I now see how important the home is, it can either be filled with the peace and love of Jesus Christ, or it can be empty, hostile and indifferent, or somewhere in between. At school, where Christ was, I was at peace and filled with joy; at home, I was not a fulfilled child. I had toys and friends, but I was missing the family. Since my family were not believers, our lifestyle at home did not support Christ whereas my scholastic life did.

"And then, Father, I suddenly found myself in a life where I no longer had Christ filled people in it. My parents removed me from a Christian school environment and placed me into the public-school system. Life suddenly got hard and I was introduced to conflict. I used to look back at this with a critical eye, but now I see that school had nothing to do with it, it was the lack

of Christ in the home. I started to live life based on the example of those around me and that is when things really began to shake. I was a lamb following a lost herd mentality. I was a lamb that felt rejected, and I was about to walk into the world as a sheep, still lost, and still feeling rejected.

"Father, I see that I started my path already stuck in my wilderness, but You, Lord, You did not give up. This will remain on my heart today as You continue to show more visions of my heart wounds. You were laying out highways in the wasteland for me, giving me roads and paths to take that would take me out of the wilderness and into the promised land. My father may have been responsible for my spiritual care and my soul while I was a child, but when I left the nursery, I was responsible for myself. I recognize that I was wrong in blaming my father for anything after I left home. That was my opportunity to be my own man, a man that was destined to walk in relationship with You; yet, I retained my youthful soul as is, remaining a sheep wandering lost in the wilderness. I wanted to be obedient, but I did not recognize what I was to be obedient to.

"I will continue this project with the eyes of my heart open, the ears of my heart ready, the mind of my heart prepared. I will see that, even though I swore to be a better father than my dad, he still passed on his sins to me as well as some of his wounds, traits, and behavior patterns.

"Lord, thank You for Your grace, Your love, Your mercy, Your compassion, and Your thoughtful guidance. Thank You for Your mentorship and opening my eyes to truths that I had not seen before. Thank You for showing me that I was blind, even after accepting You into my life. Thank You for preparing my heart, right now, at this moment, for what it is that I am about to witness. I move forward with no guilt, no remorse, no ill fillings, and no hateful thoughts about who I was. I recognize that I was a flawed man, struggling to find the path. I see that You loved me then, just as You love me now. I recognize that I have no right and no authority to hate myself. I am destined to love. And with that Father, I am ready."

Shepherd watched the sheep close out his prayer to the Heavenly Father. He could see that the Lord was well pleased. Shepherd could also see that the sheep was ready to examine his own conduct, and his attitude towards others with a heart of love and not a heart full of guilt and remorse. His heart was prepared.

The sheep had now left the nursery.

PART 3

THE SHEEP WANDERS

CHAPTER 15
LEAVING THE NURSERY

*"Always be prepared to defend with anyone a reason
for the hope that is in you, with gentleness
and respect of course."*
(1 Peter 3:15)

THIS WAS THE DAY *that the sheep was leaving the nursery, so Shepherd lowered His head and prayed words over him that He heard from the Lord. "My little lamb is leaving the nursery, becoming the sheep that he was intended to be. For I know the plans I have for you, Steve, plans for your future, and hope. I have sent an angel before you to guard you along the way and bring you to the place I have prepared; but make no mistake, you will be tested in order, and in ways, to teach you to discern the will of God. No matter what happens, there is a future; although, you may not see it at the time.*

"You will suffer more bitterness, resentment, wrath, and anger, you will act out with malice and you will clamor for things that are not intended for you. You will feel more rejection out of this place, but know that there is something more, a reason for "all of this." More importantly, you will learn to act like a man, building strength for what is to come: today you are still but a child. You will glean that a true brother is born from adversity, not ease. I will make a way in this wilderness for you as well as rivers in the desert so that you will learn to seek first the kingdom of God and His righteousness. This is the way I have prepared for you."

After Shepherd finished praying over Steve these words that the Lord had given him, he vanished through a misty veil already knowing the path that Steve would be taking. Steve was about to learn his true name and the power of faith.

▥

LOS ANGELES, CA, JUN 1987

IT WAS 21 JUNE 1987 and the day was warmer than usual for Southern California, but this was also the day that Steve would begin his new life, his new adventure. He was finally getting away from his dad and the dreary memories of his past – or so he thought anyway.

Ten months earlier, Steve had enlisted into the United States Army. He had done OK in school, even with his checkered past. He probably could have made it through college but he was sick of school. Plus, if he went to college, he knew that he would have to stay home, and that was just not an option for him.

Steve had applied for, and gotten close to, acceptance into the Naval Academy. As silly as it sounded to him and others, Steve's dream of becoming an astronaut was still very real to him, and a path to get there was flying jets for the US Navy. Unfortunately, during his interview, his history of drug use had disqualified him and the naval academy was out. This nearly destroyed Steve, as he woke up to the idea that his dream was shot because his history was going to haunt him.

So Steve talked to a recruiter for the US Army, wanting a position that would allow him to fly helicopters. It was unfathomable and ridiculous as he thought about it, but he had actually lied to his friends in the past that his dad was paying for helicopter flight lessons for him. "What an idiot I was!" he thought. He was embarrassed that he did not have the same type of relationship with his dad like his friends had with theirs, so the lie was a way of embellishing a life he wanted versus the life he had. He wanted his friends to believe that there was something there that really wasn't. And it wasn't his first and only lie, nor would it be his last.

To fly for the Army, he was told that he would have to enlist as a helicopter crew chief and serve as a mechanic for a few years before applying to flight school and serving as a Warrant Officer. So Steve signed up into the Delayed Enlistment Program to serve in the Army as an OH-58 Scout Helicopter Crew Chief, convincing his parents that this is what he wanted to do. Since he was only seventeen he needed his parents' signature to sign up.

Two weeks after graduating from high school he was off, to join the ranks and "Be All That He Could Be, In the Army." Or so he thought, anyway. Steve would learn two things this day.

He kissed his girlfriend Susan goodbye; they had been preparing for this day for a few months. They were unofficially engaged but Steve instinctively knew that this was never going to work. "Another stupid and immature thing," he thought to himself. She would later tell him that she never had intentions of following him in the military. Naïve, gullible, and immature as he may have been, he was also relieved.

His parents and sister dropped him off at the MEPS (Military Entrance Processing Station), said their goodbyes, and Steve walked into the station. With orders in hand and his bags in tow, Steve walked up to the front desk. "I am Steve Remington and I am reporting for duty today," he told the female Sergeant.

"Hey, welcome, Private. Take this board and paperwork and go into that room. Fill the forms out and you will be called. Welcome to the US Army, Soldier." She pointed to a glass door and the room on the other side as she simultaneously handed him a clipboard with papers on it and a pen dangling from a ridiculously long chain.

Steve walked into the room next door where a dozen other recruits were sitting, his heart racing. He was excited, exhilarated. "It's getting real now, Dude," he said to himself, waiting in eager anticipation for what was next.

Paperwork was basic details, name, age, home of record address, payroll signature, etcetera.

About 30 minutes later, an older looking sergeant walked into the room and called his name. "Private Steve Remington?" Steve raised his hand. "Follow me," he was instructed.

A few minutes later, he was sitting at a gray metal desk in the middle of an open floor and the sergeant was quickly typing away on a typewriter.

"Has anything changed in your life over the last year Private?"

"No Sir," he replied.

"Call me Sergeant, not Sir. OK, please sign your payroll signature here," as the Sergeant pointed on a line on the form. Steve signed his name and handed the paper back.

A few seconds after reviewing the paperwork, the Sergeant looked at Steve glaringly. "Private, I said to sign your payroll signature; please sign again," he was handed a new form to sign and did as instructed.

Upon handing the form back, the Sergeant looked at him in deep frustration. "Look, I have a long day and a long line of soldiers out there waiting for me. Payroll signature, I said. Why can't you follow instructions, Private?"

Steve was confused, "I did sign it."

"Your payroll signature is the way your name appears on your birth certificate," was the response.

"Huh?" he asked confusedly. The Sergeant pointed at his birth certificate. The name that appeared was not Steve. It was Stephen.

"STEPHEN?" STEPHEN WAS BEFUDDLED, CONFUSED. He had no idea that his real name was Stephen. He had gone by Steve his entire life. His driver's license and his social security card all said Steve, as did all of his diplomas, certificates, and trophies gathered over his short life. This issue of "attention to detail" was a significant lesson for Stephen that day. He had never looked at his birth certificate before. He had just learned that he had a new name – to him anyway.

He looked the Sergeant in the eye. "I swear that I had no idea that was my name. I know that seems weird, but it's true."

The Sergeant handed Stephen a new form and this time, Stephen signed his new name, which, even though it was close, still felt foreign to him.

A few minutes later, the Sergeant transitioned to a large monochrome computer monitor on his desk and started typing away. After a minute or two passed, the Sergeant stopped what he was doing to verify an entry on the green monochrome screen. "Uh, there is a problem Private...........You have been disqualified from serving as a crew chief because of your drug use," the Sergeant told him matter-of-factly.

"But all of that was ironed out when I enlisted," Stephen protested. "Why is this an issue now? I was honest and upfront about it. Nobody said anything about it until now."

"It doesn't matter. Army Aviation has decided that they don't want anyone that has a history of drug use, I'm afraid you're out of that specialty and need to select a new one."

"Well, I'm leaving then. I enlisted to be a crew chief and I was honest; the Army has not honored that. I'm out!" Stephen retorted.

"That's your choice, Private, but some day, in the future, MPs are going to show up at your door to arrest you for desertion," Stephen was told.

This frightened him. He had been involved in, and made, enough trouble in his life and, if he were going to start afresh, then he needed to start clean. "So", he asked, "what do we do now?"

"We have to determine what options are available and find you a new MOS," was the response. The Sergeant made a few more clicks, and after a few short minutes looked at his screen and offered Stephen three different skill specialties. For ten months Stephen had had his heart set on the plan he had made. And now he needed to make a decision in just a few short minutes that would impact his life, a decision that would change everything.

"You can join the Infantry," – that's a nonstarter, Stephen thought. "You can join the artillery," was the second option, "or, you can be a medic," was the final option given.

Stephen laughed, "OK, so I can't work on helicopters because of my past with drugs, but I am going to be allowed to work on people and have access to drugs where there is some risk of abuse?" he thought.

"Really?" he asked

"I don't make the rules but that's what the computer is telling me," the Sergeant replied.

"OK, I will be a medic, but there is no way that I am signing up for the six years I had originally agreed to when I thought I was going to be a crew chief."

The Sergeant nodded, made a few clicks on the computer, and informed Stephen that he could sign him up for two years.

"Really, two years?........OK, let's do that but I feel that I am getting screwed and am wasting my life," Stephen said. "This sucks!" Stephen decided to add to his verbal diatribe.

After all of the paperwork was completed and payroll signatures were applied, Stephen had a new active duty date of 22 July 1987. He would call his parents and explain what happened, minus the issue of the drug use of course. "No need for them to know that," he thought. It was embarrassing and humiliating enough.

He would spend the next thirty days contemplating what he had learned. His past drug use was going to haunt him. He was also assimilating the idea that he could not work on helicopters but would be allowed to work on people.

However, and, most importantly, he learned that he had a new name.

THE SHEPHERD AND THE SHEEP materialized in a new environment, one completely unrecognizable from the one that they had left. While the previous one was beautiful and comforting, this one was a world that appeared devoid of life, filled instead with destruction, dismay, and chaos.

"Where are we?" the sheep asked. He continued to look around him, keying in on the dead trees that looked like they had been burnt, and scorched earth where grass should have been growing. Instead of colorful birds and animals grazing the lands, there were shadows and outlines of things he could not identify.

"This is the way you viewed the world when you left your home to start your new life, Brother. Chaotic. Destructive. Depressed. And neglected. You viewed the world this way because this is how you viewed yourself, this is how you saw your heart. This is how you began, the condition of your wilderness journey," Shepherd explained.

"Wow, I guess I knew it was bad, but not like this. There is no life here."

The Shepherd pointed through the burnt trunks and branches to a nearby group of trees. *"Look through those trees over there; not at them, through them. What do you see?"*

The sheep had to focus but eventually he could see what looked like a small fire, burning in the opening of what he believed to be a cave in a small hill. "I see a small fire, like a cook fire, sitting at the opening of a cave."

Shepherd nodded, *"That is the Spirit of God, serving as the source of light in this place. At this point, He is only a spark of what He will become in your life, growing larger as you nourish*

Him, commune with Him, and love Him. He will never leave you, but you can push His fire farther back into the cave. In our previous experiences together, the world around you is how both you, and God, viewed you in the present; not perfect but definitely brighter, more joyful, content, peaceful and beautiful."

The sheep chuckled, "You sure like Your metaphors. The temple, the path, the rooster, and now a fire in a cave."

Shepherd laughed *"The Lord is a very visual God. He will not hold back in describing various ways that you can see Him operating in your life or ways in which you can just...see Him and experience Him. He wants you to know that He loves you and He will never forsake you. But He also wants you to know that, while you can depend on Him, much of it also depends on you. What's important for you to note is that this moment in your story is a critical milestone for you; this world around you is how you viewed yourself. It represents what you were offering to God, even how you thought He looked at you. This is everything about the condition of your spirit at that time; the Lord wanted you to see this."*

"I don't like it," the sheep said. "It's ugly, dark, and it...smells funny."

Shepherd nodded in agreement. *"There is beauty here that you don't see, but the Lord sees it. You are His creation; you are His child. He knew you before you were born and He does not make ugly things. He sees the hope in you, the hunger, a desire to be better, a desire to improve, and a desire to be loved."*

"Look down, Brother; what do you see at your feet?" Shepherd asked.

The sheep looked down, "I see a gravel path, but the gravel is sharp and pointed. If I were barefoot, it would cut me, but I also see that I have on a nice pair of shoes with thick leather protecting my feet."

"You see a path and you see that you have been equipped to walk along it. Do you see the difference in how you and I see things?" Shepherd asked.

"Yes, Sir. I focused more on the sharpened gravel and less so on my shoes. You saw a hard path, but a path that I had been equipped to walk on."

"The Lord does things even when His children fail to see it. They despair when they should be celebrating. They cry out in pain when

they should be shouting in praise. They fail to see the blessings set before them. Take, for instance, the challenges you faced when you were leaving to join the military. What are your thoughts about what the Lord just showed you?" Shepherd asked.

"IT WAS ON THAT DAY THAT I LEARNED MY NAME. It was also the day that I learned to distrust authority, that while I am expected to honor my obligations, they don't have to honor theirs," the sheep answered. He was referring to the Army signing him up to be a helicopter mechanic and then taking that away at the last minute.

"And what do you believe about God and these two things today?" Shepherd asked.

"Well, for starters, the Lord gave me both a new name and an old name, on the exact day that I was to become my own man. In the Bible, there are numerous examples of people who received new names as they started a new phase in their lives. For example, Abram became Abraham, Jacob became Israel, and Saul became Paul. Their lives were different after their names were changed."

"Was your life different?" Shepherd asked.

The sheep reflected, "Sort of. I did feel like something had changed, but not really. Perhaps there was something that I instinctively knew had been started, but then it passed in a fleeting moment."

"There was a spark that ignited that day, Brother," Shepherd told him. *"You were changed by the knowledge of your name. You grew in spirit – that was the change you sensed. But you soon acclimated to it, which is why it was fleeting for you. That name was yours and no one can take it from you, because it was given to you by God. It was God that had laid the path towards revealing your true name. He knew that in your heart you wanted, you needed, a fresh start. A new beginning. What better way than to start with a new name? Even if it was an old one."*

The sheep was in awe. "You know, I am aware of people that changed the name they use to their middle names or a nickname. I never caught on to the idea of new beginnings, fresh starts. Thank You, God, for revealing that to me."

Shepherd smiled in glee that the sheep was seeing how God was operating in his life at that time. *"What about the issues with the job you were signing up for in the Army?"*

The sheep was quick to answer this, as it had bothered him for years. "I felt betrayed. I felt that, even though I was honest and had done everything right, that I was lied to. I had planned my life around this, my career, my future. I felt lost, that I had lost control," he cried in dismay.

Shepherd nodded and then He laughed a joyful laugh. *"Your spirit hungered for love and honest companionship – that we already know. But what did you want to do, in your heart? What happened as a result of this supposed setback in your life?"* he asked.

The sheep raised his arms in mock surrender, and then he smiled back. "I know why You're laughing at me. The Lord already revealed this one to me. You're teasing me." Both of them were just having fun; they both knew where this was going but Shepherd was walking him through it anyway.

"For starters, I am the only person that I am aware of, even after a twenty-year military career, that signed up for an initial two-year enlistment. I suppose there are some, but I never met one. When my two-year assignment was coming to a close and the Army was working to convince me to re-enlist, the Army allowed me to change my MOS from Medic to something better suited for me."

Shepherd looked at him quizzically, *"And?"*

"Even with my history of drug use, the Army would later approve my re-enlistment to Aeroscout Observer, a job requiring me to fly in the left seat of the OH-58 Helicopter." The sheep could not help smiling.

Shepherd slapped his knee in laughter. *"And the significance of this is multi-fold, Brother. First, the Lord knew that it was your heart's desire to fly and He delivered. Second, there was the obstacle of your history; yet the Lord assisted in working past that. Third, you were flying in two years. If you had served as a mechanic on the very helicopter you would be flying, it would have taken more than two years, would it not?"*

"By most estimates, it may have taken four years or so, depending on certain variables that no longer matter," the sheep remarked, laughing back at Shepherd.

SHEPHERD COULD NOT STOP LAUGHING. *"And we are not done yet, Brother, are we? What else happened as a result of this* *catastrophe that you thought had happened to you in 1987?"* He asked in eager anticipation.

"I met my wife," the sheep answered embarrassed. He was not ashamed of the question; he was embarrassed that he had been so distraught by his losing control of his life that he had failed to see the biggest benefit of all.

Shepherd kept laughing. *"Yes, Praise God! The very woman that would finally open your eyes to the truth, that one that would lead you back to God. The very woman that would honor you, cherish you, and love you – even though you were a stinker. You mean, that wife?"* he said teasingly.

"Yes, yes, yes, I surrender!" the sheep laughed back. "And the irony is not lost on me that she and I would become soul mates at the exact same time that I was transitioning from Medic to Aeroscout."

"Do you see that the miracles of God were working around you, even when you were ignoring His plea? He was trying to get your attention, Brother, and you missed it. But, it is also no surprise that the revelation of this moment was immediately thrust upon you more than twenty years later when you accepted Him into your heart. Oh, what a Glorious God, yes?"

"Yes, glory to Him. Thank You, Father. Even if You must apply humor, it not only shows how much You love us, it also shows that You are a fun God, not the dull God that too many are taught about. You enjoy it when we recognize the little twists and turns of You operating in our lives. But I also repent, Father, right now in Jesus' Name, for not recognizing You when I should have. For ignoring You when I should have been paying attention. For blocking You when I should have been allowing You. Forgive me, Lord."

"Amen!" Shepherd said heartily.

"Even when you were at your lowest, the Lord was operating," Shepherd declared. *"The Lord lays the highways in the wilderness and rivers in the desert so that His children may find their way. Brother, as you ponder these mysteries as they appear before you, know that they are intended to teach you to learn that you are to seek first the kingdom of God and His righteousness."*

"Yes, Praise Him! I have no regrets."

Shepherd acknowledged this with a nod. *"Let this be one of those moments the Lord prepared for you that you shall use to defend with anyone a reason for the hope that is in you, Brother, a gentle and respectful reminder."*

The sheep and Shepherd stood there, on that sharpened gravel path for a minute, just basking in His presence, soaking in the moment.

"Well, perhaps we should move on, Stephen. Love that name by the way; it suits you and I am happy to call you by it," said Shepherd encouragingly. *"Up ahead, there is a grove of trees that the path will take us through. Let's go see what else the Lord has to show you. Shall we?"*

Stephen didn't answer verbally, but he slowly turned his body and started taking small steps down the path with Shepherd a step behind him. Stephen knew that it was his time to lead on the path. This was between him and God. It was time that he meet his story head on, and take in a breath of fresh air.

CHAPTER 16
A BREATH OF FRESH AIR: A WIFE

"A good woman is hard to find, and worth far more than diamonds. Her husband trusts her without reserve, and never has reason to regret it."
(Proverbs 31:10-11. MSG)

SHEPHERD BEGINS *by telling a story about a beauty who dreams of a day when her prince will come; he is a man who realizes that he wants to be the one that wins her heart. He pauses to let that soak in. "But, unfortunately, Stephen, chivalry today is fading away, considered cheesy, old fashioned. You think masculinity has its challenges? But it's nothing compared to what the world is doing to femininity.*

"Godly courtship has lost its touch, Stephen, because the world has taken lead in the mastery of what it means to be a woman. Being a woman is both extreme and perplexing when God and the devil are both trying to dominate her, and a way to do that is through the heart of the man."

Stephen did not know who this guy was talking to him, but, he somehow knew that he needed to listen, that he could trust him. Something was telling him that this was ..."Shepherd?"

Stephen and Shepherd were walking a brightly lit pebble path, with both sides lined by dark green grass that was neatly manicured as far as he could see. "OK, I get it, but what has that to do with me and why are you sharing this with me? And who are you?" Stephen asked.

"A woman wants a champion to win her, to answer the cry of her heart that is seeking the one that will let her know that she is exquisite and that he wants her." Shepherd looked at Stephen to see if he understood.

"So what you are saying is that what a woman truly wants, what she needs, is not necessarily what the world is offering? And I still don't know who you are and why you're talking to me," he asked.

"The issue is that men hesitate. Men are overly consumed and focused on themselves, resulting in them neglecting to provide true and loving pleasure to the other. Men work hard, spurred on by lust, for the body of the woman; however, they are blind to what true love really is, that is, the actual heart of the woman."

"It almost sounds like you are saying that part of our world is losing what true godly love between a man and woman is. Some men engage with a woman a few times and then they leave, but a true man is in it for the long haul. Is that right?" Stephen asked.

"You're getting close. Too many women have been taught that, in order to find their prince, they must sacrifice that which is most precious to them, so they give in. What she really wants, and needs is a prince that is committed, a prince that will help her grow, develop, not be stagnant. And most of this has to do with the man, not the woman," Shepherd offered.

He continued, "The other issue is that some men are simply looking for security, to improve their character or to boost their self-esteem; others think of a woman as a grade on a report card that is some kind of sign or reflection of their strength and worth."

Stephen coughed a laugh at that observation; his life had definitely been one of working to master the conquest and experimentation. But he had also been astute enough to see on daytime TV where men marry women because of what the man gains in social status.

"A woman and her prince, when joined, are a force to be reckoned with...they are powerful. There is a strength that is exponentially multiplied when this type of union manifests – under God," Shepherd stressed.

Shepherd stopped walking and turned to Stephen beside Him. "You are about to enter a union, Stephen; this is God's plan for both you and her. God knows that it is not good for a man to be alone, so He has found a suitable helper for you. How you both choose to live is up to you, but if you listen to Him, as a couple, then your union will be one of joy and happiness. If you fail to listen, as a couple, then there will be pain and struggles."

There was silence as Stephen thought about this for a minute. "Oooookkaaaaayyy, I think I understand," he replied hesitantly.

"You're listening to your head, Stephen, looking for logic in this; but we'll wait to see if you are truly listening to your heart. Your past experience with women has been based on sexual ignorance; this is what the world has taught you and you succumbed to it. Your bride has not had the same life as you; this is something that you will want to consider. You are a wounded man, Stephen, and you are wise enough to recognize that much of that comes from your father. The remainder of your wounds have been caused by your own temptations. But, just like your wounds, a woman's wounds also predominantly come from her father. You may not easily see it because you are self-focused. Love her like you would love yourself, Stephen. That is the doorway for you to understand your needs as a couple.

"You may look to her to help validate you as a man, but remember that she, too, will be looking for you to validate her as a woman. You will want to live with her in a way that she understands that you honor her. She will want to be loved, pursued, delighted in, enjoyed, protected, and fought for. You will want her to respect you, love you, nurture, and take care of you. Most of all, you will desire that she understand you.

"God has a plan for you, a destiny that He wants for you and your wife. You are both heirs of the grace of life. Listen to Him, Stephen, and you will find the joy and happiness you want." On saying that last word, Shepherd suddenly vanished. Gone – he was there, and then He wasn't. Stephen was still asking himself, "Who was that guy and why was he talking to me about a bride?"

Stephen woke up from his dream in a start. "What the heck! That was a really odd dream! Wow! Holy cats that was weird!" It took him 15 minutes to fall back asleep, and only a few hours to completely forget about that dream.

Three days later, Stephen would start his long drive from Fort Rucker, AL to Clarksville, TN, where his beauty awaited him.

CLARKSVILLE TN AND FORT HOOD TX, MAY - NOVEMBER 1989

IT WAS MEMORIAL HOLIDAY WEEKEND and she said, "Yes," as he placed the ring on her finger. A few minutes earlier, Stephen and Jamie had pulled up to the backyard of her house after a short date night. He had recently started attending flight school at Fort Rucker and had a strong urge to make things official before his training became intense. Now, it seems that they were official, though they still had to talk with her parents. Jamie was seventeen and Stephen was twenty, so they both knew it was awkward. The good news was that her parents loved Stephen; he didn't doubt they would be supportive.

Later that evening, as Stephen lay in the bed of a 90-foot RV parked in Jamie's backyard, he reflected on how he and Jamie had met. "This is going fast," Stephen said to no one in particular. "And it sure is strange how we got here," he thought and laughed.

Three months earlier, Stephen had a date with another girl who was a friend of Jamie's. This was not their first date but everywhere Tammy went, Jamie was always with her since Jamie had the car. But something changed that evening, where Stephen learned something about both himself and Tammy, that made him realize that it was wrong, and that he needed to cut it off with her. He also figured out that there was something about Jamie that was interesting.

A few weeks later, Stephen broke it off with Tammy and asked Jamie if she wanted to go out. After that things moved fast, culminating in Stephen asking Jamie to marry him a little more than a month after their first date. As she and Tammy were friends, it was only right that Jamie inform her that they were dating. That discussion went OK but things were never the same between Jamie and Tammy afterwards.

The next day, after their unofficial engagement, they informed her parents that they wanted to get married. Stephen talked to her dad and Jamie spoke to her mother. As expected, they were both supportive, though they did ask that Jamie complete some college before they got married. Truth be told, neither Jamie nor Stephen had any issues with that as they had not really discussed a marriage date, or made any plans for that matter. It would be a few days later before Stephen would say anything to his parents, but when he did tell them, he received a cursory response as his parents did not think that he would really marry Jamie based on his pattern when it came to women.

Stephen thought he had a strong desire to find someone that he could love, that he could share his life with. However, what was really on his heart was finding someone that could love him, that really wanted to love him and not be phony. Jamie was on the same path as Stephen. She, too, was wanting someone that would love her and care for her. And this is where they both found themselves, both hungry for someone to love them while both being limited in their capacity to love the other – Stephen more limited than Jamie. Neither of them was mature enough for the future they were about to undertake. They would both need to learn how to love each other, with Jamie developing that ability much faster. She felt an emotional attraction to Stephen and "just knew" that he was the right one for her.

In August of that year, Stephen graduated from flight school and was on orders to go to Fort Hood, TX. He had originally been on orders to go to Germany, but he had asked the Army for a one-year delay due to his engagement with Jamie. His request was miraculously approved, reassigning him to an Apache Training unit at Fort Hood, TX, and then to Germany exactly a year later. He hadn't even filled out official paperwork for his request; he simply wrote a letter and hoped for the best.

But he had thirty days to burn before reporting to Ft. Hood, so Jamie and Stephen decided to take a 1500-mile cross country road-trip from Clarksville, TN to Los Angeles, CA, where Jamie would meet Stephen' parents for the first time. Jamie was scheduled to attend college courses at the local college, so she would fly back to Tennessee, alone, after two weeks in CA, her first plane ride; whereas Stephen would drive direct to Ft. Hood and continue his military career.

In early October, Jamie would share with Stephen that she could not afford college, she could not get a student loan and her parents could not provide her with any money. So they both decided that they would get married the weekend after Jamie turned eighteen, two weeks away. There was no reason to wait, in their mind anyway. Their plan included a quick elopement but, after Jamie told her mother, her mother planned and put a wedding together in one week, with a dress and everything. As Jamie came walking down the staircase of her sister's home, Stephen knew that he had made the right choice. In his eyes, she was beautiful.

By November, seven months after their first date, Jamie and Stephen were living as Newlyweds in a tiny apartment in Copperas Cove, Texas. They had also learned that Jamie was pregnant with their first son and they were on orders to move to Germany in ten months. Things were moving really fast.

WHILE THE SHEPHERD WORKED with Stephen, so was that ever ready demonic pest, the wolf. When Stephen had first arrived at Ft. Hood, he had met a young lady, who was married, and they decided to share an apartment together. The fox had worked hard for this meetup as the young lady's husband was currently stationed hundreds of miles away, so it was just Stephen and her in the apartment alone, agreeing that the relationship was purely platonic.

After a few short weeks, the young lady had started to flirt and Stephen fought the urges. While his lustful past was coming back to haunt him, he was working hard to remain loyal to Jamie. Shepherd whispered to him, *"Stephen, it is better to marry than to burn with passion."* But the wolf was also telling him, *"Go ahead, man, Jamie would never find out. She wants you, Bro."* Stephen' own temptations, and his own thoughts, were confused. He wanted to but he didn't want to.

"Jamie is the one for you, Stephen. Listen to your heart," Shepherd said to him.

He and Jamie had already purchased their wedding rings, so Stephen wore his ring and lied to his roommate by telling her that he and Jamie were already married. However, this was not necessarily a concern for the other. Jamie was aware of Stephen' living conditions and that Stephen had told his roommate he and she were already married. But, even with this knowledge, Jamie was unhappy, fearful, and felt a layer of concern and sense of betrayal. The wolf had been whispering and giggling in Stephen' ear over those weeks, continuing to suggest that he go for it. But he was just as thrilled to see Stephen struggling with his temptations; he was tormented. and it was wonderful.

And then, the call from Jamie came, informing Stephen about the college problems which evolved into them setting their wedding date a few weeks ahead. Stephen was saved, the Shepherd praised

God, and the wolf got angry. Of course, it never crossed Stephen'
mind to move out and back into the barracks with the rest of the
single soldiers, for this would mean sacrificing independence and
giving up control, which Stephen enjoyed.

*"That's OK, Stephen; I have much more in store for you and
your...bride,"* the wolf scoffed. *"It's not over yet."*

*"Stephen, do not step into fear. You shall keep loving one another
earnestly, for love will cover a multitude of sins. Enduring love is
living in light of the future and you will find that offenses are quickly
forgotten."*

BACK IN THE VISION SPACE, Stephen was standing next to
Shepherd, and he felt dizzy. This vision had been the oddest one for
him so far as it included both the natural realm and a dream state.
Not to mention that it still felt weird seeing a much younger version
of himself, as if it were happening in real time in front of him. He
jokingly thought to himself, "I wonder if this is why I always felt
that someone was watching me."

But, it was the vision of the wedding, once again seeing Jamie
walk down that staircase to the living room that filled his heart. This
caused him to fall to his knees in the middle of the scorched forest,
and weep. Shepherd paused behind Stephen, allowing him to go
through the experience.

After a few minutes, Stephen finished his silent prayer, reveling
in the knowledge that the Lord had orchestrated life events during
that period of time. He recalled his short tenure as an Infantry Medic
at Fort Campbell, dreading the entire experience, and his plans to
leave the military and go to college. He marveled at how things just
seemed to come together at the last minute, the door opening for
him to qualify to fly the very same helicopter that he had originally
planned on serving as a mechanic. His heart pumped in awe at how
the Lord had brought him and Jamie together, both desperately
needing each other, and setting a bond so tight, that they would
marry six months later.

He pondered at the strangeness of how his request for a one-year
extension to remain in the US was approved for exactly one year,
which further allowed him and Jamie to marry and experience the

birth of their first child. He meditated on how strong his temptation was to have relations with his roommate, but how his will was stronger, and, just when he thought he might fail, he received the call from Jamie that changed their lives forever.

More importantly, he recalled his ongoing battle with bitterness at the Army for messing up his life and his own struggles to maintain good solid relationships. And then, he fell into praise of how God was operating in his life, protecting him not just from others, but also from himself, even when he was not seeking Him. He recognized that the Lord had a plan for him even when he did not understand his own plans. He woke up to the truth that he never had control, and the more he struggled for control, the more he would not only lose it, but become more aggravated in the process.

Stephen could, of course, see the patterns now, regretting that he missed them at that time, but thankful and grateful that he could see them now. And then, there was Jamie his mate, the one who would end up being the one person in his life that would spend decades working to save his eternal soul. The one person that would come to know him, and understand him, better than he knew himself.

As he stood up with Shepherd still standing a pace behind him, he whispered, "Thank You," and turned to look at Him.

"Brother, I can see it in you. Discipline isn't enjoyable while it's happening; even Our Creator knows that it's painful! But afterward, as you can now see, there is a peaceful harvest of right living for those who are trained in this way."

Stephen nodded, "Yes, I see that. But, unfortunately, even now I can remember some of the events that follow, and it breaks my heart to think of them."

"That is because you have not truly forgiven yourself in your heart. It's one thing to remember what a fool you've been and be happy that you aren't that way anymore; it's another to continue to allow past events to depress you and tear you down. But, then again, seeing this experience in front of you is dredging up old feelings as well as an area where your heart was being wounded – by yourself."

The sheep raised an eyebrow, "How was my heart being wounded?"

"You had placed expectations on yourself that you cherished and valued, such as loyalty, integrity, respect, honor, and commitment, all of which you had dedicated in your heart to Jamie. But you also

still wanted to be desired, flattered, wanted, accepted, and loved. Even though you weren't married yet, you had already given your heart to Jamie. But the rest of you? That is a different story.

"Hence your struggle, your conflict, and your temptation. Even though you never followed through in your temptation, you carried around both guilt and disappointment. You felt guilty for allowing yourself to be tempted, but you were also disappointed that you didn't take advantage of the opportunity. This event in your life is something that you buried, but you still carried it around with you. You hated yourself for even having the desire to follow through, regardless of the fact that you didn't do it."

"Wow! Yeah, I was really hard on myself. Why did I do that? Why do I carry stuff like that around?" Stephen asked.

THE SHEPHERD, ANTICIPATING THE QUESTION, did not bat an eyelid. *"Because you idolized your value system, Brother. We can get into how these idols grew in your life, but, the fact is that you placed your value system in higher regard over anything else in your life, including your wife, your children, your friends, your personal success – and God Himself. To the depths of your soul in this period of your life, when you compromised your values, it would tear you apart. In your mind, if you were capable of violating that which you cherished the most, then what good were you?*

"The side effect of your value system processing, is that you would carry your failures around with you, causing you to seek anyone in your life to give you the affirmation to show that you were worthy and necessary. A psychologist would probably have prescribed you drugs but that wouldn't have helped. Your issue was with your spirit, and that required a different kind of prescription – love. So, the Lord did what He does best: He issued His prescription and brought you and Jamie together as quickly as possible. You see, she needed you just as much, if not more, than you needed her.

"Stephen, you have nothing to feel guilty over; actually, you need to stand proud, the way the Lord sees you. Your path in the wilderness, the one laid out in front of you, had offered multiple turns and you needed to decide which path to take. You chose the path that avoided temptation, but one that also required that you lie. It's not the one the Lord wanted you to take, but it was one that averted destroying your soul and your relationship with Jamie. Men

do this all of the time; you are not alone. Quite a few men would have taken that path to temptation and paid a price with their soul later down the road. Your price was your own heart, the one that you wounded in this process, by placing your value system at risk as an idol in your life."

Stephen stared in both awe and admiration. He wanted to ask about which path he should have taken and how he could have avoided that whole mess to begin with, but he knew that it didn't really matter. He knew that he should have prayed to God about it, only he didn't see God at that time of his life.

"Holy cow! I do hold on to my value system above everything. I used to brag about it to any and everyone. 'You can take away my money but you will never take away my integrity – that is mine!' I would say. In fact, I carried that value system around for years after I was born again. Good Lord, over twenty-five years!" Stephen remained silent, contemplating the fact that he had been carrying this system around as an idol, placing his so-called values at a higher level than God. This revelation suddenly filled him with remorse.

"If I had honored God above everything, then those values would have come naturally – as second nature anyway – because they are consistent with the nature of God. But, instead, I separated them from God and, even though I love Him and cherish Him, I carried them in my left-hand pocket and God in my right-hand pocket. They should have all been in the same pocket. Wow!" Stephen stopped, shaking his head at how he had allowed himself to be duped. Not just back in 1989, but up to the present. He thought he was honoring God with his values, but he was actually honoring his values above God.

Shepherd smiled and then joked in His manly sort of way, *"Yes, Brother, I can see the wheels of revelation churning. What else do you think is relevant from this vision?"*

Stephen took only a few seconds, "Well, I need to get better about writing down my dreams. The dream part of the vision was very revealing to me. Secondly, I must open myself to prayer and communion with Him about everything, no matter how mundane I think it is. Finally, I must never forget to give all honor and glory to God for the goodness in my life. I see how He brilliantly brought Jamie and me together at the exact same moment I was transitioning to a job that had been a personal dream of mine. Not only did God honor my dream, He also honored my heart and my soul."

With that, he fell to his knees once again and clasped his hands in front of him.

"Father, I come before You in Jesus' name. I want to thank You that You care about everything that I care about. You have numbered all the hairs on my head. You know everything about me, and all my days were already written in Your book before any of those days existed. Father, You knew that I earnestly desired a mate, but You knew what I didn't know, that it was not just any spouse, but the exact spouse that You had in store for me. You knew what I wanted, and what I needed, before You even created me.

"Lord, THANK YOU for sending me such an incredible partner, best friend and wife. Next to Your grace, her love is the greatest gift in my life. Please never let me take her for granted. Help me to love, cherish, respect, adore, and protect her the way that she deserves. I know she's not only my wife...she's YOUR daughter, and You've trusted me to be her husband. Please help me to love her the way You love her, and be willing to lay down my life for her the way You have done for us.

"Father, we live in a world where Your daughters are being objectified and used as images for lust and selfish gratification. Please help me keep my eyes and my heart pure in a world of sin and exploitation. Help me have eyes only for my wife. Give her the confidence to know that she'll never have to compete for my attention against an airbrushed image of another woman. Let her know that I'm now and always captivated by her inner beauty and her outer beauty as well. Please keep her away from the 'Comparison Trap' that would shatter her confidence and replace it with insecurity. Help her know she doesn't need to compare her life or her accomplishments to anyone else's because Your plan for her is masterfully unique. Help me to be her biggest encourager, and never her biggest critic. Give me the words to say when she needs encouragement and give me the wisdom to know when to shut up and be quiet when she just needs me to listen.

"Help me to support her dreams and passions to propel her to achieving all You have for her. For all she will achieve, please don't let her fall into the trap of believing her identity is wrapped up in achievements (or failures). But her identity is secured in

Your love for her. Never let her lose sight of the fact that she's eternally loved by You and let her find strength in my love for her as well. Fill her heart with joy. Let laughter fill the soundtrack of our life together. Even in the difficult seasons, help us choose joy as we're reminded that our struggles are temporary, but because of You, Lord, our joy will be eternal. Help me be strong for her on the days she's feeling weak, and help her be strong for me on my weak days, and, Lord, please give us both strength for all that's ahead. Help us to NEVER lose faith in You or give up on each other.

"Thank You, Lord, for my amazing wife! She's a priceless gift to be treasured, and I pray that You help me to be a gift to her as well. Please give me the wisdom, courage and strength to be the best husband I can be today and every day.

"Also, Lord, thank You for honoring my dreams, even when I was failing to see You in them. You knew what was in my heart and I recognize that this was an opportunity for me to see You. Forgive me for neglecting You and Your hand in my life. I repent, Father, for placing my own personal values above You. I had thought that my values honored You; but I now see that I had placed them above You, and this was hurting me. Thank You, Lord, for revealing a wound of my heart that I would never have seen without Your divine intervention.

"Thank You, Lord, for the lessons in my life and working to guide me along the path away from the Wilderness. Thank You for bringing me to the River, the One that contains the Water of Life to nourish my heart and my soul. In Jesus' name, Amen."

"Amen," Shepherd declared when Stephen had finished. *"It's amazing what we see when we see the Lord's handiwork, isn't it, Brother!"* He said gleefully.

"Yes, there is no coincidence, but I also see that we still have control over our own fate. God may be guiding us, but He is not controlling us," Stephen answered.

Shepherd nodded, carefully weighing His next words. *"The Lord has more to share with you. Your journey in the wilderness is still just getting started, Stephen, and it will get darker before it gets brighter,"* He cautioned.

Stephen looked all around him. The pathway was still sharp but it was no longer gravel: it was obsidian. He also noticed that his shoes were wearing out, but still protecting him from the sharp shards. He had considered walking alongside the path rather than on it – but that is when he noticed that the landscape was covered in thorns, thistle bushes, and jumping cactus. He couldn't walk off the path if he even wanted to do.

The trees were more scorched than before and they had thinned out, revealing nothing but darkness beyond them. He could still see the same cave he had noticed earlier, but it did look as if the fire had moved deeper inside, with the light from the flames creating a dance on the cave walls. There was also a humid mist rolling in, but not too thick to not see through. Above him, he couldn't see a single star, something that he had not considered before.

Shepherd kept his eyes on Stephen, watching as this...secret place...got darker and creepier. *"This was the condition of your heart, Brother. You had witnessed incredible events in your life but you just as quickly rewarded yourself for accomplishing them, and moved on. Yet, you also started punishing yourself, feeling as if you had increased your responsibilities when you had no more room for more. You were dealing with personal circumstances in your military career, your friendships, your apparent inability to be a better soldier, not to mention fear of failure at being a husband and future father. They were consuming you."*

"Yes, Sir, I remember. I was frightened. I was afraid of being a disappointment and a failure. I was afraid of being rejected and shamed."

"Yes, all true. And in only a few short months after getting married, you experienced your first marital mistake."

"Yeppers! I will never forget it. A few months in, I created a condition where we were completely broke."

CHAPTER 17
THE STOREHOUSE IS LOST

"For which one of you, when he wants to build a tower, does not first sit down and calculate the cost to see if he has enough to complete it? Otherwise, when he has laid a foundation and is not able to finish, all who observe it begin to ridicule him, saying, 'This man began to build and was not able to finish.'"
(Luke 14:28-30)

STEPHEN WANDERED THE BATTLEFIELD, *a subset of the Wilderness that he had been walking, wondering what went wrong. How did he lose this battle? The attack from the enemy was obvious, so his counterattack should have worked. How did this happen?*

The wolf, who was hungrily watching him, spoke up, "The battle you thought you were in was actually a diversion, you fool. You were fighting from the wrong front."

"But you stole from me; you took the wealth from my storehouse. How did you do it? How did I not see it coming?" Stephen protested.

"You see there, you continue to show your weakness," the wolf shot back. When it comes to spiritual warfare, not everything is about what I do to you, but what you do to yourself. You sheep are so easily swayed and blinded. Whenever something bad happens to you, you think that you are under some form of spiritual attack, never taking ownership of where and how you focus, or neglecting the rules of the land," the wolf said smugly.

"I did not steal your wealth. It was you who created the condition that allowed it to flow out. It didn't take any effort on my part. You were blinded by what was in our storehouse; you failed to follow the rules of your Creator," the wolf lectured.

"But I thought I was OK; yet, I also see that you're right. I knew the rules and yet I ignored them anyway. Now our wealth is gone and I have let those closest to me down. Oh God, please listen to my plea. I have failed and require wisdom on how to continue on this path."

Stephen'prayer was heard, allowing the Shepherd to walk through the shroud.

COPPERAS COVE, TX, FEB 1990

STEPHEN WAS HUMILIATED AND DESPERATE. He had screwed up big and his new and pregnant wife was going to pay the price. She just didn't know it yet.

Four months earlier, Stephen and Jamie were very fortunate to have received military leased housing. However, Stephen had still been receiving his housing allowance from the military, something that should have stopped when he and Jamie signed for the military leased apartment.

At an amount of $600 a month, Stephen had accrued more than $2000 in excess pay, but, instead of saving it for what he knew was inevitable, he continued to spend this money. And then, in February 1990, it caught up with him.

The military finance team at Fort Hood, TX had finally stopped his housing allowance, AND, they garnished his pay for the money he had been overpaid for the last four months. At his pay scale, this meant that Stephen had absolutely no money for himself and his wife for the entire month of February. They had no savings whatsoever, not even a credit card. They had nothing for groceries, no money for gas to get him to work, nothing. He was devastated.

Stephen was sitting on the floor at the foot of his bed. His mind was being flooded with thoughts. "I am such a screw-up. I'm an idiot. What did I do? Why did I do that? I failed. I'm worthless. What am

I supposed to do now?" With that, he started to cry, tears streaming down his face, sobbing loudly. His wife heard him and walked in from the living room. He had not told her yet.

"What's wrong, Sweetie?" she asked.

He continued to look down, thinking of what to say. "I screwed up," he admitted finally. "I was spending money that I knew might be taken back." He then explained to her the issue about the housing allowance. "I guess I thought the Army had messed up and we would get away with it. I thought we were lucky and I was wrong – what an idiot!"

Jamie sat down next to him and put her arm around him.

"We have a roof and all the utilities are paid for by the Army," he shared with her, "but we have no money for groceries, no gas for the truck, nothing. We're 100% broke."

Jamie looked at her husband with love in her eyes as she tightened her arm around him. Although full of sorrow, she did not cry. She could see the burden her husband was carrying and she knew that, while he had made a mistake, he cared that deeply about her.

"What do we do now?" she asked.

"I am going to have to let my chain of command know. We will have to apply for an Army Emergency Relief loan. Sometimes they give grants, but mostly loans. I am so humiliated!" He then began to sob deeply again. As a young couple, they had not built up anything in case of emergency. "I am a horrible husband, I am so sorry for letting you down," he blurted out before crying deeply again.

"Seems we have an option with the AER loan. We'll get through it," she responded solemnly. She then laid her head against his shoulder and held him tight. This caused Stephen to cry that much more deeply.

The next day, Stephen reported to his platoon sergeant and let him know what was happening. Sergeant First Class Eastwood listened and looked at Stephen with obvious contempt. "Whatever, I deserve it," he thought to himself. He was already earning a strong reputation as a screw-up anyway and this was only more proof that they were right.

"Let's just get the paperwork done for your AER loan; we'll deal with your poor judgment later," Eastwood said in his South Carolina drawl.

Stephen could see in Eastwood eyes that he did not like him; in fact, that he despised Stephen for this. "He thinks I'm a fool. I agree," he thought. "I am so embarrassed."

As the day moved along, Stephen spent time gathering and filling out the minutiae of paperwork. And then, in an instant, a thought suddenly came to him around mid-day that might free him from the burden of applying for the loan.

"Wait," he thought, "I am still owed flight pay. I've been on flight status since October and they haven't paid me yet. If I can get the back pay I am owed, that might be enough to get us through the month," he figured. This thought partially lifted him out of the funk he was in. He walked to the S-1 office and discussed this with the PAC clerk.

Stephen was assigned as an Aeroscout Observer and was flying left seat in the OH-58 Scout Helicopter. As an active crew member on flight status, he was supposed to be paid an extra $125 a month in flight hazard pay. If his math was correct, he was owed more than $600. He might be able to stretch this.

"That might be an option," the clerk told him. "Let me make a few calls to the finance office and see what we can do."

A half hour later, Stephen was rewarded with an approval for the back pay. He would drive to the finance office a little later where he could pick up a printed check and take it to the bank for cashing.

Upon informing Eastwood and other members of his chain of command, he was relieved that he would not have to be looked at with contempt.

And, even though he had rectified the situation, his chain of command was still aware that he had screwed up by spending that housing allowance money. This brought Stephen back down to the hard facts again. Even though he had worked out a solution, he had still let down his wife, his chain of command, and himself.

SHEPHERD STOOD BEFORE STEPHEN'S SPIRIT, *"The Lord has heard your prayer and will address it. But He has judged that there will still be repercussions."*

"That is OK; just remove this burden from me," Stephen pleaded.

"Your storehouse will receive what is necessary to continue your journey, but, because you disobeyed and failed to plan, the Lord

assures you that you must learn that a good name is more important than even wealth and that His favor is better."

Stephen thought on this for a second, "How will the Lord accomplish that?" But, looking Shepherd in the eye, he said, "I understand. What must I do?"

Shepherd prophesied, "Because you lacked discipline, you will still experience poverty and a degree of shame. Your name will be blemished. But, if you remain true, this will be limited to a season according to the Lord's will. He will make sure that you are taught how to profit and the way you should go."

"I accept the judgment of the Father and agree. If I honor His reproof, then my honor will be restored."

"God bless you, Stephen, and may the wisdom of protection be seen in your life with the understanding that knowledge and wisdom shall preserve the life of him who possesses it." And with that said, Shepherd vanished.

The wolf stood back, observing the discussion between the sheep and Shepherd. "You will fail again – you know you will. You're a failure and you're stupid. I don't care what that godlicker said."

"Shut up! I'm not listening to you. The Lord has seen to my needs and He's taken my burden away from me," Stephen retorted.

"Oh, you might feel OK today, Mr. Sheep, but tomorrow, after word spreads about your dishonesty, you will be humiliated. You are worthless – you can already see it in the eyes of those around you. Your new bride is ashamed of you and scared now. Remember what your father always told you? Let me remind you. You aren't worth it. You aren't worth the process it took to create you," the wolf pontificated.

The wolf's words were strong and Stephen could not help but let them seep in. "The wolf's right. I am worthless and a loser," he cried even as he walked out of the battlefield and back onto the path within the Wilderness.

As he walked away, Stephen could not see a pair of loving eyes, brown and piercing, looking over him. A small tear appeared in the corner of one, "No, My Brother, the wolf is wrong. You are everything to Me and Our Father."

THERE WAS A LOUD CRACK, like thunder, that echoed across the land as Stephen found himself right back on the path of the Secret Place. His skin tingled with electricity and his heart was beating enthusiastically. He felt euphoric and excited but did not know why.

"Hello, Brother," a soothing voice said behind him. Stephen turned around and saw someone that was not the Shepherd. He was looking at the most beautiful man he had ever seen. And there was a glow about Him. Stephen instantly knew why he was feeling excited.

"Hi," he said, somewhat shaken. "I know You!"

"Yes, and I know you, though we did have some challenges early on, didn't we?" He then pointed with His hand to a bench nearby and invited Stephen to take a seat next to Him.

When not speaking, the man had a loving smile on His face, with a slight crack allowing Stephen a tiny view of His perfect teeth. The man was leaning forward towards Stephen' with His hands clasped together in His knees.

Stephen started, "In the visions, I saw something new that I had not seen before. I was watching my spirit speaking with You, wasn't I?" he asked.

"Yes, My Spirit is always speaking and sometimes your spirit can hear. But in the earthly realm, you were not experiencing the fullness of the Holy Spirit because you had pushed Him away: you were quenching Him. In 1 Thessalonians 5:19 of My Word, Paul tells the church, 'Do not quench the Spirit.' Quenching the Spirit is what happens when you don't listen to Him and you do what you know is wrong because you are following your own worldly desires. But this doesn't mean that He stops speaking."

Stephen welcomed His words, "Yes, Lord, but I need a little more clarity. In the vision, it appeared that my spirit was both listening and speaking with Your Spirit at that time, but I don't recall any experience like that. Did I miss something?"

The Man looked at Stephen, focusing His attention on him, *"But We did engage with you! You just tossed it off as if it was merely a conversation with yourself. When a man is prepared to do something that he knows is wrong, he will typically look inside himself and ask, 'Should I or shouldn't I?' or 'You know this is wrong, right?' They will hear a voice tell them not to do it, but they also hear a competing voice directing them to do it. It's as if they are having an argument within themselves. Yet, whether they do the wrong thing or not, they will judge that conversation as an internal dialogue, not recognizing the truth that the conversation was held at the spiritual level.*

"As you were spending that money, you knew it was wrong and you told yourself it was wrong. But you spent it anyway. So I allowed the end result to happen because that was your choice. And then, as you were being judged for your actions later, you knew you were wrong and you could feel yourself being punished for it. You saw things happening on the outside, but I could see everything happening on the inside.

"I judged you but you also judged yourself because you couldn't see My judgment. If you had been paying attention to My Spirit and My judgment, you would have seen that I was admonishing you with loving discipline – and that would have been enough. Instead, you added to My judgment and judged yourself unworthy, a failure, a mistake. That is not what I saw in you. Men have a nasty habit of judging themselves much more harshly than Our Father.

"If a judge sentences you to a year in prison, do you add solitary confinement to that sentence of your own accord? The judgment of self-indignation is not of God. His judgment is the right judgment. If you would stop judging yourself and accept His judgment as is, you might just find that love for yourself, the love that Our Father has for you, surface rather than condemnation. It was because of your self-judgment that you struggled with loving others."

Stephen curled up his mouth and nose, recognizing His truth for what it was. "It's my value system again, elevating it over anything and everything. Not only did I fail to live in honor, I dishonored myself further when I devalued my worth as not being worthy of God."

THE MAN THAT HE KNEW WAS JESUS NODDED IN CONFIRMATION. *"Many men continue to tumble even after they realize they are, in fact, tumbling when all they have to do is just…stop. But alas, the temptation of the flesh is strong and when you succumb to it, you lose that which I have given you…but it's the spirit, My Brother, that is stronger. Much of this has to do with the pressure the world places on men. But that is not God, that is man placing pressure on himself. God is Peace, God is Love, God is Comfort – anything lower than that is not God. Also, you were* *trying to control things that were not yours to control. That is always a losing proposition."*

"Thank you, Lord, for helping clarify this moment. I know this was an event that I carried with me for many years as a lesson to never repeat; but I also carried the burden that came with it. My wife and I would even joke about it for years, but inside, I was still seething at what I had done," Stephen confessed.

"Ah, but do you want to know what the Father and I witnessed? What we saw?" Jesus said.

"Yes, Lord. Absolutely, please."

"We saw a man who desired to honor his wife. We saw a man that cherished and loved the gift that he had. We saw a man fully repentant, a man that would live to not make this mistake again. We saw a man that understood his responsibilities to family, a man that recognized when he did not live up to them. We saw a man who was everything to his wife, but a man who was also everything to Me and to Our Father. We saw a man whose wife loved him dearly, and we saw a woman who We were in complete agreement with."

Stephen wept as He listed out His accolades and completely forgot what it was that he was lamenting about.

"But we also saw a man who neglected God in everything he was doing. We saw a man who ignored the wisdom being imparted to him. We saw a man who was operating under his own righteousness and not the righteousness of God. We saw a man who was undisciplined and we saw a man who needed correction. We saw a man that was walking down the wrong path, a man who needed to be nudged onto the right path. We saw a man who would miss the subtle hints of where to go, a man who would only listen to harsh correction.

"Therefore, you were judged and the judgment placed was one that We knew would get your attention, a judgment that We knew would direct your path to the River. We saw a man that We loved and a man who needed saving. Which is also why we kept your flight pay from you for five months and then illumined to your mind about the back pay owed to you. Do you see the Father's perfect timing? Do you understand what I am saying to you, Brother?"

"Yes, Sir. Wow! If I had been getting my flight pay on schedule, then I would not have had the back-pay waiting for me in lieu of that loan. You knew I was making a mistake and would need that money later. Thank You, Father. I also understand that the judgment applied was the judgment needed, no more, no less. I understand that the judgment meted to me was done in love and compassion, under mercy and grace to save me and not to condemn me."

Jesus nodded, smiled, and laughed. He wrapped his right arm over the back and shoulders of Stephen and jiggled him. *"Yes, Brother, yes. We needed you to find your name, your identity, and your purpose. Do you know that a man judged in this way learns how to judge others for the same mistakes? Do you know that a man judged in this way can see another man about to make the mistake before he does? Do you know that, as you cross each threshold of judgment, that you gain the gift of discernment to save others from the same fate you yourself suffered?*

"The best way to do that was to make you search for it. It is amazing how events like you just witnessed, a mistake as tiny as an insect, smaller than a mustard seed, can evolve into significant lessons of life – but life under God."

STEPHEN LOOKED UP HIM with an embarrassed grin. "Yes, Lord, I sure knew how to make a small hill into a mountain. But I am curious. Why would You appear to me now, in this place, instead of the Shepherd who has been guiding me this entire time so far?"

"I figured it was time for you to see the true Way, the Trinity. When you see Shepherd, you also see Me, for He is My Spirit as I am of the Father." The Man laughed and grasped Stephen' hands in His hands. This is when Stephen noticed the holes in His wrist for the first time. *"I can see your mind churning, Brother, but you will figure this out one day – that I promise you. Know that you commune with My Spirit and I am advocating for you before the Father. But when you commune with the Spirit, you are communing with all of Us. And We are looking forward to the day when We get to behold you in the throne room of grace. But, that is for another day. Come, let's continue down the path."*

With that, Stephen and Jesus stood up together and walked side by side. As Stephen looked around, it was still dark but he could now see stars, only a few, shining down upon them. The mist he walked through earlier was clearing up and it was starting to feel cooler. As he walked with Jesus at his side, the love he felt was overwhelming. Even though Jesus had corrected him, there was no malice. There was only peace, comfort, joy and contentment. He did not want to leave.

"Brother, you are about to witness your true threshing, that point in your life where you would change physically, spiritually, and in your soul. This is related, in part, to the judgment I placed upon you. Of course, you didn't know it at the time."

Stephen was wondering which event He spoke of as he could think of a few rough patches.

"You are about to understand what it means to be reputable, trustworthy, wise, and disciplined. You are about to learn what it means to be resilient and how to persevere. However, these lessons will come at an extreme cost. This is what scripture, My Word, refers to as the 'Threshing Floor'"

Stephen felt like getting to his knees and bowing down at His feet, but before he could do it, Jesus looked at him and slowly faded with that ever-present smile on His face. Just before He vanished completely, Stephen could swear that Jesus winked at him.

CHAPTER 18
ON THE THRESHING FLOOR: OPERATION DESERT STORM

"O my threshed people, and my afflicted of the threshing floor!
What I have heard from the Lord of hosts,
The God of Israel, I make known to you."
(Isaiah 21:10)

WITH THE SNAP OF A FINGER, Stephen found himself in a world that he knew was spiritual. The flavor of the visions the Lord was allowing him to see was each unique. When they had first started, he was simply a witness to what was happening in the earthly realm, as if he was actually there but nobody could see him. But now, now he was seeing things not only on earth, but also in his spirit during the times and events of the vision. It was blurred as if looking through a glass full of water.

As he looked through the watery window, he could see Shepherd near his younger self. But as before, it was not the earth he was seeing. He was watching a spiritual discussion, something that he had blinded himself to, or perhaps, a discussion where God was trying to get his attention but he had chosen not to listen with his heart. Stephen knew this was part of his Wilderness Project and his heart journey, his spiritual education. For him to understand himself, he needed to see what was happening, not just in the world but also below the surface, in his spirit and in his soul.

THE LOCATION WAS SURREAL, a place of history, where legends are made and lives are often lost as a result. The sheep was being led by Shepherd; the wolf being held at bay due to the light of Shepherd. The wolf hates the light and Shepherd knew that.

Shepherd and the sheep were walking alone, across a vast desert landscape full of bodies, destruction, and fire. Off in the distance, just shy of the horizon, the sheep could see others like him walking away from the desolation. But, somehow, the sheep knew that he was different than the others.

"Shepherd, why am I here alone while the others of my kind are off in the distance? Why can't I be with them? They feel…distant," he wanted to know.

"They are the ninety-nine who are following the Way. You are the one that is lost, off the path. I am here with you to pick you up and carry you to the rest of the pack, if you are willing. So, we are here alone while you observe, you learn, and you choose," Shepherd responded.

He continued, "You are still making decisions that drive you away from the path and you have allowed influencers, to guide you rather than the One that you need to hear. But do not listen. You are burdened because you believe their lies and your heart is hardened to the Truth. Because your heart is hardened, you listen to your head, which is causing you to live a dead life, one filled with negative emotions, negative thoughts, fear, rejection…and more. This dead life is keeping you away."

The sheep stopped where he was, suddenly filled with anxiety, "I want to live; I don't want to die. I don't want to be alone; I want to be with my brothers and sisters. I want life. What do I need to do to get back on the path?"

"You will need to be sifted, My little Brother. Your heart needs to be awakened so that you can see the chaff and allow it to be removed. You need to keep the good stuff and get rid of the bad. You, My friend, are about to be trampled on the threshing floor, in order to crush and separate the bad material from that which is good."

Shepherd turned to look squarely at the sheep, making sure that he had His attention. "You see all of this destruction around you?" He waved his arm around.

There were volcanic fires crossing the desert reaching heights of more than a hundred feet. There were military vehicles of many types destroyed and unrecognizable, and an upturned helicopter of the type the sheep was familiar with. He saw the heart of several men filled with malice and ill intentions, and bodies – lots of bodies. But there is one thing he saw above all others that got his attention – he saw himself, on his knees, with his face buried in his hands, shaking uncontrollably.

"Yes, Sir," the sheep replied meekly. "But I also see me on the ground filled with grief."

"This will be your experience, but it will also be your witness. You will be tested, but it will also be your testimony. You won't change completely, but your spirit and soul will be sifted. The bad that is about to be removed will allow you to change direction. Your vision will become less impaired – for the most part anyway," Shepherd added calmly.

"How does that work? Destruction, desolation, the desert? How is this removing the bad stuff? What does this have to do with a threshing floor?" The sheep shot off the questions one after the other.

"Your forefathers did not have machinery to separate edible pieces of grain from the scaly parts. So, people with sticks –or beasts of burden if they had the means – would beat the wheat, the grain, relentlessly on a flat smooth surface which is the threshing floor. This beating would loosen the materials, allowing the good parts of the harvest to be removed from the inedible parts surrounding it. You see, the grain is useless until this separation happens."

"Oh OK, I think I get it so far. There is obvious symbolism. Is there a more...um...I don't know...practical message here that is easily understood making it more relevant to me?"

"Brother, the threshing floor is symbolic of judgment. You are about to be judged so that the separation of good and bad can occur. Prophets of old have shared several examples of what happens when people repeatedly turn from God and towards false idols, of which you have been party. The Lord has judged, and will judge, those that continue to turn from Him and will scatter them to the wind, just as chaff is removed from the threshing floor. There is even one story

told in His Word about the Lord empowering His people to trample their enemies just as oxen trample the grain on the threshing floor.

"You also have the Messiah, the One we know as Jesus; now He is the One that is the most relevant to the threshing. His cousin, John the Baptist, described the Messiah as the One who will separate true believers from non-believers. True believers, the good stuff, will be gathered to Him, while those who reject Him will burn in unquenchable fire. To be clear, My Brother, the wicked are the same as the chaff removed during the threshing."

"Oh OK, I get it. You are giving me a warning that I am about to go through a threshing that will remove some of the bad parts of me from the good parts, the parts that the Messiah desires for me. Right?" said the sheep in a resigned voice.

"Yes, but not all of your bad stuff will be removed. This threshing will remove blinders that keep you from the path to allow and prevent you from changing direction; but you won't be simply lifted and placed directly on the path. This threshing is just a place where you will change direction, walking to the path which will lead you to the River. What you do with that will be up to you. The Lord will give you directions but is up to you to follow them."

▦

And with that, Stephen watched Shepherd vanish, leaving the soul of his younger self to ponder what was about to befall him next, as he entered this land of desolation in the desert wilderness. Stephen stared off in the distance, knowing what he was about to see – his life pivot.

▦

SAUDI ARABIA AND IRAQ, DEC 1990 - MAY 1991

STEPHEN HAD NOT BEEN PERFORMING as well as other soldiers in his unit, and it had been breaking his heart for a while. But this was a burden that he kept secreted away. He had friends such as David, but even that relationship didn't look anything like what others had. Stephen was prone to make mistakes or say silly things that would bring unwarranted attention on him, but he carried on with bravado and false confidence nonetheless. He was trying to improve, get better, be a better soldier, but he just kept failing and making mistakes – he couldn't understand why. The result was that those he desired respect from were the ones that would tease him, call him names, make fun of him and send him off on fool's errands. And now, his unit was heading off to war. They had been called and it was time to serve.

Stephen felt that this war was his opportunity to finally find the glory and honor he so desperately wanted, to move out in a grand display of honor, showing his buddies that he had their back and fight tenaciously.

"I've been called, Sweetie. We are heading to Saudi Arabia," he told his nineteen-year-old wife. They had just arrived in Germany a few months earlier after Jamie gave birth to their son. They had also just celebrated their first wedding anniversary. "I don't know what will happen in this war but this is what I signed up for, what our life is about now."

"I support you, Steve, you know that. Don't worry about me or Chad; we'll be OK," she said confidently. Stephen still marveled at everything that he and his wife had been through over the last twelve months. Marriage. Pregnancy. Birth. Moving to a foreign country. And now war. That is a lot for anyone to handle, and he felt guilty about leaving her and their five-month-old son in a land they didn't know.

Stephen cried as he walked out the door of their apartment in Rossdorf, Germany on 30 December 1990, not knowing if this would be the last time. But he was focused; he intended to bring honor and glory to the family, and also to his brothers-in-arms.

Stephen was twenty-one, having dreamt about an opportunity just like this to serve in battle. "I just want one battle, and then I can look at myself as a man! Baptized in fire," he had convinced himself.

While he despised his father, the one thing that he always admired him for was his service in Vietnam. His father had become handicapped via combat but he never allowed his handicap to stop him, and now he had shown his worth to the Long Beach Naval Shipyard, having moved up the civilian ranks. Perhaps this is what Stephen thought he would gain from serving in battle.

Would he finally achieve the success which always seemed to elude him? But the harder Stephen tried, the more he seemed to mess up. For those that mocked him, all Stephen wanted was to be in the club, and it hurt him deeply that he still felt like an outsider. Well, at least he had Jamie, Chad and the small circle of friends that still hung out with him without judgment.

Stephen knew that this war would somehow play a significant role in his life. So he decided to maintain a personal journal during the war, something that might have stories that he could share with his children and grandchildren. Or, if he died in combat, maybe his journal would survive and Chad could read the experiences of his father up to the day he died.

Stephen was not afraid of dying; this never crossed his mind. He was more afraid of failing or falling short, above anything else. And, as his journal now reads, Operation Desert Shield and Desert Storm did not let him down. It did change his life though, but not before being humiliated, embarrassed, placing himself in danger, almost breaking a multi-million-dollar aircraft, and almost dying in a helicopter crash.

Stephen' job was to perform navigation, aerial reconnaissance, and coordinate close air support with Air Force aircraft and AH-64 Apache gunships. Almost from the day of arriving in theater, his escapades would kick off.

ON ONE PARTICULAR EVENING in early February, Stephen was scheduled for guard duty on the airfield. Their unit had recently flown to a barren location a hundred miles south of the Iraqi border, a staging location for when the ground war would start. As his journal reads, it was freezing and he was miserable. So he decided to climb into the cockpit of one of the Apaches, hoping to get warm while still having a view of his area.

The warmth overtook Stephen and he fell asleep. Sometime later, when Stephen was reporting as missing because he failed to report in, the entire unit was awoken in a search for the missing soldier. He was found, but he was now a problem for his leadership, and life became almost unbearable. Stephen knew that he deserved it. His dad was right. Worthless! But, that was not all…

THE GROUND WAR WOULD COMMENCE in the latter half of February. On 16 February, the unit would move north to a Tactical Assembly Area about 20 km south of the border of Iraq. Just prior to the move, all vehicles were packed and loaded, soldiers were ensconced in their seats, and the movement of thousands upon thousands of ground vehicles was ready to commence. Aircrews were in their aircraft, initiating startup procedures for the flight to the TAA.

Stephen' pilot directed him to go ahead and start the aircraft as he called out the startup procedures from the checklist. However, in the middle of the engine start, Stephen' thumb slipped off the startup button causing the aircraft to heat up burning the engine and consuming the battery. A secondary startup failed to start the aircraft, potentially leaving the aircraft abandoned in position. However, a radio call to one of the crew chiefs met with success and they were able to start the aircraft on the third attempt. Even though it started, Stephen still felt humiliated and embarrassed.

The next day, the unit was tasked to go out and search for another helicopter crew that had crashed, nose diving into the ground. Stephen and his pilot were the first on the scene. After landing and taking the aircraft down to idle, the pilot looked at Stephen to his left. "Stephen, I am going to check on the crew to make sure they are OK. You have the controls. I will be back in a few minutes," he stated as he stepped out.

"Yes, Sir," Specialist Stephen Remington replied.

After what was much more than several minutes, Stephen could see his pilot still speaking with the crew, who had survived their crash. "Why is he taking so long?" he asked himself. "What are we waiting for?"

Another pilot from another aircraft in the area with whom Stephen was in communication was wondering the same thing over the team frequency on the radio. "Stephen, go ahead and shut the aircraft down. Follow the steps I give you." He then started to read through a checklist as Stephen completed each task.

"Why is he taking me through these steps?" Stephen wondered. "I know how to shut down the aircraft."

One of the instructions the pilot read to Stephen was to shut down the radio – "Stupid!" Stephen would think later. After shutting down the radio and locking down the cyclic and collective into position,

Stephen climbed out of the bird, leaving it unmanned while it was still running, and ran over to his pilot.

"Sir, what's going on? If the crew is OK, we need to get going."

When the pilot turned around and saw Stephen standing there while the aircraft was still running, his face changed to utter terror. He ran over to the airplane and proceeded to shut it down. While the knowledge of this screw up would be limited to a few people, Stephen viewed it as another notch against his already damaged reputation.

ON 24 FEBRUARY, the ground war started with tens of thousands of tanks and vehicles of all types and sizes traipsing across the land as far as eye could see. "Wow!" thought Stephen, "the Iraqis have no idea what they are in for."

However, the following day, a call came across the radio that one of the brothers in their unit had received a Red Cross message from his wife and needed to be immediately evacuated and redeployed back to Germany. Three scout aircraft were sent out to look for him, searching for one large truck in an unending sea of tanks, trucks, 5-ton vehicles, miscellaneous armored vehicles and more. "What a fantastic sight!" Stephen thought.

The vehicle that had the soldier was found, by Stephen and his pilot, of course. The thought had crossed Stephen' mind that they seemed to always be the aircraft to find these things. They landed a few dozen feet away from the vehicle where Stephen dismounted and ran to the truck to get the soldier's attention and relay the message.

As the back of the aircraft was loaded with equipment needed during the ground campaign, Stephen needed to give up his seat so that the pilot could take the soldier back to port. Here is Stephen journal entry regarding this exchange:

> "SGT M got a Red Cross call today, so I had to give up my left seat to him and had to get on the back of a truck for the convoy. I got screwed on this one cause I had to go all night, with the convoy with no equipment. I messed up by forgetting my mask and my weapon (I left them on the aircraft in my urgency to get SGT M out of there). We drove for about 9 hours and then camped about 5 miles from the border. And still, my pilot never returned to pick me up or drop off my stuff."

The next day, Stephen drove north across the berms that divided Saudi Arabia and Iraq, and he had no weapon and no chemical protection. "Here we go again!" Stephen said to himself. "I screwed up again and now I have become a burden to the team on this truck."

However, as luck would have it, Stephen would reconnect with his aircraft later that day at a Forward Arming and Refuel Point and recommence his mission. "With NBC gear and weapon," he reminded himself.

AFTER ONLY A FEW HOURS into the ground campaign, many of the coalition forces would witness mass surrenders of the Iraqi Republican Guard, even to unarmed aircraft. But, it was during a midday mission on 27 February that Stephen would see his first dead Iraqi:

> "It's 1700 right now and I just got away from another battle. We went all the way to Kuwait. I saw my first dead guy today. He was about 10 feet from a blown-up unidentified vehicle. He was in one piece but it looked like (I was about 25-30 feet above him) his elbow was shattered. And it also looked like he had several broken bones in his legs because they were bent every which way. I got fired upon by artillery again today. This time they were close. I just happened to look up and I saw a tracer round coming down. I screamed, 'Break right,' several times to the pilot, who immediately did so. He then saw two more rounds and took immediate action. All three rounds landed pretty close to us."

The aircraft shook from the explosions and debris would hit the canopy.

> "Seeing that dead guy really made me think about life. Even though he was enemy, I actually felt sorry for him. He died for nothing. He probably has a wife and child back home just like me and now they have to pay the price for Saddam Hussein."

THE COALITION FORCES WOULD DECLARE A CEASE FIRE on 28 February, followed by a decrease in excitement. They would finally end up in a compound a few miles north of Kuwait City. This is where they would remain until their redeployment back to Germany.

Sometime in April 1991, flight missions had decreased, so Stephen was tasked to serve as a driver for the Aviation Liaison Officer to the 3rd Armored Brigade. The mission was to serve as the onsite coordinator and planner for aviation assets to that brigade. At some point, Stephen would spark up a friendship with the brigade Chemical Officer, a young Lieutenant. Stephen was unaware he was a homosexual.

To Stephen, the officer always seemed depressed, so one day, he decided to ask, "Sir, are you OK?" The lieutenant, intrigued by this question, seemed to presume that Stephen was interested in more, so he dared to share his inner sexual thoughts with Stephen, and what he wanted to do with him.

"Holy crap! What did I just walk into?" Stephen thought quickly to himself. He had always figured if he were hit on by a man, that he would punch the guy; but the chances were so slim, he never thought it would happen. But, that impulse did not come to him, an act that Stephen would later be proud of.

"Uh, sorry, man. I am very much heterosexual and very much in love with my wife," Stephen responded. "I'm sorry."

"OK, that's fine," said the Lieutenant backing off.

"Look, I have to hit the latrine. We can touch base later. Cool?" Stephen said.

"Sure."

Stephen found the Aviation LNO a few minutes later and told him that he needed to get back to the unit in Kuwait. A few hours later, they arrived at the aviation compound and Stephen reported the incident to his chain of command. An investigation was started but some of those in Stephen' leadership chain were unable to keep this incident to themselves.

Word got out that Stephen had been compromised by a homosexual; his first line sergeant and a few others teased him and laughed at him. Stephen was humiliated and felt betrayed.

"Why does this keep happening to me?" he cried to no one in particular.

IN MAY 1991, THE UNIT RECEIVED the good news that they were redeploying back to Germany. On 9 May 1991, while on the final leg back to a Saudi Arabian Port from their assembly area in Kuwait, the helicopter that Stephen was flying would experience engine failure at 300 feet. They were going down. As the aircraft auto-rotated, things were going smoothly until they were 15 feet above the ground.

The pilot pulled up on the collective to slow their descent, but he performed the maneuver too soon. While they still had some forward momentum, the helicopter fell almost straight down the final feet to the ground rather than glide. In those final seconds, Stephen did not panic, but he did pray a silent goodbye to his wife and son, "I'm sorry!"

And then they made impact.

The helicopter hit the ground hard, splitting the skids and busting the downward view window. They had impacted on the downward slope of a hill, which caused the helicopter to slide forward, further causing the front of the skids to dig into the sand and lift the rear of the helicopter into the air. The rotor blades, still turning, hit the side of another slope pivoting the helicopter over and backwards. They finally stopped, landing on the right side (pilot side) of the aircraft before the helicopter came to a halt. The entire crash sequence lasted about 5 seconds.

Stephen and the pilot had been flying doors off, his side of the aircraft was now the top. When he looked down at the pilot, he was laying sideways in the sand where his door would normally have been.

"Sir, are you OK?" Stephen shouted out. The engine was still winding down.

"Yes," he heard in reply. This is when Stephen smelled smoke, followed shortly by both crew members quickly unbuttoning and climbing from the aircraft. They walked 25 feet from the airplane, before sitting in the sand to contemplate what had just happened.

Stephen was angry, no, he was pissed, bitter, and deeply frustrated. "How can this keep happening to me? Why? Why? First, a judgment mistake on my part that almost cost me my career, then a lack of protection when we invaded Iraq, then the humiliation of being propositioned. Now a helicopter crash! Really! God, please stop this." This is when Stephen remembered that after 5 months in theater, he was 30 minutes away from port, and then it would have all been over. They would be headed home and he would return to his wife and child.

"Why?" he screamed. And then the tears started to flow. He suddenly realized that, if he had died in that crash, he would have left nothing for his family. No money, no legacy, no memories. And this fueled his anger – at himself.

"That's it," he shouted out to no one in particular. "I'm done. No more taking crap from anyone, no more depending on others to take care of things. No more screwing up. I can only take care of myself; no one else will," he determined.

"I am going to get my act together. I am going to succeed. I am going to change, get better. This is bullcrap," he muttered to himself.

Ten days later, he would rejoin his wife and son. And things were about to change.

𝍫

"HA!" THE WOLF SCOFFED AT THE SHEEP. "That was exhilarating! You have been beaten and battered. You have been humiliated, estranged, and defeated. No glory for you dork; you have been devalued. Your dad was right – once again."

The sheep grew angry – a victim of defeat? Perhaps, maybe. But he was done being the victim; he was done allowing others to talk junk about him. He was infuriated.

"I left nothing for my wife and son," the sheep thought to himself. "Nothing but regret, that is."

This thought broke his heart but added fuel to the fire that was starting to burn. "That's it, this life of crap is over," the sheep declared. "I am getting my life around; I will be successful. I will leave an inheritance for my children and I will make my wife proud. I will prove to my father that he was wrong: that I am worthy; and when I do, I will shove it in his face."

The wolf stood back in awe, "Wow, where did that come from? Didn't see that coming!"

But then the wolf snickered, "But wait, he missed something. He completely left the Creator out of it; he is still in it for himself. The sheep's current vision may seem consequential to him for now, but he is still misguided. He did not surrender to Him; he simply intended to defeat those that embarrassed him."

The wolf was right, the sheep had become angry and bitter at the world, with everyone, except for those that most mattered to him.

Shepherd, with vigilant eyes, watched the sheep change direction; while only subtle, it was at least a change in the right direction.

"Thank You, Father. His fire has been ignited. He still doesn't see the River but he can smell it. He is still self-seeking, and even more self-righteous while in pursuit of his own comforts. But his heart has opened to possibilities. His mind is whirring as he considers his options. The chaff of rejection has been removed on top of other strongholds.

"Though he still doesn't yet see his true purpose, He has been awakened, Lord. Praise You, Father! Now, Father, I ask that we continue to guide him to the altar that has been built on top of the threshing floor, the place of sacrifice where his burdens, his fears, and his strongholds, can be sacrificed and surrendered to You, Lord. That special place of reconciliation and separation.

"Allow him, Father, to reconcile his heart and his spirit with Your Heart and Your Spirit. Alas, he still requires sifting, which will require that he go through further shaking. Thank You, Father! Your grace and mercy forever!"

"Also, Father, with Your guiding hand, we have guided the sheep's spouse back to You. With her guiding hand and her presence in his life, she will serve as the city upon the hill, providing light in the darkness, allowing Your Presence to reign in their life – even if the sheep does not see You today. For we know, Lord, that He will see You tomorrow, and that, Father, is due to Your righteousness and grace in the lives of Your children. Thank You, Father, in the Name of Your Son, Jesus Christ!"

And with that prayer over the sheep, the eyes of Shepherd slowly vanished, but not before the sheep witnessed the twinkle of a star in the sky, giving him a direction to walk in. And so, the sheep continued his journey through the wilderness but with a sudden change of heart.

STEPHEN OBSERVED THE ENTIRE VISION with tears. Even though he knew what was going to happen in the earthy realm, it still weighed heavily upon him. His witness in the spiritual realm was an altogether more dramatic experience. He looked up to heaven in joy, recognizing that he was not the same man. As his head came down, he could see Shepherd standing a few feet in front of him, with his arms folded in his sleeves, his staff long forgotten. As Stephen looked upon Shepherd, the landscape around them changed from a desert of destruction and war to the more familiar world of his secret place. Though it was still dark, he could see color.

Stephen had already figured that the secret place would change as he continued along this journey, but he never knew what would change, how it would change, or what changes would be represented inside of him. But then he remembered that this part of the journey would represent the condition of his spirit, and his heart, in the season that the visions represented.

Focusing back on his Desert Storm experience, he looked at Shepherd. "I recently started referring to this period of my life as my life pivot," Stephen stated, "where I changed course with a renewed focus. But I realized that I missed a more critical component of this period: this was also the time that my wife came back to Jesus. I now see that that was the most significant event."

Shepherd nodded, *"Do you see how much you have grown, Brother? Do you see how the Lord's plans work when people are obedient to His Will? You can see that His Spirit was warning you: He was speaking to your spirit, but you did not let it sit in the mind of your heart – which is why you forgot about it within minutes."*

Stephen considered the questions as he wasn't sure if they were rhetorical or if he was supposed to answer. "Yes, Sir, I can definitely see a different me today than the young man I was then or even the man I became later. But something else stands out to me from this experience, something that I had not considered until now."

"What was that, Brother?"

"The evidence shows that my life changed upon my return, much for the better, though, admittedly, there were aspects that also became darker. But overall, I improved and I changed after this war. That tells me that what I needed was sitting in me the entire time. Yet, prior to the war, no matter how hard I tried, no matter how much I wanted it, I kept messing up, doing stupid things, bringing unwanted attention to myself. I remember how people who I wanted respect from would mess with me, push me to a corner, excluded from what they were doing. And I felt it was deserved, which served to tear me down further."

"Do you think you know why you changed after this war? What was different about you?" Shepherd asked.

"I think a fire was ignited in me. While I may have wanted to be a better soldier and a better father, I barely had a spark in me, which means I couldn't ignite the desires within me," Stephen confided.

"OK," Shepherd answered, *"that's good. But it's also OK to admit that your earthly father had spent eighteen years of your life building a legacy in you through the words that he spoke over you. When you joined the military and the people around you treated you harshly, they were unknowingly building on your father's legacy, continuing to snuff the flame in you. What if I were to say to you that your Desert Storm experience, the events you were involved in, actually ministered to you? How does that resonate with you?"*

"Ministered to me?" Stephen retorted. "I had not thought about that but I do know that as each stupid event happened in that war, one after the other, I could feel something building inside of me, ready to burst out and scream 'ENOUGH!!' It wasn't suicidal or depression or anything like that; it was more like an energy."

SHEPHERD GRABBED STEPHEN' face in His hands and looked into his eyes. *"I want you to realize that all these experiences have shaped who you are today, whether you like it or not. God didn't cause all these things to happen to you, but He did allow them to happen to you. God wanted you to use all of those experience, mostly bad, but there were some good, to help you grow spiritually. He wanted to mold you into the likeness of Jesus and shape you for the unique purpose He has in your life. He didn't want even one of those experiences to go to waste.*

"God takes all of your life experiences – whether positive or painful, intentional or accidental, caused by you or by someone else, to shape you for His unique calling upon your life. Romans 8:28 may be the most personal verse in the Bible as it reminds you that in all things God works for the good of those who love Him, who have been called according to His purpose. We have used this verse before; it is a verse applicable to all of your life experiences. Men fail to realize that their life experiences are some of the most overlooked ways that God uses to shape them for the way He wants them to serve Him and others in this world.

"Your life experiences are like a ministry of flaming fire. Many men experience a turnaround in their life after something traumatic. But, sadly, some men will allow events to quench their flame, taking

out the rooster, and they give up. For some, it leads to a destitute life, lacking anything life giving, while for others it leads to suicide. This is not what God wants; this is what He hates."

"Brother, this journey was about an inspection of your heart wounds into how your heart was wounded so that you can properly heal. However, this event, your Desert Storm experience, was a series of heart wounds, one right after the other, until finally, you did what? You caught yourself, you woke up, you found that fire which healed parts of you. You found yourself at rock bottom and declared 'Enough!' You were broken, Stephen...and what does God love? A broken spirit because this is when He can use you, when you realize that you need something more to help you get out of the pit."

"But I didn't come to God – at least I don't remember doing that. I recall my taking ownership of myself, doing things myself, driving myself. I was completely focused on myself and not on Him. Or was I?"

"God created you and it was God that placed that fire inside of you, whether you recognized Him or not. Let's not forget that you accepted Christ in your youth, so there was always a part of Him operating in you, even though you weren't nourishing your spirit. Remember when you walked away from those boys with who you were living a drug induced life? You found the fire in you then, too, to have the courage and fortitude to walk away. You found that fire once again in your Desert Storm experience, because you, Brother, had been sifted on the threshing floor and some of the chaff that had been taking you down and suffocating you was removed. Your fire had been tossed off, to be carried away in the wind."

"But I also became more bitter, angry, and aggressive in going after the mission – as long as I would benefit from it. I became a hurtful person," Stephen added.

"You see there, you're still focused on the negative, Brother. You need to move past that stuff. Yes, not all of the chaff was removed, but some of it was and that should be considered a victory. Treat life as a series of battles that make up a larger war. You will win some and you may lose some, but it's how you fight the war and Who you fight the war with that matters. Bitter and angry? Possibly. But you also became determined, resolute, intent on doing things that would change the world. The Lord saw your heart; these things were coming to the surface now so that they could be sifted later.

You did behave in a way on the outside that was contradictory to Christ, but you were acting out in the way that your flesh had been trained. Meanwhile, the Lord could see your heart and He was also training your heart."

"God wants to use every experience in your life – good and bad – to help somebody else. God is telling you, 'Don't waste your experiences. Use them to help others who are going through the same thing.' These painful experiences, as well as the ones previous and the ones that come later that you keep locked away in the inner recesses of your soul could become your greatest ministry. That is what God has planned for you, answering the question about 'All of this,' that all men ponder."

"So, you've been sifted. You've been healed of some of your wounds and things in your life that were distracting you. Your wife has come to Jesus and she is now enjoying all that He has to offer for her. As for you, you are beginning to recognize your name, your identity, and your purpose for that phase of your life leading to the events that will ultimately change you forever. Your spirit can smell the River and you are walking in a path towards that River.

"But, the Lord had more in store for you, didn't He?" He then asked.

"Yes, Sir, while I knew that I was going to grow and be more successful, I didn't know what that would entail. Within two years after the war, my life would take a completely unexpected turn."

Shepherd laughed and patted Stephen on the shoulders. *"The first step in the attainment of victory, Brother, is to understand your enemy. But victory is also attained when you understand your strengths and the abilities of the One who has your back. Let's go take a look and witness the wondrous Hand of God."*

217

CHAPTER 19
DENIAL

"For the unbelieving husband is sanctified through his wife,
and the unbelieving wife is sanctified through her believing
husband; for otherwise your children are unclean,
but now they are holy."
(1 Corinthians 7:14)

STEPHEN WAS BROUGHT BACK to the secret place that he had originally started in…beautiful, serene, peaceful. But this time the vision wasn't about him; it was about his wife and for his wife, and this place represented her heart. A younger version of his wife; but it was her, nonetheless.

▉▉

SHEPHERD, WHO WE KNOW to be the Spirit of God, strode along the shore of the lake in the secret place with a young woman. "You have been called to be one of His servants, My Sister, but understand that this will come with trials. You may even likely be belittled," He revealed to her.

She stared at nothing in particular for a few seconds and then looked up into the eyes of Shepherd, "Please tell the Father that I am willing and able," she stated confidently.

"Hallelujah! Know that you have entered into the city of the living God where you are joined with thousands of angels in joyful assembly. Praise Him! I will do My part, as the Lord commands Me, to work with the sheep to guard him in his ways. But now that you recognize yourself as a true child of God, you are now a living example of His goodness. The sheep will perceive Our Father based on how you exhibit the love of God in your life. That is a road not easily traveled; it will be very difficult," Shepherd advised.

"I understand. I will work to do nothing in rivalry or conceit and will not wage war with my husband based on the feelings of my flesh. To exhibit Him, who is Love, is to be like Him, which is love. I will do my best. I do ask that the Father give me the courage, the endurance, and the patience to do what must be done."

"Amen, Sister, He has heard your petition. Know that, even though you are dealing with the flesh, you are not warring according to the flesh. It is your husband's spirit and his soul that requires reconciliation, not his body. This will require your spiritual intervention and His divine power to overcome the strongholds that have possession of his life."

"Yes, Sir and Yes, Father," she replied.

And as Stephen had already become accustomed, the woman watched as the Shepherd was just...gone. She stood alone, along the shore of the lake, pondering what would happen next.

AFTER DESERT STORM and his return to Germany, Stephen fulfilled what he had vowed that day in the middle of the desert standing beside his destroyed aircraft. He got his act together. He performed. And he grew. And his wife watched it all happen in front of her. Her husband was a changed man.

He signed up for college and started attending courses. He took some of the combat and hazard duty pay saved up from the war and started investing in mutual funds; he also played with currency market speculation using the multiple currency denominations across Europe. He studied multiple aspects of investing and he got good at it.

He and his family started touring Europe and getting to know the history and culture of various locales. And, most of all, he started behaving and acting like a soldier. It would take two years, but the memories of his antics in the war, and his character prior to the war, if he were honest, began to fade as old soldiers departed and new ones came in. He had captured the eyes of his leadership. But there were some older soldiers that remained and their memories tended to last longer, figuring that Stephen could never change, waiting for him to screw up once again.

In November 1992, Stephen was promoted to Sergeant, something that he had previously thought would never happen; the idea of becoming a Non-Commissioned Officer was out of his grasp. And then, in April of 1993, six months after pinning on his Sergeant stripes, his First Sergeant told him that he wanted him to go to the Staff Sergeant promotion board, bypassing his direct supervisor. This was the same supervisor who was responsible for him during Desert Storm, and he was not happy. Stephen was suddenly overwhelmed. He did it. He had crossed over into true leadership. But, as with his supervisor, there were those in the organization who were not happy with the speed in which he was being promoted.

There were those still hanging around that believed Stephen to be the same soldier he was years earlier. They could not believe that he could change. Their personal attacks and name calling were no longer working; in fact, they were surprised when Stephen started returning the favor in their direction. Stephen grew in favor, gaining the confidence of his senior leadership, while those same leaders were losing confidence in those who were in positions superior to Stephen.

Shepherd surveyed the scene unfolding before him, with a mixture of both happiness and sorrow. The fire ignited in Stephen' heart had worked; he had changed his life and modified his focus. Shepherd was joyful, thanking God that Stephen was starting to realize his potential to see a future, to take action into becoming the man that the Lord wanted for him. Yet, He was also sorrowful. Stephen was moving further away from the Lord, failing to see the work that He was doing in his life.

Stephen was becoming obstinate, aggressive, and brash. His newly discovered courage to retaliate at those who attacked him was improving his confidence in himself and his own ability to overcome obstacles. His deep held resentment towards his father and those that disrespected him in the past was coming to the surface, and it was not pleasant.

Stephen had become resolute in his desire to succeed, for himself and his family. His primary motivation was to prove others wrong and to make sure they knew that they were wrong. He was becoming a rough and tough soldier, but he was hurting everyone around him as a result, including his family, the same ones that he thought he was working for.

※

Hanau, Germany, April 1993

IT WAS A PERFECT SUNDAY. The sky was a deep blue and the weather was wonderful, a beautiful day and Jamie was feeling exhilarated. She had just left a great church service and was walking back to the apartment she shared with her husband, pushing the baby carriage with three-year-old Chad sitting comfortably inside. He could walk but it was just easier to use the baby carriage rather than drag him along the one-mile walk.

As she entered the main entrance to the apartment, she paused to catch her breath. Their apartment was four storeys up and, for some reason, there were no elevators installed. "Why don't Germans believe in elevators?" she asked herself for the nth time. She would make the four-storey climb with son and carriage, just as she did many times a week, complaining within.

She asked herself for the hundredth time, "Why does Steve always insist on keeping the truck, the only vehicle they owned? He never goes anywhere and it would make things easier for me." – but she loved him dearly just the same.

"Chad, stand here while I fold this up, OK?" she said to her son as she pulled him out of the carriage. He just stared at her; no response. At three years old, he was a good kid, who always did as he was told, a blessing in the midst of all the mess she had around her. Several minutes later she completed the long and dreadful climb up the stairs, holding both the hand of her son and dragging the baby carriage up. As usual, she was exhausted and prayed that Steve would be in anything but a bad mood.

She opened the door and he was at his desk playing a game on his computer – typical of him on Sunday afternoons. He rarely did anything else. She wished that he would spend some time with Chad and play with him.

"Hey, how was it?" he asked her as she placed the carriage in the corner of the hallway.

"It was really nice," she responded, "the pastor had a great teaching on how to love and…" she tried to finish but he cut her off.

"Awesome, but remember what I always say. That church stuff will never run our lives; it stops at the door, right?" he said curtly.

"Yes, I know, you remind me about that every week," she replied thinking, "Why does he always do that?"

Then he started up again, "I support you going to church because I know you like it; but if Chad ever says he doesn't want to go anymore, he stays home."

"Yes, something else you tell me every week or so," she replied coldly, and then felt bad about it. He ignored her as he usually did and went back to playing his game on his computer. He would focus on his game up until dinner, consumed in his own world.

Jamie looked at him and tears started to build up in her eyes. She walked as quickly as possible to their bedroom so that he could not see her, presumably to change her clothes, but also because she would cry.

"Lord, please help me to love my husband more. I don't know why he ignores us but I desire his attention and love in return. Lord, I call peace upon this household, even when I don't feel like it, in Jesus' Name. I am calling my husband saved, in Jesus' Name. I call him blessed and I bind the devil from speaking through him. I don't like the words he uses and they are not allowed in my house. The devil is NOT ALLOWED in my house, in Jesus' Name. I call down the fruit of love on my son and a prosperous relationship between father and son. I pray all this in Jesus' Name."

Jamie had reconnected with Jesus Christ two years earlier when her husband was deployed to Saudi Arabia in support of Operation Desert Storm. Her prayer life and Christian walk were still maturing; she was learning a lot about her heart and the Truth that can be found in Jesus Christ.

"Lord, I pray on behalf of my husband, in Jesus' Name. He does not know You but I know there is space in his heart for You. I ask

that you help me soften his heart and get to know the life that can be found in You. I love him, Lord, and never give up on him."

She knew, without a doubt, that nothing was going to pull her away from Jesus – not even her husband. He may say that Jesus would have no part in their life but He most definitely did in her life. And since He was in her life, He was in their family's life. And since He was in the family, He was in her home. Steve may not believe it, but she was adamant that her husband would be saved.

THE WOMAN WAS WALKING, alone in her thoughts but enjoying the feeling of the presence of God. Her spirit was on fire and she was in love with Him beyond measure.

Her thoughts meandered from thanksgiving in the Spirit to the thoughts of the sheep, her husband, and his antics in trying to put her down. "Shepherd told me with this would happen; I just had not realized how hard it would be," she told the Lord. She knew that the Lord loved conversation, not religious platitudes and legalism.

"However, Father, thank You for giving me a strong husband. He knows what he wants and he is going after it. Thank You for sparking a new drive in his heart to ensure that I and our child are well taken care of. Thank You for seeing to his promotion and success in his military career.

"Thank You, Father, for what you are doing in our lives. Father, I simply ask that You not give up on my husband. I see things in him that he doesn't recognize yet. If I see it, then I know You can see it as well. However, Father, please give me the courage to continue, the ability to wipe away his remarks to me, and a strength of will to move forward.

"Father, finally, please put upon his heart the desire him to spend more time with his son. His child needs a father; he needs his father. I pray all in Jesus' Name. Amen!"

Shepherd's eyes were always on Jamie because He was with her. *"Oh lovely bride, the Lord hears you and He loves you. Know that you are the protective covering for your husband in this period. Your love for him is not unnoticed by your husband or the Father.*

*Through your love as a believing bride of Christ, both your husband
and your son are sanctified and your son is clean and holy in His
eyes. Patience, My little Sister; you will experience a long season
but your patience will be rewarded. This the Lord promises. Your
faith will make your household complete. In Jesus' Name."*

HANAU, GERMANY AND FT. BENNING, GA: AUG 1993-JAN 1995

STEPHEN' MILITARY CAREER WAS SKYROCKETING. He
pinned on his Staff Sergeant stripes in August 1993, placing him
two ranks above those that he had been peers only eight months
earlier. His supervisor was transitioned into another unit and Stephen
assumed the leadership mantle of the section. This made several
that had been around for several years angry. They still considered
Stephen a screw up and his promotions undeserving: how could they
forget what happened three years earlier in Saudi Arabia? For his
part, Stephen used his Desert Storm experience to push him.

Stephen was fully aware of these opinions, but they didn't bother
him. In fact, these opinions served to inspire him further – he found
it thrilling. And then, in late 1993 a military reduction in force was
announced and Stephen's career came to a screeching halt, tossing
everything into question. Stephen began to doubt his future once
again. His specialty was being retired from the army inventory. He
had three months to consider options that the Army had given him
and he hated all of them. If he failed to choose one, he would be
discharged from the Army. He wasn't ready to get out of the military
yet, and this aggravated him. The Army had once again taken control
of his life, and he hated it.

A month after the RIF was announced, Stephen' Company
Commander called him into his office. "SSG Remington, I know
that you aren't happy about what is happening. Have you made any
decisions?"

"No, Sir, I feel let down. I worked hard and now the options the
Army is giving me don't make sense. They don't match who I am
or who I want to be."

"I figured," CPT Smith offered. "So I have been in discussions with the Battalion Commander. LTC Ford and I would like to suggest that you consider Officer Candidate School. We think you would be a welcome addition to the Officer ranks and, we would like to see you come back into the Aviation Corp. What do you think about that?"

Stephen was stunned. He had never considered becoming an officer: this came out of the blue. This would be a very significant career jump if he were to apply and be accepted. In a flash, Stephen was inspired once again; this was a way that he could take control back. But he had his fill of aviation and was not sure that is what he wanted to do. After a few seconds, he answered, "Well Sir, I never thought of that being an option. I'm humbled and flattered that you and the BC would think of me in that regard, thank you. I do, yes, Sir. I think that OCS would be a good fit for me, but I am not sure Aviation will do it for me."

"Well, think about it, Staff Sergeant. Either way, know that you have the full support of the BC and I. In fact, we have already written our letters of recommendation." He reached into a desk drawer and handed Stephen a file folder. The paperwork for OCS, along with the letters of recommendation was contained within.

"We even pulled the application together for you. Here you go, SSG Remington. I have no doubt that you will be accepted and I have no doubt that you will make a fine officer. So, let me be the first to say, 'Welcome to the ranks, Stephen.'"

Stephen had to focus in order not to tear up. "Thank you, Sir, I sincerely appreciate this." He stood up and saluted CPT Smith who saluted back, "Dismissed, Stephen!"

"Yes, Sir."

The summer of 1994 was an extravaganza. Stephen was accepted to attend the Officer Candidate School and he would be branched into the Army Signal Corp.

In January 1995, Stephen would finish his Officer training and pin on his gold bars; he was now a Second Lieutenant. And, to make it better as well as awkward, his father was there. While Jamie would pin a bar on one shoulder, Stephen' father would pin on his other bar. His emotions were mixed.

But he did it! He had achieved more than he'd ever imagined. And his dad was there to watch and participate in the promotion that Stephen used to prove to his father that he was wrong: "I am worth it! I am not a mistake, and there is an organization that wants me, the US Army!"

⌗

STEPHEN AND SHEPHERD WERE WALKING ALONG the same lake shore where he had watched his wife walking with Shepherd earlier. However, in his world, the water was dirty with debris floating on the surface. Stephen glanced around the land-based surroundings noticing that there were at least some...positive changes? He had noted some color earlier but now he could see where the color was coming from.

He could see tiny leaves starting to sprout from the twisted branches of the trees, and small patches of green grass were trying to force their way through the earthly sludge. The path was still littered with the sharp obsidian but his shoes appeared to be newer with thick soles. The sky was dark but there were more stars breaking through the atmosphere. But, more notably, was the fire, which had moved back to the mouth of the cave he could still see through the trees. It also looked like the fire was larger and brighter – which was comforting.

Shepherd was standing nearby, allowing Stephen time to take in the surroundings. He could tell that Stephen was thrilled to see some positive changes.

Finally, He spoke, *"The reflection in this world you see is perseverance, discipline, focus, resoluteness, loyalty, insightfulness and ambition, amongst others. However, this world is still contaminated with negative attitudes of bitterness, anger, hatred, boasting, greed, meanness, ruthlessness and one sin that is above all – pride."*

Stephen lowered his head, unable to look at Shepherd. Even though this was in reference to a life lived 25 years earlier, he still felt a degree of shame at his behavior. "Yes, Sir, I know. Even though I've repented for my behavior to both God and my wife, as well as forgiven myself, I still feel a degree of guilt. And I know I carried those traits with me for years which are reflected in many ruined relationships."

"Oh, you don't need to feel guilty, Brother; the Lord has forgiven you as has your wife. The fact that you still carry a degree of guilt

indicates that you have not fully healed from your past behavior. So, let's deal with that now, shall we?" Shepherd offered.

> *"Father, we lift up Stephen to you right now, in Jesus' Name. He is still carrying around feelings of guilt and remorse from his past conduct. These are things, Father, that he has already repented of and we know, because Your Word says that You have forgiven him and wiped this past behavior from Your memory. Lord, he also recognizes that with faith in Your loving hand he can wipe this blemish from his heart and out of his mind. It is OK that he remembers the past as this is his testimony. But his past should have no bearing on his conduct today.*

> *"Lord, we are still working through this Wilderness Project and there is yet more to be revealed and experienced. His conduct weighs heavily on his conscience and it will impact his ability to be open to what is still to be revealed. We both know that in Your great mercy You have not only forgiven, Stephen, but You have healed him, in Jesus' Name. Amen."*

Stephen could feel a burden lift off his shoulders. He had prayed this before, or something similar to it, but there is something about including the Holy Spirit in it that makes it more powerful.

Shepherd smiled. *"Yes, Brother, let it go. I can see your shoulders lifting and a blemish removed from your heart. From this point forward, you will need to remain diligent and steadfast in guarding your heart. If you aren't careful, that burden can return."*

A few seconds passed, *"Now, we need to discuss one of the greatest gateways to sin that was impacting you: pride. Tell me what you know about pride."*

Stephen had studied this in the past, "Pride is mentioned in the Bible somewhere between 49 and 58 times depending on the Bible translation. By most accounts, it is considered the original and most deadly of the seven deadly sins, because it perverts humans into believing they are equal to or superior to God. It serves as a gateway to other sins such as lust, envy, anger, and greed amongst others."

SHEPHERD NODDED IN APPROVAL. *"Awesome! And what is the antithesis of pride?"*

Once again, Stephen did not need to think, "Humility."

"Yes. The Lord says in James 4:6 that God opposes the proud, which is quoted from Proverbs 3:34, but that He also gives grace to the humble." Shepherd added, *"Do you see where pride was operating in your life?"*

"Yes, Sir, and I had plenty of warning signs, too: conflict, unmet needs, disparaging others, bragging, and doing things that I knew were wrong," Stephen admitted.

Shepherd nodded in agreement, *"OK, explain."*

"I was creating a conflict of interest in my home the way I treated Jamie and her faith. There would have been quarrels and fights, if she had ever decided to fight back at me – which she didn't. I felt that I was right and she was wrong. Even if I supported her going to church, it was cursory at best. My position was also one of control: I was in control and nothing else was. This was one of the negative side effects of my Desert Storm experience, I think."

"I agree. You can find scripture on that in James 4:1-2, where you coveted control and, if you didn't have it, or believe you lost it, it would anger you. This is a false sense of self-sufficiency, by the way...Well, good! What else?"

"Even with my worldly success, there was one thing that I wanted above anything else: I wanted the respect of others, and solid relationships. But other than my family, relationships all came and went, normally with my military change of station moves. I knew, or strongly suspected, that my behavior and attitude were the cause. With each fleeting relationship, I would become more bitter until I finally gave up in the idea of true friends. I thought friends would make me happy and since I could not easily make friends, I grew more and more unhappy," Stephen shared.

Shepherd reflected on this for a moment. *"I agree. Your issue was your self-centeredness. There were people that entered your life, but it was you that turned them away because you were trying to make yourself happy, thereby dominating the relationship. From God's viewpoint, you were placing your relationships with men above a relationship with Him; and God is a fiercely jealous lover. You were cheating on God because you wanted it your own way, flirting with the world at every opportunity.*

"Well, Stephen, you are doing well. What else?"

Stephen raised his eyes at Shepherd, grinning, "Straight to the gut, just the way I need it."

"The Lord knows your heart, Stephen. He knows what you need and He knows how you will receive it. But it's better to get it from Him, the true Judge, than from yourself, or others."

"OK. Anyway, as I grew in the ranks, I became cocky. I was also learning who was in my court and who wasn't. If I felt they weren't for me, then I would become their largest critic, complaining that they could never meet my standards. If I wasn't complaining about them, I was mocking them and making fun of them, oftentimes in their face. I was becoming more and more intimidating. I knew it, accepted it, and reveled in it. People were intimidated by me. Oddly enough, because of this I was typically rewarded with favor, helping me to accomplish many complex missions, and cutting through a lot of red tape. I learned to use this to my advantage but at the same time I grew to hate myself more and more for it," said Stephen, calmly appraising the situation.

Shepherd nodded again. *"No disagreement, Stephen. While you were growing professionally, you were simultaneously devolving spiritually. You figured out that you could not critique someone without raising yourself up to the position of 'chief critic.' You weren't keeping the law: you were sitting in judgment on it. That self-hate you mentioned was actually your spirit working to get your attention to stop. But your behavior became a part of who you were, eventually becoming what people expected of you. And that, challenged you spiritually and professionally for many years. A review and meditation of James 4:11-12 is a good scripture reference for you...So what else?"*

"I often bragged of my accomplishments, many times under the presumption that I was trying to help others get through a challenge in their life. However, in my heart, I was touting my resumé and the hurdles I crossed over while pumping my own chest. This is exactly what I did with my father when he pinned my Lieutenant bars on me when I received my officer commission. In my heart, I was showing him that I had control, not him. I did this, not him. I was telling him that I accomplished this, even after he had demoralized me. I wanted him to know that I did this despite him and that he had no part in it – at all. I may not have said anything to him verbally, but this was rolling through my heart and mind. My heart was definitely in the wrong place," Stephen confessed.

Shepherd was stoic and neutral, not really smiling but not show-ing any signs of being upset either. *"Recognizing the impurities of the heart is a key ingredient to healing the heart. You did not come to these realizations of your own accord; you were awakened to these truths because He revealed them to you. Praise God! Men need to wake up and realize that they are not masters of their own destiny. They can either follow the destiny God has ordained for them or they can follow a false destiny that the world has for them. But follow they do,"* and then He smiled, patting Stephen on the back once again.

"And this, My Brother, is the man you are today. A man that still struggles with past behaviors, but a man who recognizes who he is in God. You learned, perhaps later than you would have preferred, but you learned that when you come near to God, He will in turn come near to you. And when you humble yourself before Him, He will in turn lift you up. Hallelujah! Glory to Our Father!

"Brother, during that time of your life, you were on a path full of pride, trying to set your own course. Even though you knew, in your heart, that you ought to behave one way, you chose another, believing that it would somehow come out OK. You felt that you were smarter than everyone else around you – unless they had your personal respect, anyway. You were procrastinating in not doing the good that you knew to do – until the bad behavior consumed you, became a part of you. The result was that you could no longer see the man you were supposed to be; that man was unrecognizable to you. You knew that you needed to be different; you just didn't know who that different person was. So, you continued to live your life the way you knew how: being arrogant, brash, manipulative, and so on."

Shepherd then added, *"And yet, you somehow continued to find favor in your career. Other men would have fallen. Why do you think that is so?"*

"You know, since my born-again experience, I have gone back and forth with the Lord on that. I think my personal opinions on that question are blurring the truth that the Lord is trying to tell me. I was very obviously operating of my own accord, doing my own thing, not listening to God, much less seeking Him. Biblically speaking, the Lord had every right to ignore me."

Shepherd completed Stephen' assessment with the following: *"For the unbelieving husband is sanctified through his believing wife…It was because of your wife, Brother, the one given to you by God. But your pride never allowed you to see it. You thought you were in control, while, in fact, she was believing in God to lead you. Your wife was believing in the Lord Jesus and she was saved as well as everyone else in her household. It was her faith that saved you."*

CHAPTER 20
A HEART DIS-HEARTENED

"Let all bitterness and wrath and anger and clamor and slander
be put away from you, along with all malice.
Be kind to one another, tenderhearted, forgiving one another,
as God in Christ forgave you."
(Ephesians 4:31-32, ESV)

AFTER HIS OFFICER COMMISSION and basic officer training, Stephen was fortuitous enough to fulfill his first assignment for on the Islands of Hawaii – Oahu to be exact. Usually reserved for the US Navy and a large contingent of Air Force, for a US Army soldier, it was a dream assignment – a Tropical Paradise.

His first position was to serve as the Signal Officer for the 3rd Squadron, 4th Cavalry – a unit that Stephen immediately fit into based on his enlisted experience. The position was normally slotted for an Army Captain, two grades above Stephen' current grade, but it was an assignment he was able to jump right into.

Shepherd marveled at how the Lord was regularly able to craft such things. He was making sure that the sheep was placed in positions that would best utilize his strengths and capabilities. But then, the Shepherd looked downcast: "The sheep continues to experience the Creator's love and grace; yet, he is still bitter and full of resentment because of his past."

The position Stephen was filling was being vacated by another signal officer that had earned him a poor reputation. The unit immediately loved Stephen simply because he wasn't "that other guy."

The wolf, that "thing" that we have not heard from for a bit, was still operating in the sheep's life. He had found a way to manipulate the sheep's newfound drive, strength, ingenuity, and discipline into a force that set the same expectations on those that would report to him. If his soldiers showed an ounce of weakness, they were sure to incur the wrath of their leader.

At home, Jamie and Stephen were very fortunate to find a nice house to rent in a community called Mililani. After four years of living in military housing in Germany, they had decided that they would do whatever it took to always live away from the installation.

Shepherd continued to spend time with Jamie, guiding and working with her to help her understand and move in the role of His Spirit. He helped her manage the forces in her life that were discouraging her, as well as assist with spiritual operations that provided her with the strength and encouragement she needed. But it still wasn't easy.

Jamie was good about telling Stephen weeks in advance of any special activities happening, so she had told him about the Easter Service at the church she had found. "I might be a few hours late getting home that day," she had told him.

"OK, thanks for letting me know," he responded.

"Go with her, Stephen," Shepherd whispered to him.

OAHU, HI, APR 1996

IT WAS THE DAY BEFORE EASTER SUNDAY and Stephen decided that he would attend the church that Jamie had been attending with Chad. "Hey, Sweetie, I will go to church with you on Sunday, if that is OK?"

He could see that Jamie was stunned, "Really? You want to go?"

"Sure, it's Easter. Why not?" He knew that this would make Jamie happy. She had been asking him to go since she had found the church a few months earlier.

"It will be a different kind of service, just to let you now since it's Easter. They will also have communion," she told him.

"That's fine. Communion is when you eat a piece of bread and drink a shot of wine, right?" he asked.

"Sure. There's more to it than that, but yes, that is the part that I know you are familiar with," she laughingly told him.

"Cool! Let's do it!"

Stephen didn't know it, but Jamie's hopes had just leaped forward. By this point she had been praying for him for several years. "Is this the moment?" she hoped.

The following day, they arrived at the church dressed in typical Hawaiian fashion. Shorts, t-shirts and sandals were the norm for attendance in Hawaii, and they fit the profile.

The service was a message about the crucifixion, death, and resurrection of Jesus Christ. Stephen was rarely fully engaged; he did not really believe in the message. He was willing to recognize that Jesus existed and was a man with a lot of charisma and a message for that particular time, but not that he was actually the Son of God and rose from the dead in whatever number of days.

The pastor was five minutes into the service.

"The question before the house is very simple. Did Jesus really rise from the dead? Can we know for sure? Acts 1:3 says there are 'many convincing proofs' that Jesus Christ rose from the dead. What are those proofs? And can we trust them?" The pastor paused for a few seconds as he scanned the crowd, and then he continued.

"As we begin our investigation, let's start by simply looking at the facts as we have them in the gospel accounts. Here are seven pieces of evidence surrounding the events on that Sunday morning in Jerusalem in AD 33."

Stephen listens as the pastor says something about the Roman guard at Jesus' tomb and the stone that had been moved away from the tomb itself. The pastor then lists out some items that Stephen can barely hear. Finally, the pastor makes mention about the appearances of Jesus after His resurrection.

"Whatever!" he thought to himself. "The message so far is partially interesting." But there was nothing shared that changed his mind.

THE PASTOR CONTINUED.

"We tend to forget what it was like on that first Easter morning. It is worth asking ourselves: If we had been there, would we have believed or would we have doubted? Or to put the question another way, what would it take to convince you that someone you loved had come back to life after being dead three days? Suppose it was a close friend or family member and you saw them die? What would it take to convince you? Or is there any way you could be convinced? Rising from the dead is not a common thing. At best, it hasn't happened for centuries.

"If I just saw a man in front of me that I had just seen crucified three days earlier, that would be evidence enough for me," Stephen thought. "But there is no way that could happen. I can't believe these folks have faith in this phony fairy tale," he said rolling his eyes.

The service continues for another half hour and then the pastor prays and dismisses the church. After a few minutes, the pastor is making his way to the rear of the church from the podium and walks up to Jamie.

"Hey, Jamie, good to see you, praise God! How are you today?" he asks.

"I'm doing OK, thank you for asking, Pastor. Can I introduce you to my husband, Stephen?" looking at Stephen with love in her eyes and then back to the pastor.

"Absolutely! Hey, Stephen, I am so happy that you are here today. We just love Jamie and Chad. It has been a blessing getting to know her and have them in our lives," he tells Stephen.

"Glad to be here, Sir. It's good for me to be here and see what Jamie and Chad are involved in. The people seem nice," he responds.

"Yes, Sir, we have a wonderful and blessed congregation," he says.

Jamie jumps in at the pause and asks to be dismissed while she goes to get Chad from the youth group. "I'll only be about five minutes. I'll be right back," she says.

"OK, Sweetie, I'll be around here, somewhere that you can find me."

Jamie thanks the pastor, turns and walks away.

"Stephen, we truly love Jamie and Chad. She is full of the Spirit and really loves God. Thank you for allowing us to spend time with her every Sunday," the pastor warmly says to Stephen.

"Sure. I know she loves coming here. She loves church in general," Stephen replies.

"Well, my marriage was in trouble as well before I came to the Lord. Been about twenty years and it has been a thrill ride ever since."

Stephen' heart stopped for a second…and then that familiar angry feeling popped up. He suddenly felt…offended and disrespected. The shape of his eyes immediately changed as what the pastor said began to sync up.

His voice changed. "Who says my marriage is in trouble? Our marriage is just fine. It's because of people like you who make presumptuous statements like the one you just made that keeps people away from church. And I want you to know, Sir, that because of you, I will not come back to this church, or any church for that matter," he stated very curtly.

Before the pastor could even respond, Stephen turned and walked away. He walked outside to the parking lot but waited in an open area so that Jamie would see him when she came out.

Ten minutes later, they were in their Ford Windstar minivan, driving back to their house in Mililani. During that drive, he shared his experience and, while not directed at Jamie herself, he ranted about the statements that were made.

Whether he cared or not, Stephen had just shot an unpleasant arrow into Jamie's heart. She knew he wasn't yelling at her but she felt just as responsible, as if she had said those things herself, even knowing that Stephen took it the wrong way. She cried herself to sleep that night – again!

SHEPHERD PLACED HIS ARMS around Jamie to comfort her, while she cried into His shoulder. "I am sorry I failed," she sobbed. "I was so excited when he told me that he was going to church. I don't know what happened!"

"It's alright, My Sister. You are not responsible for his heart or the condition of his soul. Let peace operate in your spirit. Know this and let it rest in your heart: it may not seem like it now, but you should rejoice in these sufferings because they will give you added strength and endurance for what is yet to come. Maintain peace in the hopeful expectation that the love of God will, someday, pour into his heart like the river of living water it is," Shepherd said softly and tenderly.

"How much longer am I supposed to endure this?" she cried.

"As long as it takes, My love. The Father said, 'Believe in Me,' so, we are to believe in God and not allow our hearts to be troubled. Your husband will join the flock; this much the Lord has 'revealed.'"

Shepherd illumined her heart to pray for Stephen again, just as she had been doing every day for seven years.

"Lord God, Your word says that You chose us before the foundation of the world to be holy and blameless in Your sight. Lord, my husband is living contrary to Your word. He has chosen to walk in the way of sinners; Father, help him. May he come to the end of himself by knowing the truth that is found in Your word. Save his soul from the lies of the enemy. Show him that Jesus is the way, the truth and the life. Lord, I bless Your name, for You are doing something new in his life. In Jesus' name.

"O Lord, thank You for Your unconditional love. It is because of this great love that I live in the freedom that Jesus has given me. Thank You for opening my eyes to the truth that is found in Your word. Lord. Thank You for rescuing me from the kingdom of darkness into the kingdom of your Son, Jesus. But, Father, I am so heartbroken because my husband is lost. Continue using me as Your vessel to preach to him the gospel so that he will return back to Your family. In Jesus' name.

"God, I pray that You send Your Holy Spirit to convict his heart. Prepare his heart to once again receive the gospel of Jesus Christ. Let him know how much I love him and how much You love him and the great sacrifice You made at the cross. Lord, we thank You, and we honor You. In Jesus' name, we pray, Amen."

This time, rather than just vanishing, Shepherd remained with the woman until she was sound asleep.

As Jamie was crying on the shoulder of Shepherd, Stephen was still wandering, lost, disoriented, dizzy with everything that the world was throwing at him. He was growing more belligerent and hostile, embarrassing even himself.

Stephen was operating in fear, worried that someone or something was going to completely derail his aspirations; yet, ironically, he wasn't even sure what his aspirations were. Shepherd kept an eye on his wandering spirit. A few months ago, Stephen was on a path that would take him to the River. Today, he took a left, wandering away from it once again. And the wolf was nipping at his heels the whole time.

❖

THE SHEPHERD AND STEPHEN were once again in the secret place. Stephen was starting to acclimate and adjust to the cycle of seeing visions in both the earthly realm and the spiritual realm. But the ones about Jamie impacted him the most.

"She reminds me periodically of how often and strongly she prayed for me over the years, but actually seeing it, for me, is powerful. She really went to war for me." Stephen wept, feeling his love for her increase – if that were possible.

Shepherd smiled and nodded. *"Yes, she was, and is, a true prayer warrior, but even she could not understand the power of her prayers and the strength of her faith. She stood firm, deeply rooted in Him and in the promises of His Word."*

"I had not realized how much I'd hurt her, leaving her disappointed and heartbroken. Yet, even in the midst of that chaos, she never relented, never gave up," Stephen observed.

"Oh, she was challenged, Brother. You are seeing her prayers on behalf of you but you are not seeing her prayers of complaint and bitterness; those are between her and the Lord. She almost gave up, a few times," the Shepherd confided. *"You lashed out at the pastor, and missed an opportunity to reconnect with Jesus and his redemption and salvation at the cross. We don't need to revisit how it made you feel. But what did you see?"* He asked.

"I saw a man struggling with his identity, a man who knew there were problems with his marriage, while also not wanting to address them. The pastor was reminding me of my failure as a husband and a father – and I didn't like it. I saw a man that was worried but was not willing to deal with it."

"Yes, Brother. Your pride had taken a firm hold on you, taking your insecurities hostage and not allowing you to let them go. If you could have washed away your insecurities, you would have been able to deal with your shortcomings as a husband and a father. Your pride was causing you to be immature and short, which is why you

were hostile and defamatory towards others. This is why pride is considered one of the most severe of sins, a gateway to other sins."

Shepherd paused for just a few seconds. *"But here's the good news, Stephen. You now have a gift and an ability to see this behavior in other men, men who have allowed their pride to control them. Not only that, you now know how to talk to them based on their maturity levels. Your experiences have trained you to be an expert in how this will destroy their lives, while also serving as a living example that it does not need to be that way. Do you know how valuable that is to the Lord?"*

Stephen looked down, embarrassed by the compliment, but also hiding a burden. "But I still do things that indicate I still have pride operating in my life today. It bothers me and I don't like it, but even that hasn't seemed to stop me from operating in pride now. It makes me feel inadequate, a poor example for other men."

"Ah, but Brother, today you know the difference. Today you hate that sin. Today you are working with the Creator to fight against it, diligently working to cleanse it from your heart. Yesterday? Yesterday you didn't recognize it and didn't care when you did. Today? Today you strive to operate in love, compassion, and empathy; the Lord knows this and He is proud of you. Yes, you struggle with pride today – all men do – even experienced pastors. But, you are on guard against it, and that is what's important.

"Also, your pride was not only hurting you: it was hurting your wife, while also harming your son. The harm to your child is something the Lord will address later. But part of this heart wound quest is to understand that some wounds expand out beyond yourself and are transferred to others. You know this yourself based on your relationship with your own father. Your wife and son were placed in your care, your responsibility, and some healing was necessary to pass through you and on to your family. This was partly done when you were born again, but it was fulfilled when you later acknowledged this before your family and asked for their forgiveness.

"When you accepted Christ, the process was started to heal your heart from the blinders that were impeding your ability to see pride when He showed it to you. Once you saw it, you were able to deal with it under His guiding hand," Shepherd explained.

"But, there is more for you to see; this journey isn't over yet. You had forty years of bad learning, poor judgment, and a hateful

heart that need to be dealt with. While there is some immediate cleansing once you are born again, it can still take time to remove all of that bitterness, wrath, anger and slander, to reach that point where you are consistently kind, tenderhearted and forgiving – not only of others, but of yourself, just as the Lord Himself forgave you."

Chapter 21
SHOT THROUGH THE HEART.
BUT IT'S OK.

"Behold, children are a gift of the Lord,
the fruit of the womb is a reward."
(Psalm 127:3)

"... husbands..., live with your wives in an understanding
way,..., since she is a woman; and show her honor
as a fellow heir of the grace of life,
so that your prayers will not be hindered."
(1 Peter 3:7)

AFTER SERVING A LITTLE more than a year with the cavalry squadron, the Squadron Commander decided to place Stephen in a platoon leader position for one of his ground troops. This resulted in an outcry from the current platoon leaders – those positions were reserved for Armor Officers. They were insulted that the commander believed that a technology officer could do the same job as they.

"This is crap! It's insulting!" one of them told Stephen to his face. "No offense to you, man, but you are a signal officer, not armor. Does the boss think that we can't handle it, so he has to reach into another branch?"

The wolf was nearby, taking advantage of the situation. *"Go after him, Sheep! Don't let him insult you like your father did, or all of those other jerks in your past. Look where you are and where they are. You are better than them."*

"How is that not insulting, Brother?" Stephen responded. "Do you think that I, the person, can't do the job? Disregard my branch, look at me, Stephen. Also, I didn't ask for this. The boss pulled me into his office and told me what he was doing. And I happily accepted; didn't really seem that I had a choice, to be honest."

Stephen continued to curry favor with leadership and some of the best positions as far as career advancement was concerned. Yet, ironically, he would regularly complain to his wife about...well... everything! He just could not find joy and happiness.

"I hate it; it sucks!" he would tell his wife. She in turn, was getting tired of hearing it; it was tearing her down.

When the Commander of the Signal Battalion learned that one of his signal officers was being slated for a ground troop position, he used his authority and immediately reassigned Stephen to the Signal Battalion to serve as one of his platoon leaders. Stephen later learned that two of the squadron ground troop platoon leaders had complained to a more senior signal officer – resulting in Stephen' immediate reassignment. The result was, in January 1997, Stephen would be given one of the hottest sought-after platoons in the organization, providing tactical and strategic communications for the Division Main Headquarters when deployed.

Shepherd was also watching the event unfold. *"This is where the Lord has placed you Stephen. Honor the commitment, but also honor your wife, your son, and your daughter."*

By the time Stephen was assigned to the Signal Battalion, his platoon had been preparing for several months for a deployment to Australia; he had a little more than thirty days to catch up. Making the mission more complex and personal for Stephen was that his wife was pregnant with their second child...and her due date was the week before Stephen would deploy.

This complicated an already complicated situation in their marriage. And the wolf laughed as he watched the situation play out.

But Shepherd represented the heart of the Lord, and the Lord loves His children. Over the woman and the sheep, Shepherd sang: *"The Lord is my rock and my fortress and my deliverer, My God, my rock, in whom I take refuge; My shield and the horn of my salvation, my stronghold."*

"It will be OK,*"* He declared.

OAHU, HI, FEB 1997

STEPHEN WAS PREPPED AND READY to deploy on what he believed was going to be one of the best peace time missions of his military career. In two weeks he would be deploying for a planned thirty-five-day mission to Australia. His equipment was already enroute via ship; the paperwork was completed, and his soldiers were eager. First Lieutenant Remington was ready to go. But there was just one problem.

The second child of Jamie and Stephen, a daughter, had an expected due date of 18 February, but Stephen was scheduled to fly out to Australia on 25 February. This meant that he would leave his wife seven days after the birth of their daughter Keri, leaving his wife with not only a newborn baby, but now her parents as well, who had decided to visit for the birth of their granddaughter and who could be just as needy as a newborn.

Stephen was stressed as he contemplated his situation. Does he ask his commander to let him remain at home with his new baby and help take care of his wife and their six-year-old son Chad? Or, does he honor the military commitment and deploy to Australia, which would be a once-in-a-lifetime mission – not to mention fun? His inner struggle was real, but his priorities were out of balance and he knew it. He hated that he wanted to go on the Australia mission when he knew that he needed to be committed to his wife. He hated himself because this should not be a struggle, the answer should be obvious. "Why do I keep getting placed in these situations?" he complained to himself.

Jamie and Stephen had tried to talk about it but Stephen was leaning heavily towards the mission to Australia. He never discussed it with his commander as he was non-committal and fighting his heart. Jamie tried to share her views with Stephen but he wouldn't listen. "If you leave, you will be leaving me with a one-week old baby, our six-year-old son, and my parents. You know that my parents are not easy to deal with. That's not fair!" she argued.

"What am I supposed to do? My platoon was tasked with this mission before I was assigned to it as platoon leader. I've only been in the unit a month! What kind of picture do I send if I ask to be excused from this mission?" he would reply.

In his mind, he had nothing to do with it; it wasn't his fault. He didn't ask to be assigned to the signal battalion, much less that particular platoon. Nor had he asked to go on the Australia mission. It was thrust upon him by others. It wasn't fair.

However, Jamie was still distraught.

"Your mom is coming to help you, Jamie," Stephen would say.

"You know that she can't help. She can barely help herself; she can't even get around much," Jamie protested.

Stephen was aware that her mother had health and weight issues that hampered her. And her dad, well, he would spend time with Chad; he loved that kid. Stephen would remind Jamie of this, while knowing that her dad wouldn't do anything around the house. "Your dad will pretty much take care of Chad. He may not do much around the house or with our baby, but at least Chad will be off your hands."

Jamie shook her head in disgust. "Yeah, sure. And I will be stuck cleaning up after them and my mother, on top of taking care of the baby. And then I have to handle my own physical and mental issues that come after giving birth."

Stephen thought he understood it all, but he didn't. He was too blinded by the opportunity laid in front of him on this Australia mission. He had decided that the mission was more important to him.

Keri was born at the large pink military hospital on the island of Oahu on 18 February. Jamie wanted an epidural before Keri was born but the doctors didn't get to her on time and their daughter was born naturally – and painfully – for Jamie.

There were also complications. Keri was born with the umbilical cord wrapped around her neck and she had swallowed some of the material in the birth canal around her as she was being birthed. After the doctors cut the cord and resuscitated Keri, she was immediately taken to another room and placed in an oxygen tank – that's what Stephen considered it anyway.

Keri would recover and be allowed to go home on 21 Feb, three days after her birth. Three days after that, Stephen left the house for Helemano and the beginning of his Australia mission.

Jamie's parents would arrive the next day and Jamie would have to drive to pick them up at the airport, while dealing with physical issues of her own. In her mind, Stephen was oblivious to it all. In Stephen' mind, Jamie didn't understand the position he was in – that it was not his fault. They were two forces competing on opposite ends of the rope in a game of tug of war. In Tug of War, someone has to lose. In this case, they both lost.

Stephen' thirty-five-day mission ended up lasting forty-two days as the 25th Infantry Division forgot to plan the return flight for the soldiers. Jamie's parents would remain on Oahu for two weeks before heading back home, and, as Jamie had predicted, she did most of the work the entire time they were at the house.

Jamie was relieved when Stephen finally made it home and was able to spend time with his now six-week-old daughter. However, something was lost between them, and it would take time for proper reconciliation.

THE WOLF WALKED THE PERIMETER of the dwelling while the Shepherd wrapped his arms of protection around the sheep and the woman. *"Be of strong courage and good cheer; your children will require it."*

There was a distance between Stephen and the woman, but there was also relief, that they were together once again. The woman was flustered but she was committed to honoring her husband.

Stephen loved his daughter and held her tight to his chest. While there, she was resting her head on his chest, with her ear placed over the heart of her father, giving her the peace and the loving trust that only a father can provide. And she rested.

Off in the corner, the firstborn son would observe. He, too, loved his new sister but he was also envious of the love his father showed to her. He wanted that; he craved that; he wanted more; no, wrong – he needed more. "I love you, Daddy! Can you love me?"

BACK IN THE SECRET PLACE, Stephen fell to his knees leaning forward with his head on the ground and his hands over his head. "Oh, Lord, please forgive me. Oh God, why was I like that?" he cried as he rocked his body back and forth.

Shepherd stood back. He and the Lord had worked to prepare Stephen' heart ahead of this vision as well as the next one, but the distress of his past behavior was still strong.

"Oh God, Jamie, I am so sorry! I was so selfish!" Stephen began to shake, losing control and having difficulty catching his breath. This lasted for a few minutes before Stephen was able to breathe again. And then he remembered the final words that his son silently cried out to him at the end of the vision. He collapsed once more.

"Chad, I am sorry, Son! I loved you!" he cried out again, beginning to shake uncontrollably as he had previously. "I was a fool! I was stupid!" he screamed out, slamming his arms on the ground, unable to sit up.

Shepherd kneeled down beside him on his right side, placing his left arm across Stephen back, not a hug, but a slight pull to let Stephen know that He was there to comfort him. *"It's OK, Brother, repent, let it out. Release that stronghold from your heart."* With the exception of his born-again experience, Stephen cried like he had never cried before, and this went on for many minutes.

When the shaking finally stopped and Stephen' cries slowed to quiet sobs, Stephen lifted himself up to his knees while the Shepherd gently helped him up. "I was such a horrible person," Stephen confessed.

Shepherd shook his head. *"No, Brother, you were not. You were misled, deceived, and foolish, maybe. And, while it is true that you were ruled by pride, your heart was always for your family, even when your flesh was being selfish.*

"You may have once been foolish, disobedient, deceived, enslaved by your own lusts and pleasures while wallowing in envy and hate, BUT, when God revealed Himself to you, showing His kindness and love, He saved you. Not because of anything you did, but because of His mercy. He, Brother, He washed away your sins and gave you a new birth and a new life through the Holy Spirit.

"Also, we shall never forget the power of repentance and forgiveness. You repented to your wife and she forgave you. You repented to your son and he forgave you. You repented to your daughter and

she forgave you. You repented to God, and He forgave you. That is powerful, Stephen. You are free from any regret, guilt, or remorse. Don't waste that forgiveness. Allow the love of forgiveness to flow through your veins and into your heart. Don't let your past conduct hold you hostage, but allow it to motivate you, to push you, to show others what love can do. Show others that, no matter their past, true and heartfelt repentance can save you from a future enslaved to sin. Don't allow any of that to go to waste. You are NOT a victim, Stephen; you are a victor in Jesus' Name."

"But I can't forget my past; it hurts."

"Stop it!" Shepherd sharply admonished him. *"It's true that you may not forget, or perhaps some things in your life will bring some of those memories back to the surface. But you are stronger than any pain, any hurt, and any grievance you hold against yourself. Because you, Stephen, have the Holy Spirit inside of you and He is stronger than any negative forces and influences. You are the light and salt of the earth, Stephen, and no darkness can exist in that environment. When those ill feelings re-surface, you have the authority to cast them aside by the blood of Jesus. Your heart is troubled by this no more, in Jesus' Name. Receive it, Stephen! Receive it now! NOW! In Jesus' Name!"*

The power and authoritative voice of the Holy Spirit fell upon Stephen, causing him to once again fall to his knees. Clasping his hands together and raising them towards heaven, he declared in a loud commanding voice, "I receive it, in Jesus' Name!" He began to weep again. "Thank You, Lord, for Your mercies. Thank You, Lord, for Your saving grace! Thank You, Lord, for saving a wretch like me." He then lowered his head into the palm of his hands and laid on the ground with his knees in his chest.

"Stephen, in your early years, it was your father that wounded you; you blamed him for this for many years. But then, one day, you cast that aside and started blaming yourself, and this, Stephen, this is what wounded you the most – yourself. You are no longer burdened by the sins of your father; you actually let that go many years ago. The truth is that you are burdened by your own sins. This is what the Lord wants to reveal to you." Shepherd lowered his voice to a sound that was soft and soothing, like music in Stephen' ears.

"You started this quest to understand how your father wounded your heart and how to heal from that. But it wasn't his wounding

that you needed healing from: it was your own wounding. Your own regrets, your own actions as a father and as a husband. Your own behavior and attitude towards others. Stephen, this has nothing to do with other people in your life or from your past: this journey has been about you. Do you see that now?" And Shepherd looked him squarely in the eye.

"Yes, Lord!" he cried out.

"Stephen, you say that you have forgiven yourself, but your heart doesn't believe you. You've repented often enough, but your own past still haunts you. Stephen, it is actually easy to forgive others...but forgiving oneself? That is harder. The Word says that "If we confess our sins he is faithful and just and will forgive our sins and purify us from all unrighteousness." You may have confessed your sins to Him, but you did not have faith in His ability to live up to His part of the bargain because you were placing your own abilities above His."

*"**A PRAYER FOR FORGIVING YOURSELF** can work, but your prayer must be uttered with true sincerity and faith in Him above faith in yourself. You don't have to empty your heart of your shame before you come to God. You should come to God exactly as you are with that shame and allow Him to take it! Don't feel like you have to be perfect and don't think you need to forget your past. You just need to learn to let go of that guilt that you are carrying around."*

"I understand and I believe, but the struggle is..." Stephen started to say, but Shepherd cut him off before he could finish. *"The struggle is in your head, Brother; let it go. Use that energy for good and use that energy to love others who are suffering the same thing,"* He commanded.

"Take as much time as you need. I will be around if you need Me. But this day is yours. When you are ready to move forward, when you are ready for peace, when you are ready in your heart, to let it go – ask Him, for He is waiting for you. And remember, there is no such thing as perfect people, but the Lord is always there to keep perfecting you." And with those words, Shepherd turned and walked away, slowly vanishing until he wasn't there.

Stephen, still sitting upright on his knees, closed his eyes, meditating on what had been revealed to him, and relaxing in His presence. His skin felt like it was on fire, but in a good way. He focused on scriptures that he had memorized while picturing his earlier vision of Jesus in his mind. Keeping his eyes closed, he remained there as his heartbeat slowed, his breathing relaxed. He moved on from mentally reciting scripture to worship, praising God for opening the eyes of his heart to the truth of his heart wounds.

"Thank you Father. Praise You, Lord! I love You, Jesus! Thank You! Thank You, Father!" Stephen continued repeating words of thanks, waiting in hopeful expectation for what he needed to say to God.

Then Stephen heard these words enter his heart, *"Indeed there is no one on Earth who is righteous, no one who does what is right and never sins."*

"Father, I come before You humbly today asking You to help me forgive myself. I have looked back on my past way too long. And I am tired of feeling like I could have done better every single day. I feel oppressed by my past and my sins. The devil wants me to remain in my guilt and shame instead of embracing Your love. I feel the weight of the harm I have caused, and I am ashamed.

"You say that nothing can separate me from Your love. Fill my mind with Your light, and chase out the darkness. Free me from the guilt and pain of my past. Deliver me from this long night in my soul. I really could have made better choices, but I cannot go back and change them. The only thing I am in control of now is my future. I cannot live life backward. Lord, right now, I release all my anxiety into Your hands. It is not Your will that I hate myself for all the things that I have done. Lord, when I hate myself, I hate the very person that You have created.

"Father, not only do I pray for myself but I also pray for other people that are struggling with forgiving themselves. Unforgiveness makes us feel insecure. Help me, and others, accept ourselves for our shortcomings because Your Holy Word states: 'For all have sinned and fall short of the glory of God.'

"Lord, as You cleanse and purify our hearts from unforgiveness, help us understand that 'all of us have become like one who is unclean, and all our righteous acts are like filthy rags.' God, imperfection is a considerable part of our earthly nature. Help us accept our flaws and know that You love us in spite of them. In Jesus' name, Amen."

As Stephen prayed those words, he could feel his heart change, like it was lifted in the air to a state of constant levitation. He felt euphoric and at peace with everything around him. Stephen remained in that state for many minutes, enjoying the loving embrace of the Lord. "Thank You, Father."

Stephen opened his eyes and slowly stood to his feet, shaking the debris from his knees. He looked around his environment, trying to gather his bearings and shake the wooziness from his head. It was still dark, but he could see more stars as well as a full moon. Under the light of the moon, he could see the path extending further into the trees, pulling him forward.

With his heart lifted and his eyes open, Stephen started walking in the direction he felt called to walk. "I'm ready, Lord." After a few more steps, there was a sudden snap and Stephen was gone.

CHAPTER 22
ANOTHER LAMB IS PROVOKED

"Children, obey your parents in the Lord, for this is right.
Honor your father and mother, so that it may be well with you,
and that you may live long on the earth."
(Ephesians 6:1-3)

However...

"Fathers, do not provoke your children to anger, but bring them
up in the discipline and instruction of the Lord."
(Ephesians 6:4)

AS HAD BEEN THE PATTERN, the fox was once again passed from father to son. And, as with his father before him and his father before, the fox would use situations to create dishonor between father and son, to spike the relationship and make it toxic for both. While the fox played with the son, the wolf and the coyote were with the father, doing their part to bring harm to the man, and hence, the family.

Stephen had moved on from his assignment in Hawaii and, in 1999, was assigned to Fort Gordon, GA. While most Lieutenants of the time only served in platoon leader positions for six months before being reassigned, he was given the opportunity to serve for a full year and had earned a reputation as one of the top performers. However, he had also earned a reputation for being mean spirited, egotistical, arrogant, and selfish. His journey across the wilderness was still taking him to the River the Father laid before him, but he was still far from it.

Now at Fort Gordon, an opportunity for a command had presented itself. Stephen asked for the command and was given it. While it was not necessarily on the career trajectory he had planned, it seemed the appropriate move at the moment. Stephen and Chad, now ten years of age, had been having conversations which caused great concern to Stephen. Chad was depressed and had no desire to make friends or build relationships. This is when the command had presented itself.

In September 2000, Jamie had given birth to another son, a ten-year age gap between the brothers, and a three-year-old sister stuck in the middle. Chad once again felt he was losing out on his father's attention, which was now focused on Samuel.

However, something changed in his mom and dad, the way they treated Samuel versus the way he was treated. They were speaking life over Samuel, positive words of growth, encouraging him, in a way that hurt Chad, making him believe he was being disregarded, punished. "It's not fair, "Chad often thought to himself. "They are always yelling at me, telling me about how bad I am doing at school; I'm a disappointment."

Chad had tried talking with his dad about it. "Chad, I understand, Son, and I am sorry. Your mom and I were very young when you were born and we were much less tolerant about things than we are now."

"But it's not fair. You let him get away with everything and I get in trouble for the same things. I hate it, Dad."

"Did you think it was fair when we punished you for things when you were little? I don't either, Son, and I am sorry about that; but, if it wasn't fair to punish you then, how could it be fair to punish Samuel now?"

"But it's not fair," Chad would continue to argue. He fought back tears because his dad always said that crying solves nothing and he would give him a hard time if he did.

"I know, Son. But as I said, your mother and I were very immature when you were born. She and I have grown since then," his father said conclusively.

Chad stopped at that point. In that conversation, what he heard was: "You were an accident and we should not have had you then."

WHILE HIS PARENTS DID LOVE HIM dearly, they would periodically joke with others that Chad's middle name was "Oops." And this is what Chad felt like, an "oops." This created an emptiness in his life, allowing the fox to sow in his parasite, who injected thoughts of "rejected," "unwanted," "unloved," and "not important." Like father, like son.

The saving grace was that Chad had Shepherd in his life, who was hugging him now, comforting him. "Why does he not like me? Why doesn't he see that I want to spend time with him? Why don't they want me?" he would cry.

"Your father is misguided, My child, but he does truly love you. He wants you to succeed and wants to spend time with you, but he is being misdirected and detoured through life right now. I know you hurt and so does he; he just doesn't know what to do about it and is not asking Our Father for instructions."

"But...," he would start before Shepherd would soothingly place his hand on Chad's heart. *"Oh, My poor Lamb, you know how to love and this is what is important. You love but don't feel that love being returned – and that hurts. His Word tells us that, no matter how a person treats you, including your father, you should continue to treat others the way you want them to treat you. Continue to love your father; he will come around. This is the hope I have for him, and for you."*

Chad looked away so Shepherd wouldn't see his tears. Shepherd continued to hold Chad in that loving embrace until he slowly faded away.

AUGUSTA, GA, MAY 2001

CHAD CONSIDERED HIMSELF BELOW AVERAGE, low in self-esteem, a boy who missed his father. He was slightly overweight and, while he was getting through school, he was a below average student by most standards. Even at eleven years of age, he never felt that his dad respected him.

On his part, he adored his father, a career soldier, who had recently taken command of a Company on nearby Fort Gordon. His father loved what he was doing, but it never seemed like he enjoyed being home. His dad would spend most of his time by himself, on his computer doing whatever he did, or reading books. He would also spend a lot of time in the garage building or restoring something, normally furniture.

Chad wanted his dad to love him but was generally ignored, apart from getting a laugh here and there occasionally, a movie, or eating out. But it wasn't enough. Chad needed more. He often wondered if his dad really loved him. But when he and his did spend time together, this is when he had his dad's undivided attention; and Chad loved it. But the time together was scarce. Chad was lonely and he had struggled with sharing this with his dad.

So, his grades suffered a bit, he gained weight, and his parents worried.

Recently, his dad had been stressed about things at work, Chad didn't understand any of it, but his dad would always be angry about something, upset at someone, complaining that something was not going the way it should. His dad would come home in a bad mood and avoid everyone. This would disappoint Chad because all he wanted was his dad's attention.

And then, the day came when his dad came home and the backyard was flooded with hundreds of gallons of water. His dad started yelling at him.

"Chad, what did you do in the backyard?" he screamed. It was his dad's eyes that hurt Chad the most.

"Nothing, I haven't touched the hose or anything in the backyard, Dad. I promise; I swear!" he cried back.

"I know Keri didn't do it or your one-year old brother. Why are you lying to me? We have water all over the backyard; there must be hundreds of gallons dumped out there," his dad yelled back.

Chad was sobbing at this point and all he could do was plead to his dad that he did not touch the water hose. After a few minutes, his dad stormed off to check hoses and faucets. His dad did not talk to him the remainder of the evening.

Chad ran to his room and cried for an hour. He couldn't cry in front of his dad. This would irritate him more.

"Why does he hate me? He blames me for everything. What am I doing wrong?" he cried to himself.

These thoughts would dominate eleven-year-old Chad for the remainder of the night; unfortunately, no answers came to him. He prayed that his dad would come to his room and check on him, but, then again, he didn't.

Things got harder for Chad two days later.

CHAD WAS IN THE LIVING ROOM when Dad came home, grumpy as usual. Dad went upstairs, changed out of his military BDUs and put on shorts and a t-shirt before coming downstairs to get a beer and head to the garage. At least, this was his usual pattern as he enjoyed wood working to relax before his mom made dinner.

"Hey Son, you're good today?" his dad asked.

"Yeah, I'm alright," he answered.

"That's good," as his dad glanced out the window into the backyard.

"What the heck!" his dad suddenly barked. "The backyard is covered in water again! Come on Chad – why?"

"I don't know, Dad, I didn't do anything," he insisted.

"Why are you lying? Just tell me. Be honest!"

"Dad, I have not touched anything. I don't know." He could feel the tears welling up. "Why does Dad think I am lying? Why can't he trust me?"

"Go to your room," his dad said angrily. "You're grounded for a week until you can be honest with me."

Chad could see his dad's anger building up and he started getting scared. "Dad is going to smack me," he thought. But he ran to his room crying, before his dad could do anything. "I didn't do anything," Chad screamed at him as his final parting words.

"I am getting the paddle and will be up to your room in a few minutes," his dad shot back.

At those words, Chad lost it. He felt betrayed – at least as from an eleven-year-old's point of view.

"I can't make him happy; I can't make him love me. I didn't do anything and now I am about to get paddled. It's not fair! Life is not fair!"

His dad couldn't see it during those moments, but he was losing the trust, respect and confidence of his oldest son. Needless to say, Chad received the customary two paddles to his behind that night. Chad cried for several hours before falling asleep.

The next day, the truth would be made clear.

Chad's dad came home on Friday and the backyard, once again, was fully flooded. However, this time there was something different. As his dad observed the backyard, he noticed that water was pouring out of a pipe near the bottom of the foundation of the house.

"What the heck?" he mentioned loud enough for Chad to hear. He then walked out the deck door to get a more up close and personal look. Sure enough, water was pouring out of the pipe and his dad knew immediately what was happening. Their water tank pressure relief valve was going off, blowing over a hundred gallons of water into the backyard.

Thirty minutes and a full inspection later, it was confirmed, sure enough, that the pressure relief valve on their water heater was going off. Not only that, it had become apparent that this valve had been going off all week and flooding the backyard with water.

Chad's dad was devastated and Chad could see it in his eyes. Even at eleven, he knew that his dad now knew the truth that he was not responsible for flooding the backyard.

But, an apology never came. Life simply moved on. Chad was acclimating to the condition that his dad did not care for him, and it pained him to feel that way. Chad was crying again, "Why don't you understand me?"

Later that evening, Stephen was sitting at his desk in silence. A close-up view showed that tears were streaming down his face. "What have I done?" he cried in remorse.

▥

THE WOLF WAS CELEBRATING. He really didn't have to do much – just a little nudge and the father's own flesh took over. The fox, standing off a short distance away, grinned at the wolf.

"Great job, but you're still a meathead," the fox joked. "I myself have been able to fill that empty void in the little lamb's heart with my parasite. His feelings of despair are taking hold."

"Good, you little ankle biter! Keep him that way because you know that the godlicking butt kisser is always around, intervening. He will sway him if you don't remain on guard," the wolf retorted.

They both wagged their tails in delight. However, the wolf was just as much a coward as the fox. They hated the light and most times, when Shepherd showed up, they would both run and hide in whatever hole they could find. But the wolf was stronger; he held more demonic power than the fox. If he could perceive doubt, fear, or unbelief in his prey, he could use that to walk in the shadows close by.

At this moment, Shepherd was glowing with the fully glory of God, His light keeping both demonic figures at a far-off distance. Shepherd was sitting on a bench in a marble hallway and the little lamb was sitting on his lap. His head was on the shoulder of Shepherd, who had his left arm around the lamb's back with his hand resting on his left shoulder.

"My little Lamb, My Child, God has given you a spirit of love and self-control. He loves you more than you know. Love will always protect you; you can always trust in love because love never fails. Your father loves you and your mother adores you. Do not resent them because of the attention given to your younger brother who requires necessary attention at his age. You are not forgotten, Child; He knows you."

The lamb was experiencing the greatest peace he had ever felt. He smiled...at rest.

SHEPHERD WAS SITTING on the same bench that He and Stephen had been using earlier in the journey. Stephen once again glanced around the environment; this was something that he had become accustomed to doing as a measure of the spiritual walk.

He could see more green in the trees as leaves were beginning to sprout and he could see more grass appearing from within the bleak landscape. The fire at the mouth of the cave was the same but it also looked like the sky was becoming grayer rather than dark, almost as if the sun was ready to show its face. The moon was still full and extremely bright and he could see more stars. He also noticed that the mist that had been blanketing the area was gone.

"Seems like a good sign." He knew that this represented him during the times of the vision and was not representative of him now.

"There is power in words." Shepherd said. "Both death and life are in the power of the tongue and they that love it shall eat the fruit thereof. What does that mean to you?" Shepherd asked.

Stephen answered, "It means that if I speak negative words or positive words, then my life will become like the words I speak."

Shepherd nodded, *"How do you think that works as we speak with our children and about our children?"* He asked.

Stephen and Jamie had shared a few conversations on this topic with each other. "If we speak life over our children, even if they are not around, then they have an excellent chance of living godly and loving lives. However, if we speak negative things to them, or about them, then we are speaking that power over them and they are likely to not live joyful and fruitful lives.

"Jamie and I recognize that over our own children today. We spoke lively and positive things to Samuel, and over Samuel, throughout his entire life, and he has grown into someone that is much more confident and assured than our other two children. We see that and recognize it now, but we completely missed it with our other two children. We do speak life over our daughter now, but that restoration does take time."

"Yes," Shepherd said. *"Scripture says a lot about words and how we use them either for good or for negative consequences. Proverbs 6:2 says, 'If you have been snared with the words of your mouth, Have been caught with the words of your mouth...' Proverbs 12:13 says, 'An evil man is ensnared by the transgression of his lips, But the righteous will escape from trouble.' Proverbs 12:18 says, 'The tongue of the wise brings healing.'*

"What people say can make the difference between success and failure – between good and bad consequences. I stated earlier that death and life are in the power of the tongue and they that love it shall eat the fruit thereof. This verse implies that those who enjoy talking must bear the fruit of that talk, whether good or bad. Productive words can bear a good fruitful harvest."

Shepherd then gave Stephen the punch he expected. *"You did not have a lot of positive things to say during certain parts of your life. And, like many parents, you failed to realize that your children heard those words and those words became a part of their lives. You were also not very nice in your choice of words with many of those that you worked with."*

Stephen nodded, "Yes, Sir, my wife and I can see that in the lives of our children both then and now. It's been a tough one for me to swallow personally. And with others, to be honest, I am still paying a price for that today as I destroyed a lot of positive relationships. I have requested and received forgiveness from some of them, but for others, I simply had to pray for forgiveness, and to forgive myself, as I don't know how to contact them. It's just not the same thing not apologizing face to face, or at least personally over the phone."

Stephen continued, "I have learned the hard way. The devil loves it when we talk negatively. It not only drags us down, but it gives a door to the evil one to continue us down that spiral. But, I can also say that I don't dwell on it as much as I used to; I just work harder every day to live by example, and be a role model to my children now. I still mess up from time to time as portions of that habit resurface occasionally, but the people around me know that I'm trying and working on it."

SHEPHERD NODDED HAPPILY. *"Yes, Brother. Now, when we speak positive things, the scriptures also show that you don't just glibly say things, but it has to be backed up by faith. Sometimes people say, "I'm going to be a millionaire, hah, hah, hah!" Or "I'm going to be President of the United States" or other such things. Those statements lack faith, hard work, discipline, and preparation. They fail to see that saying things is action oriented.*

"A hard concept for people to understand, especially for young Christians, men in particular, is that following Christ is not a magic formula, pushing buttons make things happen. It's not saying superficial words that have no substance because they won't hold up under the test of waiting for the answer. But scripture does provide principles to follow that will help Christians develop their faith and it does provide assurance that prayers will be answered. They will begin to see God's blessing come into their lives because they are planting and planning for a good harvest – and good fruit."

Stephen agreed. "Yes, Sir, change takes place with words, but they must be words spoken from the heart and with faith."

Shepherd nodded back, *"Too many times people pray the wrong way, begging God to do this or that. Too many times they conclude a prayer by weakly saying, 'If it be Thy will' when scripture already says, 'It is God's will.' Weak prayers like that are ineffective. The Lord's children must reframe their words with authority, assurance, and action. The power of speech, the power of words, puts a handle on things. People pray knowing that God has the answer to our needs."*

Stephen was fired up, loving conversations like this. "My wife and I have learned through personal and wondrous experiences that speaking it out in faith starts the process of bringing it out of the realm of the spiritual into the realm of the here and now. It breaks our heart when we hear people say, 'Oh, I just don't have any faith.' We want to yell at them to stop! What you just said is not scriptural. We have been given the faith we need. Romans 12:3 says, 'Everyone has been given the measure of faith.' Not a measure, but the measure. He meets our needs with our words of faith. We also know that Luke 17:6 says, 'If you have faith as small as a mustard seed you can say to this mulberry tree, be uprooted and planted in the sea and it will obey you.'"

Shepherd slapped Stephen on the back in happiness. *"Yes, Brother, all of this plays into the idea of words."*

"Ow!" Stephen said jokingly, rubbing his shoulder in mock pain.

"There is life or death in the tongue, be it with words said to and about children, workmates, or other family members. Or be it in prayer life," Shepherd concluded.

Shepherd paused for a bit, looking at Stephen in a particular way. *"Stephen, the Lord sees that your heart didn't react to your young condition in this vision the way you did the last time. How did that vision make you feel?"*

Stephen pursed his lips. "It hurt, Shepherd. It still hurts a lot. I remember that issue with the water heater and I remember crying off and on for a few days about how I'd treated Chad. I remember being so humiliated and embarrassed that I couldn't even look at him. This is why I didn't apologize for it until a few years later. However, because I sought forgiveness and received it, I am OK with it now. However, I can also remember dozens of conversations with workmates and soldiers where I hurt them. As a commander, an officer, I should have known better. But, this is something that I accept was part of my flawed character back in those days, and has nothing to do with my character today – minus the occasional slip-ups."

Shepherd slapped Stephen on the back again, this time because he knew Stephen would playfully react.

"Come on, man," and Stephen stated rubbing behind his right shoulder again.

"Yes, Brother, forget the past because the past does not define who you are today. You are a new man, with a renewed heart and a renewed mind. Absolutely, yes!" He said, slapping Stephen on

the back again, not as hard this time, and earning a look of respect from Stephen.

"Alright, Brother, we are coming to that critical point, to that moment in time where your life changed forever. But, before we get there, the Lord wants to visit another season of your life, a season of volatile change. But it was this season that brought you home, the season that took you to the River."

CHAPTER 23
THE WAY HOME

*"For I know the plans that I have for you,' declares the Lord,
'plans for welfare and not for calamity to give you
a future and a hope."
(Jeremiah 29:11)*

*"... for I have learned to be content in whatever
circumstances I am."
(Philippians 4:11)*

*"There is an appointed time for everything.
And there is a time for every event under heaven..."
(Ecclesiastes 3:1)*

THE LAST SIX YEARS for Stephen were a blur. It was a long season of changes filled with drama, violence, death, questions, doubts, while also with excitement, danger, adventure, and history. To go into detail, dear Reader, would make this telling too long, so we shall only recognize the highlights.

As seasons end, so do military assignments, and as these seasons change, so do the whims of the military. The Shepherd knew that this was the time for change for the sheep and his little lambs, a few more appointments before it was all said and done. One of these would require that the sheep revisit a location where his life had first been dramatically changed, the same location that the woman was running away from.

The sheep could smell it...the River afar off in the distance, the one that would take him from this blasted desert to a place of freedom and comfort. But, the wilderness journey would continue a little longer for him, bringing him to places both foreign and familiar.

The evil one lodged an attack against New York, killing over 3000 in a single battle that was part of a much larger and significant war that had been waging for millennia. Many sheep and lambs were slaughtered in that battle, but many more would perish in the years to follow. The wolf was jubilant at the master plan that his master had beautifully executed and stood bemused at what his master had yet to reveal.

After changing command at Fort Gordon in 2002, the family was reassigned to Aberdeen Proving Grounds. The new mission was to build out and support a new organization specifically tailored to fight and defend against future attacks across the homeland via weapons of mass destruction – at least the aftermath of such attacks. This required that the sheep become knowledgeable of intelligence gathered about the events that immediately followed the attacks of 9/11. He loved a challenge and this would prove fruitful.

Shepherd spoke, *"My Brother, can you not see how the Lord has been operating in your life? Can you not see that this was another assignment, ordained for you to be a blessing, to be honorable, above all, compassionate and graceful?"*

The sheep would be challenged in his undocumented capacity, a position off the books, to develop new technology, new communications capabilities, and new methods of operating in an environment that was predicated on chaos, extreme destruction, and massive casualty rates. Many would fight against him and the sheep would fight the system back, but without an ounce of grace or mercy for those that got in his way.

He would participate, from a distance, in the search for WMD across Iraq after the initial invasion, and support the communication of situation reports and updates to the White House. He would beat out dozens of others with top ratings from very senior military officials; yet, he was still inward bent and still carried that constant feeling he was messing up. "Let's see how this can benefit me," he would figure. But, even with success, he still felt like a failure.

In 2004, the family would once again move, this time back to where their life had started – Fort Campbell, KY. This would also bring the woman back home and to what she had been running from. However, just prior to this move, there was an earth-shattering moment in the life of the sheep, it was a word of praise that he had been seeking his entire life.

His mother and father had visited over Christmas of 2003. During that visit, in a short talk with his father, he heard words that he had long forgotten that he even longed for. "I want you to know that I am proud of you, Son," his father said to him.

"What just happened?" said the sheep confused, now bereft of the yearning that had consumed him for so long. How could something he so deeply wanted more than anything not bring the joy he expected? Because he knew that his desire was a lie, a façade of what he knew to be true. He was succeeding based on outward appearances, the way that his father had also been attuned. But the truth was that he still felt like a failure. His inward man was…empty.

"That's it, you cowardly sheep; move away from the River. Death is so much more pleasant than the life He is trying to give you," the wolf bayed.

"No, Brother, the wolf is wrong again. The Father knows your heart and He knows what you yearn for. That was the crack in your father's heart, a beacon of light, of hope for him. Your earthly father gave you what you wanted, but you have allowed the wolf to distract you. Listen to the knocking on your heart, for what lies beyond that door is what you have truly been seeking. That emptiness you feel is the place allocated for Him, your Savior, the True Lamb of God. Open the door and let Him in!"

"He's rambling, sheep – a mess of words that nobody can understand. You've seen a bible? Can you make any sense of it? He's speaking the same words found within it. Ignore Him. He's an imbecile!" the wolf snarled into the sheep's other ear.

Faking earthly success while hiding the pain of emptiness inside of him was the condition in which the sheep walked: dead and living at the same time. And this, my dear Readers, is when he began serving in the 160th Special Operations Aviation Regiment, side by side with some of the most elite soldiers that the US Army had to offer. He would stand in awe of their courage, strength, honor, and silent glory.

But, this assignment would also take him back to an area that had almost killed him both emotionally and physically more than a decade earlier – Ancient Babylon in Iraq.

"A time of reconciliation, Stephen. An opportunity to restore honor where you feel you had originally lost it." Shepherd spoke to his heart.

SEVEN TIMES OVER THREE YEARS Stephen would revisit that side of the world. Except this time, he would be more intimate and up close with violence and the most horrifying and vicious carnage that the enemy was capable of committing against the weak and helpless.

"That is the world the Creator made for you, helpless sheep. Who would make such a terrible thing?" the wolf sneered.

His oldest son would come to appreciate his own intelligence and resourcefulness, experiencing firsthand that he was able to get good grades in school and live with a servant attitude. And, of course, the opportunity for a driver's license and access to a car helped a little. But Stephen would make sure that his son could see that this ability had been inside of him the entire time – Chad just needed to see it for himself.

Nonetheless, even with the positive conversations and time together, Stephen would become more distant with his oldest son and his daughter. Only his youngest son would cry when he would leave for war, talk to him on the phone when he called, and give him a hug when he returned home. Stephen and his daughter were once close when she was a toddler, but even that had been lost.

"Brother, this is the difference between speaking life over a child and neutral or nominal words. Speak love and love will be returned," Shepherd commented.

In 2007, Stephen would decide that he was done; his military service was over. However, his motivation for retirement was not about time served because he would have happily served three more years. It was just that he had become disenfranchised with the war effort in Iraq. He witnessed events that shaped him, causing him to rethink what the war was about, while asking himself if it was worth it.

"Why are we here? What are soldiers dying for? Not for America, that much I am convinced of. And, it doesn't really matter what we do, whenever we leave, be it today or ten years from now, within six months after we leave, this place will burn again." His motivation was not political. It was his challenge in defining what the loss of life for all sides meant in the grand scheme of things. It felt... useless and meaningless.

But, it was the brutal savagery of the enemy that did it in for him. The degree of evil and senseless violence displayed in that part of the world would take generations, by his personal estimation, to cleanse and it was neither possible nor even the responsibility of America to do so. Not militarily, anyway. This belief came to rule his soul and Stephen felt he could no longer ask his soldiers to put themselves on the line for a cause he no longer believed in – so he retired.

"Witness the evil of man you ignorant sheep. This is their inherent nature; it is a part of who they are; who you are," the wolf pressed in aggressively. The wolf was sensing a change and knew that he needed to ramp up the lies, the deceit, manipulating Stephen to focus on his flesh and what it wanted to do.

This is why the details of these final years in military service are best left behind, my dear Reader. While likely the most dramatic and exciting of his twenty years of service, it was also the most horrific and vile period of the sheep's life...until the events of February 2011 – a story for another time.

"No, My Son, do not listen to the wolf, for his words are wrong and slanted. You may have been born in a spirit of sin but that is not what your spirit naturally leans towards. You are born to be free, due to His grace and mercy. It was He that died for you, the One that created you. You are created for something more. Yes, you did witness the evil of man firsthand, My Brother. Now you understand why it is important that we crush it. We must save every spirit we can before the unquenchable fire takes hold of them for eternity."

Shepherd continued, *"Now, take a right, My friend, and walk towards the River once more."*

This period of his wilderness journey is wrought with massive bolts of lightning and rolling thunder, along with heavy pellets of rain and hail that made travel very difficult and treacherous. Stephen may have turned away from the River earlier, but it was a diversion to walk around a large boulder sitting along his path.

STEPHEN HAD RETIRED. He was both excited and scared about what the next stage of his life would bring. He would be able to spend more time with his family; but he had to get established first. Then he would have time to spend with the family.

Shepherd could see that Stephen was on the hunt for something, but his focus was off. He said one thing with his mouth but his actions spoke something else entirely. Success sickness had overtaken him; a newfound energy drove him since his original motivation had been removed by the confession of his father, "I'm proud of you, Son!" And the wolf, seeing his opportunity, unlocked the door intended for another.

With sudden notice, a door opened in a far-off land and Stephen walked through it, leaving his family behind. However, the room he entered was not a fit.

Shepherd was listening to Jamie's prayer as well as the others who were in agreement with her:

> *"Lord, bring him home. The family does not need to move, we can sense it in our spirit that the time is not right. Open the doors, Father, that need to be opened and close the doors that are keeping him away. We ask this in Jesus' Name."*

Shepherd spoke, *"He has heard you, My Sister."*

Shepherd turned his attention to Stephen' heart, *"The Lord has a plan for you, Brother. And it does not include the calamity you will undertake if you remain. Leave. Go home. Be encouraged and have faith!"*

"Remember that other door, you sniveling sheep. I bet you it is unlocked. Try it. I think you will find it accommodating," the wolf urged.

Before the first door had been opened, the sheep had come across another door that he had previously thought was locked. Now he found it unlocked – so he opened it and walked through door number two. This took him to a completely new land, leaving his family behind once again.

Jamie continued her prayer where she had left off.

> *"Lord, thank You for closing the first door. Now Father, he still isn't home as another door opened that was not intended for him. We ask, in His Holy Name, that that door close and another door*

open that will bring him home. Thank You, Father for Your continued grace and mercy."

A month after walking through the second door, door number three opened for the sheep. But this one was different. This was the door that brought him back home.

"AArggh! Why did you have to do that, You blubbering interloper!" the wolf screamed at Shepherd. *"It isn't fair! You cheated!"*

"He is a child of God; he is not your plaything, wretched Wolf. As His Father, the Creator has a plan and laid things out for the sheep. The sheep is the one who decided, just like he decided on those other positions. The Lord knows his destiny. While he took two wrong turns to get there, any child will always find his way back. You would be smart to remember that, you vile creature!"

Shepherd watched over Jamie and her three little lambs. *"Keep praying, little Sister; your faith is working. Your endurance and diligence will pay off; He honors His promises. The time is getting near, a time of discovery for Stephen."*

Shepherd shifted his gaze to Chad, chasing the fox away that was haunting him. *"Don't cry, little one; his wilderness journey is almost over. Your father is coming home; and he will soon find the River that will take him to our Savior!*

NASHVILLE, TN, AUG 2008

STEPHEN WAS ON AN EMPLOYMENT ROLLER COASTER that had been going on for the last five months, and he was exhausted.

A year earlier, he had opted to retire from the military after twenty years of service. The truth was that he was tired of Iraq and had lost faith in the purpose for being there. Having been across the pond seven times since 2004, he no longer believed in the war effort. His retirement date was 1 August 2007 but he had built up so much leave time that his last day in the Army was the last week of March.

He had just been offered the position of IT Director for the Tennessee State Attorney General, a position he would start in late August 2007, but it had been a long and bizarre road getting there.

This position would be his third civilian job since leaving the military in April, just five months earlier.

Stephen had wanted to take thirty days to himself after retirement but the first company to hire him was based in Seattle, and the CEO that had hired him as a Vice President for Information Management had encouragingly requested that he start two weeks after he left the military. What made it more difficult was that he was living in Clarksville, TN, thousands of miles away.

He and Jamie had decided he would move to Seattle first and then Jamie and the kids would join him a year later. Chad had one more year of high school left and they didn't want to disrupt his studies during his last year. This tended to be good news because the CEO had not been completely honest with Stephen when she hired him. She had sold her company to another larger organization and this significantly larger company had a different plan for Stephen.

Stephen tried his best but after sixty days, it was obvious that what his new boss wanted from him was something that he could not provide, so he decided to resign. A few months previously, he had been offered another position as a contractor supporting a project with the National Guard Bureau in the Pentagon. He reached out to them, asked them if the position was still available; they said yes and he was re-offered the position. However, this position would require him to live near Washington DC, on the complete opposite side of the country from his family.

After leaving Seattle in late June, Stephen stopped off in Clarksville for a week, before heading off to Washington DC. The team being put together consisted of Stephen, another retired military soldier, and a retired Colonel. Together, these three were charged with putting together a strategic communication initiative plan for the National Guard Bureau (NGB). However, the boss of the team was a significant micro manager, which grated on Stephen' personality and his drive for control.

Then, just a few weeks after starting his position in DC, he was contacted by an IT Service Management organization based out of Nashville, looking to hire a Senior Project Manager. After interviewing Stephen on the phone, the interviewer, thinking Stephen would be perfect for the role, recommended him to his Vice President, who also completed a telephone interview. A few days later, the VP called Stephen back and invited him to meet with the Tennessee State Attorney General.

Two weeks later, Stephen was offered the position of IT Director for the Attorney General for the State of Tennessee, wherein he submitted his contract termination with the Bureau. So, by the end of August, Stephen was back where he had originally started five months earlier, in Clarksville, TN. Five months had passed, along with over 6000 miles and two job terminations. He was tired but he was also thrilled with the idea that he would not have to move his family. As the years moved on, Stephen liked to say that the wear and tear on his body had nothing to do with age – it was the mileage.

However, the toll on Stephen was nothing compared to the yo-yo effect on his family. While Stephen thrived on change, the constant stress of not knowing what was happening next had been wearing thin on his wife and oldest son, in particular, who was struggling with changes he saw in his father. Of course, Stephen' youngest son Samuel was thrilled that his daddy was back home.

Throughout 2007 something inside had changed Stephen, with seventeen-year-old Chad commenting to his mother, "What changed with Dad? He's not the same person he was before he left for Seattle – and I don't like it."

"I don't know, but we can pray for him and ask the Lord to help him find peace for whatever is bothering him. Yes, we can do that," she decided. With that, she and Chad knelt down together.

"Heavenly Father, I lift my husband up before You and pray for peace in his heart. Show him Your grace, Lord. He obviously has some things troubling him, and I ask that You conquer those worries and bring him peace. Help him with solutions where there is anxiety and doubt. Be the Lord of all things in his life. Thank You, Father, in Jesus' Name."

On his part, Stephen had convinced himself that he thrived on change. But the dramatic changes over the first half of 2007 had actually taken a toll in his soul, causing him to question his decision to retire from the military – and everything else about his life. In the military, he thought he knew who he was and why he was there, but since retiring, he no longer knew. Life had become…unpredictable. He was losing awareness of self and this was making him lash out more than usual, while being blinded to his own actions.

Stephen thought he was fine, but he wasn't. His character was changing, and not for the better in the eyes of those closest to him.

He had imagined what he and his family could do now that they were back together, things that they had not been able to do in twenty years. He felt free, but he also felt trapped and he didn't know why: this bothered him. He was surrounded by people but he also felt lonely, and he felt like a failure in everything.

His changing condition would cause his kids to become more distant, his wife to become more unsettled and fearful, and his heart more hardened. He was lost but did not recognize the new feelings and didn't know what to do about it. This made him more erratic, vociferous and domineering in his opinions and thoughts. And it was hurting his family and his professional life.

SHEPHERD SPOKE *what the Lord told him to: "Stephen, there is an appointed time for everything, just as there is a time for every event under heaven. You have experienced birth, but you have also experienced death. You have experienced home planting many times but you have also experienced numerous occasions where it was time to uproot your family and move.*

"You have experienced a time when you had to kill, but you have also experienced times of healing. You have cried out and you have laughed. You have learned when to speak and when to be silent. You have torn things down and you have rebuilt. And, you have experienced both war and peace.

"And what have you gained from all of that time you have spent, Stephen? You have spent a life searching for your identity and your purpose; it is now time that you find it. I see you, Stephen. Can you hear Me knocking on the door of your heart?"

"Sense the River, Stephen. Go to the River. I have shown you the way."

"Believe in Me, Stephen, I am the River you are looking for. I am the Way from the wilderness. With Me in your heart, out from it will flow the rivers of living water you have been seeking. I am the way to your identity and purpose. Deny me no further. Follow Me!"

Somewhere off in the distance, a rooster started crowing.

PRESENT DAY STEPHEN watched the vision of this season unfold before him like a deck of cards being shuffled, pausing at particular moments long enough for him to add in memories that he had long forgotten. But, it was when he heard the rooster crow that his heart started beating more excitedly. He knew what was going to happen next, causing his breathing to catch up with his beating heart.

Instead of meeting up with Shepherd back in the secret place, the vision slowly faded until he was completely surrounded by nothingness, darkness. Yet, he could hear a sound as if he were wearing a pair of headphones – crystal clear. He could hear the rush of a river crashing over rocks as it flowed downstream. He could hear someone walking across the water, the splashing of feet as they hit its surface.

And then he saw a light, growing larger and brighter. It finally reached a point where it was so bright, that he had to close his eyes and eventually cover his eyes with his hands. Even then he could still see a red glow through his folds of skin.

And then, he heard the tap-tap-tap of someone typing on a keyboard. He opened his eyes as he removed his hands and found himself in old but familiar territory – his old basement office.

PART 4

THE ROOSTER CROWS

CHAPTER 24
KNOCK KNOCK

"Be prepared and ready and keep the lights on. Be like men
who wait for their master and immediately open the door
for him when he comes and knocks. Blessed are those who
he finds alert, because he himself is going to take on the
role of servant and serve them while also allowing them
to recline at the table; he will wait on them. Whether it be
early or late, those that he finds as such will be blessed...
Be ready, for the Son of Man is coming
at a time you don't expect."
(Luke 12:35-38, 40, personalized)

Now the Lord is the Spirit, and where the
Spirit of the Lord is, there is freedom.
(2 Corinthians 3:17)

THE WOLF AND THE COYOTE *could sense Him coming. But*
something was different. "What is this?" the coyote asked the wolf.
"Knock, knock, knock...knock, knock, knock."
There was power in the air, something new, something personal.
As the seconds ticked by, so did His power summarily increase...and
then...they knew. Shepherd was not coming alone; He had Someone
with Him.

"Knock, knock, knock...knock, knock, knock," the sheep had been stressed for several weeks, a building emotional torment unlike anything he had ever experienced.

Shepherd materialized through the misty veil, but as the wolf and coyote had sensed, He was accompanied by a Being so bright that they could feel their skin immediately begin to burn by His very presence. This sent them scattering into far off shadows to hide.

"Him? Why did He bring Him?" the wolf and coyote howled together. They were completely blind now and their skin burned like fire. *"Where is our master?"*

"Knock, knock, knock...knock, knock, knock." The sheep began to shake, neither understanding nor comprehending what was happening.

Shepherd pulled out a sword and approached the wolf and coyote while the light turned and approached the sheep. The light lowered and caressed the sheep's heart, completely enveloping him.

Shepherd stood before the creatures and looked down at them. *"Your master hides like a coward just as you do now. Stay away in the name of the Messiah, the Holy One and the Way; for the sheep is ours. He is about to be given his options and a choice,"* He commanded.

"Knock, knock, knock...knock, knock, knock." The sheep began to tremble. Losing his strength and unable to stand, he fell to the ground and landed on his belly.

"He will fail," they replied. *"His flesh is stronger; it rules his mind and his body."*

"Come to Me, Sheep. Hear Me. Follow Me. Accept My love," the light spoke softly to the sheep.

"Knock, knock, knock...knock, knock, knock." The sheep began to sob.

"Stop the torment and stop the pain, My Brother. Take My peace, love, and joy," the light continued.

"Knock, knock, knock...knock, knock, knock." The sheep began to cry hysterically.

"You have been found wanting, My Brother, and you have led a sinful life. But, I have sought you out. You are forgiven but you must ask and you must make your choice now," the light stated with compassion.

"Knock, knock, knock...knock, knock, knock." The sheep couldn't breathe.

"Choose life. Choose love. Choose forgiveness and righteousness. Or, choose an eternal prison. Choose death; choose hate; choose condemnation."

"Knock, knock, knock." The sheep looked up with his eyes buried in cloudy tears and opened the door, "I choose ... "

░▓░

CLARKSVILLE, TN, SEP 2008

STEPHEN HAD BEEN SERVING the Attorney General for a year as his IT Director and had been in charge of implementing a major project at a cost of $1.2 million. Ten months of effort and the project was coming to a successful close. They had built a brand-new data center in the basement of the building, had replaced and upgraded over 350 computers, upgraded over 100 software applications in their portfolio, and migrated the entire AG Office to the new technical environment from the antiquated state-owned network.

It had been very complicated and stressful, but also selfishly rewarding. Many of the young attorneys in the office had taken to calling Stephen "Moses," hailing him as their leader into the promised land "of technology."

"If they only knew the details of what it had taken to get there!" he thought to himself.

Two months earlier, Stephen was able to promote one of his staff from help desk technician to systems analyst on a very constrained, and impossible, payroll budget. Yet somehow, his now vacated help desk position was immediately and miraculously filled via a chance phone call with another IT Director, serving another state department, who was recommending an IT intern. "Odd how that happened," Stephen remembered thinking.

In the beginning of his tenure a year earlier, Stephen had told another of his staff members that he didn't think he was a fit in the revamped organization Stephen was building. Stephen was encouraging him to look for an opportunity with his full support and endorsement. The tall Jamaican didn't bat an eyelid. Showing no concern at all, he simply smiled and said, "No problem, Stephen; thanks for telling me," which had shocked Stephen. He had expected a little drama, but Owen had shown no fear or concern at all.

A month later, Stephen ended up promoting the same Owen to Manager, thanks to an opportunity that had suddenly opened for Stephen. He was thrilled that he was able to keep Owen as they had developed chemistry together.

Now that the stress had pretty much gone away – "mission complete" as Stephen liked to say – he now had time to ponder all that had been accomplished. And then…the voices started, out of nowhere. And Stephen began to feel…frightened.

Those feelings had started almost two weeks ago. It was now labor day weekend and Stephen was sitting at his desk in his basement home office – and he was trembling. "What is happening to me?" he cried.

Over those two weeks, feelings and emotions had been increasing, tormenting him: a sense of dread, fear, failure. His emotions were flaky. But today, this was different. He was shaking and couldn't stop. Tears were forming, he had no idea why. His heart was racing and his breathing was stressed.

Powerful. Intense. Insane? Stephen was afraid to say anything to anyone, including his wife. It was as if his entire life was falling upon him all at once, all of the bad stuff, the weird stuff, the humiliation, the failures.

Today, he couldn't shake the voices. *"You are going to die, Stephen…You are not who you think you are. You have been in denial of your true self."* It was as if the voices were centered in his heart and trying to get into his head.

"You have not been a nice person…they are going to figure you out."

"You are going to prison, Stephen…you are going to pay the price for everything you've ever done if you don't submit to who you really are."

"Your family will fall right after you…"

"Stop! Why won't it stop?" he gasped hysterically. He didn't want his voice to carry upstairs.

Stephen began to cry uncontrollably. "Why would I go to prison? What have I done? What am I doing wrong?"

Off in the corner, Shepherd observed as the One spoke to Stephen. *"As in the days of Ezra, when the king gave him authority over his people, it had been proclaimed that for those who fail to observe Our Father, judgment will be placed upon them and strictly enforced, whether it be death, banishment, confiscation, or even imprisonment.*

"You are heading down a dark path and are going to lose every-thing, Stephen...even the love that some still hold for you," the voices continued.

Stephen could no longer function. His shaking body turned into violent trembling and he could not stop crying. "I don't cry," he thought to himself as he began to cry harder.

"Come to the One that can save you, Stephen. Hear Me, Stephen; I am the Father's voice. Let Me be your Comforter," the Light spoke.

STEPHEN WAS SUDDENLY overcome with overwhelming grief and guilt, sensing the horror of who he was. He felt terrified about what he started to sense was going to happen to him.

"Why is this happening now? What have I done?" he continued to ask over and over. The same fears in his head about what was going to happen to him kept repeating.

The Light continued speaking to Stephen: *"The Creator of the heavens, who spread out the earth and gives breath and spirit to people, has called you, Stephen. In righteousness He will hold you by your hand and watch over you. He is your light in the darkness, Stephen. He can open your eyes and He can bring you up and out of the prison, even from the darkness of the prison you are in."*

"What do I need to do?" Stephen could barely breathe. He stood up from his chair to see if he could get more breath into his lungs.

His knees buckled and he crashed to the floor behind his chair. He got up to his knees and crawled to a brown futon couch in his office. From there, Stephen cried more than he had ever cried in the last thirty years.

"Help me!" he cried out.

Mucus poured from his nose and something thicker than water poured out of his eyes with his tears. His lungs were burning as they fought for air that he was struggling to take in.

"You must choose, Stephen. Choose Jesus. Choose Life. Choose Truth. Choose Life. Choose Joy. Time is short for you, Stephen; you must choose now."

Stephen couldn't see it but a serpent had risen from the ground and was slithering towards him, but neither the Light nor the Shepherd stopped it.

Stephen felt a heaviness in his body with almost every joint feeling the stress of pain as his body continued to heave and shake violently. He thought he was going to pass out.

"You are feeling the Lord's Presence, Stephen; that is the heaviness. Go to the River that you have been seeking, the one that will lead you from the wilderness. The stronghold of unbelief is being removed as you begin to see who you have been, as well as who you are intended to be."

The wolf and the coyote could not see, but they could hear everything. "Nooooo!" they squealed. They were so blinded by the Light that they couldn't see the snake crawling closer to Stephen, just a few more feet to go. The snake was there for a purpose: therefore the Light did not touch him.

"Sense His light enter your heart, Stephen. Walk into the River. He can cleanse all unrighteousness in your life, Brother. He is merciful. He is compassionate. You are forgiven for everything."

The heaviness in his body began to push pressure upward towards his mouth, his eyes, and his ears. Taking off his t-shirt because there were was nothing nearby, Stephen heaved globs of mucus from his throat and his nose. As the heaviness dissipated, his ears popped and the pain across his entire body began to subside.

The snake was now in striking distance as it raised its head, opened its mouth, and bared its fangs.

The tears were still flowing as his breathing normalized. "I know what I have to do." And with that, Stephen entered the River. "I believe!"

A BLOODIED FOOT APPEARED from out of the Light and stomped on the snake's head, smashing it as the snake's body quivered and trembled until finally, the writhing ceased and it simply vanished.

"Your identity is now with Me, Stephen," the One told his heart. *"Your purpose, your reason for being will be made clear to you as you follow Me."*

His body suddenly felt relaxed but he was physically and emotionally exhausted. He continued to sob on his knees, with his head between his folded arms on the futon couch.

"Thank You, Lord!" he cried out.

"Praise God! Another lost sheep has been found!" Shepherd proclaimed to the heavens.

Later that afternoon, Stephen walked up to his wife, who was sitting on the couch reading. "We need to go to that Christian bookstore you like. It's time for me to get a bible."

***

THE WOLF AND COYOTE HOWLED out as they, too, vanished, but Shepherd knew they would be back.

"Praise the Lord God Almighty!" Shepherd proclaimed. He walked up to Stephen and gave him a hug. "Welcome to the family, little Brother."

Shepherd knew that His time with the sheep would be different now that Jesus Christ was present in his heart. He would be led by the Chief Shepherd now. For the Spirit was now infused with his spirit: they were now one.

But, Shepherd also knew, because the Lord had revealed it to him, new and life changing struggles would soon come upon Stephen. Nevertheless, because the Lord had sought him out, Jesus would lead him through the trials he was about to enter and be a part of.

"You need to get into His Word, Brother," Shepherd instructed. "Build upon that foundation. Soak Him in, learn what His voice sounds like. Listen to Him. He is your Guide and your Teacher."

Shepherd pondered the future of the sheep. "Thank You, Yeshua. Stick with Him, for We know that the future struggles will be real with this one, harder and more difficult than anything he has ever dealt with in his earthly life so far."

Jesus walked back through the dim veil, leaving Stephen with the Spirit to allow them to get to know each other, to recover the time lost since Stephen had been a child.

***

PRESENT DAY STEPHEN AND THE SHEPHERD appeared back in the secret place to the snap of crackling thunder. It all happened in the space of milliseconds, but the environment around them was immediately more beautiful than it had been since the quest had started. Stephen stood in awe as he looked around. "This is it! This is The Garden!"

Stephen noticed the lake nearby but it was different. The water was pale blue in color but also crystal clear and Stephen could feel the ebb and flow of life in it. He walked to the edge of the lake and peered into it, seeing a glow emanating from its very depths. "This isn't a lake," he discovered. "This IS the River; the River of Living Water."

Shepherd stood back joyful, as He gave Stephen this moment. As Stephen stared into the River, the words and actions of his past came back to him, everything he remembered before and everything that he had forgotten until experiencing the visions. He was at peace with all of it.

Shepherd finally spoke. *"As the Spirit of Truth reveals more to you, you will begin to realize more and more about what it means when Jesus says, 'I am in you and you are in Me.' You were made complete that day, do you remember?"*

Stephen nodded, "I remember that odd sensation of dread and despair, the voices condemning me to prison, which I thought was odd. I remember how I had been knocked to the floor and had to crawl to the couch, when I swear every bit of liquid in me came out of me.

"And I remember how, twenty minutes later, I felt completely the opposite of that: peaceful and tranquil. I had a new confidence in me, so I finally knew what I had to do and who I needed to reach out to."

"That's because you were made complete and you had no more condemnation in you. You are no longer an orphan. However, you do have to go back to the cross daily, sacrifice yourself daily, and deny yourself daily or that condemnation can return," Shepherd reminded him. Then He asked. *"What do you think you learned in this quest? And what do you think the Lord wants you to do with that knowledge?"*

Stephen looked back into the water again, soaking in the life flowing from it. "I learned that as children, we inherit things from our parents, or parental figures. They stick with us whether we realize it or not. I can now see where traits were passed on from my grandfather to my father and then on to me. And this happened, even though my father and I, I in particular, did not want it – even though we thought we had rejected it.

"But I also know that the victimization is strongest when we don't realize who we truly are. We don't know our identity and we don't understand our purpose. And, with this void in our life, we will blame everyone for our ills and problems, even blaming ourselves. This creates a never-ending circle. And, in this shell of victimhood, we stagnate in the things that we want most: to be recognized, loved, and appreciated.

"The peace and tranquility I felt that day in 2008 was just as overwhelming as the remorse and guilt I had felt previously. It is difficult to describe but I can say that I most definitely knew it."

Shepherd nodded, *"What do you now believe your identity and purpose to be?"*

"I used to think that my identity was a husband and father and that I had a duty to provide for my family. I was also a soldier, honor bound to my peers, my superiors and my soldiers. I had wrapped myself in this identity and, when I felt like I was losing it, that would destroy me.

"The military had become my church with soldiers being the congregation, and this kind of saved me from a life that would have killed me if I had not joined the military. It was kind of like when I joined DeMolay after leaving that drug addled lifestyle as a teen-ager. However, I had allowed this identity to block the true vision of who I truly was."

"AND WHO ARE YOU?" Shepherd asked.

"I now know that my true identity is a son of the Father, already made complete and whole, already at peace and filled with the power of the Spirit. My purpose is to live with Him, live like Him, and share Him with everyone. It is selfish to hold that back from others that need Him."

Shepherd looked at him patiently, *"So, as you reflect on this journey, what do you believe was holding you back? Why did it take you forty years to finally accept who you were in Christ?"*

Stephen paused, looked off in the distance at the vegetation, the forest, the cave, the sky. "I had forgotten who I was. I was blinded to my true identity and even though I was searching, I was not searching in the right place. I was clinging to what was false, thinking that the world would tell me who I was and what I was supposed to do.

"My blindness caused me to blame others, my father mostly, for what I believed to be wrong with me and I had allowed this hatred to fester and grow inside of me like a cancer. I eventually forgave him thinking it was enough. But it wasn't. I thought this journey, that this quest, was about learning where my father had wounded me so that I could heal from that, but I was completely mistaken. I was wrong."

Shepherd stood there, waiting for Stephen to finish composing what his heart was telling him.

"It was me. I had spent thirty years wounding myself, blaming the world for not being fair. I wounded myself every time I lashed out at someone, every time I neglected them, every time I behaved in a way that was arrogant, cocky, and superior. I wounded myself daily as I allowed my pride to further contaminate me, drinking in every success in an effort to prove to others that I was better than them. But I was also consuming every failure, allowing each failing to take me a foot deeper into my own pit.

"I knew something was wrong because, each time I succeeded at something, I still felt like a failure. And it was tormenting. I spent so long doing what I felt compelled to do that I was allowing the world to make me into something I was not intended to be.

"I now recognize that our journey is to learn about and believe who we truly are, a person destined to be raised from the pit into the realm of light that is the presence of Jesus Christ. And this comes through relationship, not a religious duty.

"This quest has shown me that the only way to heal and to identify with who I am supposed to be is to let go of every identity I carried around for forty years. I need to release every offense made against me, which was much easier than the offenses I made against myself and the ones I made towards others. Forgiving myself has been the most difficult struggle for me. I thought I knew this, yet I was shocked that I did not realize I was wounding myself and not healing."

Shepherd added, *"And, Brother, your self-inflicted wounds not only blocked your vision, they created vain and naïve imaginations and thoughts about other things that you thought you could use to fulfill you or save you from the troubles in your life – including people."*

"Wow!" Stephen thought, "He's right. I did use people, even if I treated them fairly and responsibly, to give me some sense of fulfillment. But it was also serving as a distraction. I had not seen that before."

"I can see you are thinking...what are your thoughts now, Brother?"

"I want everyone to know the Father, and to see what I saw and learn what I know. I want everyone who is struggling with identity and purpose to find the River of love. I want men who are weary and bored to taste what I have tasted, to find the path in their wilderness that will lead them out of their own wastelands. I want men to allow the Light to wash away every bad memory, every bad thought, every bad event, every bad thing they have done. I want men to know that their past has no bearing on the love that Jesus Christ has for them, even in their moments of torment and worry.

"I want men to know that the Way of Jesus is actually much simpler than they realize. That the pains of their past actually make them the best Disciplers for grace, mercy, compassion, and empathy through their example."

"I want men to know that they do not have to be victims of themselves or of others, and that they are victorious in Jesus Christ. I want men to see the Shepherd in their life, the Comforter, the Guide, the Teacher, and their accountability Partner.

"I want men to know that Jesus is not some wimp that won't fight for others. I want men to know that they can maintain their masculinity, that they can be a soldier and a warrior. And they need to recognize that every warrior needs a King and a Kingdom to fight for. The Lord is King, and Heaven is that Kingdom. This, Shepherd, this is what I am thinking."

Shepherd gave Stephen a one arm hug and shoulder bump. *"I can see the fire burning in you, Brother; that is the Holy Spirit working in you and speaking through you. Praise God!"*

And then He got serious. *"Men have been told that God is a gentleman, which is true. But God also meets you where you are as He knows what you need. You were, and still are in some sense, a very intense person, Stephen, but you were also very heavy hearted and heavy headed. The Lord came at you the way He needed to, to meet you where you were. He was knocking and you opened the door. And, as soon as you opened that door, He knocked you down into a position that He knew would get your attention."*

Stephen laughed, "Yes, Sir, He sure did. I have told people that my experience was very physical, but I am not sure they will ever know what that means unless they experience it for themselves."

Shepherd worked to bring things to a close. *"The Lord is not done with you yet, Stephen. There is another layer to this quest that He wants to share with you. You changed that day in 2008, but life did not get easier for you, did it?"*

Stephen shook his head, "No, Sir, while Jesus helped me find myself and my purpose, my life did not necessarily get easier. Things changed in a good way, even dramatically. But, life actually got harder."

"Yes, Brother; He got to your heart, but there was another battle ground that needed to be conquered." Shepherd paused and then continued.

"It is time for you to wake up, Stephen. Write down everything that you saw, everything that you heard, and everything that you felt. Do not leave anything out. Then, when you are ready, reach out to Me and we will begin to explore the final area that we need to conquer, the area surrounding your heart gate – the mind."

EPILOGUE
THE DAY THE EARTH
STOOD STILL

*"And do not be conformed to this world, but be transformed
by the renewing of your mind, so that you may prove
what the will of God is, that which is good
and acceptable and perfect."*
(Romans 12:2)

AS STEPHEN AND THE SHEPHERD closed out their conversation, a transition was taking place, a new beginning with a new set of challenges. Stephen was a new man in Christ, but he still had the same old characteristics. Stephen loved God and he wanted to follow God, but he was still victim to success sickness and he remained materialistic. He started following the God he wanted, instead of the God he needed. And his life was about to take a new twist, a paradigm that no one expects when they first experience the glory and mercy of Jesus Christ.

The result of his new redemption and salvation was a revised set of expectations of how he would behave. But he also held on to his perceived expectations about how others would treat him. He was confident that he would behave differently – he even felt different; but the people in his life did not change with him, and this challenged him. Stephen thought he was supposed to have some form of special power, but for some reason such power eluded him.

Stephen had a gullible sense of expectation that, once he became a Christian, life would be easier, yet new jobs, new leaders, and a new set of rules would nearly push him over the edge. Before he dedicated his life to Christ, Stephen held opinions about church and which seemed to play out in reality. What he failed to realize is that church is full of hurting people and they hurt others just as much as he does. He would learn a valuable truth: "hurting people hurt people." His experiences with people in his Christian life would almost cause him to consider giving up church – that it was not worth it – because there are some very judgmental people in church.

Shortly after accepting Christ, Stephen would be attacked by local politicians. But his new man would not allow him to fight back, which ate Stephen up, creating a new sense of bitterness and frustration. Rather than attacking back and lashing out, Stephen held it in, hoping that Christ would somehow fix it. Things did work out, but not the way he expected.

In 2008, the foundation of Jesus Christ was laid in his heart. Stephen was shown that the bible refers to Jesus serving as the cornerstone, the most critical stone in a building. As a man of almost forty years of age, he was still consumed by many of the old patterns of his life. He was a Christian now, but in many ways he still acted the same, spoke the same, and carried himself in the same way. His heart had changed, but his outward behavior did not appear to have changed much, and his mind was still running on autopilot. Nonetheless, due to the love of Jesus Christ, he adopted a new outlook on life that was positive and encouraging.

Scripture refers to toddlers drinking milk, a metaphor for new Christians as they initially consume the Word of God, allowing Him to grow in their lives. New Christians ought to take it easy while observing and serving under the mentorship and discipleship of others, and for Stephen, that was his wife and neighbor.

The exact same month that Stephen accepted Christ, he accepted a position as the IT Director in the county in which he lived. For the first time in the life of their family, Stephen would be working in a location a few miles from home so that he and his wife could actually have lunch together, and he could visit his kids at school. In their nineteen years of marriage, they had never been able to do that. Stephen was starting a new life as a new Christian, in a new job, with a new attitude, and new possibilities.

There were more jobs and new moves over the years that followed and Stephen would learn how to mature in his faith to the greatest extent possible. He came to learn that, as he matured in his faith, that he was able to start taking in solid food, things that were very deep, spiritually focused, and powerful. Stephen was beginning to learn what his spiritual gifts were, as well as what it means to have gifts and to produce fruit. Stephen learned how to transition from a position of using and living on the faith of others to a position that required him to operate in his own faith as well as God's faith.

Stephen was well on his way to a position of being dependent on God rather than on his wife and others when, one day, the floor dropped out from beneath him and his wife. Chad died while serving in the Air Force in the Middle East. His children crashed, his wife crashed, but Stephen crashed the hardest. This was the day that the earth stood still, and smacked Stephen right upside the head. His life changed forever and things were not pleasant.

Stephen' story and the challenges of his new life in Christ continue in Book 2 of *The Wilderness Project.*

COMING 2021

THE WILDERNESS PROJECT (BOOK 2)

A CALL TO ACTION

"So whoever knows the right thing to do and
fails to do it, for him it is sin."
(James 4:17)

"Therefore, preparing your minds for action, and being
sober-minded, set your hope fully on the grace that will be
brought to you at the revelation of Jesus Christ."
(1 Peter 1:13)

If this book has touched you in any way, then it is time for you, right now in Jesus Name, to take action.

!!CRITICAL!!

If you have not yet accepted Jesus Christ as your Lord and Savior, then we need to take care of that right now before you do anything else.

See the ***Prayer of Salvation*** in this book and pray that prayer out loud. There is no specific pattern to this type of prayer other than confessing that Jesus is your Lord and Savior and asking Him, and accepting Him, into your heart. The Prayer of Salvation in this book is an example, or a template, for you to use if you need it.

While it isn't necessary to pray this with someone else, it sure does add power and confidence if you can pray this with another believer.

If you had accepted Jesus Christ in your heart in the past, but believe that you have fallen short or backslidden, then you can rededicate your life to Christ. You can use the same ***Prayer of Salvation*** and pray it out loud, with a brother in Christ if at all possible.

~*NEXT STEPS*~

If you are lucky enough to find yourself surrounded by other believers, then some will advise and guide your walk through a series of steps, or a set of principles, that you need to follow in order to receive redemption and forgiveness. I am one of those that doesn't believe, other than accepting Him as your Savior, that there are a specific set of steps as outlined by God. If there is, I have not found it after a decade of my walk. God created all of us as unique beings. We all have different backgrounds, different experiences, and altering value systems that make it difficult for a series of specific steps to fit each person.

However, the one thing that I firmly believe is applicable to every single believer, regardless of who you are - maintaining a personal relationship with Jesus Christ. And this relationships absolutely requires that you build up your spirit, that you regularly nourish your spirit, that you spend daily time in prayer, and that you spend time daily meditating on scripture (quality time not just time).

Secondarily, every believer must ensure that they 1) believe, 2) accept, and 3) repent.

1. **You must <u>BELIEVE</u> in your heart, not your head; this my brother requires faith, for it is faith.** Confess this, out loud, with your mouth: **"I believe!"** Declare it **"In Jesus Name!"**. Say it 100 times if necessary. Say it every day for a year if you have to. Say it every morning. There is power in your words. And then answer this: "What do you believe?" Answer this question out loud. You may

A CALL TO ACTION

have 3 things in the beginning, but over time you will add to the list of what you believe.

> "For God so loved the world, that He gave His only begotten Son, that whoever believes in Him shall not perish, but have eternal life." (John 3:16)

> "But God shows His love for us in that while we were still sinners, Christ died for us." (Romans 5:8)

> "Because, if you confess with your mouth that Jesus is Lord and believe in your heart that God raised him from the dead, you will be saved." (Romans 10:9)

2. **Let Jesus know that you receive Him and <u>ACCEPT</u> Him. There is something about having a witness in your walk that adds power and confidence in knowing and believing that you are doing the right thing.**

> "Because, if you confess with your mouth that Jesus is Lord and believe in your heart that God raised him from the dead, you will be saved." (Romans 10:9)

> "But to all who did receive him, who believed in his name, he gave the right to become children of God," (John 1:12)

> "Jesus said to him, "I am the way, and the truth, and the life. No one comes to the Father except through me." (John 14:6)

> "For "everyone who calls on the name of the Lord will be saved." (Romans 10:13)

3. **You must <u>REPENT</u> and you must <u>FORGIVE</u>; forgiveness not just of others, but also forgive yourself. Forgiving myself was the most difficult thing for me. Refer to the Prayer for Forgiveness in this book as an aid if necessary.**

   a. <u>Ask the Lord to forgive you.</u> He will, He promised.

   > "Repent therefore, and turn again, that your sins may be blotted out," (Acts 3:19)

299

"In Him we have redemption through His blood, the forgiveness of our trespasses, according to the riches of his grace," (Ephesians 1:7)

"In whom we have redemption, the forgiveness of sins." (Colossians 1:14)

"If we confess our sins, he is faithful and just to forgive us our sins and to cleanse us from all unrighteousness." (1 John 1:9)

b. <u>You must forgive yourself.</u> I would encourage you to do this first, but, for some this may take time. I know, this one is easy to say, or easier to read. Confess this, out loud, with your mouth: **"I forgive myself!"** Demand it! Take authority! Declare it "**In Jesus Name!**". Say it 100 times if necessary. Say it every day for a year if you have to. There is power in your words. It took me five years - Yes, I said that correctly - five years!

"If we confess our sins, he is faithful and just to forgive us our sins and to cleanse us from all unrighteousness." (1 John 1:9)

"Casting all your anxieties on him, because he cares for you." (1 Peter 5:7)

"And whenever you stand praying, forgive, if you have anything against anyone, so that your Father also who is in heaven may forgive you your trespasses." (Mark 11:25)

"Pay attention to yourselves!..." (Luke 17:3-4)

"For if you forgive others their trespasses, your heavenly Father will also forgive you, but if you do not forgive others their trespasses, neither will your Father forgive your trespasses." (Matthew 6:14-15)

"Therefore I tell you, her sins, which are many, are forgiven—for she loved much. But he who is forgiven little, loves little." (Luke 7:47)

c. <u>You must forgive others.</u> As with everything, you are highly encouraged to forgive with your mouth, out loud.

For me, forgiving others came easy, probably because I was so hard on myself; even forgiving my father was easy to do. For you, you may find forgiving some people difficult based on the level of offense or grievance. Either way, you must learn to forgive or it will hamper your walk.

> "And whenever you stand praying, forgive, if you have anything against anyone, so that your Father also who is in heaven may forgive you your trespasses." (Mark 11:25)

> "For if you forgive others their trespasses, your heavenly Father will also forgive you, but if you do not forgive others their trespasses, neither will your Father forgive your trespasses." (Matthew 6:14-15)

4. If you have repented and confessed that Jesus Christ is your Lord and Savior and that you believe that He is risen, then Praise God! And Hallelujah! Welcome to the fold brother (or sister). You are now a member of Christ's Army, a Warrior. If you have just started the process of forgiveness, particularly for yourself, then know that for some this may take some time for it to fully permeate your heart. Remember, for me it took over five years before I fully believed it - I pray that it doesn't take you as long.

What's next?

a. Buy a journal for you to write in. This is not a diary. Your journal is your record of communication with God. Use this journal to write what you believe the Lord is revealing to you. Use this journal to write down questions that you have for God. Use the journal to write down scriptures or book quotes that speak to your heart. Use this journal for every single step that follows in this Call to Action.

b. If you are relatively new to the Bible, then read through the entire Book of John in one sitting. Go ahead and read through it the first time as fast as you want. And then, read it again, but this time read a few verses, close your eyes, meditate on and ponder His Words and let His Words talk to you and permeate your mind and your heart. Continue this process until you finish that book. And then, read it again, but this time ask God, "Lord, what do you want me to learn from these passages?".

c. <u>Review through the Bibliography section of this book.</u> I have listed out several books that I not only have in my own library, but they impacted me in ways that other books did not. Note: just because a book touched my heart is no guarantee that it will touch yours. Simultaneously, you may already have books, or will read books, that will touch your heart but hold no place in mine. This is perfectly acceptable.

d. If you are new to this Christian journey, then you will want to <u>find one or two Christian accountability partners</u> in addition to your spouse (if applicable). Those that you can depend on, those who will feel comfortable in correcting you when you make a mistake, but also those that you will receive correction with no offense. If you get offended, this is a check on your heart.

e. Visit www.thewildernessprojectexperience.com and join <u>The Wilderness Project Experience</u>. There you will also find resources that will help you along your Wilderness Journey.

5. During the course of reading this book, there may have been some Christian ideas and concepts that you find difficult to understand, find difficult to do in your own Christian walk, or you may even think them ludicrous.

a. <u>Hearing Gods Voice</u> - I struggled for years to hear Gods voice, not just hearing Him, but just the idea that you can hear him at all. When I finally came to believe that it is possible to hear His voice, I grew frustrated with knowing when it was Him, me, or, something worse.

> "Whoever is of God hears the words of God. The reason why you do not hear them is that you are not of God." (John 8:47)

> "My sheep hear my voice, and I know them, and they follow me." (John 10:27)

i. Review my bibliography section for books that discuss how to Hear God's Voice

ii. Visit www.thewildernessprojectexperience.com where you can join The Wilderness Project Experience as well as gain access to resources that can help you.

b. Visions - it is possible to receive visions from God. Most are familiar with dreams, but the Lord provides visions in other ways as well.

> "And it shall come to pass afterward, that I will pour out my Spirit on all flesh; your sons and your daughters shall prophesy, your old men shall dream dreams, and your young men shall see visions." (Joel 2:28)

i. Review the bibliography section for books that discuss the concept of Visions.

ii. Visit www.thewildernessprojectexperience.com where you can join The Wilderness Project Experience as well as gain access to resources that can help you.

c. The idea of a Secret Place

> "But when you pray, go into your room and shut the door and pray to your Father who is in secret. And your Father who sees in secret will reward you." (Matthew 6:6)

"He who dwells in the secret place of the Most High
Shall abide under the shadow of the Almighty." (Psalm
91:1, NKJV)

   i. Review the bibliography section for books that discuss the concept of the Secret Place.

  ii. Visit www.thewildernessprojectexperience.com
where you can join The Wilderness Project
Experience as well as gain access to resources that
can help you.

  d. <u>Prayers</u> - this book contains a bunch of prayers for
forgiveness, redemption, intercession, salvation, for
loved ones, and petition. Please feel free to go back
through the book and find the prayer(s) that apply to
your situation, the situation of a family member, or life
in general. I have found that while an entire prayer may
not resonate in my heart, portions of it do. Prayers are
your communication to God, make them your own.

6. Finally, for my brothers out there. While women have
suffered too, we, as men, statistically speaking, struggle
the most because we are the ones that predominantly have
poor behaviors, poor attitudes, and rough backgrounds.
Men are the most likely to commit suicide while women
outnumber men in church by over 50%. Men are having
a hard time understanding where they fit into the whole
Christian scene, or, how the stuff being discussed at church
fits into their life. Men have a harder time because we tend
to be more heavy-hearted and more hard-headed. Men are
like this because we have LOST THE FIRE. I am here to
share the following:

  a. You ARE NOT alone in whatever you are dealing with.
I not only promise this, I guarantee it. However, it may
be hard to find a dude that understands you. Been there
and done that.

b. Read through the entire chapter of Acts Chapter 2. If you don't walk away from that understanding the fire of the Spirit of God, then please reach out to me directly at the email listed in my About the Author section, or, you can sign up at The Wilderness Project Experience.

c. Pray about receiving the baptism of the Holy Spirit. I encourage you to take advantage of this gift from God, this is where the fire of God comes from.

d. Finally, know that God needs you in His Army. You are a Soldier for Christ with the Heart of a Warrior. This is your purpose and this is where you can find your identity. I am a 20-year military veteran and I can say, with no doubt, that there is nothing which comes closer to the military (or law enforcement) than the brotherhood of Christ.

e. Read through the bibliography section of this book for books that are focused specifically on men, about men, for men.

7. **Write your story down, your testimony, and share it with others!**

I love all of my brothers, even the ones I don't know yet. It is time for all of us to Rise UP, and join His winning team.

MY JOURNEY TO THE
WILDERNESS PROJECT – AN ESSAY

AS I SIT HERE WRITING this opening paragraph, I am swallowed up in tears and sorrow. I don't have sorrow and tears for where I am today, but for the life I missed - 40 years of emptiness and contempt. My sadness is directed at how I had been living a tiny story that was shallow, wasting many years in the Wilderness failing to find the path to the River that would take me away from the dryness of the desert and cross over into the Promised Land. I missed dozens of spiritual opportunities as a result, causing me to miss my calling when I was much younger.

Ted Dekker, a best-selling Christian author, said it best that "true spirituality cannot be taught, it can only be learned; and this learning takes place through a series of experiences". Yes, and it is these experiences that will become the outline for your story. I learned a lot through my experiences, much of which took me years to unlearn. I believe that many men are in search of themselves – their identity and their purpose. They want to know how their story meshes into the larger story – the story of existence itself. Why are we here and where do I fit in the picture? You may even ask yourself why does any of this, whatever it is, matter? You may even ask it the cliché way – what is the meaning of life?

I find the latter question too corny, almost impossible to answer as it leads to a complex string of layers and theories causing us to get lost in a resulting quagmire. However, answering the question of "why are we here and where do I fit?", that one we can answer. And the answer is found by exploring your Wilderness Journey and finding your own path to the River. And this is where the Lord gave me the idea for The Wilderness Project Book series, beginning with Breaking Free from the Shadows.

For much of the first 40 years of my life, I was a walking and functioning hate-a-holic. I did not like myself and strove to pull comfort from others, whether they wanted me too or not - rarely giving anything back. My driving force, my motivation, was to become the guy that could get anything done, no matter what and no matter the cost – and I was good at it. I wanted to prove to others that I was accomplished, that I was successful, and that I was worth their attention and approval. Why? Because on the inside I was empty, I was not a good person, and I constantly felt like a failure, that I was a nobody. So, I became obstinate, overly aggressive, overly confident, and brash, feeding the very thing that was damaging me. I hungered to be liked but was, instead, self-destructive.

And then, after a 20 year military career in the Army, I saw an opportunity to change [*even attending speech therapy to remove foul language from my natural vocabulary*], to try and become a guy that people just liked, that they wanted to be around; but this only lead me to disappointment, highly sought out and desired because of my ability to accomplish the task, complete the mission, finish the project, no matter what; not because I was a person that they wanted to hang around with or invite out for lunch. My finely-honed skills alone were what people wanted and what they expected of me. So I continued to do things the only way I knew how because I did not want to fail them – culminating with a beautiful ending, but also filled with destructive results. I was wrong and I had missed an opportunity He offered me once again.

AS I LIVED MY LIFE "for me", I was ironically destroying myself in the process. As an adult, I pretty much abandoned my wife and my three children to their own wilds, to fend for themselves while I brought home the bacon. And then one day in 2008, He, Jesus Christ, came to me in a very physical way that knocked me to my knees. I experienced His truth of grace and the Fathers tremendous love for me; but the irony is that I wasn't looking for it, not like that anyway, it just happened, and then I was suddenly awake.

However, accepting Christ did not necessarily make me better, life did not get easier, nor did life suddenly go well for me afterwards. Ted Dekker again says it best, after I was born again "I was supposed to have special powers to love others and turn the other cheek and refrain from gossip and not judge. I was supposed to be a shining example, known by the world for my extravagant love, grace, and power in all respects. And yet, while I heard the rhetoric of others, I didn't seem to have these powers myself." There was still drama playing around within me that outweighed the good stuff of life that was happening around me. My heart was still asleep and I was unable to hear the inner voices that I was supposed to be subjecting myself to. I was trying to follow the God I needed, but what I did was follow the God I wanted. I took another wrong turn at the fork in the road.

I was still lost and I was totally confused as to where and how I could possibly be lost. It took me years to realize that I was failing to understand the wounds that I was still carrying around in my heart and I was not taking steps to heal them. I had inherited a philosophy that "life was hell" from my father, learning to expect and believe in the inevitable pain that we feel "every day", either physical or emotional (forget spiritual). If I didn't feel pain before the end of the day, then by golly, I would create some if I had to – and I became a master. I was oblivious to what the Lord was trying to tell me via my inner man because my inner man was preoccupied with the continuing drive of internal self-pity parties. Ever experience those?

THE TESTIMONY AND DETAILS of my son's passing will be outlined in the next book but suffice it to say that I almost gave up. I wanted to die; I could no longer live with myself. And I lived this way for three years. I walked away from church and I walked away from God. And my life got worse as a result.

If I had not had that foundation laid in my heart more than a year earlier as partially shared in Chapter 24 of this book, I sense that I would be dead. Praise God that I got through that period, as did my wife and two other children. As of the writing of this essay, my wife and I are still together after 30 years of marriage but that is a miracle in itself.

My father passed away in 2017 but not before the Holy Spirit led me, with me by my father's side, in leading him to Jesus Christ a few weeks before he passed away. I forgave my father in 2009 after flying out to Arizona to meet him unannounced but our relationship never blossomed unfortunately, but our relationship issues were no longer a hindrance in my life.

MY CHILDHOOD WAS A STRUGGLE, for some reason I always felt abandoned and that I somehow did not belong where I was. I was untethered and always felt that I was at fault for something, that I did something wrong without knowing what it was; and this was torture, particularly for seven-year-old me. I carried this heart system with me well into my adult life, my marriage, my children, and my military career.

I was a lost child, much of which I can remember only because Jesus worked with me to destroy strongholds blotting those memories out. This doesn't mean that my parents weren't there, they were, and I had a lot of cousins, but things were just... off. These feelings would carry with me for years, creating insecurities, sensations of rejection, and loneliness. I had friends, but they did not fill that void inside of me. I was in search of something but I had no idea what it was, making me feel awkward, further feeding into my insecurities. I was alone in my Wilderness Journey, never inviting the One I needed to accompany me.

My teen years were filled with drugs, girls, and parties and I rarely saw my father, and I was ok with that. There were moments of violence, criminality, and moronic activities with some very dangerous and seedy people – and all of this before I turned 17. Some people thought I was a nerd because I was an above average student (at least until my senior year of high school), it certainly fooled my parents. I would often think to myself, "If they only knew the danger I was living around and the chaos I could create based on a simple request." "They", being everyone around me: family, friends, school mates, everyone.

THERE WERE FUN TIMES and lots of family vacations, but today I marvel at how difficult it was for me to see, to recall, those times. They were foggy in my mind while, in contrast, the times of drama and inner conflict were much clearer. When I would search my memory bank for the positive moments, I found that I needed to focus really hard before some images came to me. Sometimes it was necessary for me to actually look at a photograph to bring any recollection to my frontal lobe, and even then I still couldn't recall some of those fun times even with the picture right in front of me. Why? Because of the condition my heart during those moments, I had constructed strongholds in my spirit and locked those memories away as I travailed my chosen path along my Wilderness Journey.

Simultaneously, I had also locked away some of my own negative behavior and conduct, things I said, things I did. As I am sharing stories with people, my wife in particular will immediately correct me, filling in gruesome, yet essential details that I missed, things that are painful, things that are ugly. I hate those moments because they make me very uncomfortable, and even after she reminds me of them I still can't remember some of them - not a bit. However, Praise God!! I love my wife even more for it. When she "reminds" me of them, she is reminding me of who I used to be in order to shine the light on who I am today. Not for reasons of judgment or condemnation, but for reasons of celebration and thankfulness. And she always gives the glory and honor to God. Why can't I remember them? For the same reasons that I could not remember the fun times.

The good news is that years after being Born Again, I am truly starting to understand many aspects of my life, my upbringing, my parentage, and my spiritual life because I have spent time investigating my Wilderness Journey. But, more importantly and much more exciting for me, these times of exploration and discovery have brought me much closer to Jesus Christ, not just knowing who He is, but who I am with Him in my life. The result is that He has helped me to knock down some of those strongholds that were clogging my memory banks. Memories of fun times come to me much easier and yes, even some of my negative behavior is also much more accessible. In both cases, this has led me to understanding and revelation knowledge, which has allowed me to change because He is changing me. His mercies, His grace, and His love are all the motivation I need, something that I wish I had learned MUCH earlier in my life.

I EARNESTLY SEEK GOD EVERY DAY and have learned what it means to have a relationship with Him. That is what He wants and what our purpose is in life, to have a personal, one on one, relationship with our Creator through His Son Jesus Christ.

When I was born again in 2008, I was born a new child, but I had also become a Prodigal Father, a lost son of God that was also a father himself. I had not lived up to the life that God asks of us and to this day, the shame of this has been heavy on me. Also, while I did not share details in this book, two areas that kept me from Christ for so long was the bible and church itself. For me to grow in God, this was an area that I needed to get past, move on in order to move forward, and this was difficult for me being that I am both a logical and analytical person. But I did and I will share in Book 2 of this series, I will dig into thoughts and perspectives about the Bible and about Church, before I knew Christ and after.

As a soldier and as a man, it is rare to find someone that understands your plight, that can assure and reassure you that everything will be fine. This is where new communities become vital, most importantly, the family and the church. For I have found no other bond that can replace the camaraderie of arms but that of the church brotherhood (*gibborim* Soldiers for Christ).

When I joined the military in 1987, it had become my church and the soldiers around me were all part of the same congregation. It had structure, rules, and informal and formal norms that you were required to live by in order to survive. My colleagues and fellow soldier, my insecurities aside, kept each other sane, comforted in distress, and focused on the prize. It is no wonder that within a year after retiring from the military in 2007, I was lost. And then, He found me, in 2008, and a new brotherhood was introduced into my life. It is no longer about the blood of my fellow Soldiers, though that is still a part of me. It is now about the blood of Christ.

In my twenty years of service, the greatest fear that gripped my heart was that I would let my buddies down in the discharge of my duties, or that I would disgrace my family. Likewise, the body of Christ is a team sport, with all members making up the body. If one should "fail," then the body would feel it. However, if one should "fall," then the body would ensure that no member would be left behind. Each member of the body is there to assure that everything will be all right. The brotherhood of Christ, the *gibborim,* is there for you. You simply need to seek and then ask.

RARELY DO I PERSONALLY come across another man that came to Christ late in life like me, a man that came burdened with a past of hypocrisy, blasphemy and questionable motives (some darn near evil). I hear about them and I regularly read stories about other men like this, but I can count the number of men that I have had personal conversations with on one hand. And one thing I can say with a high degree of certainty, nobody, and I mean nobody, can relate to what a man like me has gone through, or is going through, other than God Himself and other men like me. Very possibly, men like you.

My Wilderness Journey is not unique, nor does it even come close to the degree of trauma and experiences of other men. Some may even consider my life to be a mere whisper as compared to theirs. To this you will get no disagreement, no argument - but what you will get is "Praise God! Glory to God!! Hallelujah. I am excited that we are brothers - Soldiers for Christ!" You will then hear me declare, "Lets mobilize and go on a mission together to save other men, many of whom have lived lives even harder than you and me! Let's Follow Him!".

I spent too many years trying to understand my life when what I should have been seeking was to understand His Life. I was conforming to the way the world wanted me to be versus conforming to the way He wanted me to be. I was seeking the appreciation and respect of men when I should have been seeking Him, whom I already had respect and admiration. And I was seeking love from people when I should have been receiving love from Him, and He already loved me the way I was. That void in my life, the one that made me feel like something was off, the one that made me feel like I did not belong, was the emptiness set aside for the River of Living Water. This was the River that I was searching for, the River what would serve as the path out of my wilderness.

We are all on a Wilderness Journey, sometimes we revisit that wilderness, serving as an exploration for what it is that makes us who we are. For me, that required that I ask the Lord to reveal things to me not just about myself, but also about my father and my grandfather; reasons that will become clear to you as you read this book. And this, this right here, is why my eyes were filled with tears from the onset of writing this chapter. I held a lot of blame, remorse, anger, and bitterness at my father and grandfather for several decades, for making me feel helpless, tangling me into something that I could not understand. I now know the truth and the truth has made me understand that I was wrong and has set me free from that bondage I was in. I had allowed my world, and forces around me, to manipulate me. And I blamed the wrong ones for it.

My entire life has been one long search for identity and significance in this life. After being born again, I continued to seek my identity and significance in this life, but now I knew that I was already secure for the next life, the one that I will enter into after I leave this earth. This was my Wilderness Project.

FOR ANY NAYSAYERS OUT THERE, I will persist in my principles not to contrast my experience with the watered-down culture of men who stand for nothing. Although some items were left out and some items were dramatized, I wrote this book using some of the stories and episodes about my family history and aspects of my own behavior, and I was honest while using events from my own past and the restoration of my heart. I was transparent about how I felt and how I reasoned with others and responded to their actions. But, at heart, I share in the honest pursuit of the Lord. A display of "how not to be," I recognize that this will be at odds with the moral and spiritual uncertainty of others; moreover there may be others that will mock and attempt to make me feel ashamed. But, in all of this, I am like king David who drew a line in the sand. I was who I was, but today I am who I am whether you like it or not.

The warrior spirit is a manifestation of the Holy Spirit, the Spirit of Christ. During the three wars I participated in during my military career, I was eager to engage what I thought of as the warrior spirit, but I was only engaging in self. As we view our own individual lives via the internal video playback in our heads, we are confronted with a series of revelations. I knew that my experiences in combat operations and combat support were significant to me but I had not realized the full extent. Prior to September 2008, I had been blinded by sin and my own personal desires. Then I got born again. And then, just as I started to heal my wounds, the devil rallied and started to inflict new ones while trying to revisit old ones.

After my born-again experience in 2008, the following weeks that followed were a blur of regular and frequent revelations of what had been my reality up to that point – revelation after revelation. The Holy Spirit had quickened my soul and I was reborn. I had been blind to my self-directed actions and behavior; but now I was able to see. I knew I was flawed but not to the magnitude that I now realize. This was not bad news; this was good news, for I now knew where and what needed correction – and how to do it. What I needed was the humility to seek help and the courage to confess my shortcomings and flaws that needed to be scraped away. I needed to eat some crow and humble pie.

As a man with a heart set aright, I know who I am, where I am, and the good that God is doing in my life. I recognize that my heart is fragile but I have learned how to guard it. My warrior heart, and yours, is needed. Jesus is a Warrior and He is your source of inspiration; Spiritual warfare can be difficult for some to comprehend, but the Bible constantly exhorts men to remain strong, have courage, and to [frequently] consecrate themselves.

GOD DEFIES COMPREHENSION and His very Being defies the logical and secular understanding of existence. I can say firsthand that, the more you delve into the knowledge of God, the more you will realize how shallow your previous understanding has been – at least, for me. I cannot rationalize God as I will never grasp the full measure of who He is. But, I can say with some certainty that if I had not gone through my wilderness journey, I would not be on the path I am on today. Perhaps He would have gotten to me another way, at another time, who knows? In either case, He is my redemption and my salvation, and my wilderness journey was necessary for my own evolution, a series of blips on my own timeline of life, laid before me as a part of my destiny. I have reconciled my new life with the full certainty that "The fear of the Lord is the beginning of knowledge" (Proverbs 1:7).

More importantly, the condition of my heart is what created all of the destructive conditions around me. How many of you recognize some of this in yourself, or in others that you know? How many of you think that there is no way you can come to God, or feel that God would never accept you? How many of you believe that there might be a God but you still aren't sure? The positions that readers will take away from this book are numerous and there is no answer that I can give other than, "take these questions to God." Bottom line is that a man needs to know his identity and his purpose; until that happens, he will remain feeling empty inside. A man needs to face his enemy and conquer it.

TO HAVE VICTORY we must get to the place where we no longer let events drag us down. If approval is what you seek and it is still withheld, abandon your bitterness towards the one who withholds your approval. Abandon your bitterness towards what you believe life in general has dealt you. If you want to be encouraged but still feel like you've been deliberately cut off, then you have the option of choosing to believe for a coming season of fruitfulness in those very same areas. It's your choice, and it won't happen until you choose. It never helps to allow negative circumstances to mold us into the role and identity of "the victim." We have a choice as to whether it will be temporary or if it will become our identity. We should be able to say, "I was the victim of blah blah blah but now I'm a specialist in blah blah blah." There is hope for all. You just need to grasp it and take hold of it in your heart.

The image of God, Christ in you, the mind of Christ, and whatever the Lord has gifted you with is the antidote and remedy you need. You need to take control of that jumbled mess in your victim mentality – the self-fulfilling belief that came out of a bad situation in which you were victimized, or thought you were. Cancel such a belief by tapping into your God-given resources. Let the peace of Christ be the arbiter. There is a truer ministry in righteousness.

The challenge is whether you identify yourself as the victim or the victimizer – and whether you can admit it. I was both, I was a victim and I victimized others, including my wife and my children. How can you see what is in front of you if you fail to recognize what is inside of you? When our own hearts condemn us, there is no power in prayer, no power in preaching. We are just *"sounding brass or a clanging symbol"* (1 Corinthians 13:1). If you are the victimizer, recognize it and repent to God, He will forgive you. If you feel you are a victim, forgive and repent of your unforgiveness. He is a good God and He will accept you no matter how messed up you think you are. You can join His flock – no matter what.

EVEN AS I WROTE BREAKING FREE FROM THE SHADOWS, my knowledge of Jesus continued to expand, knowing that He can help me, and you, that He can bring peace to the storms of our lives and heal the sickness that has twisted and warped our minds and bodies due to the way the world conformed us to be. In the end, we will be far more than conquerors through Christ, who is our true source of strength. We are battle tested Soldiers for Christ with a new heart, the Heart of a Warrior.

Even in the Wilderness, it is the way of Jesus that whenever we find ourselves blinded by our own grievances, judgments, and fears, we sink into darkness. But, when we trust Jesus in his way once again, we see the light instead of the darkness that we feel is overtaking us. This is the Way through the Wilderness - a beacon of light guiding you through your journey.

Man, I had allowed the world to tell me what and who I was supposed to be, and it did not work for me - at all. Paul encourages us to *"not be conformed to this world, but be transformed by the renewing of your mind, so that you may prove what the will of God is, that which is good and acceptable and perfect"* (Romans 12:2). Who do you want to follow – it's your choice. God is waiting and He will never give up on you! He loves you that much.

This is our revolution, our healing, and our resurrection - to be free from the prisons that hold us captive, to see what few see, and to rise from death with Jesus as His soldiers. Enter the Wilderness Project and see if you can witness what the sheep witnessed and experienced. Perhaps, just maybe, it may change your views and understanding of your life (purpose), your father (your past), yourself (identity), and the world you live in (significance).

Marcus Johnson

PRAYER OF SALVATION

If you are open to it, I invite you to come to know Jesus and include Him in your life by praying, out loud, the prayer below. If you have already accepted Him in the past but feel you have come short, then you can also use this prayer to recommit your life (I did).

The Prayer of Salvation begins with faith in God. We're letting God know we believe His Word is true. By the faith He has given us, we choose to believe in Him. When we pray, asking God for the gift of salvation, we're exercising our free will to acknowledge that we believe in Him. That demonstration of faith pleases God because we have freely chosen to know Him.

When we pray the prayer of salvation, we're admitting that we've sinned. To sin is simply to fall short of the mark, as an arrow that does not quite hit the bull's-eye. The prayer of salvation, then, recognizes that Jesus Christ is the only human who ever lived without sin.

When we pray the prayer of salvation, we are professing faith in Christ as Savior and Lord. With Christ as our standard of perfection, we're now acknowledging faith in Him as God, agreeing with the Apostle John that: "*In the beginning was the Word, and the Word was with God, and the Word was God. He was in the beginning with God. All things were made through Him, and without Him nothing was made that was made*" (John 1:1-3, NKJV).

Say it and mean it now! Do you agree with everything you have read so far? If you do, don't wait a moment longer to start your new life in Jesus Christ. Remember, this prayer is not a magical formula. You are simply expressing your heart to God.

Father, I know that I have broken Your laws and my sins have separated me from You. I am truly sorry, and now I want to turn away from my past sinful life toward You. Please forgive me and help me avoid sinning again. I believe that Your Son, Jesus Christ, died for my sins, was resurrected from the dead, is alive, and hears my prayer. I invite Jesus to become the Lord of my life, to rule and reign in my heart from this day forward. Please send your Holy Spirit to help me obey You, and to do Your will for the rest of my life. In Jesus' name I pray, Amen.

That's it, it is that simple. Your next step would be to immediately get involved with a local church. You will need that fellowship with fellow believers. It's also Biblical.

PRAYER OF FORGIVENESS

Part of my growing process was to forgive, and I needed to forgive a lot of people, including myself and numerous others throughout my life. Unforgiveness is a shackle: it binds you to those you fail to forgive and gives them power over you. I pray that you can find the courage and moral tenacity to let it go. If you are someone that needs to forgive and move forward, then I would encourage you to pray this prayer out loud –with a close friend, if possible. Depending on your past, this prayer could take a while. I promise, it's worth it. You can also use this prayer to forgive yourself.

Father, in the name of Jesus, I acknowledge that I have sinned against You by not forgiving those who have offended or hurt me. I repent of this and ask Your forgiveness. I also acknowledge my inability to forgive them apart from You.

*Therefore, from my heart I choose to forgive. **[Insert their names – release each one individually]**. I bring under the blood of Jesus all that they have done wrong to me. They no longer owe me anything. I remit their sins against me.*

Heavenly Father, as my Lord Jesus asked You to forgive those who had sinned against Him, I pray that Your forgiveness will come to those who have sinned against me.

I ask that You bless them and lead them into a closer relationship with You. Amen.

APPENDIX

This appendix includes all Scriptures that are quoted directly or indirectly, specifically referenced, or otherwise foundational to the story at specific points per chapter. All scriptures are from the NASB unless otherwise indicated.

PROLOGUE

Isaiah 43:19 "Behold, I will do something new, Now it will spring forth; Will you not be aware of it? I will even make a roadway in the wilderness, Rivers in the desert."

Acts 18:9 "And the Lord said to Paul in the night by a vision, "Do not be afraid any longer, but go on speaking and do not be silent;"

Joel 2:28 "It will come about after this That I will pour out My Spirit on all mankind; And your sons and daughters will prophesy, Your old men will dream dreams, Your young men will see visions."

1 John 4:1 "Beloved, do not believe every spirit, but test the spirits to see whether they are from God, because many false prophets have gone out into the world."

Psalm 89:19 "Once You spoke in vision to Your godly ones, And said, "I have given help to one who is mighty; I have exalted one chosen from the people."

Psalm 46:10 "Be still, and know that I am God."

1 Corinthians 2:12 "Now we have received, not the spirit of the world, but the Spirit who is from God, that we might know the things that have been freely given to us by God."

Proverbs 2:3-5 "For if you cry for discernment, Lift your voice for understanding; If you seek her as silver And search for her as for hidden treasures; Then you will discern the fear of the Lord And discover the knowledge of God."

Acts 2:17 "And in the last days it shall be, God declares, that I will pour out my Spirit on all flesh, and your sons and your daughters shall prophesy, and your young men shall see visions, and your old men shall dream dreams."

Acts 1:8 "But you will receive power when the Holy Spirit has come upon you, and you will be my witnesses in Jerusalem and in all Judea and Samaria, and to the end of the earth."

Habakkuk 2:1-2 "I will stand on my guard post and station myself on the rampart; And I will keep watch to see what He will speak to me, And how I may reply when I am reproved. Then the Lord answered me and said, "Record the vision And inscribe it on tablets, That the one who reads it may run.""

CHAPTER 1

Psalm 91:1 "He who dwells in the secret place of the Most High Shall abide under the shadow of the Almighty."

CHAPTER 2

Psalm 91:1 "He who dwells in the secret place of the Most High Shall abide under the shadow of the Almighty."

Job 38:36 (LEB) "Who has put wisdom in the bird, or who has given understanding to the rooster?"

Romans 8:28 "And we know that God causes all things to work together for good to those who love God, to those who are called according to His purpose."

Proverbs 30:29-31 "There are three things which are stately in their march, Even four which are stately when they walk: The lion which is mighty among beasts And does not retreat before any, The strutting rooster, the male goat also, And a king when his army is with him."

Matthew 26:74-75 "Then he began to curse and swear, "I do not know the man!" And immediately a rooster crowed. And Peter remembered the word which Jesus had said, "Before a rooster crows, you will deny Me three times." And he went out and wept bitterly."

Psalm 34:18 "The Lord is near to the brokenhearted And saves those who are crushed in spirit."

James 4:6 "But He gives a greater grace. Therefore it says, "God is opposed to the proud, but gives grace to the humble.""

Matthew 5:3-6 "Blessed are the poor in spirit, for theirs is the kingdom of heaven. "Blessed are those who mourn, for they shall be comforted. "Blessed are the gentle, for they shall inherit the earth. "Blessed are those who hunger and thirst for righteousness, for they shall be satisfied."

2 Corinthians 12:9 "And He has said to me, "My grace is sufficient for you, for power is perfected in weakness." Most gladly, therefore, I will rather boast about my weaknesses, so that the power of Christ may dwell in me."

Psalm 147:3 "He heals the brokenhearted And binds up their wounds."

James 4:10 "Humble yourselves in the presence of the Lord, and He will exalt you."

Matthew 11:28 "Come to Me, all who are weary and heavy-laden, and I will give you rest."

Acts 2:17 "And it shall be in the last days,' God says, 'That I will pour forth of My Spirit on all mankind; And your sons and your daughters shall prophesy, And your young men shall see visions, And your old men shall dream dreams;"

CHAPTER 3

Proverbs 26:27 "He who digs a pit will fall into it, And he who rolls a stone, it will come back on him."

Psalm 147:3 "He heals the brokenhearted And binds up their wounds."

Psalm 127:3 "Behold, children are a gift of the Lord, The fruit of the womb is a reward."

Matthew 18:6 "but whoever causes one of these little ones who believe in Me to stumble, it would be better for him to have a heavy millstone hung around his neck, and to be drowned in the depth of the sea."

CHAPTER 4

Matthew 7:15 (CSB) "Be on your guard against false prophets who come to you in sheep's clothing but inwardly are ravaging wolves."

John 10:10 "The thief comes only to steal and kill and destroy; I came that they may have life, and have it abundantly."

Colossians 2:2 "That their hearts may be encouraged, having been knit together in love, and attaining to all the wealth that comes from the full assurance of understanding, resulting in a true knowledge of God's mystery, that is, Christ Himself,"

Psalm 127:3 "Behold, children are a gift of the Lord, The fruit of the womb is a reward."

Titus 3:10-11 "Reject a factious man after a first and second warning, knowing that such a man is perverted and is sinning, being self-condemned."

Ezekiel 22:27 "Her princes within her are like wolves tearing the prey, by shedding blood and destroying lives in order to get dishonest gain."

John 10:12 "He who is a hired hand, and not a shepherd, who is not the owner of the sheep, sees the wolf coming, and leaves the sheep and flees, and the wolf snatches them and scatters them."

CHAPTER 5

Ezekiel 13:3-4 "Thus says the Lord God, "Woe to the foolish prophets who are following their own spirit and have seen nothing. O Israel, your prophets have been like foxes among ruins."

Luke 13:31-32 "Just at that time some Pharisees approached, saying to Him, "Go away, leave here, for Herod wants to kill You." And He said to them, "Go and tell that fox, 'Behold, I cast out demons and perform cures today and tomorrow, and the third day I reach My goal.'"

Isaiah 64:8 "But now, O Lord, You are our Father, We are the clay, and You our potter; And all of us are the work of Your hand."

2 Timothy 3:2 "For men will be lovers of self, lovers of money, boastful, arrogant, revilers, disobedient to parents, ungrateful, unholy,"

Matthew 16:24-26
    "Then Jesus said to His disciples, "If anyone wishes to come after Me, he must deny himself, and take up his cross and follow Me. For whoever wishes to save his life will lose it; but whoever loses his life for My sake will find it. For what will it profit a man if he gains the whole world and forfeits his soul? Or what will a man give in exchange for his soul?"

Hebrews 12:15 "See to it that no one comes short of the grace of God; that no root of bitterness springing up causes trouble, and by it many be defiled;"

Ephesians 4:32 "Be kind to one another, tender-hearted, forgiving each other, just as God in Christ also has forgiven you."

Luke 6:37 "Do not judge, and you will not be judged; and do not condemn, and you will not be condemned; pardon, and you will be pardoned."

1 John 4:7-21

7 Beloved, let us love one another, for love is from God; and everyone who loves is born of God and knows God. **8** The one who does not love does not know God, for God is love. **9** By this the love of God was manifested in us, that God has sent His only begotten Son into the world so that we might live through Him. **10** In this is love, not that we loved God, but that He loved us and sent His Son to be the propitiation for our sins. **11** Beloved, if God so loved us, we also ought to love one another. **12** No one has seen God at any time; if we love one another, God abides in us, and His love is perfected in us. **13** By this we know that we abide in Him and He in us, because He has given us of His Spirit. **14** We have seen and testify that the Father has sent the Son to be the Savior of the world.

15 Whoever confesses that Jesus is the Son of God, God abides in him, and he in God. **16** We have come to know and have believed the love which God has for us. God is love, and the one who abides in love abides in God, and God abides in him. **17** By this, love is perfected with us, so that we may have confidence in the day of judgment; because as He is, so also are we in this world. **18** There is no fear in love; but perfect love casts out fear, because fear involves punishment, and the one who fears is not perfected in love. **19** We love, because He first loved us. **20** If someone says, "I love God," and hates his brother, he is a liar; for the one who does not love his brother whom he has seen, cannot love God whom he has not seen. **21** And this commandment we have from Him, that the one who loves God should love his brother also.

CHAPTER 6

Mark 13:35 "Therefore be alert, since you don't know when the master of the house is coming—whether in the evening or at midnight or at the crowing of the rooster or early in the morning."

1 Timothy 2:1 "First of all, then, I urge that entreaties *and* prayers, petitions *and* thanksgivings, be made on behalf of all men,"

Romans 8:26 "In the same way the Spirit also helps our weakness; for we do not know how to pray as we should, but the Spirit Himself intercedes for *us* with groanings too deep for words;

Ephesians 6:18 "With all prayer and petition pray at all times in the Spirit, and with this in view, be on the alert with all perseverance and petition for all the saints,"

Isaiah 59:16 "And He saw that there was no man, And was astonished that there was no one to intercede; Then His own arm brought salvation to Him, And His righteousness upheld Him."

CHAPTER 7

Matthew 26:33-35 "But Peter said to Him, "Even though all may fall away because of You, I will never fall away." Jesus said to him, "Truly I say to you that this very night, before a rooster crows, you will deny Me three times." Peter said to Him, "Even if I have to die with You, I will not deny You." All the disciples said the same thing too."

Matthew 26:69–75

69 Now Peter was sitting outside in the courtyard, and a servant-girl came to him and said, "You too were with Jesus the Galilean." **70** But he denied it before them all, saying, "I do not know what you are talking about." **71** When he had gone out to the gateway, another servant-girl saw him and said to those who were there, "This man was with Jesus of Nazareth." **72** And again he denied it with an oath, "I do not know the man." **73** A little later the bystanders came up and said to Peter, "Surely you too are one of them; for even the way you talk gives you away."**74** Then he began to curse and swear, "I do not know the man!" And immediately a rooster crowed. **75** And Peter remembered the word which Jesus had said, "Before a rooster crows, you will deny Me three times." And he went out and wept bitterly.

John 21:15-19

15 So when they had finished breakfast, Jesus said to Simon Peter, "Simon, son of John, do you love Me more than these?" He said to Him, "Yes, Lord; You know that I love

You." He said to him, "Tend My lambs." **16** He said to him again a second time, "Simon, son of John, do you love Me?" He said to Him, "Yes, Lord; You know that I love You." He said to him, "Shepherd My sheep." **17** He said to him the third time, "Simon, son of John, do you love Me?" Peter was grieved because He said to him the third time, "Do you love Me?" And he said to Him, "Lord, You know all things; You know that I love You." Jesus said to him, "Tend My sheep. **18** Truly, truly, I say to you, when you were younger, you used to gird yourself and walk wherever you wished; but when you grow old, you will stretch out your hands and someone else will gird you, and bring you where you do not wish to go."**19** Now this He said, signifying by what kind of death he would glorify God. And when He had spoken this, He said to him, "Follow Me!"

Mark 13:35 "Therefore, be on the alert—for you do not know when the master of the house is coming, whether in the evening, at midnight, or when the rooster crows, or in the morning—"

CHAPTER 8

Jeremiah 1:5 "Before I formed you in the womb I knew you, And before you were born I consecrated you..."

Luke 15:4 "If a man has a hundred sheep and one of them gets lost, what will he do?" He'll go out and search for the one that is lost until he finds it."

James 1:14 "But each one is tempted when he is carried away and enticed by his own lust."

Ezekiel 14:10-11 (NIV) "They will bear the punishment of their iniquity; as the iniquity of the inquirer is, so the iniquity of the prophet will be, in order that the house of Israel may no longer stray from Me and no longer defile themselves with all their transgressions..."

Proverbs 19:27 "Cease listening, my son, to discipline, And you will stray from the words of knowledge."

2 Timothy 4:3-4 "For the time will come when they will not endure sound doctrine; but wanting to have their ears tickled, they will accumulate for themselves teachers in accordance to their own desires, and will turn away their ears from the truth and will turn aside to myths."

Proverbs 4:23 "Watch over your heart with all diligence, For from it flow the springs of life."

Matthew 22:37 "And He said to him, "'You shall love the Lord your God with all your heart, and with all your soul, and with all your mind.'"

Proverbs 22:6 "Train up a child in the way he should go, Even when he is old he will not depart from it."

1 Timothy 4:12 "Let no one look down on your youthfulness, but rather in speech, conduct, love, faith and purity, show yourself an example of those who believe."

Exodus 3:8 "So I have come down to deliver them from the [a] power of the Egyptians, and to bring them up from that land to a good and spacious land, to a land flowing with milk and honey, to the place of the Canaanite and the Hittite and the Amorite and the Perizzite and the Hivite and the Jebusite."

Ezekiel 18:20 "The person who sins will die. The son will not bear the punishment for the father's iniquity, nor will the father bear the punishment for the son's iniquity; the righteousness of the righteous will be upon himself, and the wickedness of the wicked will be upon himself."

Romans 3:23 "for all have sinned and fall short of the glory of God,"

Romans 5:18 "So then as through one transgression there resulted condemnation to all men, even so through one act of righteousness there resulted justification of life to all men."

Luke 15:4 "What man among you, if he has a hundred sheep and has lost one of them, does not leave the ninety-nine in the open pasture and go after the one which is lost until he finds it?"

John 1:29 "The next day he *saw Jesus coming to him and *said, "Behold, the Lamb of God who takes away the sin of the world!""

John 1:36 "and he looked at Jesus as He walked, and *said, "Behold, the Lamb of God!""

Isaiah 53:10 "But the Lord was pleased To crush Him, putting Him to grief; If He would render Himself as a guilt offering, He will see His offspring, He will prolong His days,

And the good pleasure of the Lord will prosper in His hand."

Psalm 95:7 "For He is our God, And we are the people of His pasture and the sheep of His hand. Today, if you would hear His voice,"

1 Peter 5:2 "shepherd the flock of God among you, exercising oversight not under compulsion, but voluntarily, according to the will of God; and not for sordid gain, but with eagerness;"

2 Thess 2:11 "For this reason God will send upon them a deluding influence so that they will believe what is false,"

Psalm 127:3 "Behold, children are a gift of the Lord, The fruit of the womb is a reward."

Matthew 24:12 "Because lawlessness is increased, most people's love will grow cold."

CHAPTER 9

Jeremiah 1:5 "Before I formed you in the womb I knew you, And before you were born I consecrated you...""

Luke 15:4 "If a man has a hundred sheep and one of them gets lost, what will he do?" He'll go out and search for the one that is lost until he finds it."

James 1:14 "But each one is tempted when he is carried away and enticed by his own lust."

Ezekiel 14:10-11 (NIV) "They will bear the punishment of their iniquity; as the iniquity of the inquirer is, so the iniquity of the prophet will be, in order that the house of Israel may no longer stray from Me and no longer defile themselves with all their transgressions..."

CHAPTER 10

1Corinthians 14:33 "for God is not *a God* of confusion but of peace, as in all the churches of the saints."

Job 7:9-10 "When a cloud vanishes, it is gone, So he who goes down to Sheol does not come up. He will not return again to his house, Nor will his place know him anymore."

2 Corinthians 4:12,16 "So death works in us, but life in you.", "Therefore we do not lose heart, but though our outer man is decaying, yet our inner man is being renewed day by day."

John 8:44 "You are of *your* father the devil, and you want to do the desires of your father. He was a murderer from the beginning, and does not stand in the truth because there is no truth in him. Whenever he speaks a lie, he speaks from his own *nature*, for he is a liar and the father of lies."

2 Thessalonians 2:9-11
"**9** *that is*, the one whose coming is in accord with the activity of Satan, with all power and signs and false wonders, **10** and with all the deception of wickedness for those who perish, because they did not receive the love of the truth so as to be saved. **11** For this reason God will send upon them a deluding influence so that they will believe what is false,"

1 Corinthians 2:14 "But a natural man does not accept the things of the Spirit of God, for they are foolishness to him; and he cannot understand them, because they are spiritually appraised."

Proverbs 14:12 "There is a way *which seems* right to a man, But its end is the way of death."

2 Corinthians 4:16 "Therefore we do not lose heart, but though our outer man is decaying, yet our inner man is being renewed day by day."

1 Timothy 4:10 "For it is for this we labor and strive, because we have fixed our hope on the living God, who is the Savior of all men, especially of believers."

1 Peter 1:13 "Therefore, prepare your minds for action, keep sober *in spirit*, fix your hope completely on the grace to be brought to you at the revelation of Jesus Christ."

2 Timothy 2:7 "Consider what I say, for the Lord will give you understanding in everything."

CHAPTER 11

Romans 12:17 "Never pay back evil for evil to anyone. Respect what is right in the sight of all men."

Matthew 4:6 "and *said to Him, "If You are the Son of God, throw Yourself down; for it is written, 'He will command His angels concerning You'; and 'On their hands they will bear You up, So that You will not strike Your foot against a stone.'"

Deuteronomy 3:22 "Do not fear them, for the Lord your God is the one fighting for you.'"

1 Corinthians 15:33 "Do not be deceived: "Bad company corrupts good morals.""

Psalm 34:14 "Depart from evil and do good; Seek peace and pursue it."

Matthew 13:11-17
"**11** Jesus answered them, "To you it has been granted to know the mysteries of the kingdom of heaven, but to them it has not been granted. **12** For whoever has, to him more shall be given, and he will have an abundance; but whoever does not have, even what he has shall be taken away from him. **13** Therefore I speak to them in parables; because while seeing

they do not see, and while hearing they do not hear, nor do they understand. **14** In their case the prophecy of Isaiah is being fulfilled, which says, 'You will keep on hearing, but will not understand; You will keep on seeing, but will not perceive; **15** For the heart of this people has become dull, With their ears they scarcely hear, And they have closed their eyes, Otherwise they would see with their eyes, Hear with their ears, And understand with their heart and return, And I would heal them.' **16** But blessed are your eyes, because they see; and your ears, because they hear. **17** For truly I say to you that many prophets and righteous men desired to see what you see, and did not see it, and to hear what you hear, and did not hear it.

Hebrews 13:6 "so that we confidently say, "The Lord is my helper, I will not be afraid. What will man do to me?""

2 Timothy 1:7 "For God has not given us a spirit of timidity, but of power and love and discipline."

Matthew 18:21-22 "**21** Then Peter came and said to Him, "Lord, how often shall my brother sin against me and I forgive him? Up to seven times?" **22** Jesus said to him, "I do not say to you, up to seven times, but up to seventy times seven."

1 Corinthians 2:11 "For who among men knows the thoughts of a man except the spirit of the man which is in him? Even so the thoughts of God no one knows except the Spirit of God."

Romans 8:28 "And we know that God causes all things to work together for good to those who love God, to those who are called according to His purpose."

Psalm 32:8 "I will instruct you and teach you in the way which you should go; I will counsel you with My eye upon you."

CHAPTER 12

Luke 10:19 "Behold, I have given you authority to tread on serpents and scorpions, and over all the power of the enemy, and nothing will injure you."

Psalm 11:5 "The Lord tests the righteous and the wicked, And the one who loves violence His soul hates."

Colossians 3:21 "Fathers, do not exasperate your children, so that they will not lose heart."

Romans 8:6 "For the mind set on the flesh is death, but the mind set on the Spirit is life and peace,"

Colossians 3:15 "Let the peace of Christ rule in your hearts, to which indeed you were called in one body; and be thankful."

2 Thessalonians 3:16 "Now may the Lord of peace Himself continually grant you peace in every circumstance. The Lord be with you all!"

1 Corinthians 14:33 " for God is not *a God* of confusion but of peace, as in all the churches of the saints."

1 Corinthians 3:16-17 "Do you not know that you are a temple of God and *that* the Spirit of God dwells in you? If any man destroys the temple of God, God will destroy him, for the temple of God is holy, and that is what you are."

CHAPTER 13

Ephesians 5:18 "And do not get drunk with wine, for that is dissipation, but be filled with the Spirit,"

Proverbs 20:1 "Wine is a mocker, strong drink a brawler, And whoever is intoxicated by it is not wise."

1 Corinthians 6:19-20 "Or do you not know that your body is a temple of the Holy Spirit who is in you, whom you have from God, and that you are not your own? For you have been bought with a price: therefore glorify God in your body."

Isaiah 53:6 "All of us like sheep have gone astray, Each of us has turned to his own way; But the Lord has caused the iniquity of us all To fall on Him."

1 Peter 1:22 "Since you have in obedience to the truth purified your souls for a sincere love of the brethren, fervently love one another from the heart,"

Proverbs 13:20 "He who walks with wise men will be wise, But the companion of fools will suffer harm."

Psalm 100:3 "Know that the Lord Himself is God; It is He who has made us, and not we ourselves; We are His people and the sheep of His pasture."

John 10:27-28 "My sheep hear My voice, and I know them, and they follow Me; and I give eternal life to them, and they will never perish; and no one will snatch them out of My hand."

1 John 4:4 "You are from God, little children, and have overcome them; because greater is He who is in you than he who is in the world."

James 4:4 "You adulteresses, do you not know that friendship with the world is hostility toward God? Therefore whoever wishes to be a friend of the world makes himself an enemy of God."

CHAPTER 14

Deuteronomy 32:10 "He found him in a desert land, And in the howling waste of a wilderness; He encircled him, He cared for him, He guarded him as the pupil of His eye."

1 John 3:1 "See how great a love the Father has bestowed on us, that we would be called children of God; and such we are. For this reason the world does not know us, because it did not know Him."

John 21:15 "So when they had finished breakfast, Jesus *said to Simon Peter, "Simon, son of John, do you love Me more than these?" He *said to Him, "Yes, Lord; You know that I love You." He *said to him, "Tend My lambs.""

Luke 15:4 "What man among you, if he has a hundred sheep and has lost one of them, does not leave the ninety-nine in the open pasture and go after the one which is lost until he finds it?"

Matthew 9:36 "Seeing the people, He felt compassion for them, because they were distressed and dispirited like sheep without a shepherd."

Numbers 27:17 "who will go out and come in before them, and who will lead them out and bring them in, so that the congregation of the Lord will not be like sheep which have no shepherd.""

Proverbs 22:6 "Train up a child in the way he should go, Even when he is old he will not depart from it."

Ephesians 6:4 "Fathers, do not provoke your children to anger, but bring them up in the discipline and instruction of the Lord."

Deuteronomy 6:7 "You shall teach them diligently to your sons and shall talk of them when you sit in your house and when you walk by the way and when you lie down and when you rise up."

Isaiah 53:6 "All of us like sheep have gone astray, Each of us has turned to his own way; But the Lord has caused the iniquity of us all To fall on Him."

1 Peter 5:8 "Be of sober spirit, be on the alert. Your adversary, the devil, prowls around like a roaring lion, seeking someone to devour."

Matthew 9:36 "Seeing the people, He felt compassion for them, because they were distressed and dispirited like sheep without a shepherd."

CHAPTER 15

1 Peter 3:15 "but sanctify Christ as Lord in your hearts, always *being* ready to make a defense to everyone who asks you to give an account for the hope that is in you, yet with gentleness and reverence;"

Jeremiah 29:11 "For I know the plans that I have for you,' declares the Lord, 'plans for welfare and not for calamity to give you a future and a hope."

Romans 12:2 "And do not be conformed to this world, but be transformed by the renewing of your mind, so that you may prove what the will of God is, that which is good and acceptable and perfect."

Exodus 23:20 "Behold, I am going to send an angel before you to guard you along the way and to bring you into the place which I have prepared."

Isaiah 43:19 "Behold, I will do something new, Now it will spring forth; Will you not be aware of it? I will even make a roadway in the wilderness, Rivers in the desert.

Proverbs 23:18 "Surely there is a future, And your hope will not be cut off."

Ephesians 4:31 "Let all bitterness and wrath and anger and clamor and slander be put away from you, along with all malice."

1 Corinthians 6:18 "Flee immorality. Every *other* sin that a man commits is outside the body, but the immoral man sins against his own body."

Proverbs 17:17 "A friend loves at all times, And a brother is born for adversity."

CHAPTER 16

Proverbs 31:10-11 (MSG) "A good woman is hard to find, and worth far more than diamonds. Her husband trusts her without reserve, and never has reason to regret it."

Genesis 2:8 "The Lord God planted a garden toward the east, in Eden; and there He placed the man whom He had formed."

Ephesians 5:28-29 "So husbands ought also to love their own wives as their own bodies. He who loves his own wife loves himself; for no one ever hated his own flesh, but nourishes and cherishes it, just as Christ also *does* the church,"

1 Peter 3:7 "You husbands in the same way, live with *your wives* in an understanding way, as with someone weaker, since she is a woman; and show her honor as a fellow heir of the grace of life, so that your prayers will not be hindered."

1 Corinthians 7:9 "But if they do not have self-control, let them marry; for it is better to marry than to burn *with passion*."

1 Peter 4:8 "Above all, keep fervent in your love for one another, because love covers a multitude of sins."

Hebrews 12:11 (NLT) "All discipline for the moment seems not to be joyful, but sorrowful; yet to those who have been trained by it, afterwards it yields the peaceful fruit of righteousness."

CHAPTER 17

Luke 14:28-30 "For which one of you, when he wants to build a tower, does not first sit down and calculate the cost to see if he has enough to complete it? Otherwise, when he has laid a foundation and is not able to finish, all who observe it begin to ridicule him, saying, 'This man began to build and was not able to finish.'"

Proverbs 22:1 "A *good* name is to be more desired than great wealth, Favor is better than silver and gold."

Proverbs 13:18 "Poverty and shame *will come* to him who neglects discipline, But he who regards reproof will be honored."

Isaiah 48:17 "Thus says the Lord, your Redeemer, the Holy One of Israel, "I am the Lord your God, who teaches you to profit, Who leads you in the way you should go."

1 Thessalonians 5:19 "Do not quench the Spirit;"

CHAPTER 18

Isaiah 21:10 "O my threshed people, and my afflicted of the threshing floor! What I have heard from the Lord of hosts, The God of Israel, I make known to you."

Deuteronomy 25:4 "You shall not muzzle the ox while he is threshing."

Isaiah 28:28 "Grain for bread is crushed, Indeed, he does not continue to thresh it forever. Because the wheel of his cart and his horses eventually damage it, He does not thresh it longer."

Hosea 13:3 "Therefore they will be like the morning cloud And like dew which soon disappears, Like chaff which is blown away from the threshing floor And like smoke from a chimney."

Micah 4:11-13
"And now many nations have been assembled against you Who say, 'Let her be polluted, And let our eyes gloat over Zion.' "But they do not know the thoughts of the Lord, And they do not understand His purpose; For He has gathered them like sheaves to the threshing floor. "Arise and thresh, daughter of Zion, For your horn I will make iron And your hoofs I will make bronze, That you may pulverize many peoples, That you may devote to the Lord their unjust gain And their wealth to the Lord of all the earth.

Matthew 3:12 "His winnowing fork is in His hand, and He will thoroughly clear His threshing floor; and He will gather His wheat into the barn, but He will burn up the chaff with unquenchable fire."

Luke 3:17 "His winnowing fork is in His hand to thoroughly clear His threshing floor, and to gather the wheat into His barn; but He will burn up the chaff with unquenchable fire."

Psalm 104:4 "He makes the winds His messengers, Flaming fire His ministers."

CHAPTER 19

1 Corinthians 7:14 "For the unbelieving husband is sanctified through his wife, and the unbelieving wife is sanctified through her believing husband; for otherwise your children are unclean, but now they are holy."

Hebrews 12:22 "But you have come to Mount Zion and to the city of the living God, the heavenly Jerusalem, and to myriads of angels,"

Psalm 91:11 "For He will give His angels charge concerning you, To guard you in all your ways."

Philippians 2:3 "Do nothing from selfishness or empty conceit, but with humility of mind regard one another as more important than yourselves;"

2 Corinthians 10:3-5
"**3** For though we walk in the flesh, we do not war according to the flesh, **4** for the weapons of our warfare are not of the flesh, but divinely powerful for the destruction of fortresses. **5** We are destroying speculations and every lofty thing raised up against the knowledge of God, and we are taking every thought captive to the obedience of Christ,"

James 4:6 "But He gives a greater grace. Therefore it says, "God is opposed to the proud, but gives grace to the humble.""

Proverbs 3:34 "Though He scoffs at the scoffers, Yet He gives grace to the afflicted."

James 4:1-2 "What is the source of quarrels and conflicts among you? Is not the source your pleasures that wage war in your members? You lust and do not have; so you commit murder. You are envious and cannot obtain; so you fight and quarrel. You do not have because you do not ask."

James 4:3-6
"**3** You ask and do not receive, because you ask with wrong motives, so that you may spend it on your pleasures. **4** You

adulteresses, do you not know that friendship with the world is hostility toward God? Therefore whoever wishes to be a friend of the world makes himself an enemy of God. **5** Or do you think that the Scripture speaks to no purpose: "He jealously desires the Spirit which He has made to dwell in us"? **6** But He gives a greater grace. Therefore it says, "God is opposed to the proud, but gives grace to the humble."

James 4:11-12 "Do not speak against one another, brethren. He who speaks against a brother or judges his brother, speaks against the law and judges the law; but if you judge the law, you are not a doer of the law but a judge of it. There is only one Lawgiver and Judge, the One who is able to save and to destroy; but who are you who judge your neighbor?"

Acts 16:31 "They said, "Believe in the Lord Jesus, and you will be saved, you and your household."

CHAPTER 20

Ephesians 4:31-32 "Let all bitterness and wrath and anger and clamor and slander be put away from you, along with all malice. Be kind to one another, tender-hearted, forgiving each other, just as God in Christ also has forgiven you."

Acts 1:3 "To these He also presented Himself alive after His suffering, by many convincing proofs, appearing to them over a period of forty days and speaking of the things concerning the kingdom of God."

Romans 5:3-5 "**3** And not only this, but we also exult in our tribulations, knowing that tribulation brings about perseverance; **4** and perseverance, proven character; and proven character, hope; **5** and hope does not disappoint, because the love of God has been poured out within our hearts through the Holy Spirit who was given to us."

John 14:1-2 "Do not let your heart be troubled; believe in God, believe also in Me. In My Father's house are many dwelling places; if it were not so, I would have told you; for I go to prepare a place for you."

CHAPTER 21

Psalm 127:3 "Behold, children are a gift of the Lord, The fruit of the womb is a reward."

1 Peter 3:7 "You husbands in the same way, live with your wives in an understanding way, as with someone weaker, since she is a woman; and show her honor as a fellow heir of the grace of life, so that your prayers will not be hindered."

Psalm 18:2 "The Lord is my rock and my fortress and my deliverer, My God, my rock, in whom I take refuge; My shield and the horn of my salvation, my stronghold."

Titus 3:3-5
"**3** For we also once were foolish ourselves, disobedient, deceived, enslaved to various lusts and pleasures, spending our life in malice and envy, hateful, hating one another. **4** But when the kindness of God our Savior and His love for mankind appeared, **5** He saved us, not on the basis of deeds which we have done in righteousness, but according to His mercy, by the washing of regeneration and renewing by the Holy Spirit,"

Ecclesiastes 7:20 "Indeed, there is not a righteous man on earth who continually does good and who never sins."

Romans 3:23 "for all have sinned and fall short of the glory of God,"

Isaiah 64:6 "For all of us have become like one who is unclean, And all our righteous deeds are like a filthy garment; And all of us wither like a leaf, And our iniquities, like the wind, take us away."

CHAPTER 22

Ephesians 6:1-4
"**1** Children, obey your parents in the Lord, for this is right. **2** Honor your father and mother (which is the first commandment with a promise), **3** so that it may be well with you,

and that you may live long on the earth. **4** Fathers, do not provoke your children to anger, but bring them up in the discipline and instruction of the Lord."

John 1:5 "The Light shines in the darkness, and the darkness did not comprehend it."

John 8:12 "Then Jesus again spoke to them, saying, "I am the Light of the world; he who follows Me will not walk in the darkness, but will have the Light of life.""

John 12:46 "I have come as Light into the world, so that everyone who believes in Me will not remain in darkness."

Psalm 18:18 "They confronted me in the day of my calamity, But the Lord was my stay."

2 Timothy 1:7 "For God has not given us a spirit of timidity, but of power and love and discipline."

1 Corinthians 13:7-8 "bears all things, believes all things, hopes all things, endures all things. Love never fails; but if there are gifts of prophecy, they will be done away; if there are tongues, they will cease; if there is knowledge, it will be done away."

John 10:14 "I am the good shepherd, and I know My own and My own know Me,"

Matthew 7:23 "And then I will declare to them, 'I never knew you; depart from Me, you who practice lawlessness.'"

Matthew 11:27 "All things have been handed over to Me by My Father; and no one knows the Son except the Father; nor does anyone know the Father except the Son, and anyone to whom the Son wills to reveal Him."

Proverbs 18:21 "Death and life are in the power of the tongue, And those who love it will eat its fruit."

Proverbs 6:2 "If you have been snared with the words of your mouth, Have been caught with the words of your mouth,"

Proverbs 12:13 "An evil man is ensnared by the transgression of his lips, But the righteous will escape from trouble."

Proverbs 12:18 "There is one who speaks rashly like the thrusts of a sword, But the tongue of the wise brings healing."

Romans 12:3 "For through the grace given to me I say to everyone among you not to think more highly of himself than he ought to think; but to think so as to have sound judgment, as God has allotted to each a measure of faith."

Luke 17:6 "And the Lord said, "If you had faith like a mustard seed, you would say to this mulberry tree, 'Be uprooted and be planted in the sea'; and it would obey you."

CHAPTER 23

Jeremiah 29:11 "For I know the plans that I have for you,' declares the Lord, 'plans for welfare and not for calamity to give you a future and a hope."

Philippians 4:11 "Not that I speak from want, for I have learned to be content in whatever circumstances I am."

Ecclesiastes 3:1-10
> "**1** There is an appointed time for everything. And there is a time for every event under heaven—**2** A time to give birth and a time to die; A time to plant and a time to uproot what is planted. **3** A time to kill and a time to heal; A time to tear down and a time to build up. **4** A time to weep and a time to laugh; A time to mourn and a time to dance. **5** A time to throw stones and a time to gather stones; A time to embrace and a time to shun embracing. **6** A time to search and a time to give up as lost; A time to keep and a time to throw away. **7** A time to tear apart and a time to sew together; A time to be silent and a time to speak. **8** A time to love and a time to hate; A time for war and a time for peace. **9** What profit is there to the worker from that in which he toils? **10** I have seen the task which God has given the sons of men with which to occupy themselves.

Romans 3:1 "Then what advantage has the Jew? Or what is the benefit of circumcision?"

Luke 12:36 "Be like men who are waiting for their master when he returns from the wedding feast, so that they may immediately open the door to him when he comes and knocks."

John 7:38-39 "He who believes in Me, as the Scripture said, 'From his innermost being will flow rivers of living water.'" But this He spoke of the Spirit, whom those who believed in Him were to receive; for the Spirit was not yet given, because Jesus was not yet glorified."

John 12:26 "If anyone serves Me, he must follow Me; and where I am, there My servant will be also; if anyone serves Me, the Father will honor him."

Matthew 9:9 "As Jesus went on from there, He saw a man called Matthew, sitting in the tax collector's booth; and He *said to him, "Follow Me!" And he got up and followed Him."

Matthew 16:24 "Then Jesus said to His disciples, "If anyone wishes to come after Me, he must deny himself, and take up his cross and follow Me."

CHAPTER 24

Luke 12:35-38, 40

"**35** "Be dressed in readiness, and keep your lamps lit. **36** Be like men who are waiting for their master when he returns from the wedding feast, so that they may immediately open the door to him when he comes and knocks. **37** Blessed are those slaves whom the master will find on the alert when he comes; truly I say to you, that he will gird himself to serve, and have them recline at the table, and will come up and wait on them. **38** Whether he comes in the second watch, or even in the third, and finds them so, blessed are those slaves. **40** You too, be ready; for the Son of Man is coming at an hour that you do not expect.""

2 Corinthians 3:17 "Now the Lord is the Spirit, and where the Spirit of the Lord is, there is liberty."

Ezra 7:25-26
> "**25** You, Ezra, according to the wisdom of your God which is in your hand, appoint magistrates and judges that they may judge all the people who are in the province beyond the River, even all those who know the laws of your God; and you may teach anyone who is ignorant of them. **26** Whoever will not observe the law of your God and the law of the king, let judgment be executed upon him strictly, whether for death or for banishment or for confiscation of goods or for imprisonment."

Isaiah 42:5-7
> "**5** Thus says God the Lord, Who created the heavens and stretched them out, Who spread out the earth and its offspring, Who gives breath to the people on it And spirit to those who walk in it, **6** "I am the Lord, I have called You in righteousness, I will also hold You by the hand and watch over You, And I will appoint You as a covenant to the people, As a light to the nations, **7** To open blind eyes, To bring out prisoners from the dungeon And those who dwell in darkness from the prison."

EPILOGUE

Romans 12:2 "And do not be conformed to this world, but be transformed by the renewing of your mind, so that you may prove what the will of God is, that which is good and acceptable and perfect."

BIBLIOGRAPHY

BOOKS

The books in this bibliography have aided me in my walk and my relationship with Christ. Some of these books I continue to reference, review, and use to this day. I have many more books in my library than those listed here, but I attempted to list the ones that have the largest impact on my life. If you read any of these books, you will very likely recognize themes within The Wilderness Project.

There are numerous books, that I do not have, out there that are wonderful and many people have testified to how they helped them in their walk, however, I am only listing those that are in my personal library and that I have personally read. For due diligence, books will resonate in a man's heart differently, just because these books impacted me, does not imply that they will have the same impact on you. Likewise, there are books I have read that did not do anything for me, but may resonate deeply with you.

Devotionals - I will ALWAYS encourage men to have at least one devotional that they read from daily.

    Sparkling Gems Vol. 1 (2003), Rick Renner
    Sparkling Gems Vol 2 (2016), Rick Renner
    Smith Wigglesworth Devotional (1984)
    Devotions for the Man in the Mirror (2015), Patrick Morley

Ministry Books for Men - specifically for men, I wish I had come across these much earlier in my walk

    Wild at Heart (2010), John Eldredge

The Heart of a Warrior (2015), Michael Thompson
Search and Rescue (2011), Michael Thompson
Man Alive (2012), Patrick Morley
Rough Cut Men (2015), David Dusek
How God Makes Men (2013), Patrick Morley
A Warriors Faith (2015), Roger Vera
Brave Rifles - The Theology of War (2017), Bradford Smith

Prayer - men MUST learn how to pray, biblically and scripturally

The Art of Prayer (1992), Kenneth E. Hagin
Prayers that Heal the Heart (2001), Mark and Patti Virkler
Dialogue With God - Opening The Door to Two Way Prayer
    (1986, 2005), Mark and Patti Virkler
4 Keys to Hearing God's Voice (2010), Mark and Patti Virkler
The Secret Place (2011), William J. Dupley

Spiritual Warfare - I recognized my old self in these books and
the challenges I experienced after being Born Again

Army of Dawn Part I - Preparing for the Greatest Event of all
    Time (2015), Rick Joyner
Army of Dawn Part 11 - A New Breed (2016), Rick Joyner
The Final Quest Trilogy (2016, 2017), Rick Joyner [compilation
    of three books originally published in 1996, 1999, and 2003
Breaking Unhealthy Soul Ties (2011), Bill and Susan Banks
The Three Battlegrounds (2006), Francis Frangipane
Battlefield of the Mind (1995), Joyce Meyer
The Bait of Satan (2004), John Bevere

General - books that may not fit a particular category but helped
me to better understand and comprehend scripture

Just Courage - Gods Great Expedition for the Restless Christian
    (2008), Gary A. Haugen
Glory Rising (2009), Jeff Jansen
The Furious Sound of Glory (2017), Jeff Jansen
Culture of Honor (2009), Danny Silk

Identity theft - Satan's Greatest Crime Against Humanity (2017), Duane Sheriff

Unshakeable Hope - Building Our Lives on the Promises of God (2018), Max Lucado

Blessing or Curse - You can Choose (2006), Derek Prince

Hardness of Heart (2008), Andrew Wommack

Christian Philosophy (2012), Andrew Wommack

Jesus Among Secular Gods - The Countercultural Claims of Christ (2017), Ravi Zacharias & Vince Vitale

Understanding the Anointing (1983), Kenneth E. Hagin

The Cost of Our Silence (2015), David Fiorazo

With My Eyes Wide Open (2016), Brian Welch

Am I Being Deceived? (2001), Mark and Patti Virkler

Speaking the Truth in Love - A Christian Approach to Assertiveness (2009), Henry Virkler

WEBSITES

For the warfighter in combat, they may have many different types of weapons at their disposal that they can select from depending on the mission they are preparing to undertake. I want men to be armed with as much information as possible. Between the books listed above and the websites that follow, the man should be well armed with an arsenal at his disposal.

As with any weapon, the warrior must spend time with it so that he knows how to use it – properly. He studies it, he trains with it, and he becomes proficient with it. Some weapons take time to master, while others are easier to use. The websites below may be loaded with information and details that take time to review. Use them if necessary, but use them wisely if you must. These websites are not listed in any type of preferred order, they are simply listed in the order in which I wrote them.

https://www.biblegateway.com – one of my favorites, a website that gives you access to dozens of bible translations (two dozen or so) without having to buy them. Type in the verse you are looking for and the translation you want and click go. I love this website and use it extensively as I can view verses across many different translations. I used this site to build the Scripture Appendix of this book.

https://bible.knowing-jesus.com – an excellent tool for scripture word and phrase searches

https://carm.org – a good resource for those that want to dig into theological and doctrinal issues. There are resources that also compare to other religions.

https://www.gotquestions.org – answers thousands of bible questions. A good resource to use when beginning a study, but, I would vet results against other sources.

https://www.churchrelevance.com – an excellent site for those considering a ministry or looking to expand their ministry

http://biblicalanthropology.blogspot.com – sometimes it helps to understand a bible verse based on the context of the time period in which it was written. Biblical anthropology traces the antecedents of practices and beliefs to shed light on why things were done, not simply how they were done. This site attempts to measure context based on culture traits, rituals and belief systems of the time.

https://www.exploregod.com – a website dedicated to answering tough and difficult questions. There are videos as well, which is something that, statistically speaking, most men prefer.

https://www.biblestudytools.com – an excellent bible search and study tool

https://www.focusonthefamily.com – an excellent resource for the family man. This website helped me to understand my role as a spiritual head of household as a Prodigal Father – a man that came to Christ later in life.

https://www.insightforliving.ca – bible teaching resources

https://biblereasons.com – a site dedicated to helping you understand your faith. This site is not afraid to call out what they believe to be false religions.

https://lavendervines.com – sometimes the best resources for us include the personal testimonies of other Christians. Meet Tiffany.

http://www.fhghministries.org – ok, this one is our personal ministry website where we blog periodically. You can subscribe if you wish. We may blog several times a week or once a month as we blog as the Lord guides us, not as the wind blows.

http://justworship.com – time with the Lord necessitates that you spend time in worship. This site is dedicated to helping you expand your worship experience.

https://www.compellingtruth.org – another site dedicated to tackling tough questions of the Christian faith.

https://www.patheos.com – I almost excluded this site as it can be controversial. This is a site that I would save for those that are very comfortable and confident in their Christian walk ; some would say spiritually mature, someone strong in heart and their faith. This site has very good Christian articles on current cultural and societal issues but it also includes articles based on multiple religions that are not of the Christian faith. It can be confusing for those not prepared or ready to read what other religions have to say on a particular topic.

https://www1.cbn.com – a site that is dedicated to the coming of Jesus Christ and the establishment of His Kingdom.

ACKNOWLEDGEMENTS

As you should be able to gather from the story in this book, I have the most sincere and deepest gratitude for my wife Julee. She has been my motivator as I wrote this book, it does take a lot of time and mucho patience. If it weren't for her, I highly doubt I would be sitting here today.

A special thanks to Neil, who ignited that fire in my heart to start speaking out by asking me that one simple question that no one had ever asked me before. Why did it take me 40 years to come to Christ?

To my kids, well, after my wife they were the ones that really needed to forgive me...thanks you and I love you.

To my mother Barbara, who freaked out when I shared with her some of the stories about me that she had no idea. Yes, I was that sneaky.

To my sister Jeannie who thanked me for not having her killed when I could have. Where did she get the idea that I hated her? Perhaps a sign of my character back in "those days" (??).

Thanks to my dad Dwayne, who showed me that anything is possible, regardless of your handicaps.

Thank you to Fleur, who's creativity and intellect played a large part in the final document you now hold in your hands.

To Jimbo, Tammy, Sarine, Heath, Jhesika, and Cindy, early beta readers for the first part of this book, allowing me to properly set course for the remaining parts. And to Lori, whose enthusiasm and encouragement helped me keep this book alive and moving when I started to doubt myself.

And to the Igniting Souls team at Author Academy Elite, just wow!

ABOUT THE AUTHOR

Marcus is a combat veteran of three wars, serving in the US Army for 20 years. Born and raised in a godless family, he was angry and frustrated at life, and lived as an ardent agnostic for 40 years before having a dramatic experience with Christ and learning his true identity. Today Marcus is a transformed man thanks to the loving grace that is found in God and now has a passion to help others recognize who they are in Christ and find the FIRE that God placed in their hearts.

After retiring, Marcus served in multiple leadership positions in both government and private sectors. He holds a Doctorate in IT Leadership (ABD) and a Doctorate in Ministry. He and his wife founded FHGH Ministries in 2019 which serves to educate others to find Faith, Honor, Glory, and Hope in their lives with honest and balanced messages that cross both faith and culture.

Marcus Johnson is a prolific writer, having authored two books to date with two more books in progress as well as having had articles published in an international Christian magazine. His publishing portfolio includes My Personal Desert Storm: Eating Crow and Humble Pie (Amazon, 2019), Breaking Free From the Shadows (2020) and numerous articles published in Rejoice Essential Magazine.

Marcus has been married to Julee since 1989 and they have three children together, Christoffer, Katelyn, and Seth. He and his wife are also a Goldstar family, having lost Christoffer in 2011 while he was serving in the Middle East with the US Air Force.

Connect with Marcus at: fhghministries@gmail.com
fhghministries.org
TheWildernessProjectExperience.com

CPSIA information can be obtained
at www.ICGtesting.com
Printed in the USA
LVHW051710090920
665454LV00001B/174